THE BAIRNSFAT … IBUS

Bulle … ts

AND

From Mud to Mufti

Also available from Great Northern Publishing:

NON-FICTION: Non-Fiction/Military History/The Great War:

Baptism of Fire
Part One of the War of the Yorkshire Gurkhas
by Mark Marsay
ISBN: 0 9535204 0 4

Bombardment! The Day the East Coast Bled
Part Two of the War of the Yorkshire Gurkhas
by Mark Marsay
ISBN: 0 9535204 1 2

Forthcoming Works from Great Northern Publishing:

Fiction/Adult Humour:
Hazardous to Health - An Obadiah Jones Novel (1)
by Mark Marsay
ISBN: 0 9535204 3 9 *(available September 2000)*

Science Fiction/Adult Humour:
Beyond The Void - An Erasmus Novel (1)
by Mark Marsay
ISBN: 0 9535204 4 7 *(available December 2000)*

Other titles under preparation:

Fiction/Adult Humour:
Under Surveillance - An Obadiah Jones Novel (2)
A Bridge Too Far - An Obadiah Jones Novel (3)
An Alien Affair

Science Fiction/Adult Humour:
The Love Colony - An Erasmus Novel (2)
Howling At The Moon - An Erasmus Novel (3)
Montana Springs

Western/Adult Humour:
Bitter Creek

Adult Fiction:
Dark Passions - Anthology
My Soul To Keep - Anthology
Intimate Strangers

Fantasy Humour:
Poddrantallingtondibble - In Search of Odenhall
Poddrantallingtondibble - Homeward Bound
Granny Capstick

Fantasy:
The Book Of Dale

Fiction/Childrens:
Teddy Buttons
A Time To Wish

THE BAIRNSFATHER OMNIBUS

Bullets & Billets

AND

From Mud to Mufti

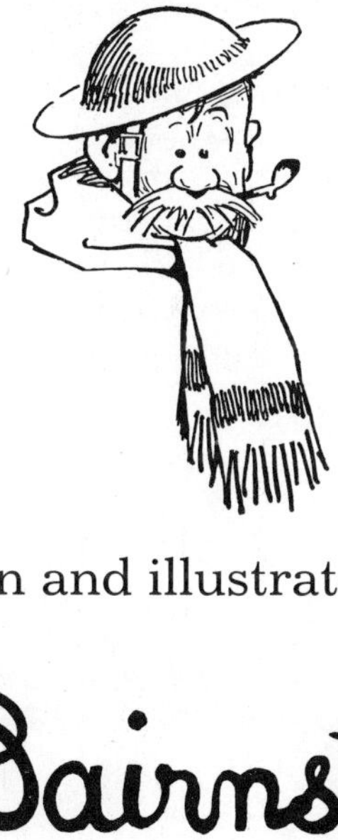

Written and illustrated by

Bruce Bairnsfather

COMPILED AND EDITED BY MARK MARSAY

GREAT NORTHERN PUBLISHING

THE BAIRNSFATHER OMNIBUS
'Bullets & Billets' and 'From Mud to Mufti'

ISBN: 0 9535204 2 0

Cover illustration:
'THE POINT OF VIEW'
"Well, if it don't get merrier than this by Christmas, it won't be up to much!"
Original artwork by Captain Bruce Bairnsfather - cover rendering by Neil Pearson.
The original cartoon appeared in *The Bystander* magazine on 5th December 1917.

~

'Bullets & Billets' first published by Grant Richards, London, 1916.
(First, Second and Third Impressions ~December 1916 ~ reprinted eight times).
'From Mud to Mufti' first published by Grant Richards, London, 1919.
This omnibus edition first published by Great Northern Publishing, 2000.

~

GREAT NORTHERN PUBLISHING
PO Box 202, Scarborough, North Yorkshire. YO11 3GE

Printed and bound by Redwood Books, Trowbridge, Wiltshire.

Captain Bruce Bairnsfather - to whom this special omnibus edition is dedicated - shortly after the war, with (inset) his most famous comic creation and lifelong companion, the irrepressible Old Bill.

A Statement From The Publisher

Having been fans of Bruce Bairnsfather's work for a number of years, and having enjoyed both his cartoons and his style of writing, the decision was taken for Great Northern Publishing to re-publish both of his autobiographical works, *'Bullets & Billets'*, first published in 1916, and *'From Mud to Mufti'*, published in 1919, in this omnibus form.

Despite the enormous success both books enjoyed at the time, testament to Bairnsfather's popularity even after the war, this is the first time the pair have been in print since those original editions were produced.

These titles were chosen because they provide the reader with a chronological account of Bairnsfather's rise to fame through his association with *The Bystander* magazine, the creation of Old Bill, and his work for the allied armies throughout the Great War, told in his own words and in his inimitable style. It is Bairnsfather's war, told by the man who lived every moment of it.

Our hope is to re-introduce Bairnsfather to old friends and introduce him to some new ones too.

It is not Great Northern Publishing's practice to simply produce a facsimile copy of a previously published work, slap on a fresh cover and then pass it off as a 'new' edition. We have gone to considerable lengths to re-set and re-design the two volumes, whilst endeavouring to keep faith with the original publications and their intent. All the illustrations from the original volumes have been used (though we apologise for the poor quality of some of the reproductions, which have been 'lifted' from previously printed copies through sheer necessity).

Had Bruce Bairnsfather been with us today we are sure he would be as proud of this work as we are.

We hope you enjoy his books as much as we do . . . and who knows, perhaps one day soon we'll see all his work back in print . . . *now wouldn't that be something!*

Contents

Bullets & Billets ~ List of illustrations

Maps

From Mud to Mufti

From Mud to Mufti ~ List of illustrations

Epilogue

Glossary

Notes

Acknowledgements

Preface

WITH BIOGRAPHY

Captain Bruce Bairnsfather was, without doubt, the finest cartoonist of the Great War. His work, which appeared regularly in *The Bystander's 'Fragments from France'* series was read and enjoyed by hundreds of thousands of British Tommies in trenches, billets and estaminets the length and breadth of the Western Front. Bairnsfather, like no other, captured the very essence of trench life - both the humour and the squalid misery of it - and it was this ability which made him practically unique amongst his contemporaries.

My grandfather, who served on the Western Front with the 5th Green Howards (Alexandra, Princess of Wales's Own Yorkshire Regiment) and won the MM on the Somme, always spoke of Bairnsfather with a broad grin and acknowledged that he was one of those rare few of the 'officer class' who knew what it was really like, day by day, for himself and his pals in the trenches.

Although Bairnsfather's cartoons have re-appeared once again in print in recent years, thanks to the efforts of the redoubtable Tonie and Valmai Holt, his literary work has been largely overlooked and forgotten, save by a few die-hard collectors who tend to snap up the original volumes which infrequently come up for sale. Bairnsfather's work is seen by many 'historians' and academics as being of little or no value in the telling of the story of the Great War, and it has largely been left aside in favour of the war poets (of which one has to say there is now something of a glut) with their often graphic depictions of the horrors of that war and their occasional somewhat lofty idealism. Indeed, horror, blood and gore seem almost to be the staple ingredient of most accounts published by authors in recent years, who write as if serving up the gruesome reality of the carnage to their readers for the very first time. I think it is fair to say that today's readers know only too well the harsh realities of the Great War, how it bled a generation dry for good intentions and how far too many young men paid the ultimate sacrifice for no other reason than the base egotism of the gold-braided élite.

But there is a place too in all that bloody detail, for the humour, prevalent in even the most dire of situations, with which the squalid British Tommy kept alive his flagging spirit, his belief in the cause, the great crusade against the barbarous Hun, and his steadfast loyalty to his homeland and his so-called 'superiors', who ever seemed intent on doing away with him. And for too many years the humour of the trenches has been overlooked and shut away in favour of that harsh realism we know all too well today.

There is certainly a place for Bairnsfather alongside his peers, the likes of Graves, Sassoon and Owen, and although his material, dealing as it does in both his cartoons and his prose, presents us with an often schoolboyish view of the war, it is no less valid for that. His insight, understanding and critical powers of observation of what the beleaguered Tommy went through are second to none.

Indeed, shortly after the war Bairnsfather was dubbed 'the man who helped win the war'. For how many other artists, writers or poets could the same claim be made, and this by the very people who won that war and returned to the land of their birth, often bitter and jaded?

And though the work of his peers continues to fascinate new generations and remains in print, is required reading in our educational establishments, is studied to the nth degree, is pored over, discussed, dissected, devoured, digested and regurgitated to be pounced on afresh by some well-intentioned academic or scholar with an alphabet of letters after his name, ever endeavouring to find deeper and deeper meaning in every word, sentence and nuance, it is for me, and for people like me with an appreciation of Bairnsfather's work, that one finds in its sheer simplicity a truth; a truth which is shown far more starkly in a simple brush-stroke or the sweeping curve of a pencil than in all the sentences, paragraphs and chapters written by the lauded, laurel-crowned few. Bairnsfather captured the essence of that terrible life, and was respected, admired and lauded by the very people who knew that life intimately, the Tommies in the trenches. Their love of the man speaks volumes for his integrity and his rapport with them. Bairnsfather was not just an 'officer cartoonist', he was seen as one of them, one who had suffered and had been through what they had been through. He was their hero, of their own choosing, and they took him to their hearts. Therefore when the debate arises, does Bairnsfather's work deserve to be presented on a par with that of his peers and contemporaries, let the humble British Tommy's voice be heard, and hear him cry resoundingly, "Yes! Yes! Yes!"

It is time Captain Bruce Bairnsfather was remembered for what he gave the nation (and for which he was never officially recognised) and in particular what he gave to the British Tommy - a heart full of mirth with which he was able to endure and eventually win that grotesque and bloody war.

*

Charles Bruce Bairnsfather was born on the 9th July 1887 at Murree, an isolated hill station on the North West Frontier some thirty miles north of Rawalpindi. Lieutenant Thomas Bairnsfather (Bruce's father), had been appointed to the Indian Staff Corps with the Bengal Infantry, and so it was that his heavily pregnant wife, Amelia Jane Every, found herself giving birth to her first-born in what could only be described as 'the middle of nowhere' in less than salubrious surroundings.

From the very beginning Bruce, as he was known, was shown great affection and, unlike other British parents of the time, Thomas and Amelia chose not to keep their son at arm's length, but encouraged him to share their own varied interests.

On the 2nd April 1890, a second son, Malcolm Henry was born. By this time the boys' father was serving as a Captain with the 29th Punjab Infantry and the family was housed at the Dalhousie hill station on the Kashmir border. Though the Bairnsfathers' new son survived an outbreak of typhoid at the station, he succumbed to meningitis a month after his first birthday in 1891.

With Bruce approaching his eighth year the family returned to England in 1895 and did the 'family rounds', staying with relatives until Bruce was offered a home with Amelia's sister and her husband, the Rector of Thornbury, near Bromyard in Herefordshire, prior to his being sent off to school. Meanwhile Thomas and Amelia returned to India.

Deprived of company, Bruce was left to his own devices a lot of the time and found some small comfort from his loneliness in drawing, and his frequent letters to his parents were often littered with small sketches and childish doodles.

In those days it was fully expected that a son would follow in his father's footsteps, and the United Services College, Rudyard Kipling's former school at Westward Ho!, was chosen as the educational establishment for Bruce. The school's founders had one principal aim uppermost in their minds at all times; to get their boys into the British Army via either Sandhurst or Woolwich. Bruce would prove to be no exception.

On the 16th October 1897, Amelia gave birth to her third son, Tom Duncan, and a year later the Bairnsfathers returned to England for a brief visit. It was whilst on this visit that the pair became convinced that Bruce's prolific artistic output had to be stemmed. This feeling was further reinforced by close relatives, who maintained the need for stricter discipline on the boy. Thus, in June of 1898, Bruce was enrolled at Westward Ho! with instructions from his father to the headmaster to 'beat his *artistic* ability out of him'! Harsh instruction indeed from a father who had doted on his son in his early years, but who firmly believed it was for Bruce's own good; for certainly it was believed that no good could come of such an artistic bent in the Army. A little less than a month later the canings began.

Bruce stayed at the school for six years, the first two of which were spent in the junior school, where he was unmercifully bullied, caned and forced to fag for the senior boys. Mischievous by nature, Bruce brought much of his punishment on himself due to his outright determination to avoid work of any kind, and this despite the fear of reprisals from members of staff who were all too free in venting their dislike of the boy with the cane. However, ironically, on one occasion, when his 'Prep-work' exercise book was discovered filled with drawings of soldiers Bruce was punished, not with the cane, but by being forced to sit and draw soldiers for two hours instead of joining in school games. It is doubtful this taught him a lesson!

In 1899 Bruce's parents and younger brother, now nicknamed Bumpy, returned to England. Thomas Bairnsfather had completed his Indian service with a deserved promotion to the rank of Major, and the family chose to settle near Bideford, to be close to their eldest son. A year later Bruce passed the entrance exam to the senior school, though he continued to do badly. The canings he had endured as a youngster continued, this time added to by the senior boys and prefects who beat him for not liking rugby, and on another occasion, for having had too many canings during the previous week!

His reports were dire and the criticism of him by his masters was unrelenting. But rather than mend his ways and buckle under, Bruce found a perverse satisfaction in filling his exercise books with caricatures, often of those masters whose ire he would have to endure afterward.

When plans were made to move the school to a more populated area in 1904 it was decided that Bruce would not join it. After all, he had achieved nothing, save a school prize for drawing and much notoriety. With his father still determined that Bruce should follow him into the Army he was sent to a 'crammer' - Trinity College in Stratford-upon-Avon - in order to learn enough to get him through the entrance exam. Bruce was not averse to going into the Army, though he did harbour rather romantic notions as to what the life involved.

With this move to a fresh and stimulating environment, and a bedroom of his own in the attic of the family home at Bishopton, Bruce began to explore his talent for art, using watercolour and oils to record the images of the Warwickshire countryside around him. However, unfamiliar with the mediums and frustrated at not being able to produce what he wanted to on canvas and paper he convinced his father to allow him to attend art classes at the newly built Stratford Technical College and here he quickly became the star pupil. Indeed, with the encouragement of the school's headmaster, Thomas Holte, Bruce blossomed and gradually his earlier enthusiasm for joining the Army began to fade. As his talent took shape Bruce soon became known as the 'resident cartoonist'

In the early days I found illustrating my career in the margin most unlucky!

The editor regrets he is unable to accept, etc., etc. From 'The Bairnsfather Case' - 1920.

"Yer know, Bert, I shouldn't be surprised if they puts up a memorial for us around 'ere some time."

at Trinity College and even began selling his drawings to his fellow students. Bolstered by these minor successes, he drew and submitted numerous designs for advertisements to various businesses, but it was a design for Players Navy Mixture which earned him his first professional payment of two guineas - Bruce was so proud he carried the cheque about with him for weeks, showing it to friends and anyone who showed any interest until the cheque was so tatty it was almost uncashable.

By the time of his Army entrance exam Bruce's mind was occupied with other things and, although he waited anxiously for the result, it was rather a foregone conclusion. He failed. He did, however, get nearly full marks for his drawing, which seemed to please him greatly, though it is likely his parents were far less pleased.

However, rather than being happy about not passing the Army entrance exam as might be expected of him, Bruce determined to get into the Army by the only other method open to him. He would sit a much simpler examination and then do eighteen months of basic training, which, it was hoped, would lead to a full commission.

In 1906, at the age of nineteen, he passed the Army exam and joined the 3rd Militia Battalion Royal Warwickshire Regiment, based at Budbrook Barracks. Army life, an endless round of drilling, bayonet practice, route-marches and shooting practice, soon reinforced his belief that he was a military flop. Even his transfer to a Regular battalion of the Cheshire Regiment (his father Thomas's old regiment) did not alleviate his disillusionment and boredom. At every opportunity he would escape his dreary Army life and lose himself in the music halls of Birmingham.

However, the escapism of those same halls was put out of his reach when his regiment was moved to Bordon, near Aldershot, and it was here that the urge to quit the Army became almost irresistible, so much so indeed that Bruce became ill and prevailed upon his parents to allow him to leave the Army to follow an artistic career.

In 1908 Bruce did just that and enrolled in the John Hassall School of Art, near Olympia. He took a room in Earl's Court and threw himself into his art, often being the last pupil to leave the school at the end of the day, when he would return to his small room and continue with his sketches. Again the music halls, this time those of West London, provided him with entertainment and relaxation. When his time at the school ended Bruce tried his hand at producing posters, but met with little success and, with abject failure on his immediate horizon, could do nothing more than take a job as an electrical apprentice with Spencer's of Henley Street, Stratford. In his spare time he continued drawing and producing posters and paintings. Some little work came his way from such companies as Liptons and Beecham's, and the proceeds from these, along with his savings, allowed him to make short trips to both France and Belgium to study the work of the masters. But by far his greatest success in this lean period was winning a poster competition organised by the Quinlan Opera Company for which he won the princely sum of £10.

Still with the firm of Spencers, Bruce gradually worked his way up to the position of lighting engineer and then to speciality salesman. Early in 1914 he was dispatched by the company to sort out a machine in Newfoundland. It was to be the first of his many seasick crossings. Bruce was a fearfully bad sailor. It was on his return from this brief sojourn to Newfoundland that the world was plunged into war and a letter from Spencer's duly informed him that due to the outbreak of hostilities his services were no longer required. Thus he found himself penniless and without employment. However, like many of his contemporaries, Bruce, swollen with patriotic pride, did the one thing least expected of him, he re-joined the Army.

Within a matter of days he was back in the uniform of the Royal Warwickshire Regiment, and on 12th September 1914 was commissioned into its 3rd (Reserve) Battalion. He moved to Albany Barracks on the Isle of Wight, and at the end of November was ordered to join the 1st Battalion, then in trenches near Armentières. He was accompanied by a company of one hundred men which he was supposed to deliver safely. It is this trip, taken over 28th and 29th November, which opens the first book of this omnibus *'Bullets & Billets'*.

For two days Bruce remained at a reinforcement camp just outside Le Havre, before orders came through instructing him to join his battalion as a machine-gun officer. The Warwickshires had arrived in France shortly after the Battle of Mons (23rd August 1914) and had taken part in the retreat.

Bruce's journey to the front took two days by train, via Rouen and Boulogne, and the further he travelled the greyer, wetter and flatter everything around him became. Finally he reached the end of the line, to find no one there to meet him and with no idea exactly where the battalion was. Once he found it he soon settled into the regular routine. Combined with a rigorous adherence to that routine he adopted (as many of his age and background did), alongside an almost caricatured sense of duty, a sort of perverse sense of public-school humour in order to conceal the very real shock of trench life, and to hide his true feelings at seeing the bodies of the slain strewn between the opposing trenches, so numerous they formed part of the trench walls. Everywhere bloated rats fed on the dead, while the living were eaten alive by lice. Coupled to this was the misery of trench-foot - where feet, agonisingly raw, swelled to balloon-size proportions - the constant chatter of machine guns and the all too frequent 'thump' and 'crump' of the artillery barrages. All of it affected him greatly, so much so in fact that he seldom took time out behind the lines for fear of not being able to face the return to the horrors of the front line. That schoolboy humour saw him through those dark early days and was to stay with him throughout the war, serving as a counterbalance to the horror and carnage all around him, though it was later mixed with hard-bitten cynicism and a critical appraisal of those above him, many of whom he felt not only unfit for command, but unworthy of the implicit trust placed in them by the humble British Tommy in the front line.

That first Christmas on the Western Front saw the most extraordinary episode of the entire war, when men from both sides held an 'unofficial' cease-fire and fraternised in no-man's-land, despite the orders from their 'back-area' superiors. Bruce was a part of this unusual tapestry and it is both described and drawn in Chapter 8 of *'Bullets & Billets'*. By this time he was a full Lieutenant and, unlike more senior officers stuck in remote and largely safe back areas well behind the lines, he suffered the same privations and conditions as did the men under his command, regular soldiers who hailed from the area of the Midlands he was so familiar with.

It was in a battle-scarred cottage in the tiny village of St Yvon that the first *'Fragments from France'* (for which he would justly become world famous) were born, when Bruce decorated the ravaged walls of the cottage with his own particular brand of humorous cartoons. His drawings, often done on scraps of paper, were at that time also becoming popular with the men, who took them and pinned them up in their trenches. The more in demand he became, the more he drew and soon anything that could be drawn on was being used, scraps of paper, ration boxes, and the pock-marked walls of that little cottage. Bruce delighted in drawing what he saw and heard around him, and in so doing, he delighted those around him. On one occasion, one which was to prove rather momentous for Bruce in particular, the cottage was evacuated as shells rained down on the village. Fortunately the cottage remained unscathed and, once the shelling had ceased, Bruce and his fellows returned to it, whereupon another shell was loosed and fell close by. To a man the group rushed to the door and exclaimed, *"Where did that one go to?"*

Ever ready with his pencils, Bruce made a quick sketch of the incident and later, during a rare rest period behind the lines, completed a finished drawing using the exclamation of his comrades as its title. Someone suggested the drawing be sent to *The Bystander* magazine, a copy of which was lying around. The drawing was duly dispatched and Bruce thought no more of it for several weeks as the routine of 'in and out' of the trenches consumed his every waking hour. On 2nd February 1915 he was promoted to Captain and on the 25th he went home on leave. However, back home, with no one to share the horrors of the war with and no longer able to sustain the pretence before his comrades, Bruce buckled and was advised to extend his leave for the sake of his sanity. At first he accepted the advice, but on impulse returned to France and to what had, by then, become all too familiar to him. He rejoined the battalion on 4th March 1915. It was therefore a moment of great surprise when a cheque and a letter of acceptance arrived from *The Bystander*, on 21st March. *"Where did that one go to?"* appeared in the magazine on 31st March 1915. Bruce's career had begun and with it the association which would bring him world-wide fame.

Sometime later the battalion was moved north of Douve at the base of Messines Ridge and, during a ten-day rest period, Bruce found himself billeted in a French farmhouse. It was here he received another letter of acceptance from *The Bystander* for his drawing entitled, *"They've evidently seen me."* which showed the head of an officer, with field glasses, poking out of a chimney through which an enemy shell is passing (the picture would eventually appear in the 21st April 1915 issue).

By mid-March 1915 the weather had improved and Bruce found himself much in demand. The Colonel wanted the walls of his Headquarters decorated with sketches, the Brigade Commander requested a drawing, and Divisional Headquarters wanted a dozen of his pictures. Within the space of eighteen months the allied countries of France, Italy and America would readily acknowledge the morale-boosting effect of Bruce's work, yet the British would never officially acknowledge him or reward him.

In April the battalion was moved into the infamous Ypres Salient, where, at 5.00pm on 22nd April, the Germans launched the first gas attack of the war. Two days later they followed it up with a second attack in the areas of Langemarck and Passchendaele. In the early hours of 25th April the Warwickshires were marched into battle and into a vicious hail of machine-gun and artillery fire. Two miles north-east of Ypres, at Wieltje, Bruce was tossed into the air by a shell exploding nearby, which damaged his hearing and left him disorientated. That day the battalion lost 500 men and 17 officers, killed, wounded or missing. At least Bruce was still alive, though his nerves had finally taken all they could and snapped. Within forty-eight hours, diagnosed with shellshock, he was in a Boulogne hospital, bound for Blighty.

A spell in the 4th London General Hospital at King's College, Denmark Hill, followed, and with it Bruce's rehabilitation began; for it was to the hospital that a representative of *The Bystander* magazine tracked him down and offered him a contract. The magazine had received a host of complimentary letters concerning his two previously published pictures and Bruce was offered the weekly sum of £4 to provide a single drawing for each publication. The rest, as they often say, is history and Bruce's rise to fame was

Top: Lieutenant Bairnsfather, in the Plugstreet Wood area, circa 1914.
Bottom: Captain Bairnsfather, the 'officer cartoonist', circa 1916.

meteoric in anyone's terms. At the end of July he was declared fit for light duties and posted back to his regiment and the 3rd Reserve Battalion at Parkhurst on the Isle of Wight. Here he was placed in charge of 200 'old soldiers' all of whom, like him, were on light duties. And it was here, among these Old Contemptibles, that the character for which he was most famous, the walrus-moustached, bulbous-nosed Old Bill took shape and cropped up more and more in his drawings. It was the beginning of a partnership which would last a lifetime, through good times and bad, and through Bruce's many ups and downs.

Two months later, at the end of September 1915, he was posted to Salisbury Plain and the Headquarters of the 34th Division at Sutton Veney. Here he became the divisional machine-gun officer, responsible for training the officers and sections for the entire division. It was at Sutton Veney, in October 1915, that Bruce was to draw what, arguably, was to become his most famous piece of work. It was the drawing of two soldiers in a shell-hole, one of whom was very disgruntled. The caption, which would soon become a common part of the English language read, *"Well, if you knows of a better 'ole, go to it."*

The drawing featured in *The Bystander* in the issue of 24th November 1915 (the Christmas edition). The country took to this drawing and its message as to no other image of the war, and spurred on by the nation's enthusiasm *The Bystander* published a collection of forty-one of Bruce's drawings in booklet form early in 1916. The booklet was entitled, *'Fragments from France'* and *'The better 'ole'* was used for the cover. It sold out. A second print run was ordered and that too sold out. In all the booklet was printed a staggering eleven times and sold over a quarter of a million copies. The original drawing of *'The better 'ole'* now resides in the Victoria and Albert Museum in London.

Though Bruce was now something of a celebrity, he was still in the Army and eventually he was posted back to France as a staff captain (special reserve) with the Fourth Army railheads at Montrelet in the Albert and Doullens sector.

Meanwhile, back home in May 1916, an exhibition of Bruce's work was held at the Graphic Gallery on the Strand, with offers for the originals being made from all quarters. The original of *'The better 'ole'* was sold to an unnamed general in the War Office. With such success Bruce's work was ripe for exploitation and *The Bystander* seized its opportunity by following up fragments with, *'More Fragments from France'*. The magazine increased Bruce's weekly fee from £4 to £20, though often he was producing a number of cartoons for the same fee.

However, Bruce's health again deteriorated and on 15th May he was hospitalised at Rouen, suffering from exhaustion with the added misery caused by a huge and painful carbuncle on his neck. But though in hospital he continued to produce his daily quota of sketches and drawings for *The Bystander*. Bruce was sent back to the hospital at King's College, Denmark Hill, Camberley and was formally classified as 'not fit for active service in France'. He was then sent home to Bishopton to recuperate until 20th June 1916.

It was now that the book he had been collecting notes for, and which would become *'Bullets & Billets'*, was begun in earnest. He also began work on material for the stage, translating his characters into music-hall figures. It was Old Bill who was to feature most prominently in these staged versions of his cartoons. Indeed, with the first presentation to the public of Bruce's stage work, in a revue titled *'Flying Colours'*, the 'establishment' was far from pleased, questions were asked in the House and generals complained vociferously about Bairnsfather's vulgar images of the British soldier.

Towards the end of August 1916, with the carnage of Verdun only just beginning to

Captain Bairnsfather, as the newly appointed 'officer cartoonist' makes haste to return to the Western Front, this time to draw cartoons for the French, November 1916.

fade, the French requested that Bruce be loaned to them to create for France what he had created for the British - high morale through the medium of laughter. Reluctantly the War Office agreed and Bruce was appointed 'Officer Cartoonist' in the Intelligence Department. Once again Bruce was in France, this time travelling throughout the French sectors. His cartoons were published in the French Army's official publication *'Bulletin des Armées'* and decorated the French Headquarters at Coxyde-les-Bains (near Ostend).

The year was a hectic one. In November Cassell's published a book by Captain A. J. Dawson, titled *'A Temporary Gentleman in France'* for which Bruce provided the cover illustration. Hodder & Stoughton published another of Dawson's books, *'Somme Battle Stories'* which featured eight of Bruce's drawings. December saw the publication of *'Bairnsfather, A Few Fragments From His Life'* by Vivian Carter, the editor of *The Bystander*. And in the same month Bruce's own autobiographical work, *'Bullets & Billets'* was published by Grant Richards of London, in which he recounts his adventures from landing in France to his return home after being wounded at Ypres.

Early in 1917 Bruce returned to England to work on his French drawings, as well as a new stage piece for a revue titled *'See Saw'*. The year would prove frenetic as Bruce endeavoured to translate his work into a hit London show, produced books for both the home and French markets, and entered the film world, as well as continuing to provide material for *The Bystander* as *'Fragments'* approached sales of a staggering two million.

Then came an invitation to tour the Italian front from the Italian Army which he took up and describes in his second book (published by Grant Richards in 1919) *'From Mud to Mufti'*. The book takes up his story where *'Bullets & Billets'* left off (one reason they appear together in this omnibus edition).

The stage play *'The Better 'Ole'*, built around the character of Old Bill and the *'Fragments from France'* cartoons, opened on 4th August 1917. Despite everyone believing it would be a disaster it was a major hit and the audience loved it. That successful opening night began a two-and-a-half-year run which would see up to a dozen companies touring the globe and a successive 817 performances at the Oxford Music Hall. The stage magazine *Play Pictorial* devoted an entire issue to the play and *The Weekly Despatch* called it, 'A real war play at last'. Also in August 1917 the fourth volume of *'Fragments from France'* was published and the total copies in print topped 1,725,000. A Midlands based pottery company, Grimwades, created pottery pieces which carried reproductions of the cartoons on them, everything from shaving mugs to flower pots, all cheap and produced in abundance. *The Bystander*, capitalising still further on its most famous artist, issued a pack of playing cards which featured the *'Fragments from France'* cartoons and introduced a monthly set of six postcards.

Then the Americans entered the war and Bruce was once again in demand by an allied army. This time the Americans wanted him in France to capture the spirit of their troops and to do what he had done for the British, French and Italians, namely to relieve the tension of war through laughter. In December 1917 Bruce left for France and Neufchâteau in the Alsace-Lorraine region. The Americans turned out to be the most friendly people he had ever known and he returned home, with sketchbooks bulging, to a hectic round of charity functions.

At the beginning of 1918, Welsh-Pearson turned Bruce's *'The Better 'Ole'* into a motion picture and it was released in Britain on 1st July. Next the Australian Government wanted him 'down under' to raise their troops' morale. The trip took Bruce via America and in October he was in New York, besieged by autograph hunters and well-wishers. While he was there *'The Better 'Ole'* opened to a packed house and was as much a success in America as it had been at home. However, Bruce's health now took a turn for the worse and his trip to Australia was cancelled. On his return rumours of an armistice were in the air and the war finally came to an end. It was shortly after this he put the finishing touches to *'From Mud to Mufti'*.

1919 saw Bruce embark on a gruelling lecture tour around the country, which tired him greatly. Back in London he entered into a new five-year contract with *The Bystander* to continue working for the magazine which had helped make him famous, and to produce a weekly magazine of his own simply titled *'Fragments'*. Meanwhile he was also contributing articles (and later his first 'comic strip') to the *Daily Graphic*. His popularity was at its peak. The magazine was well received and sold well, even by today's standards. In September 1919 it was selling 500,000 copies a week, and by the beginning of October this had risen to 700,000. With what he regarded as a steady income for the foreseeable future Bruce began to look for somewhere to settle down and call home. He bought the Old Spa house at Bishopton (where he still had a studio) for his parents, and then turned his attention to acquiring a property for himself, somewhere close to his 'income' (Tallis House, the headquarters of *The Bystander*) but not too far from his parents. He settled on an Elizabethan house, Waldridge Manor, in Buckinghamshire, with 250 acres of grounds. However it would take him more than a year and several thousand pounds to make the place habitable. To enable him to bring the interior up to modern standards Bruce sold off almost 200 hundred acres.

In October 1919 *'From Mud to Mufti'* was published and sold well. And with Old Bill now a household name, with mascot images and impersonators of him all over the country, Bruce continued to prosper.

January of the following year (1920) saw him off on a lecture tour of the United States. The hectic schedule caught up with him and by the end of the month he was hospitalised, having collapsed. Unable to continue with the tour, Bruce returned to England in February.

Examples of his work were springing up all over the place. The Staffordshire pottery company, Grimwades, extended their range considerably, renaming it *'Bairnsfather Ware'*, and included full dinner services, tea sets and even items of fine china. In May an 'Old Bill' motor mascot was advertised through the *'Fragments'* magazine. The mascot, the tin-helmeted head of Old Bill, was cast in a choice of bronze (by far the most popular), brass, nickel and chromium plate. Bruce, proud of his old friend, mounted one on his own car.

The *'Fragments'* magazine went from to strength to strength with many famous writers and artists contributing to its success. By November, Bruce was again in America entertaining audiences with his lectures and anecdotes. Following the 10,000 mile tour he returned home just after Christmas and on 15th January 1921, at the age of thirty-three, he was married at the London City Registry Office to Australian divorcée, Cecilia Agnes Scott, aged thirty-four. Everyone was caught by surprise, for Bruce had kept his private life private, and few knew of the pair's relationship. The wedding was a low-key affair and was not reported in the press until some ten days later. The pair (along with Cecilia's daughter, teenager Heather, from her former marriage), with the renovations on the Manor House at Waldridge complete, bought a London town house situated in John Street off the Strand. He also bought his parents a new home, a house named White Cliff at Princes Riseborough and moved them there lock, stock and barrel.

As well as his regular magazine work, Bruce was also working on a new stage show featuring Old Bill. The show would be called *'Old Bill MP'* and would follow the character from his work down a pit, through industrial strife and on to Westminster. The show finally opened on 17th April 1922, Easter Monday. It was another success. However, a suitable London venue had not been found and it was decided to take the show on tour. It was at this time that *The Bystander* group of magazines and periodicals (which included the *Graphic*) was sold and Bruce's contract with them terminated. It was a severe blow. Meanwhile the play went on and opened at the Lyceum on 12th July. It ran for 159 performances, which ended, rather symbolically, on 11th November.

Bruce then found himself in the limelight as he agreed to appear in a variety show for the princely sum of £110 a week. His act was titled *'Old Bill and Me'* and was booked for a twenty-two week tour. It was during this tour, on 26th December 1922, that Bruce's first and only child was born, a girl, Barbara Bruce Bairnsfather.

In March 1923 the *Ideal Home* magazine did a seven-page illustrated feature on Waldridge Manor, described as *'the residence of Captain Bruce Bairnsfather, a time-honoured relic'*. Film offers for the rights to his work began coming in from both the UK and USA, and with work underway on *'Old Bill Through the Ages'* at Elstree, Bruce accepted a £150 a week arrangement to tour America with his stage act. Before the Bairnsfathers travelled abroad Waldridge Manor was put up for sale. Realising he would need to spend more time in the USA (for that was where the real money was to be made) and that he had spent far too much on the manor's restoration, Bruce had reluctantly decided to rid himself of the place. In the event he got less than half of what he had paid for it. That year, 1923, he spent Christmas in Kansas City.

His next business move, in 1924, was to sign with King Features for a syndicated comic strip throughout America and Canada. Thus the Bairnsfathers took the first of a succession of furnished apartments in New York and Bruce settled down to producing comic strips for the North American newspapers. Meanwhile, back home in May, the film *'Old Bill Through the Ages'*, billed as a *'film that is going to make the world laugh'* opened. Though it was a box-office success at the time, it is believed Bruce made very little from it. Bruce briefly returned home to produce and launch another revue, *'Ullo'* (Old Bill's famous catchword), before returning to the States to fulfil his many commitments. The revue did not do well. Indeed, it fared so badly that he was forced to return to England and to his new base at 33 Tedworth Square, there to attend a panicked conference of agent and bookers. It was decided to add a 'star' name to the production, but rather than help, this tactic actually backfired and the star's £100 a week salary was not covered by increased attendance. In desperation Bruce borrowed £1,000 from a friend to keep the show afloat. He further raised money against an expected inheritance and managed to secure some work from the *Sunday Express*.

In October of 1925 the immediate future began to look a little brighter. The failing revue *'Ullo'*, was re-titled *'Carry On Sergeant'* and re-launched on 28th October. It ran for eight weeks and cost Bruce some £8,000. It was a financial consequence from which he would never fully recover. Broken by what he saw as his failure Bruce sold his only remaining asset, his car, and returned to the States.

In 1926 things began to pick up. Charlie Chaplin's brother Syd negotiated the rights for a film version of *'The Better 'Ole'*, a contract was signed for a daily comic strip and another to write an 'Old Bill' book. Bruce was also contributing to *Life* magazine. His coffers were further enhanced when Warner Brothers, producers of the Chaplin film, accepted and paid him for twelve advertising posters. The film opened in New York on 23rd October 1926 to generally good reviews and consistent houses well into 1927. Back home in Britain it received a mixed reception for Chaplin's version of Old Bill bore little

Top: Cecilia Agnes Scott, before she became Mrs Bruce Bairnsfather on 15th January 1921.
Bottom: Barbara 'Barbie' Bairnsfather, Bruce's only child, at a chess tournament, circa 1932.

resemblance to Bruce's original character. The year also saw the founding of the MOTHS (the Memorable Order of Tin Hats) by Charles Evenden of South Africa. The organisation, which took Old Bill as its mascot, was set up for veterans and each branch was known as a Shell-Hole with a name of its own. Their officials were known as Old Bills. The first British 'shell-hole' was Windy Corner, founded in Reading three months later.

1927 also saw the publication by Bobbs-Merrill of the book, *'Carry On Sergeant'*, consisting of reminiscences of Bruce's wartime experiences, now a little more considered and matured than his own earlier efforts in *'Bullets & Billets'* and *'From Mud to Mufti'*. Sadly the book was written specifically for the American market and very few copies were imported to Britain. While all this was going on around him Bruce continued with his 'vaudeville' act, playing a week at the Palace, New York in January of 1927. Towards the latter part of the year he received a proposition which would provide him with the most spectacular disaster of his career.

The newly formed Canadian International Films approached him to write their first screenplay. Bruce agreed and wrote *'Carry On Sergeant!'* It was the story of a sergeant in the Canadian Scottish, and followed him from his enlistment, through his arrival on the Western Front, his martial and amorous adventures and his final death in action during the Second Battle of Ypres in 1915, a period and place Bruce knew only too well. He was appointed director and moved from New York to Trenton, Canada, where Cecilia and Barbara (then aged five) joined him. Production on the film began in September, though actual filming did not start until November due to poor weather. The film premiered on Saturday, 10th November 1928 and was released to good reviews, for the film had been heavily cut from 14 reels to just 9. However, after a promising start the film faltered and by the end of December was on its last legs, with audiences walking out during performances. In January 1929 Canadian International Films Limited was declared bankrupt.

The whole experience left Bruce seriously disillusioned and very much poorer, for he had worked for almost a year without a salary, having agreed to be paid when the film made money! It was with reluctant resignation that Bruce uprooted from Canada, where his future had seemed promising, to return to New York. His first priority was to resurrect Old Bill, who was now appearing as a waxwork at Madame Tussaud's (and in fact remained on show there until 1934), which he did for the magazine *Judge*.

By 1930 Bruce and Cecilia were estranged, her drinking (a problem from their very earliest days together), wild swings of temperament and constant interference with his work, coupled with such an impoverished time for them, led her back to England, whilst Bruce took up with the actress and producer Constance Collier. Cecilia began divorce proceedings and she was granted alimony. This in turn led Bruce into another round of touring and live performances to meet his financial commitments.

Early in 1931 he was again hospitalised. Cecilia discontinued divorce proceedings and in May Bruce sailed for England, having told reporters that his domestic affairs were straightened out and that he was returning to his wife. In actual fact he did not land at Portsmouth, much to the chagrin of the waiting reporters there, but sailed on, to be reunited with Cecilia in Paris. The pair, on returning to England, made their home at Piltdown, Sussex, and it was here that Bruce converted a disused chapel in the garden into a studio.

In September the pair returned to the States, ready for Bruce to embark on yet another lecture tour. This was followed in the Spring of 1932 by his first World Tour. Honolulu

1. *From 'Laughing Through the Orient' - 1932.*

2. *From 'Laughing Through the Orient' - 1932.*

3. *From 'Carry On Sergeant!' - 1927.*

4. *From 'Laughing Through the Orient' - 1932.*

was followed by Yokohama Bay and Fujiyama in Japan, then on to China and Hong Kong, Macao and Singapore, Johore and Penang and thus to India. But it was not to the India of his memories to which he returned, but to the commercialised, tourist packed and impoverished place it had now become. They passed on to Aden, Suez and Port Said, on to Naples and in June finally disembarked at Marseilles to travel to Paris by night train. They then returned to Piltdown, where Bruce could recharge his batteries before returning to the States in the Autumn for another lecture tour.

Now he set to work on a new book, *'Laughing Through the Orient'*, which detailed his recent world tour, on preparing for his new 'show', and in producing sketches and comic strips for the various newspapers and periodicals he was committed to. On 1st August he wrote an article for the *Daily Herald*, titled 'Old Bill Comes Back', it was inspired by the erection of the Thiepval monument to over 73,000 British dead who gave their lives on the Somme, but who have no known grave. The monument also commemorated the 200,000 soldiers from all nations who died fighting to gain possession of the hill upon which the memorial was built. The article was in the form of a dialogue between the 'Capting' and Old Bill and was rather bitter. It set out the argument that the true war memorials were the maimed soldiers who still inhabited the many war hospitals throughout the country, and that had the soldiers known their reward (if they survived) or compensation (if they died) for enduring the horrors of the war would be an impressive brick or stone structure, it would not have been sufficient motivation for joining up, nor for continuing to endure that fearful conflict. In essence Bruce was expressing the feelings of a vast majority of war veterans; industrial unrest, mass unemployment, and the lack of understanding, gratitude or remembrance by those who had remained civilians during the fighting were all fuel added to the raging fires of discontent and bitterness.

That same year, 1932, Bruce's fortunes plummeted. Not only had his unwise investments, unfavourably-termed contracts and unbusinesslike ventures become readily apparent with regard to his lack of wealth, but on 23rd August a bankruptcy notice was served against him by an American businessman tired of chasing him for payment of a small, outstanding bill. Publicity was rife about his financial status and affairs, but gradually the excitement died down and Bruce and Cecilia, with whom he was reconciled, returned to New York. Whilst Bruce embarked on a mammoth eight thousand mile tour of thirty-five cities, Cecilia ensconced herself in their New York apartment.

With the bankruptcy revelations still hanging over him Bruce began 1933 in a surprisingly optimistic mood. The book *'Laughing Through the Orient'* was published in March and received good reviews. He was then invited to do a series of articles for the *Daily Express* and travelled through Germany (where Hitler was on the rise) and Russia (where Stalin was all-powerful). The articles appeared from the end of May 1933 and Bruce used the familiar guise of Old Bill to make his observations. The European trip was swiftly followed by yet another American tour, and on his return to England he embarked on a music-hall tour.

During 1933 Bruce also began work for *'The Passing Show'* magazine, in which he drew a weekly 'Old Bill and Bert' cartoon strip until 1938. A number of the cartoons from the magazine were also reproduced as postcards by Tucks. Life was busy and hectic, but far from profitable. And to make matters worse the truth of his financial state was made public and everyone knew how far he had fallen from those heady wartime heights.

Old Bill proudly displays his 'British Legion' membership badge.

The next few years were to prove difficult. One bright period was his association with the Royal British Legion (formed in 1921 to promote the interests of ex-servicemen of the Great War), which Old Bill joined and for whose *Journal* Bruce drew a steady supply of sketches based on Old Bill's Great War memories. He also produced a postcard for the Legion (reproduced on page xxx) which assisted greatly in recruiting.

In late 1934 Bruce's bankruptcy was discharged and some relief was brought to bear on his perilous financial situation, though he was by no means out of the woods and needed to work steadily to keep the wolf from the door. The following year, in April 1935, twenty years after he was injured there, he returned to Ypres in an act of personal pilgrimage. It was a moving experience and one he wrote about for the Royal British Legion's *Journal*.

1936 saw another lecture tour of the States, where his popularity was still high, followed by another music-hall tour of England. The same year also saw the beginning of publisher George Newnes' weekly magazine *'Twenty Years After'* which was edited by Major-General Sir Ernest Swinton. The magazine was *'dedicated to the memory of those who marched away and returned no more, and to those who survive, in gratitude for all they did and all they suffered'*, and its stated aim was to describe the Great War. One of its main features was the use of contrasting photographs of famous landmarks as they had been during the war and as they were now, twenty years after, hence the title. Bruce appeared in Chapter 8 and alongside his article were examples of his work.

One of the most memorable events in Bruce's up and down career occurred on the 1st October of that year, when his drawings were featured in the first ever programme of experimental transmissions from the BBC's Alexandra Palace. There then followed a music-hall pairing of Bruce with popular comic of the day, Billy Russell. The pair toured Britain to approbation. More work followed with the *Evening Standard*. On the 14th August 1937 Bruce joined the Uckfield Branch of the Old Contemptibles Association and was proud to have been one of the few who had served in France between 5th August and 22nd November 1914.

As the clouds of war gathered over Europe in 1938 Bruce began work on his memoirs. The autobiography was titled *'Wide Canvas'* and was far removed from his earlier attempts (as produced in this omnibus). Early the following year Hutchinson published a thirty-six page book titled *'Old Bill Stands By, An Old Friend in a New Emergency'*. Old Bill had aged and put on more than a few pounds, yet he was once again ready to do his bit, for war looked certain. The book sold some 20,000 copies and proved popular enough for postcard publishers Valentines to produce a series of postcards titled *'Old Bill Again'*.

As the prospect of war loomed ever nearer Bruce was asked by the War Office to produce a poster to aid recruitment into the Territorial Army. A number of newspapers and periodicals trumpeted the fact that Old Bill was back, but the *Sunday Graphic* went further with words that must have stung Bruce to the quick:

"After twenty years Captain Bruce Bairnsfather, creator of Old Bill is making a come-back. Old Bill has made a come-back too, on 10,000 posters. For twenty years he has been dead, his fat jolly face thrown in the disused attic with the rest of the war relics. He was called the 'greatest inspiration of the last war'. He was equalled in fame only by his creator, once the world's most famous cartoonist."

Once again Old Bill was hitting the headlines. By bringing Bruce and his most famous character back at this time of crisis the War Office, was, in effect, paying recognition to the part the pair had played in the Great War - yet there was still no formal acknowledgement of Bruce's part in the allied victory.

1. *From 'Jeeps & Jests' - 1943.*

2. *Yes, it was on board a Corvette at an American naval base that he was asked to join the Merchant Service . . . just for a while.*

3. *Anglo-American relations.*
From 'Jeeps & Jests' - 1943.

4. *Old Bill.*
From 'Jeeps & Jests' - 1943.

5. *They both went through the 'last one', so there's plenty to talk over.*
From 'Jeeps & Jests' - 1943.

6. *'Over My Sandbags'*
The artwork for
Bruce's column in
Defence magazine - 1939.

7. *If he'd been in the American Army.*
From 'No Kiddin'!' - 1945.

As preparations for war increased, drawings of Old Bill amongst the new army appeared regularly in the *British Legion Journal*, and Bruce took up his association with *The Bystander* again, producing material for the magazine until 1942. A company approached Bruce for permission to make models of Old Bill and to use his image for advertising purposes. A contract was signed with Alexander Korda Film productions for the exclusive film rights to *'Old Bill'*. And the *Sunday Chronicle* engaged Bruce on a story competition for the armed services; *'Laugh again with Bairnsfather'* ran the caption, *'the famous comic artist who saw the funny side of things more brilliantly than anyone.'*

The various service magazines also sought him out and Bruce's recognition as the foremost cartoonist was re-established with his caricatures of Hitler, Stalin and Mussolini among others.

On 12th October 1939 *'Wide Canvas'* was published to excellent reviews. It was perhaps more than a little fortunate that by this time Bruce was re-establishing his reputation in Britain and in part this may have contributed to his acclaim. Also, Bruce had established the character of Young Bill (Old Bill's son, and of the generation which would fight this new war) in a regular comic strip for *Illustrated Magazine*. Young Bill would also come to life on the 'silver screen' as the film of *'Old Bill and Son'* went into production.

Bruce was given permission to visit the front line in France and he left London on 11th December 1939. During the three week trip he drove over one thousand miles, filling his notebooks and sketchpads with the drawings and observations he would later use in his many contributions to the magazines and periodicals of the day.

The Bairnsfathers had now settled in an old forge at North Chapel, near Petworth in Sussex, and things began to look up. In November 1940 the book *'Old Bill and Son'*, featuring stills from the film, was published. But with things going so well it was only a matter of time before everything fell apart again.

The film of *'Old Bill and Son'*, featuring a fresh-faced John Mills as Young Bill, opened on 9th February 1941. Already poorly received by the press in a private showing, the film fared little better on general release and was considered less than successful. As if to reinforce Bruce's growing sense of disquiet, his sudden and meteoric rise came to a shuddering halt as his contributions were cut, or reduced to allow room for other work. It was almost as if his star had blazed once more, brighter than ever, before finally sinking in the heavens.

However, though his homeland once again snubbed him, in America it was a different story and he found himself more in demand than ever. In 1942 Bruce was appointed an official cartoonist to the American Forces in Europe and contributed to the famous forces newspaper *Stars and Stripes*. With the rank of Captain, Bruce wore the American uniform with pride and to all intents and purposes became an American representative in Europe and travelled from American base to American base in both England and Ireland. In 1943 he was attached to the 8th Air Force's 305th Bomber Group at Chelveston, near Bedford. There was even an American bomber nicknamed Old Bill, upon whose nose Bruce himself painted the old soldier's likeness. Incidentally, the crew of that bomber became the most decorated in the 305th Bomber Group, with 2 DSCs (Distinguished Service Cross), 8 Silver Stars and 7 Purple Hearts.

In 1945 Bruce's last book, *'No Kiddin''* was published in America. With the end of the war work slackened off considerably and Bruce returned to the States on another lecture tour, followed by another in 1947. If nothing else, it kept the wolves at bay, for Bruce had very little work to do at home.

The last known photograph of Bruce Bairnsfather, taken in June 1959, just three months before his death at the age of 72.

The following year, on 14th August, Barbara, Bruce's only child, married William Littlejohn in Providence, Rhode Island. In 1949 Bruce put the Old Forge up for sale and moved into Barn Close nearby. However, near penury forced the sale of this home too and Bruce took a room at The Feathers Inn at Ledbury, until he was recognised and, for his own peace of mind was forced to move on again, this time to the secluded privacy of the Brecon Hills at the Old Cross, Winforton. In September 1951 Bruce and Cecilia moved again, to Dial Cottage, Evendine, Colwell. By this time, although not widely known, and overshadowed by Cecilia's growing ill health, Bruce was seriously ill with a growth in his bladder.

1952 saw Bruce become a grandfather, and Barbara's son was named Bruce Every Littlejohn, after Bruce and Bruce's mother, Amelia Jane Eliza Bairnsfather, formerly Every.

In 1954 Bruce moved home yet again, this time to Thames Ditton and a cottage called Two Rivers. His condition continued to worsen despite regular treatment. The year also saw Ceclia moved into a nursing home for treatment for her addiction to alcohol and general ill health. Indeed Bruce's own health and need to be closer to his surgeon prompted the sale of Two Rivers cottage and a move to Chapel Cottage, Littleworth, near Worcester. With no work his finances were once more under strain and eventually he was forced to sell his faithful old Morris with its Old Bill mascot on the hood.

On 31st December 1958 Bruce's mother passed away, aged 98 and, coincidentally, on the same date as his father had died in 1944. Writing from the Private Ward of the Royal Infirmary in Worcester, where he was seriously ill, Bruce informed his daughter of the event. But he kept from her the fact that he had been in hospital for five weeks.

Bruce's final work began in early 1959 when a series of articles appeared in the *Weekly Post*. By July he was able to travel to London and spent three weeks there, though he refused an invitation from Field Marshal Montgomery (himself an officer in the Warwickshires during the Great War) to a party for the officers of the Royal Warwickshire Regiment.

Following three major operations and eighteen examinations, Bruce succumbed to cancer of the bladder (which had to be removed), and died on 29th September 1959 of acute renal failure. He was just 72. The following day many newspapers carried warm tributes and detailed his long, although not always distinguished career. His daughter Barbara, still living in America, was shocked to hear the news of her father's death on the radio and hastily returned for the cremation service at Cheltenham.

Through successes and failures Bruce had continued through his life with his companion from the trenches ever constant by his side, Old Bill. The two were inseparable. Bruce died without the recognition rightly due him for his part in raising morale and presenting, albeit in a humorous fashion, the life of the trench-bound Tommy. Though he received approbation and acclaim at his peak from the general public the establishment never took to him and, while many of his contemporaries were honoured in one form or another, Bruce was constantly forgotten and deliberately overlooked.

The 1970s saw a growth in the demand for Bruce's work and for items connected to it and the man himself, and to this day collectors keep his memory alive with their collections of ephemera.

In 1978 Tonie and Valmai Holt published the *'Best of Fragments from France'*.

On 24th August 1981, Bruce's daughter, Barbara, proudly unveiled a Blue Commemorative Plaque on the wall of the artist's former home at 1 Sterling Street, Westminster, London.

In 1984, the Editor of the *British Postcard Collectors Magazine* produced a limited edition commemorative postcard to mark the 25th anniversary of Bruce's death, and the following year, 1985, saw the publication of the most authoritative Bairnsfather biography yet produced (along with a detailed catalogue of all the collectables associated with him) by Tonie and Valmai Holt (from which much of this greatly edited biography has been culled, and to whom I am greatly indebted for their permission to use material from their work).

And in 1987, to mark Bairnsfather's centenary, Mark Warby, one of his most ardent fans and one of the country's leading Bairnsfather authorities, was largely responsible for producing a special postcard featuring a portrait of the artist from 1942.

Thus, though largely overlooked, Bruce has never been forgotten.

*

That my grandfather thought so highly of Captain Bruce Bairnsfather (he would always use his rank when speaking of him) and could still recall him with a smile though he was 101 and the war some 78 years past, proves to me beyond any doubt that the man had what was sadly lacking in a lot of his contemporaries and superiors (and to a degree remains so to this day); empathy with the common soldier stuck in the trenches, rotting in the mud, being eaten alive by lice and flies, riddled by machine-gun bullets, blown to oblivion by constant shelling and eaten when dead by the rats which proliferated over the killing fields of France and Belgium. That he chose to turn the horror of what he saw and experienced first-hand, into cartoon form and humorous prose, says as much about the frailties of the human mind to comprehend the slaughter going on around it as it does about his obvious and very real talent to capture those moments and feelings which were common to all men, from all armies, in that terrible conflict. The war brought him an attention and 'stardom' that he was never able to recapture, as much a product of his time as the conflict which gave birth to his comic talents.

No doubt collectors will continue to collect, and readers continue to read, his work, even though he is largely forgotten now. But wouldn't it be comforting to think that one day, just maybe, we may yet see Old Bill in animated cartoon form, perhaps brought to life by the likes of Disney, transferred to film, video tape or DVD to recount his adventures in the Great War, the adventures of a doomed and lost generation.

Though Bruce Bairnsfather was without doubt a 'hero' to the British Tommy, one of their own whom they took to their hearts like no other, his praise remains unsung by his superiors and successive generations of government. Perhaps it is now time for the country to acknowledge the very great debt it owes this very singular man. A memorial plaque (one of only two 'memorials' known to exist - and sponsored by the Holts) in the Gardens of Remembrance at Cheltenham Crematorium reads in part, *'In loving memory of Captain Bruce Bairnsfather, 1st Royal Warwickshire Regiment. Creator of Old Bill.'*

I humbly suggest the addition of the single line, *'Who kept the Empire's spirit alive with his mirth in its darkest hours and who a grateful nation will never forget.'*

Mark Marsay
Author in Residence
Great Northern Publishing
Scarborough
April 2000

THE BAIRNSFATHER OMNIBUS

Bullets & Billets

Written and illustrated by

Bruce Bairnsfather

1916

Taken from the original frontispiece for 'Bullets & Billets',
the first part of Bairnsfather's wartime experiences.

The original title page for Bairnsfather's first book, 'Bullets & Billets', published by Grant Richards in December 1916.

Foreword

Down south, in the valley of the Somme, far from the spots recorded in this book, I began to write this story. In billets it was. I strolled across the old farmyard and into the wood beyond. Sitting by a gurgling little stream, I began, with the aid of a notebook and a pencil, to record the joys and sorrows of my first six months in France.

I do not claim any unique quality for these experiences. Many thousands have had the same. I have merely, by request, made a record of my times out there, in the way they appeared to me.

TO MY OLD PALS,
'BILL', 'BERT', AND 'ALF',
WHO HAVE SAT IN THE MUD WITH ME.

The original foreword and dedication by the author.

Chapter 1

LANDING AT HAVRE ~ TORTONI'S ~ FOLLOW THE TRAMLINES ~ ORDERS FOR THE FRONT

Gliding up the Seine, on a transport crammed to the lid with troops, in the still, cold hours of a November morning, was my debut into the war. It was about 6.00am when our boat silently slipped along past the great wooden sheds, posts and complications of Havre harbour.

I had spent most of the twelve-hour trip down somewhere in the depths of the ship, dealing out rations to the hundred men I had brought with me from Plymouth. This sounds a comparatively simple process, but not a bit of it. To begin with, the ship was filled to bursting point with troops, and the mere matter of proceeding from one deck to another was about as difficult as trying to get round to see a friend at the other side of the ground at a Crystal Palace cup final.

I stood in a queue of Gordons, Seaforths, Worcesters, etc., slowly moving up one, until, finally arriving at the companionway (nearly said staircase), I tobogganed down into the hold and spent what was left of the night dealing out those rations. Having finished at last, I came to the surface again, and now, as the transport glided along through the dirty waters of the river, and as I gazed at the motley collection of Frenchmen on the various wharves, and saw a variety of soldiery and a host of other warlike props, I felt acutely that now I was *in* the war at last - the real thing! For some time I had been rehearsing in England, but that was over now, and here I was, to use the common or garden vernacular, 'in the soup'.

At last we were alongside, and in due course I had collected that hundred men of mine and found that the number was still a hundred, after which I landed with the rest, received instructions and a guide, then started off for the base camps.

These camps were about three miles out of Havre, and thither the whole contents of the ship marched in one long column, accompanied on either side by a crowd of ragged little boys shouting for souvenirs and biscuits. My hundred men and I were near the rear of the procession, and in about an hour's time arrived at the base camps.

I don't know that it is possible to construct anything more atrociously hideous or uninteresting than a base camp. It consists, in military parlance of nothing more than 'fields, grassless; one - tents, bell; five hundred'; in fact, a huge space, once a field, now a bog, on which are perched rows and rows of squalid tents.

I stumbled along over the mud with my troupe, and having found the Adjutant (after a considerable search), thought that my task was over and that I could slink off into some odd tent or other and get a sleep and a rest. Oh no! The Adjutant had only expected fifty men, and here was I with a hundred.

Consternation! Two hours of telephoning and intricate backchat with the Adjutant eventually led to my being ordered to leave the expected fifty and take the others to another base camp hard by to see if they would like to have them there.

The rival base camp expressed a willingness to have this other fifty, so at last I had finished and having found an empty tent, lay down on the ground with my greatcoat for a pillow and went to sleep.

I awoke at about three in the afternoon, got hold of a bucket of water and proceeded to have a wash. Having shaved, washed, brushed my hair and had a look at the general effect in the polished back of my cigarette case (the rest of my kit was still at the docks), I emerged from my canvas cave and started off to have a look round.

I soon discovered a small café down the road, and found it was a place used by several of the officers who, like myself, were temporarily dumped at the camps. I went in and got something to eat. There was quite a good little place upstairs, where one could get breakfast each morning - just coffee, eggs and bread sort of thing. By great luck I met a pal of mine here, he had come over in a boat previous to mine, and after we had had a bit of a refresher and a smoke we decided to go off down to Havre and see the sights.

A tram passed along in front of the café, and this we boarded. It took about half an hour getting down to Havre from Bléville, where the camps were, but it was worth it.

Tortoni's Café, a place we looked upon as the last link with civilisation: Tortoni's with its blaze of light, looking-glass and gold paint, its popping corks and hurrying waiters, made a deep and pleasant indent on one's mind, for *tomorrow* meant *the Front* for most of those who sat there.

As we sat in the midst of that kaleidoscope picture, formed of French, Belgian and English uniforms, intermingled with the varied and gaudy robes of the local nymphs, as we mused in the midst of dense clouds of tobacco smoke, we could not help reflecting that this might be the last time we should look on such scenes of revelry, and came to the conclusion that the only thing to do was to make the most of it while we had the chance. And by Gad, we did!

A little after midnight I parted from my companion and started off to get back to that base camp of mine. Standing in the main square of the town I realised a few points which tended to take the edge off the success of the evening: number one, it was too late to get a tram; number two, all the taxis had disappeared; number three, it was pouring with rain, and number four, I had three miles to go.

I started off to walk it; but had I known what that walk was going to be, I would have buttoned myself round a lamppost and stayed where I was; I made the fatal mistake of thinking I knew the way.

Leaning at an angle of forty-five degrees against the driving rain, I staggered along the tramlines past the casino, and feeling convinced the tramlines must be correct, determined to follow them. After about half an hour's walk, mostly uphill, I became rather suspicious as to the road being quite right. Seeing a sentry-box outside a palatial edifice on the right, I tacked across the road and looked for the sentry. A lurid thing in gendarmes advanced upon me and I let off one of my curtailed French sentences at him.

"Pour Bléville, Monsieur?"

I can't give his answer in French, but being interpreted, I think it meant I was completely on the wrong road and that he wasn't certain as to how I could ever get back on it without returning to Havre and starting again. He produced an envelope, made an unintelligible sketch on the back of it and started me off again down the way I had come.

I then realised what my mistake had been, for there was evidently a branch tramline, which I had followed, and this, I thought, could only have branched off near the casino. So back I went to the casino and started again.

I was right about the branch line, and started merrily off again, taking, as I thought, the main line to Bléville.

After another half-hour of this, with eyes feverishly searching for recognisable

'RATIONS'

landmarks, I again began to have doubts as to the veracity of the tramlines. However, pretending that I placed their honesty beyond all doubt, I plodded on, only to round a corner and find the outlook so unfamiliar that I determined to ask again.

There was not a soul about. Presently I discovered a small house, standing back off the road and showing a thin slit of light above the shutters of a downstairs window. I tapped on the glass and a sound as of someone hurriedly trying to hide a pile of coverless umbrellas in a cupboard was followed by the opening of the window, where a bristled head was silhouetted against the light.

I squeezed out the same old sentence, "Pour Bléville, Monsieur?"

A fearful cataract of unintelligible words burst from the head, but left me almost as much in the dark as ever, though with a faint glimmer that I was 'warmer'. I felt that if I went back about a mile and turned left, all would be well.

I thanked the gollywog in the window, who, somehow or other, I think must have been a printer working late, and started off once more.

The birth of 'Fragments': scribbles on the farmhouse walls.

After another hour's route-march I came to some scattered houses, and finally to a village. I was indignantly staring at a house when suddenly, joy! . . . I realised that what I was looking at was an unfamiliar view of the café where I had breakfasted earlier in the day. Ten minutes more and I had reached the camp. The time was now 2.30am and I thought I would just take a look in the Orderly Room tent to see if there were any orders for me. It was lucky I did. Inside I found an orderly asleep in a blanket and woke him.

"Anything in for me?" I asked. "Bairnsfather's my name."

"Yes, sir, there is," came through the blanket, and getting up he went to the table at the other end of the tent. Sleepily he handed me the wire which read, 'Lieutenant Bairnsfather to proceed to join his battalion as machine-gun officer.'

"What time do I have to push off?" I inquired.

"By the eight o'clock from Havre tomorrow, sir."

The time was now 3.00am.

Tomorrow the Front!

And then I crept into my tent and tried to sleep.

Chapter 2

TORTUOUS TRAVELLING ~ OFF FOR THE FRONT ~ CLIPPERS AND TABLETS ~ DUMPED AT A SIDING ~ JOINING MY BATTALION ~ OFF TO THE TRENCHES

Not much sleep that night. Instead a sort of feverish coma of wild dreams in which the gendarme and I were attacking a German trench, the officer in charge of which we found to be the Base Camp Adjutant! However, I got up early, packed my few belongings in my valise - which had mysteriously turned up from the docks - and went off on the tram down to Havre. That hundred men I had brought over had nothing to do with me now, I was entirely on my own and was off to the Front to join my battalion.

Down at Havre the officials at the station gave me a complicated yellow diagram, known as a travelling pass, and I got into a carriage on the train bound for Rouen. I was not alone now, for a whole forest of second-lieutenants like myself were in the same train, and with them a solid, congealed mass of valises, packs, revolvers and haversacks.

At last the train started, and after the usual hour spent in feeling you have left all the most important things behind, I settled down on a mound of equipment and tried to get a bit of sleep.

That astronomical annoyance, the star shell, which momentarily enables you to scrutinise the kind of mud you are in.

So, what with sleeping, smoking and talking, we jolted along until we pulled up at Rouen. Here I had to leave the train for some obscure reason, in order to go to the Palais de Justice to get another ticket. I padded off down over the bridge into Rouen, found the Palais, went in, and was shown along to an office that dealt in tickets.

In this dark and dingy, oak-panelled saloon, illuminated by electric light and the glittering reflections of gold braid, there lurked a general or two. Here I was given another pass, entitling me to be deposited at a certain siding in Flanders.

Back I went to the station, and in due course rattled off on the train again towards the north.

A fearfully long journey we had up to the Front. The worst of it was that nobody knew - or if they did, wouldn't tell you - which way you were going, or how long it would take to get to your destination.

For instance, we didn't know we were going to Rouen till we got there. And we didn't know we were going from Rouen to Boulogne until, after a night spent on the train, the whole outfit jolted and jangled into the 'Gare de Something', down by the wharf at that salubrious seaport. We spent a complete day and part of an evening at Boulogne, as our train did not leave until midnight.

Another chap, who was going to the next railhead to mine at the Front, and I went off together into the town and had lunch at a café in the High Street. We then strolled around the shops, buying a few things we needed. Not very attractive things either, but I'll mention them here to show how we thought and felt. We first went to a 'pharmacie' and got some boxes of morphia tablets, after which we went to an ironmonger's (I don't know the French for it) and each bought a ponderous pair of barbed-wire cutters. So, what with wire cutters and morphia tablets, we *were* gay.

About four o'clock we calmed down a bit and went to the same café where we had lunched. Here we had tea with a couple of French girls, exceedingly good to look upon, who had apparently escaped from Lille. We got on splendidly with them, till a couple of French officers, one with the Legion of Honour, came along to the next table. That took all the shine out of us, so we determined to quit and cleared off to the 'Hotel de Folkestone', where we each had a bath to console ourselves.

Dinner followed, and then, feeling particularly hilarious, I made my will. Not the approved will of family lawyer style, but just a letter announcing, in bald and harsh terms, that in the event of my remaining permanently in Belgium, I wanted my total small worldly wealth to be disposed of in a certain way. Feeling better after this outburst I rejoined my pal and off we went into the town again, and by easy stages reached the train.

At about 1.00am the train started and we creaked and groaned our way out of Boulogne. We were now really off for the Front, and the situation, consequently, became more exciting. We were slowly getting nearer and nearer to the real thing. But what a train! It dribbled and rumbled along at about five miles an hour, and, I verily believe, stopped at every farmhouse within sight of the line. I could not help thinking that the engine driver was a German in disguise, who was trying to prevent our ever arriving at our destination. I tried to sleep, but each time the train pulled up I woke with a start and thought that we'd got there. This went on for many hours, and as I knew we must be getting somewhere near, my dreams became worse and worse. I somehow began to think the engine driver was becoming cautious (he was by now a Frenchman once again) and had perhaps to get down occasionally and walk ahead a bit to see if it was safe to go on. Nobody on the train had the least idea where the Front was, how far off, or what it was like. For all we knew our train might be going right up into the rear of the front-line trenches.

Somewhere around 6.00am I reached my siding. All the others, except myself and one other, had got off at previous halts. I got down from the carriage on to a cinder track and went along the line to the station. There was nobody about except a few Frenchmen, so I went back to the carriage again and sat looking out through the dimmed window at the flat, rain-soaked country. The other fellow with me was doing the same.

A sudden, profound depression came over me; here was I and this other cove, dumped down at this horrible siding with nothing to eat and nobody to meet us. How rude and callous of someone, or something. I looked at my watch. It had stopped; and on trying to wind it I found it was broken.

I stared out of the window again, but gave it up and stared at the opposite seat instead. Suddenly my eye caught something shiny under the seat.

I stooped and picked it up . . . it was a watch!

I have always looked upon this episode as an omen of some sort, but of what sort I can't quite make out. Finding a watch means finding 'time'. Perhaps it meant I would find time to write this book. On the other hand, it may have meant that my time had come. Who knows?

At about eight o'clock, by my new watch, I again made an attack on the station and at last found the RTO, which, being interpreted, means the Railway Transport Officer. He told me where my battalion was to be found, but didn't know whether they were in the trenches or out. He also added that if he were me he wouldn't hurry about getting there as I could probably get a lift on an ASC (Army Service Corps) wagon later on. I took his advice, and having left all my tackle by his office, went into the nearest estaminet to get some breakfast.

The owner, a genial but garrulous little Frenchman, spent quite a lot of time explaining to me how those hateful people, the Boches, had occupied his house not so long before and had punched a hole in his kitchen wall to use a machine gun through.

After breakfast I went to the station and arranged for my baggage to be sent on by an ASC wagon, and then started out to walk to Nieppe, which I learnt was the place where my battalion was billeted. As I plodded along the muddy road in the pouring rain, I became aware of a sound with which I was afterwards to become horribly familiar.

BOOM!

That was all. But I knew it was the voice of the guns, and in that moment I realised that here was the war and that I was in it.

I ploughed along for about four miles down uninteresting mud canals - known on maps as roads - until, finally, I entered Nieppe.

The battalion, I heard from a passing soldier, was having its last day in billets prior to going into the trenches again. They were billeted at a disused brewery at the other end of the town. I went on down the squalid street and finally found the place. A crowd of dirty, war-worn-looking soldiers were clustered about the entrance in groups. I went in through the large archway past them into the brewery yard. There were soldiers everywhere, resting, talking and smoking. I inquired where the officers' quarters were and was shown to the brewery head office. Here I found the battalion officers, many of whom I knew, and went into their improvised mess-room, which, in previous days had apparently been the brewery boardroom.

I found everything very dark, dingy and depressing. That night the battalion (1st Royal Warwickshire Regiment) was going into the trenches again, and last evenings in billets are not generally very exhilarating. I sat and talked with those I knew, and presently the Colonel came in and I heard what the orders were for the evening. I felt very strange and foreign to it all, as everyone except myself had had their baptism of trench life, and consequently, at this time, I did not possess that calm indifference, bred of painful experience, which is part of the essence of a true trench-dweller.

The evening drew on. We had our last meal in billets - sardines, bread, butter and a cake sort of thing - slung on to the bare table by the soldier servants, who were more engrossed in packing up things they were taking to the trenches than in anything else.

And now the time came to start off. I found the machine-gun section in charge of a sergeant, a most excellent fellow, who had looked after the section since the officer (whose place I had come to fill) had been wounded. I took over from him, and, as the battalion moved off along the road, fell in behind with my latest acquisition - a machine-gun section, with machine guns to match.

It was quite dusk now, and as we neared the great Bois de Ploegstert, known all over the world as 'Plugstreet Wood', it was nearly night. The road was getting rougher, and the houses, dotted about in dark silhouettes against the skyline, had a curiously deserted and worn appearance. Everything was looking dark, damp and drear.

On we went down the road through the wood, stumbling along in the darkness over the shell-pitted track. Weird noises occasionally floated through the trees; the faint 'crack' of a rifle, or the rumble of limber wheels. A distant light flickered momentarily in the air, cutting out in bold relief the ruins of the shattered château on our left.

On we went through this scene of dark and humid desolation, past the occasional mounds of former habitations, on into the trenches before Plugstreet Wood.

Chapter 3

THOSE PLUGSTREET TRENCHES ~ THE FIRST NIGHT ~ MUD AND RAIN ~ FLOODED OUT ~ A HOPELESS DAWN

It was an extraordinary sensation, that first time of going into the trenches. The first idea that struck me about them was their haphazard design. There was, no doubt, some very excellent reason for someone or other making those trenches as they were, but they really did strike me as curious when I first saw them.

A trench will, perhaps, run diagonally across a field, will then go along a hedge at right angles, suddenly give it up and start again fifty yards to the left, in such a position that it is bound to cross the kitchen garden of a shattered château, go through the greenhouse and out into the road. On getting there it henceforth rivals the ditch at the side in the amount of water it can run off into a row of dugouts in the next field. There is, apparently, no necessity for a trench to be in any way parallel to the line of your

'Plugstreet Wood'
An impression of the famous Bois de Ploegstert.

enemy; as long as he can't shoot you from immediately behind, that's all you ask.

It was a long and weary night, that first night of mine in the trenches. Everything was strange and wet and horrid. First of all I had to go and fix up my machine guns at various points, and find places for the gunners to sleep. This was no easy matter, as many of the dugouts had fallen in and floated off downstream.

In this, and subsequent descriptions of the trenches, I may lay myself open to the charge of exaggeration. But it must be remembered that I am describing trench life in the early days of 1914, and I feel sure that those who had experience of them will acquit me of any such charge.

To give a recipe for getting a rough idea, in case you want to, I recommend the following procedure. Select a flat ten-acre ploughed field, so sited that all the surface water of the surrounding country drains into it. Now cut a zigzag slot about four feet deep and three feet wide diagonally across, dam off as much water as you can so as to leave about a hundred yards of squelchy mud, delve out a hole at one side of the slot, then endeavour to live there for a month on bully beef and damp biscuits, whilst a friend has instructions to fire at you with his Winchester every time you put your head above the surface.

Well, here I was, anyway, and the next thing was to make the best of it. As I have said before, these were the earliest trenches in the war, days when we had none of those desirable 'props' such as corrugated iron, floorboards and sandbags *ad lib*.

When you made a dugout in those days you made it out of anything you could find, and generally had to make it yourself. That first night I was 'in', I discovered after a humid hour or so, that our battalion wouldn't fit into the spaces left by the last one, and as regards dugouts, the truth of that mathematical axiom, 'Two into one won't go', suddenly dawned on me with painful clarity. I was faced with making a dugout, and it was raining, of course. (Note: whenever I don't state the climatic conditions, read 'raining'.)

After sloshing about in several primitive trenches in the vicinity of the spot where we had fixed our best machine-gun position, my Sergeant and I discovered a sort of covered passage in a ditch in front of a communication trench. It was a sort of emergency exit back from a row of ramshackle, waterlogged hovels in the ditch leading to the communication trench. We decided to make use of this passage, and arranged things in such a way that by scooping out the clay walls we made two caves, one behind the other. The front one was about five yards from the machine gun and you reached the back cave by going through the outer one.

It now being about 11.00pm, and having been for the last five hours perpetually on the scramble through trenches of all sorts, I drew myself into the inner cave to go to sleep. This little place was about four feet long, three feet high and three feet wide. I got out my knife, took a scoop out of the clay wall, and fishing out a candle-end from my pocket, stuck it in the niche, then lit it and a cigarette. I now lay down and tried to size up the situation and life in general.

Here I was in this horrible clay cavity, somewhere in Belgium, miles and miles from home, cold, wet through and covered with mud. This was the first day, and, so far as I could see, the future contained nothing but repetitions of the same thing, or worse.

Nothing was to be heard except the occasional crack of the sniper's shot, the dripping of the rain and the low murmur of voices from the outer cave. In the narrow space beside me lay my equipment; my revolver and a sodden packet of cigarettes. Everything was damp, cold and dark. The candle-end gutters and I suddenly think of something like the 'Empire' or the 'Alhambra', or anything else that's reminiscent of brightness and life, and then, *swish bang,* back to the reality that the damp clay wall is only eighteen inches in front of me; that here I am; that the Boche is just on the other side of the field; and that there doesn't seem the slightest chance of leaving except in an ambulance.

My machine-gun section, for the gun near by, lay in the front cave a couple of feet from me and their spasmodic talking gradually died away as, one by one, they dropped off to sleep. I gave one more indignant glare at the flickering candle-end, then pinched the wick, curled up and went to sleep.

*

A sudden cold sort of peppermint sensation assailed me. I awoke and sat up.

My head cannoned off the clay ceiling, so I had to partially lie down again. I attempted to strike a match, but found the whole box was damp and sodden. I heard a muttering of voices and a curse or two in the outer cave and presently the Sergeant entered my sanctum on all fours.

"We're bein' flooded out, sir. There's water a foot deep in this place of ours."

That explains it. I feel all around the back of my greatcoat and find that I have been sleeping in a pool of water.

I crawled out of my inner chamber, and the whole lot of us dived through the rapidly rising water into the ditch outside. I scrambled up on to the top of the bank and tried to focus the situation. From inquiries and personal observation I found the cause of the rising tide was the fact that the Engineers had been draining the trench, in the course of which process they had apparently struck a spring. We accepted the cause of the disaster philosophically and immediately discussed what was the best thing to be done. Action of some sort was urgently necessary, as at present we were all sitting on the top of the mud bank of the ditch in the silent, steady rain, the whole party being occasionally illuminated by a German star shell - more like a family sitting for a flashlight photograph than anything else.

We decided to make a dam.

Having found an empty ration box and half a bag of coke, we started on the job of trying to fence off the water from our caves. After about an hour's struggle with the elements we at last succeeded, with the aid of the ration box, the sack of coke and a few tins of bully beef, in reducing the water level inside to six inches. Here we were, now wetter than ever, cold as polar bears, sitting in this hygroscopic catacomb at about 2.00am. We longed for a fire and a fire was decided upon. We had a fire-bucket, which had started life as a biscuit tin, a few bits of damp wood, but no coke.

"We had some coke, I'm sure! Why, of course, we built it into the dam!"

Down came the dam, out came the coke and in came the water.

However, we preferred the water to the cold, so finally, after many exasperating efforts, we got a fire going in the bucket.

Five minutes of bliss was followed by disaster. The fire-bucket proceeded to emit such dense volumes of sulphurous smoke that in a few moments we couldn't see a lighted match. We stuck it a short time longer, then, one by one, we dived into the water and out into the air, shooting out of our mud hovel to the surface like snakes when you pour water down their holes.

The time is now 3.00am and we've had no sleep, but plenty of rain, water and smoke. A board meeting is held immediately and decides to give up sleep and dugouts for the night. A motion to try and construct a chimney with an entrenching tool is defeated by five votes to one.

Dawn is breaking, and my first night in trenches comes to an end.

Chapter 4

MORE MUD ~ RAIN AND BULLETS ~ SHELLING A CHATEAU ~ VISITING POSITIONS ~ A BIT OF CAKE ~ 'WIND UP' ~ NIGHT ROUNDS ~ 'NARROW SQUEAKS'

The rose-pink sky fades off above to blue,
The morning star alone proclaims the dawn.
The empty tins and barbed-wire bathed in dew
Emerge, and then another day is born.

I wrote that poem in those damned trenches, so you can see the sort of state to which I was reduced. Well, my first trench night was over, and the dawn had broken. Everything else left to break had been seen to by the artillery, which generally started off at about eight o'clock. And what a fearful long day it seemed, that first one. As soon as it was light I began scrambling about, having a good look at the general lie of things.

In front was a large expanse of turnip field, at the further side of which a long irregular parapet marked the German trenches. Behind those again was more turnip field, dented here and there with shell-holes filled with water, beyond which stood a few isolated remnants which had once been cottages. I stood at a projection in one of our trenches, from where I could see the general shape of our line, and could glimpse a good view of the German arrangements.

Not a soul could be seen anywhere.

Here and there a wisp of smoke indicated a fire-bucket. Behind our trenches, behind the shattered house at the top of a wooded rise in the ground, stood what once must have been a fine château. As I looked, a shrieking hollow whistle overhead, followed by a momentary pause, and then 'CRUMPH!' showed clearly what was the matter with the château. Every morning, as we crouched in our mud kennels, we heard those 'crumphs' and soon got to be very good judges of form. We knew they were shelling the château, because when they didn't shell the château, we got it in the trenches. So we looked on that dear old mangled wreck with a friendly eye; that tapering, twisted, perforated spire, which they never could knock down, was an everlasting bait to the Boche, and a perfect fairy godmother to us.

Oh, those days in that trench of ours! Each day seemed about a week long. I shared a dugout with a platoon commander after that first night. The machine-gun section found a suitable place and made a dugout for themselves. Day after day, night after night, my companion and I lay and listened to the daily explosions, read and talked, and sloshed about that trench together. The greatest interest one had in the daytime was sitting on the damp straw in our clay vault, scraping the mud off one's saturated boots and clothes. The event to which one looked forward with the greatest interest was the arrival of letters in the evening.

Now and again we got out of our dugout and sloshed down the trench to scheme out some improvement or other, or to furtively look out across the waterlogged turnip field at the Boche trenches opposite. Occasionally, in the silent, still, foggy mornings, a voice from somewhere in the alluvial depths of a miserable trench would suddenly burst into a scrap of song, such as *'Old soldiers never die, They simply fade away'*, in a voice full of 'fed-upness' and steeped in determination. Then all would be silence for the next couple of hours. And so the day passed.

At dusk, my job was to emerge from this horrible drain and go round the various machine-gun positions. What a job! I generally went alone, and in the darkness struck out across the sodden field, tripping, stumbling, and sometimes falling into various shell-holes on the way. One does a little visiting at this time of day. Having seen a gun in another trench, one looks up the nearest platoon commander. You look into so-and-so's dugout and find it empty. You ask a sergeant where the occupant is.

"He's down the trench, sir."

You push your way down the trench, dodging pools of water and stepping over fire-buckets and mess-tins, brushing past men standing, leaning or sitting, right on down the trench, where, round a corner, you find the platoon commander.

"Well, if we can't get any sandbags," he is probably saying to a sergeant, "we will just have to bank it up with earth, and put those men on the other side of the traverse." Or something like that.

He turns to me and says, "Come along back to my dugout and have a bit of cake. Someone or other has sent one out from home."

We start back along the trench. Suddenly a low murmuring, rattling sound can be heard in the distance. We stop to listen. The sound gets louder. Everyone stops to listen. The sound approaches and is now distinguishable as rifle-fire. The firing becomes faster and faster, then suddenly swells into a roar and now comes the phenomenon of trench warfare, 'wind up' - the prairie fire of the trenches.

Everyone 'stands to' the parapet, and away on the left a tornado of crackling sound can be heard, getting louder and louder. In a few seconds it has swept on down the line, and now a deafening rattle of rifle-fire is going on immediately in front. Bullets are flicking the tops of the sandbags on the parapet in hundreds, whilst white streaks are shooting up with a swish into the sky and bursting into bright, radiating blobs of light - the star shell at its best.

A curious thing, this 'wind up'. We never knew when it would come on. It is caused entirely by nerves. Perhaps an inquisitive Boche, somewhere a mile or two to the left, had thought he saw someone approaching his barbed-wire; a few shots are exchanged, a shout or two, followed by more shots, panic, more shots, the panic spreads, then suddenly the whole line of trenches on a front of a couple of miles succumbs to that well-known malady, 'wind up'.

In reality it is highly probable there was no one in front near the wire, and no one has had the least intention of being there. Presently there comes a deep 'boom' from somewhere in the distance behind, and a large shell sails over our heads and explodes somewhere amongst the Boches. Then another and another, and then all becomes quiet again. The rifle-fire diminishes and soon ceases altogether. The total result of one of these 'firework' displays is several thousand rounds of ammunition squibbed off, hundreds of star shells wasted, and no casualties. It quite put the 'wind up' me at first, but I soon got to know these affairs and learnt to take them calmly.

I went along with the platoon commander back to his lair. An excellent fellow he was too. No one in this war could have hated it all more than he did, and no one could have more conscientiously done his very best at it. The poor fellow was afterwards killed near Ypres.

"Well, how are things going with you?" I asked.

"Oh, all right. They knocked down that same bit of parapet again today. I think they must imagine we've got a machine gun there, or something. That's twice we've had to build it up this week. Have a bit of cake?"

So I had a bit of cake and left him. He was going back to that old parapet again, whilst I struck off into the dark, wet fields towards another gun position, falling into an unfamiliar 'Johnson 'ole' on the way.

No one gets a better idea of the general lie of the position than a machine-gun officer. In those early, primitive days, when we had so few of each thing, we, of course, had few machine guns, and these had to be sprinkled about a position to the best possible advantage. The consequence was that people like myself had to cover a considerable amount of ground before our rambles in the dark each night were done. One machine gun might be, say, in 'Dead Man Farm', another at the 'barrier' near the crossroads, whilst another couple were just at some effective spot in a trench, or in a commanding position in a shattered farm or cottage behind the front-line trenches.

I would leave my dugout as soon as it was dark and do the round of all the guns every night. Just as a sample, I will carry on from where I left the platoon commander . . .

"The Knave of Spades."

I slosh across the ploughed field at what I feel to be the correct angle to bring me out on the crossroads, where, about two hundred yards away, I have another machine gun. I scramble across a broken gateway and an old bit of trench, and close behind it come to a deep cutting into which I jump. About five yards along this I come to a machine-gun emplacement, with a machine-gun sentry on guard.

"Where's the Corporal?" I ask.

"I'm 'ere, sir," is emitted from the slimy depths of a narrow, low-roofed dugout, and the Corporal emerges, hooking back the waterproof sheet as he comes out to prevent the light showing.

"How about this gun, Corporal - is everything all right?"

"Yes, sir. But I was looking around today and thought that if we was to shift the gun over there, where the dead cow is, we'd get a better field of fire."

Our meeting is adjourned to inspect this valuable site from the windward side. After a short, bloodthirsty conversation relative to the perforating of the enemy, I leave and push off into the bog again, striking out for another visit.

Finally, after two hours' visiting, floundering, bullet dodging, and star shell shirking, accompanied by a liberal allowance of 'narrow squeaks', I get back to my own bit of trench. Tobogganing down where I erroneously think the clay steps are, I at last reach my dugout, and entering on all fours, crouch amongst the damp tobacco leaves and straw and light a cigarette.

Chapter 5

MY MAN FRIDAY ~ SUSTAINING LIFE ~ "CHUCK US THE BISCUITS" ~ RELIEF ARRIVES ~ BILLETS

It was during this first time up in the trenches that I got a soldier servant. As I had arrived only just in time to go with the battalion to the trenches, the acquisition had to be made by a search in the mud. I found a fellow who hadn't been an officer's servant before, but who wanted to be. I liked the look of him, and so feeling rather like Robinson Crusoe, when he booked up Friday, *I got me a man.*

He lived in a dugout about five yards away, and from then onwards continued with me right to the point where this book finishes. This fellow of mine did all the cooking, such as it was, and worked in conjunction with my friend, the platoon commander's servant. Cooking, at the times I write about, consisted of making innumerable brews of tea, and opening tins of bully and Maconochie. Occasionally bacon had to be fried in a mess-tin lid. One day my man soared off into culinary fancies and curried a Maconchie. I have never quite forgiven him for this, but I am nearly right again now.

These two soldier servants never had to leave the trench. It was their job to try and find something to make a fire with, and to do all they could to keep the water out of our dugout; a task which not one of us succeeded in doing.

My plan for sustaining life under these conditions was to change my boots as often as possible. If there wasn't time for this, I used to try and boil the water in my boots by keeping my feet to the fire-bucket. I always put my puttees on first and then a pair of thick socks, and finally a pair of boots. I could, by this means, hurriedly slip off the sodden pair of boots and socks and slip on another set which had become fairly dry by

A Hopeless Dawn.
Rain, mud, damp coke and dugout off downstream.

the fire. We lived permanently damp, if not thoroughly wet. My puttees, which I rarely removed, were more like long rolls of the consistency of nougat than anything else, thanks to the mud. Dugouts had no wooden linings in those days, no corrugated iron roofs, and no floorboards. They were just holes in the clay side of the fire-trench, with any old thing for a roof and old straw or tobacco leaves - which we pinched from some abandoned farm - for a floor. So, you see, there was not much of a chance of dodging the moisture.

The cold was what got to me. Personally, I would far rather have gone without food than without a fire. A fire of some sort was the only thing to cheer me. Coke was scarce and always wet, and it was by no means uncommon to overhear the remark, "Chuck us the biscuits, Bill; the fire wants mendin'." At night I would frequently sally forth to a cracked up village behind, and perhaps procure half a mantelpiece and an old clog to stoke our 'furnace' with.

After the usual number of long days and still longer nights spent under these conditions, we came to the day when it was our turn to go out to rest billets, and a relieving battalion's turn to come in. What a splendid day that is! You start 'packing' at about 4.00pm. As soon as it is dusk the servants slink off across the turnip morass behind and drag our few belongings back to where the limbers are. These limbers have come up from about three or four miles away, from the Regimental Transport headquarters, to take all the trench 'props' back to the billets. We don't leave ourselves until the 'incoming' battalion has taken over. After what seems an interminable wait, we hear the clinking of mess-tins and rattling of equipment, the sloshing of feet in the mud and much whispered profanity, which all goes to announce to you that they're here. Then you know the other battalion has arrived, and are now about to take over these precious slots in the ground.

When the exchange is complete, we are free to go. To go out for our few days in billets. The actual going out and getting clear of the trenches takes a long time. Handing over, and finally extricating ourselves from the morass, in the dark, with all our belongings, is a lengthy process, and then we have about a mile of country, which we have never been able to examine in the daytime and get familiar with, to negotiate. This is before we get to the high road and really start for billets!

I had the different machine-gun sections to collect from their various guns, and this not until the relieving sections had all turned up. It was a good two hours' job getting all the sections with their guns, ammunition and various extras finally collected together in the dark a mile back, ready to put all the stuff in the limbers and so back to the billets. When all was fixed up, I gave the order and we started plodding along back down the narrow, dreary road towards our resting place. But it was quite a cheerful tramp, knowing as we did, that we were going to four days' comparative rest, and anyway, safety.

On we went down the long, flat, narrow roads, occasionally looking round to see the faint flicker of a star shell showing over the tops of the trees, and to think momentarily of the poor devils left behind to take our place and go on doing just what we had been at. Then, finally, getting far enough away to forget, songs and jokes took us chirping along, past objects which soon became our landmarks in the days to come.

On we went, past estaminets, shrines and occasional windmills, down the long winding road for about four miles, until at last we reached our billets, where the battalion willingly halted and dispersed to its various quarters. I and my machine-gun section had still to carry on, for we lived apart, a bit further on at the Transport Farm. So we continued on our own for another mile and a half, past the estaminet at Romerin, out towards Neuve Eglise to our Transport Farm; the usual red-tiled Belgian farm, with a rectangular *smell* in the middle.

Chapter 6

THE TRANSPORT FARM ~ A GLORIOUS TIME ~ FLEECED BY THE FLEMISH ~ A STRAW-MATTRESS BED ~ RIDING ~ NEARING CHRISTMAS

It was about 9.00pm when we turned into the courtyard of the farm. My Sergeant saw to the unlimbering and dismissed the section, whilst I went into the farm and dismantled myself of all my tackle, such as revolver, field glass, greatcoat, haversacks, etc.

My servant had, of course, preceded me, and by the time I had made a partial attempt at cleaning myself, he had brought in a meal of sorts and laid it on the oilcloth-covered table by the stove. I was now joined by the Transport Officer and the Regimental Quartermaster. They lived at this farm permanently, and only came to the trenches on occasional excursions. They had both had a go at the nasty part of warfare though, before this, so although consumed with a sneaking envy, I was full of respect for them.

We three had a very merry and genial time together. We now had something distinctly resembling a breakfast, a lunch and a dinner each day. The Transport Officer took a lively interest in the efforts of Messrs. Fortnum and Mason, and thus added generously to our menus. It was a glorious feeling, pushing open the door of that farm and coming in from all the wet, darkness, mud and weariness of four days in the trenches. After the supper, I disappeared into the back kitchen place and did what was possible in the shaving and washing line.

The Belgian family were all herded away in here, as their front rooms were now our exclusive property. I have never quite made out what the family consisted of, but, approximately, I should think mother and father and ten children. I am pretty certain about the children, as about half a platoon stood around me whilst shaving and solemnly watched me with dull brown Flemish eyes. The father kept in the background, resting I fancy, from his usual day's work of hiding unattractive turnips in enormous numbers under mounds of mud (the only form of farming industry which came to my notice in Flanders).

The mother, however, was 'all there' in more senses than one. She was of about observation balloon proportions and had an unerring eye for the main chance. Her telegraphic address, I should imagine, was 'Fleecem'. She had one sound commercial idea - charge as much as you can for everything they want, hide everything they do want, and slowly collect any property, in the way of food, they have in the cellar, so that in the future there shall be no lack of bully beef and jam, in our farm at any rate.

They had one farm labourer, a kind of epileptic who, I found out, gave his services in return for being fed - he received no pay. He will regret this contract of his in time, as the food in question was bully beef and plum and apple jam, with an occasional change to Maconochie and apple and plum jam. That store in the cellar absolutely precludes him from any change from his diet for many years to come. Of course I must say his work was not such as would be classed amongst the skilled or intellectual trades; it was, apparently, to pump all the accumulated drainage from the subterranean vault out in the yard in front, about twice a week, the rest of his time being taken up by assisting at the hiding of the turnips.

After I had washed and shaved under the critical eyes of Angèle, Rachel, André and company, I retired into an inner chamber which had once been an apple store, and went to bed on a straw mattress in the corner. Pyjamas at last! And an untroubled sleep. Occasionally in the night one would wake and, listening at the open window, would hear the distant rattle of rifle-fire far away beyond the woods.

These four days at the Transport Farm were days of wallowing in rest. There was, of course, certain work to be done in connection with the machine-gun department, such as overhauling and cleaning the guns, and drilling the sections at intervals; but the evenings and nights were a perfect joy after those spent in the trenches. One could walk about the fields near by, could read, write letters and sleep as much as one liked. And if one wished, walk or ride over to see friends at other billets. Ah yes! Ride. I am sorry to say that riding was not, and is not, my forte; unfortunate this, as the machine-gun officer is one of the few privileged to have a horse. I was entitled to ride to the trenches, and ride away from them, and during our rest, ride wherever I wanted to go. But these advantages, so coveted by my horseless pals in the regiment, left me cold. I never will be any good at the 'Haute Ecole' act I'm sure, although I made several attempts to get a liking for the subject in France. When the final day came for our departure to the trenches again, I rode from that Transport Farm.

Riding in England, or in any civilised country, is one thing, and riding in those barren, shell-torn wastes of Flanders is another. The usual darkness, rain and mud pervaded the scene when the evening came for our return journey to the trenches. My groom (curse him) had not forgotten to saddle the horse and bring it round. There it was, standing gaunt and tall in front of the paraded machine-gun section.

With my best equestrian demeanour I crossed the yard, and hauling myself up onto my horse, choked out a few commands to the section, and sallied forth on to the road towards the trenches.

Thank heaven I didn't go into the cavalry. The roads about the part we were performing in were about two yards wide, with a precipitous ditch at each side. In the middle, all sorts and conditions of holes punctuated their long winding length. Add to this the fact that you are either meeting, or being passed by, a motor-lorry every ten minutes, and you will get an idea of the conditions under which riding takes place.

Well, anyway, during the whole of my equestrian career in France, I never came off. I rode along in front of my section, balancing on this 'ship of the desert' of mine, past all the landmarks, cracked houses, windmills, estaminets, etc. I experienced innumerable tense moments when my horse - as frequently happened - took me for a bit of a circular tour in an adjacent field, so as to avoid some colossal motor-lorry with one headlight of about a million candle-power, which would suddenly roar its way down our single narrow road. At last we got to the dumping-ground spot again - the spot where we horsemen have to come to earth and walk, and where everything is unbaled from the limbers. Here we were again, on the threshold of the trenches.

This monotonous dreary routine of 'in' and 'out' of the trenches had to be gone through many, many times before we got to Christmas Day. But during that Christmas period, there was one outstanding feature above the normal dangerous dreariness of the trenches. It was a slight affair in the nature of our attack on the 18th of December, so in the next chapter I will proceed to outline my part in this passage of arms.

Chapter 7

A PROJECTED ATTACK ~ FIXING UP ~ DIGGING A SAP ~ AN 'ELL OF A NIGHT ~ THE ATTACK ~ PUNCTURING PRUSSIANS

One evening I was sitting, coiled up in the slime at the bottom of my dugout, toying with the mud enveloping my boots, when a head appeared at a gap in my mackintosh doorway.

"The Colonel wants to see you, sir."

So I clambered out and went across the field, down a trench, across a road and down a trench again to where the headquarters dugouts lay all in a row. I came to the Colonel's dugout, where, by the light of a candle-end stuck on an improvised table, he was sitting, busily explaining something with the aid of a map to a group of our officers. I waited till he had finished, knowing he would want to see me after the others, as the machine-gunner's job is always rather a specialised sideline.

Soon he explained to me what he wished me to do with my guns, and gave me a rough outline of the projected attack. He pointed out on the map where he wished me to take up positions, and closed the interview by saying he thought I should at once proceed to

reconnoitre the proposed sites and lay all my plans for getting into position, as we were going to conduct an operation on the Boches at dawn the next day.

I left, and started at once on my plans. The first thing was to have a good look at the ground and examine all the possibilities for effective machine-gun co-operation. I determined to take my Sergeant along with me, so that he would be as familiar with the scheme in hand as I was. It was raining, of course, and the night was as black as pitch when we started out on our Sherlock Holmes excursion. I explained the idea of the attack to him and the part we had to play. The troops on our right were going to carry out the actual attack, and we, on their left flank, were going to lend assistance by engaging the Deutschers in front and by firing 'half-right' to cover our men's advance.

My job was clear enough. I had to bring as many machine guns as I could spare down to the right of our own line, to assist as much as possible in the real attack. My Sergeant and I went down to examine the ground where it was essential for us to fix up. We got to our last trench on the right and, clambering over the parapet, did what we could to find out the nature of the ground in front and see how we could best fix our machine guns to cover the enemy. We soon saw that in order to get a really clear field of fire it was necessary for us to 'sap out' from the end of our existing right-hand trench and make a machine-gun emplacement at the end. This necessitated the digging of a sap of about ten yards in length, collecting all the materials for making an emplacement, and mounting our machine gun. It was now 11.00pm, and all this work had to be completed by dawn.

Having rapidly realised there was not the slightest prospect of any sleep, and that the morrow looked like being a busy day, we commenced with characteristic fed-up vigour to carry out our nefarious design.

A section, myself and the Sergeant, started on digging the sap, and what a job it was! The Germans were particularly restless that night and kept squibbing away whilst we were digging, and as it was some time before we had the sap deep enough to be able to stand upright without fear of a puncture in some part of our anatomy, it was altogether most unpleasant. About an hour before dawn we had got as far as making the emplacement and this we started to put together as hard as we could. We filled sandbags with the earth excavated from the sap, and with frenzied energy tried to complete our defences before dawn. The rain and the darkness, both very intense that night, were really very trying. One would pause, shovel in hand, lean against the clay side of the sap and hurriedly contemplate the scene. There we were, five men, a sergeant and myself, wet through and muddy all over, with no sleep and little to eat, silently digging and filling sandbags with an ever-watchful eye for the breaking of the dawn.

Light was breaking across the sky before the job was done, and we still had to complete the top guard of our emplacement. Then we had some fireworks.

The nervy Boches had spotted our sap as something new, and their bullets, whacking up against our newly thrown-up parapet, made us glad we had worked so busily.

We were bound to complete that emplacement, so, at convenient intervals, we crept to the opening, and after muttering, "One, two, three!" suddenly plumped a newly filled sandbag on the top. Each time we did this half a dozen bullets went zipping through the canvas or just past overhead. This operation had to be done about a dozen times. A warm job! But at last it was finished and we sank down into the bottom of the sap to rest. The time for the artillery bombardment had been fixed to begin at 6.00am, if I remember rightly, so we got a little rest between finishing our work and the attack itself.

Of course the whole of this enterprise, as far as the bombardment and attack were concerned, cannot be compared with the magnitude of a similar performance in 1915. All the same, it was pretty bad, but not anything like so accurately calculated, or so mechanically efficient as our later efforts in this line. The precise timetable methods of the present period did not exist then, but the main idea of giving the opposition as much heavy lyddite, followed by shrapnel, was the same.

At about half-past six, as we sat in the sap, we heard the first shell go over. I went to the end of the traverse alongside the emplacement, and watched the German trenches. We were ready to fire at any of the enemy we could see, and when the actual attack started, at the end of the bombardment, we were going to keep up a perpetual sprinkling of bullets along their reserve trenches. A few isolated houses stood just in line with the German trenches. Our gunners had focused on these, and they gave them a good pasting.

'Crumph! Bang! Bang! Crumph!' - hard at it all the time, whilst shrapnel burst and whizzed about all along the German parapet. The view in front soon became a sort of haze of black dust, as 'heavy' after 'heavy' burst on top of the Boche positions. Columns of earth and black smoke shot up like giant fountains into the air. I caught sight of a lot of the enemy running along a shallow communication trench of theirs, apparently with the intention of reinforcing their front line. We soon had our machine gun peppering up these unfortunates, and from that moment on kept up an incessant fire of the enemy.

On my left, two of our companies were keeping up a solid rapid fire on the German lines immediately in front.

At last the bombardment ceased. A confused sound of shouts and yells on our right, intermingled with a terrific crackle of rifle-fire, told us the attack had started. Without ceasing, we kept up the only assistance we could give: our persistent firing half-right.

How long it all lasted I can't remember; but when I crept into a soldier's dugout, back in one of our trenches, completely exhausted, I heard that we had taken the enemy trench, but that, unfortunately, owing to its enfiladed position, we had to abandon it later.

Such was my first experience of this seesaw warfare of the trenches.

A few days later, as I happened to be passing through poor, shattered Plugstreet Wood, I came across a clearance amidst the trees. Two rows of long, brown mounds of earth, each surmounted by a rough, simple wooden cross, was all that was inside the clearing. I stopped, and looked, and thought - then went away.

The usual line in billeting farms:
A three-sided, red-tiled building, with a rectangular smell in the middle.

Chapter 8

CHRISTMAS EVE ~ A LULL IN HATE ~ BRITON CUM BOCHE ~ IMPRESSIONS ~ CUTTING THE HUN'S HAIR

Shortly after the doings set forth in the previous chapter we left the trenches for our usual days in billets. It was now nearing Christmas Day, and we knew it would fall to our lot to be back in the trenches again on the 23rd of December, and that we would, in consequence, spend our Christmas there. I remember at the time being very down on my luck about this, as anything in the nature of Christmas Day festivities was obviously knocked on the head. Now, however, looking back on it all, I wouldn't have missed that unique and weird Christmas Day for anything.

Well, as I said before, we went 'in' again on the 23rd. The weather had now become very fine and cold. The dawn of the 24th brought a perfectly still, cold, frosty day. The spirit of Christmas began to permeate us all, and we tried to plot ways and means of making the next day, Christmas, different in some way to others. Invitations from one dugout to another for sundry meals were beginning to circulate. Christmas Eve was, in the way of weather, everything that Christmas Eve should be.

I was billed to appear at a dugout about a quarter of a mile to the left that evening to have rather a special thing in trench dinners - not quite so much bully and Maconochie about as usual. A bottle of red wine and a medley of tinned things from home deputised in their absence. The day had been entirely free from shelling, and somehow we all felt that the Boches, too, wanted to be quiet. There was a kind of invisible, intangible feeling extending across the frozen swamp between the two lines which said, "This is Christmas Eve for both of us - *something* in common."

About 10.00pm I made my exit from the convivial dugout on the left of our line and walked back to my own lair. On arriving at my own bit of trench I found several of the men standing about, and all very cheerful. There was a good bit of singing and talking going on, and jokes and jibes on our curious Christmas Eve, as contrasted with any former one, were thick in the air.

One of my men turned to me and said, "You can 'ear 'em quite plain, sir!"

"Hear what?" I enquired.

"The Germans over there, sir; you can 'ear 'em singin' and playin' on a band or somethin'."

I listened; away out across the field, among the dark shadows beyond, I could hear the murmur of voices, and an occasional burst of some unintelligible song would come floating out on the frosty air. The singing seemed to be loudest and most distinct a bit to our right.

I popped into my dugout and found the platoon commander.

"Do you hear the Boches kicking up that racket over there?" I said.

"Yes," he replied, "they've been at it some time!"

"Come on," I said, "let's go along the trench to the hedge there on the right - that's the nearest point to them, over there."

So we stumbled along our now hard, frosted ditch, and scrambling up on to the bank above, strode across the field to our next bit of trench on the right. Everyone was listening. An improvised Boche band was playing a precarious version of 'Deutschland,

Deutschland über Alles', at the conclusion of which some of our mouth-organ experts retaliated with snatches of ragtime songs and imitations of the German tune. Suddenly we heard a confused shouting from the other side. We all stopped to listen. The shout came again. A voice in the darkness shouted in English, with a strong German accent, "Come over here!" A ripple of mirth swept along our trench, followed by a rude outburst of mouth organs and laughter. Presently, in a lull, one of our sergeants repeated the request, "Come over here!"

"You come halfway, - I come halfway," floated out of the darkness.

"Come on, then!" shouted the Sergeant. "I'm coming along the hedge!"

"Ah! but there are two of you," came back the voice from the other side.

Well, anyway, after much suspicious shouting and jocular derision from both sides, our Sergeant went along the hedge which ran at right-angles to the two lines of trenches. He was quickly out of sight; but, as we all listened in breathless silence, we soon heard a spasmodic conversation taking place out there in the darkness.

Presently the Sergeant returned. He had with him a few German cigars and cigarettes which he had exchanged for a couple of Maconochies and a tin of Capstan, which he had taken with him. The séance was over, but it had given just the requisite touch to our Christmas Eve - something a little human and out of the ordinary routine.

After months of vindictive sniping and shelling, this little episode came as an invigorating tonic and a welcome relief to the daily monotony of antagonism. It did not lessen our ardour or determination; but just put a little human punctuation mark in our lives of cold and humid hate. Just on the right day, too - Christmas Eve! But, as a curious episode, this was nothing in comparison to our experience on the following day.

On Christmas morning I awoke very early, and emerged from my dugout into the trench. It was a perfect day: a beautiful, cloudless blue sky; the ground hard and white, fading off towards

the wood in a thin low-lying mist. It was such a day as is invariably depicted by artists on Christmas cards - the ideal Christmas Day of fiction.

"Fancy all this hate, war, and discomfort on a day like this!" I thought to myself. The whole spirit of Christmas seemed to be there, so much so that I remember thinking, "This indescribable something in the air, this Peace and Goodwill feeling, surely will have some effect on the situation here today!" And I wasn't far wrong; it did around us anyway, and I have always been so glad to think of my luck in, firstly, being actually in the trenches on Christmas Day, and, secondly, being on the spot where quite a unique little episode took place.

Everything looked merry and bright that morning - the discomforts seemed to be less, somehow; they seemed to have epitomised themselves in intense, frosty cold. It was just the sort of day for Peace to be declared. It would have made such a good finale. I should like to have suddenly heard an immense siren blowing; everybody to stop and say, "What was that?" Siren blowing again; appearance of a small figure running across the frozen mud waving something. He gets closer - a telegraph boy with a wire! He hands it to me. With trembling fingers I open it: "War off, return home. - George, R.I." Cheers! But no, it was a nice, fine day, that was all.

Walking about the trench a little later, discussing the curious affair of the night before, we suddenly became aware of the fact that we were seeing a lot of evidences of Germans. Heads were bobbing about and showing over their parapet in a most reckless way, and, as we looked, this phenomenon became more and more pronounced.

A complete Boche figure suddenly appeared on the parapet, and looked about itself. This complaint became infectious. It didn't take 'Our Bert' long to be up on the skyline (it is one long grind to ever keep him off it). This was the signal for more Boche anatomy to be disclosed, and this was replied to by all our Alfs and Bills, until, in less time than it takes to tell, half a dozen or so of each of the belligerents were outside their trenches and were advancing towards each other in no-man's-land.

A strange sight, truly!

I clambered up and over our parapet, and moved out across the field to look. Clad in a muddy suit of khaki and wearing a sheepskin coat and Balaclava helmet, I joined the throng about halfway across to the German trenches.

It all felt most curious: here were these sausage-eating wretches, who had elected to start this infernal European fracas, and in so doing had brought us all into the same muddy pickle as themselves.

This was my first real sight of them at close quarters. Here they were - the actual, practical soldiers of the German army. There was not an atom of hate on either side that day; and yet, on our side, not for a moment was the will to war and the will to beat them relaxed. It was just like the interval between the rounds in a friendly boxing match.

The difference in type between our men and theirs was very marked. There was no contrasting the spirit of the two parties. Our men, in their scratch costumes of dirty, muddy khaki, with their various assorted head-dresses of woollen helmets, mufflers and battered hats, were a light-hearted, open, humorous collection as opposed to the sombre demeanour and stolid appearance of the Huns in their grey-green faded uniforms, top-boots, and pork-pie hats.

The shortest effect I can give of the impression I had was that our men, superior, broadminded, more frank, and lovable beings, were regarding these faded, unimaginative products of perverted 'Kultur' as a set of objectionable but amusing lunatics whose heads had *got* to be eventually smacked.

A memory of Christmas, 1914:
"Look at this bloke's buttons, 'Arry. I should reckon 'e 'as a maid to dress 'im!"

"Look at that one over there, Bill," our Bert would say, as he pointed out some particularly curious member of the party.

I strolled about amongst them all, and sucked in as many impressions as I could. Two or three of the Boches seemed to be particularly interested in me, and after they had walked round me once or twice with sullen curiosity stamped on their faces, one came up and said, "Offizier?" I nodded my head, which means 'Yes' in most languages, and besides, I can't talk German. These devils, I could see, all wanted to be friendly; but none of them possessed the open, frank geniality of our men. However, everyone was talking and laughing, and souvenir hunting.

I spotted a German officer, some sort of lieutenant I should think, and being a bit of a collector, I intimated to him that I had taken a fancy to some of his buttons.

We both then said things to each other which neither understood, and agreed to do a swap. I brought out my wire clippers and, with few deft snips, removed a couple of his buttons and put them in my pocket. I then gave him two of mine in exchange.

Whilst this was going on a babbling of guttural ejaculations emanating from one of the laager-schifters, told me that some idea had occurred to someone.

Suddenly, one of the Boches ran back to his trench and presently reappeared with a large camera. I posed in a mixed group for several photographs, and have ever since wished I had fixed up some arrangement for getting a copy. No doubt framed editions of this photograph are reposing on some Hun mantelpieces, showing clearly and unmistakably to admiring strafers how a group of perfidious English surrendered unconditionally on Christmas Day to the brave Deutschers.

Slowly the meeting began to disperse; a sort of feeling that the authorities on both sides were not very enthusiastic about this fraternising seemed to creep across the gathering. We parted, but there was a distinct and friendly understanding that Christmas Day would be left to finish in tranquillity. The last I saw of this little affair was a vision of one of my machine-gunners, who was a bit of an amateur hairdresser in civil life, cutting the unnaturally long hair of a docile Boche, who was patiently kneeling on the ground whilst the automatic clippers crept up the back of his neck.

Chapter 9

SOUVENIRS ~ BACK TO REST ~ A RIDE TO NIEPPE ~ TEA AT HQ ~ TRENCHES ONCE MORE

A couple of days after Christmas we left for billets. These two days were of a very peaceful nature, but not quite so enthusiastically friendly as the day itself. The Germans could be seen moving about in their trenches, and one felt quite at ease sitting on the top of our parapet or strolling about the fields behind the lines.

It was during these two days that I managed to get a German rifle that I had had my eye on for a month. It lay out in the open, near one or two corpses between our trenches and theirs, and until this Christmas truce arrived, the locality was not a particularly attractive one to visit. Had I fixed an earlier date for my exploit, the end of it would most probably have been a battered second-lieutenant's cap and a rusty revolver hanging up in the inglenook at Herr Someone-or-other's country home in East Prussia. As it was, I was able to walk out and return with the rifle unmolested.

"Chuck us the biscuits, Bill. The fire wants mendin'."

When we left the trenches to 'go out' this time I took the rifle along with me. After my usual perilous equestrian act I got back to the Transport Farm, and having performed the usual routine of washing, shaving, eating and drinking, blossomed forth into our four days' rest again.

The weather was splendid. I went out for walks in the fields, rehearsed the machine-gun section in their drill, and conducted cheery sort of 'Squire-of-the-village' conversations with the farmer who owned our farm.

At this period, most of my pals in the regiment used to go into Armentières or Bailleul, and get a breath of civilised life. I often wished I felt as they did, but I had just the opposite desire. I felt that, to adequately stick out what we were going through, it was necessary for me to keep well in the atmosphere, and not to let any exterior influence upset it.

I was annoyed at having to take up this line, but somehow or other I had a feeling that I could not run the war business with a spot of civilisation in it. Personally, I felt that rather than leave the trenches for our periodic rests, I would sooner have stayed there all the time consecutively, until I could stick it out no longer.

During this after-Christmas rest, however, I so far relapsed from these views as to decide to go into Nieppe to get some money from the Field Cashier. That was my first fall, but my second was even more strange. In a truculent tone I said I would ride!

"Smith, go and tell Parker to get my horse ready!" It just shows how reckless warfare makes one.

A beautiful, fine, still afternoon. I started off. Enormous success. I walked and trotted along, past all sorts of wagons, lorries, guns and dispatch riders. Nearly decided to take up hunting, when the time came for me to settle in England once more. However, as I neared the outskirts of Nieppe, and saw the flood of interlacing traffic, I decided to leave well alone - to tie this quadruped of mine up at some outlying hostelry and walk the short remaining distance into the town where the cashier had his office. I found a suitable place and, letting myself down to the ground, strode off with a stiff bandy-legged action to the office. Having got my 100 francs all right, I made the best of my short time on earth by walking about and having a good look at the town. A squalid, uninteresting place, Nieppe; a dirty red-brick town with a good sprinkling of factory chimneys and orange peel; rather the same tone as one of the Potteries towns in England. Completing my tour I returned to the horse, and finally, stiff but happy, I glided to the ground in the yard of the Transport Farm.

Encouraged by my success I rode over to dinner one night with one of the companies in the battalion which was in billets about a mile and a half away. Riding home along the flat, winding, waterlogged lane by the light of the stars I nearly started off on the poetry lines again, but I got home just in time.

During these rests from the trenches I was sometimes summoned to Brigade Headquarters, where the arch-machine-gunner dwelt. He was a captain of much engineering skill, who supervised the entire machine-gun outfit of the Brigade. New men were being perpetually trained by him, and I was sent for on occasion to discuss the state and strength of my section, or any new scheme that might be on hand.

This going to Brigade Headquarters meant putting on a clean bib, as it were; for it was here that the Brigadier himself lived, and after a machine-gun séance it was generally necessary to have tea in the farm with the Brigade staff.

I am little or no use on these social occasions. The red and gold mailed fist of a General Staff reduces me to a sort of pulverised state of meekness, which ends in my smiling at everyone and declining anything to eat. As machine-gun officer to our battalion I had to go through it, and as everyone was very nice to me, it all went off satisfactorily.

On this time out we were wondering how we should find the Boches on our return, and pleasant recollections of the time before filled us with a curious keenness to get back and see. A wish like this is easily gratified at the Front, and soon, of course, the day came to go into trenches again, and in we went.

Chapter 10

MY PARTIAL ESCAPE FROM THE MUD ~ THE DESERTED VILLAGE ~ MY 'COTTAGE' ~ MOVING IN

Our next time up after our Christmas Day experiences was full of incident and adventure. During the peace which came upon the land around the 25th of December we had, as I mentioned before, been able to stroll about in an altogether unprecedented way. We had had the courage to walk into the mangled old village just behind our front-line trenches, and examine the ruins. I had never penetrated into this gloomy wreck of a place, even at night, until after Christmas. It had just occasionally caught our attention as we looked back from our trenches; mutilated and deserted, a dirty skeleton of what once had been a small village - very small - about twelve small houses and a couple of farms. Anyway, during this time in after Christmas we started thinking out plans, and in a few days we heard that it had been decided to put some men into the village, and hold it, as a second line.

The platoon commander with whom I lived happened to be the man selected to have charge of the men in the village. Consequently one night he left our humble trench and, together with his servant and small belongings from the dugout, went off to live somewhere in the village.

About this time the conditions under which we lived were very poor. The cold and rain were exceedingly severe, and altogether physical discomfort was at its height. When my stable companion had gone I naturally determined to pay him a call the next night, and to see what sort of a place he had managed to get to live in.

I well remember that next night. It was the first on which I realised the chances of a change of life presented by the village, and this was the start of two months' 'village' life for me. I went off from our old trench after dusk on my usual round of the machine guns. When this was over I struck off back across the field behind our trench to the village, and waded up what had been the one and only street. Out of the dozen mangled wrecks of houses I didn't know which one my pal had chosen as his residence, so I went along the shell-mutilated, waterlogged road, peering into this ruin and that, until, at the end of the street, about four hundred yards from the Germans, and two hundred yards from our own trenches, I came across a damp and dark figure lurking in the shadows: "'Alt! 'Oo goes there?"

"Friend!"

"Pass, friend, all's well." Evidently the sentry, posted at the end of the village.

I got a tip from him as to my friend's new dwelling-place. "I say, Sentry, which house does Mr Hudson live in?"

"That small 'un down t'other end on the left, sir."

"Thanks." I went back along the deserted ruin of a street, and at the far end on the left I saw the dim outline of a small cottage, almost intact it appeared, standing about five yards back from the road. This was the place the sentry meant right enough, and in I went at the hole in the plaster wall. The front door having apparently stopped something or other previously, was conspicuous by its absence.

All was dark. I groped my way along round to the back, stumbling over various bits of debris on the ground, until I found the opening into what must be the room where Hudson had elected to live. Not a light showed anywhere, which was as it should be, for a light would be easily seen by the Boches not far away, and if they did see one there would be trouble.

I came to an opening covered with an old sack. Pulling this a little to one side I was greeted with a volume of suffocating smoke. I proceeded further, and diving in under the sack, got inside the room. In the midst of the smoke, sitting beside a crushed and battered fire-bucket, sat a man, his face illuminated by the flickering light from the fire. The rest of the room was bathed in mysterious darkness. "Where's Mr Hudson?" I asked.

"He's out havin' a look at the barbed-wire in front of the village, I think, sir; but he'll be back soon, as this is where 'e stays now." I determined to wait, and, to fill in the time, started to examine the cottage.

It was the first house I had been into in the firing line, and unsavoury wreck of a place as it was, it gave one a delightful feeling of comfort to sit on the stone-flagged floor and look upon four perforated walls and a shattered roof. The worst possible house in the world would be an improvement on any of those dugouts we had in the trenches. The front room had been blown away, leaving a back room and a couple of lean-tos which opened out from it. An attic under the thatched roof with all one end knocked out completed the outfit. The outer and inner walls were all made of that stuff known as wattle and daub - a sort of earth-like plaster worked into and around hurdles. A bullet would, of course, go through walls of this sort like butter, and so they had. For, on examining the outer wall on the side which faced the Germans, I found it looking like the top of a pepper-pot for holes.

A sound, as of a man trying to waltz with a cream separator, suggested to my mind that someone had tripped and fallen over that mysterious obstacle outside which I had noticed on entering, and presently I heard Hudson's voice cursing through the sack doorway.

He came in and saw me examining the place. "Hullo, you're here too, are you?" he exclaimed. "Are you going to stay here as well?"

"I don't quite know yet," I replied. "It doesn't seem a bad idea, as I have to walk the round of all the guns the whole time. All I can and have to do is hitch up in some central place, and this is just as central as that rotten trench we've just come from."

"Of course it is," he replied. "If I were you I'd come along and stay with me, and go to all your places from here. If an attack comes you'll be able to get from one place to another much easier than if you were stuck in that trench. You'd never be able to move from there when an attack and bombardment had started."

Having given the matter a little further consideration, I decided to move from my dugout to this cottage, so I left the village and went back across the field to the trench to see to the necessary arrangements.

I got back to my lair and shouted for my servant. "Here, Smith," I said, "I'm going to fix up at one of the houses in the village. This place of ours here is no more central than the village, and any one of those houses is a damn sight better than this clay hole here. I want you to collect all my stuff and bring it along; I'll show you the way." So presently, all my few belongings having been collected, we set out for the village. That was my last of that fearful trench. A worse one I know could not be found. My new life in the village now started, and I soon saw that it had its advantages. For instance, there was a slight chance of fending off some of the rain and water. But my knowledge of the 'Front' by this time was such that I knew there were corresponding disadvantages, and my instinct told me that the village would present a fresh crop of dangers and troubles quite equal to those of the trench, though slightly different in style. I had now started off on my two months' sojourn in the village of St Yvon.

Chapter 11

STOCKTAKING ~ FORTIFYING ~ THE ONLY SOUVENIR ~ AN EMERGENCY EXIT ~ NEBULOUS *'FRAGMENTS'* ~ DEFENDING OURSELVES

Hudson, myself, his servant and my servant, all crushed into that house that night. What a relief it was! We all slept in our greatcoats on the floor, which was as hard as most floors are, and dirtier than the generality; but being out of the water and able to stretch oneself at full length made up for all deficiencies. Hudson and I both slept in the perforated room; the servants in the larger chamber, near the fire-bucket.

I got up just before dawn as usual, and taking advantage of the grey light, stole about the village and around the house, sizing up the locality and seeing how my position stood with regard to the various machine-gun emplacements. The dawn breaking, I had to skunk back into the house again, as it was imperative to us to keep up the effect of 'deserted house in village'.

We had to lurk inside all day, or if we went out, creep about with enormous caution,

"Shut that blinkin' door, there's a 'ell of a draught in 'ere!"

and go off down a slight slope at the back until we got to the edge of the wood which we knew must be invisible to the enemy. I spent this day making a thorough investigation of the house, creeping about all its component parts and thinking out how we could best utilise its little advantages. Hudson had crept out to examine the village by stealth, and I went on with plots for fortifying the 'castle', and for being able to make ourselves as snug as we could in this frail shell of a cottage. I found a hole in the floorboards of the attic and pulled myself up into it thereby.

This attic, as I have said before, had all one end blown away, but the two sloping thatched sides remained. I cut a hole in one of these with my pocket-knife, and thus obtained a view of the German trenches without committing the error of looking out through the blown-out end, which would have clearly shown an observer that the house was occupied. Looking out through the slit I had made I obtained a panoramic view, more or less, of the German trenches and our own. The view, in short, was this: one saw the backs of our own trenches, then the 'no-man's-land' space of ground, and beyond that again the front of the German trenches. This is best explained by the sketch map which I give on page 41. I saw exactly how the house stood with regard to the position, and also noticed that it had two dangerous sides, i.e., two sides which faced the Germans, as our position formed two sides of a triangle.

I then proceeded to explore the house. In the walls I found a great many bullets which had stuck in between the bricks of the solitary chimney or embedded themselves in the woodwork of the door or supporting posts at the corners. Amongst the straw in the attic I found a typical selection of pathetic little trifles: two pairs of very tiny clogs, evidently belonging to some child about four or five years old, one or two old and battered hats, and a quantity of spinning material and instruments. I have the small clogs at my home now, the only souvenir I have of that house at St Yvon, which I have since learnt is no more, the Germans having reduced it to a powdered-up mound of brick-dust and charred straw. Outside, and lying all around, was a miscellaneous collection of goods: half a sewing machine, a gaudy cheap metal clock, a sort of mangle with strange wooden blades (which I subsequently cut off to make shelves with), and a host of other dirty, rain-soaked odds and ends.

Having concluded my examination, I crept out back to the wood and took a look at it all from there. "Yes," I thought to myself, "it's all very nice, but, by Gad, we'll have to look out that they don't see us, and get to think we're in this village, or they'll give us a warm time." It had gone very much against my thought-out views on trench warfare, coming to this house at all, for I had learnt by the experiences of others that the best maxim to remember was: 'Don't live in a house'.

The reason is not far to seek. There is something very attractive to artillery about houses. They can range on them well, and they afford a more definite target than an open trench. Besides, if you can spot a house that contains, say half a dozen to a dozen

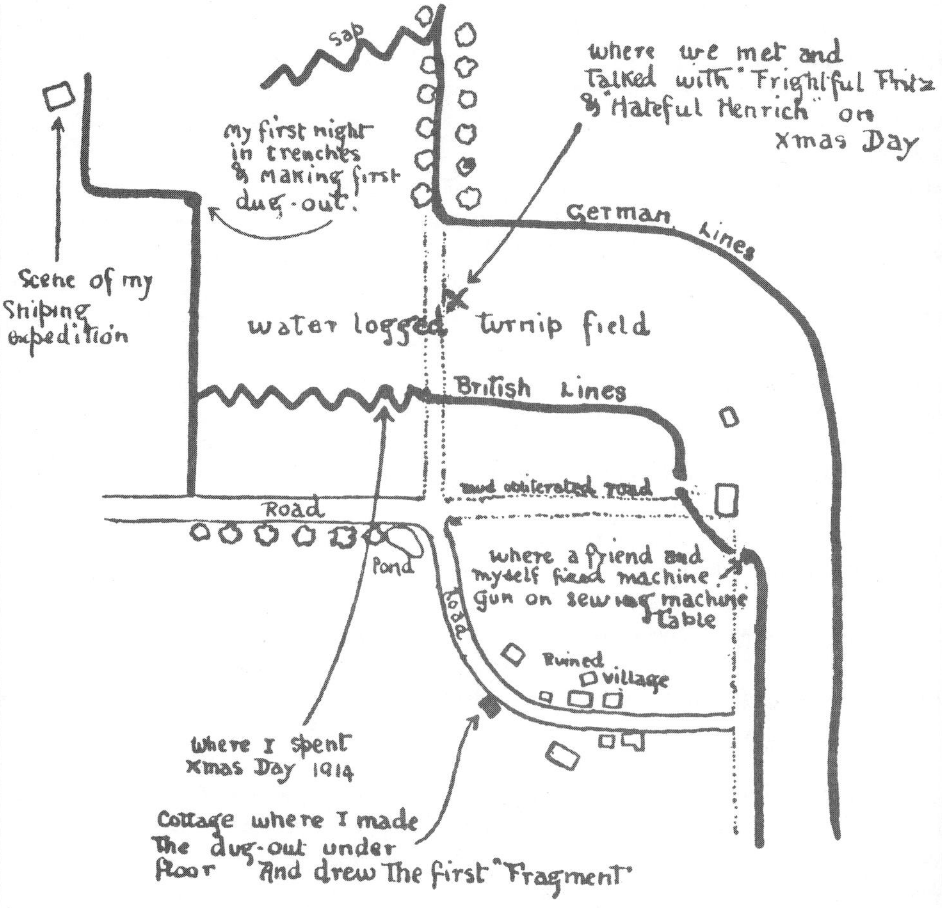

The Bairnsfather map of Christmas 1914, showing exactly where the 'truce' and fraternisation took place.

The hand-drawn map as it appears in 'Bullets & Billets', 1916.

people, and just plop a 'Johnson' right amidships, it generally means 'exit house and people' which, I suppose, is a desirable object to be attained, according to twentieth century manners.

However, we had decided to live in the house, but as I crept back from the wood, I determined to take a few elementary and common-sense precautions. Hudson had returned when I got back, and together we discussed the house, the position, and everything we could think of in connection with the business, as we sat on the floor and had our midday meal of bully beef and biscuits, rounded up by tea and plum and apple jam, spread neat from the tin on odd corners of broken biscuits. We thoroughly talked over the question of possible fortifications and precautions. I said, "What we really want is an emergency exit somewhere, where can stand a little chance, if they start to shell us."

He agreed, and we both decided to pile up all the odd bricks, which were lying outside at the back of the house, against the perforated wall, and then sleep there in a little easier state of mind. We contented ourselves with this little precaution to begin with, but later on, as we lived in that house, we thought of larger and better ideas, and launched out into all sorts of elaborate schemes, as I will show when the time comes.

Anyway, for the first couple of sessions spent in that house in St Yvon, we were content with merely making ourselves bullet-proof. The whole day had to be spent with great caution indoors; any visit elsewhere having to be conducted with still greater caution, as the one great thing to be remembered was: "Don't let 'em see we're in the village." So we had long days, just lying around in the dirty old straw and accumulated dirt of the cottage floor.

We both sat and talked and read a bit, sometimes slept, and through the opening beneath the sack across the back door we watched the evenings creeping on, and finally came the night, when we stole out like vampires and went about our trench work. It was during these long, sad days that my mind suddenly turned on making sketches. This period of my trench life marked the start of *'Fragments from France'*, though it was not till the end of February that a complete and presentable effort, suitable for publication in a paper, emerged. It was nothing new to me to draw, as for a very long time before the war I had drawn hundreds of sketches, and had spent a great amount of time reading and learning about all kinds of drawing and painting. I have always had an enormous interest in Art; my room at home will prove that to anyone. Stacks of bygone efforts of mine will also bear testimony to this. Yet it was not until January, 1915, that I had sufficiently resigned myself to my fate in the war, to let my mind turn to my only and most treasured hobby. In this cottage at St Yvon the craving came back to me. I didn't fight against it, and began by making a few pencil scribbles with a joke attached, and pinned them up in our cracked shell of a room. Jokes at the expense of our miserable surroundings they were, and these were the first *'Fragments'*. Several men in the local platoon collared these spasms, and soon after I came across them, muddy and battered, in various dugouts near by. After these few sketches, which were done on rough bits of paper which I found lying about, I started to operate on the walls. With some bits of charcoal, I made a mess on all the four walls of our back room. There was a large circular gash, made by a spent bullet I fancy, on one of the walls, and by making it appear as though this mark was the centre point of a large explosion, I gave an apparent velocity to the figure of a German, which I drew above.

These daubs of mine provoked mirth to those who lived with me, and others who occasionally paid us visits. I persisted, and the next 'masterpiece' was the figure of a soldier (afterwards Private Blobs, of *'Fragments'*) sitting up a tree staring straight in front of him into the future, whilst a party of corpulent Boches are stalking towards him through the long grass and barbed-wire. He knows there's something not quite nice going on, but doesn't like to look down. This was called *'The Listening Post'*, and the sensation described was so familiar to most that this again was apparently a success. So what with scribbling, reading and sleeping, not to mention time occupied in consuming plum and apple jam, bully, and other delicacies which a grateful country has ordained as the proper food for soldiers, we managed to pull through our days. Two doses of the trenches were done like this, and then came the third time up, when a sudden burst of enthusiasm and an increasing nervousness as to the safety of ourselves and our house, caused us to launch out into really trying to fortify the place. The cause of this decision to do something to our abode was, I think, attributable to the fact that for about a fortnight the Germans had taken to treating us to a couple of dozen explosions each morning - the sort of thing one doesn't like just before breakfast; but if you've got to have it, the thing obviously to do is to try and defend yourself; so the next time up, we started.

Chapter 12

A BRAIN-WAVE ~ MAKING A 'FUNKHOLE' ~ A UNIQUE ROOF ~ PLUGSTREET WOOD ~ SNIPING

On arriving up at St Yvon for our third time round there, we - as usual now - went into our cottage again, and the regiment spread itself out around the same old trenches. There was always a lot of work for me to do at nights, as machine guns always have to be moved as occasion arises, or if one gets a better idea for their position. By this time I had one gun in the remnant of a house about fifty yards away from our cottage. This was a reserve gun, and was there carrying out an idea of mine, i.e., that it was in a central position, which would enable it to be rapidly moved to any threatened part of the line, and also it would form a bit of an asset in the event of our having to defend the village.

The section for this gun lived in the old cellar close by, and it was this cellar which gave me an idea. When I went into our cottage I searched to see if we had overlooked a cellar. No, there wasn't one. Now, then, the idea. I thought, "Why not make a cellar, and thus have a place to dive into when the strafing begins." After this terrific outburst of sagacity I sat down in a corner and, with a biscuit-load of jam, discussed my scheme with my platoon-commander pal. We agreed it was a good idea. I was feeling energetic, and always liking a little tinkering on my own, I said I would make it myself.

So Hudson retired into the lean-to and I commenced to plot this engineering project. I scraped away as much as necessary of the accumulated filth on the floor and, my knife striking something hard, I found it to be tiles. Up till then I had always imagined it to be an earth floor, but tiled it was right enough - large, square, dark red ones of a very rough kind. I called for Smith, my servant, and telling him to bring his entrenching tool, I began to prise up some of the tiles. It wasn't very easy, fitting the blade of the entrenching tool into the crevices, but once I had got a start and had got one or two out, things were easier.

I pulled up all the tiles along one wall about eight feet long and out into the room a distance of about four feet. I now had a bare patch of hard earth eight feet by four to contend with. Luckily we had a pickaxe and a shovel lying out behind the house, so taking off my sheepskin jacket and balaclava, I started off to excavate the hole which I proposed should form a sort of cellar. It was a big job, and my servant and I were hard at it, turn and turn about, the whole of that day. A dull, rainy day, a cold wind blowing the old sack about in the doorway, and in the semi-darkness inside, yours truly handing up Belgian soil on a war-worn shovel to my servant, who held a sandbag perpetually open to receive it. A long and arduous job it was, and one in which I was precious near thinking that danger is preferable to digging. Mr Doan, with his backache pills, would have done well if he had sent one of his travellers with samples round there that night. However, at the end of two days, I had got a really good hole delved out, and now I was getting near the more interesting feature, namely, putting a roof on, and finally being able to live in this underground dugout.

This roof was perhaps rather unique as roofs go. It was a large mattress with wooden sides, a kind of oblong box with a mattress top. I found it outside in a ruined cottage. Underneath the mattress part was a cavity filled with spiral springs. I arranged a pile of sandbags at each side of the hole in the floor in such a way as to be able to lay this curiosity on top to form a roof, the mattress part downwards. I then filled in with earth all the parts where the spiral springs were placed. Total result - a roof a foot thick of earth, with a good backbone of iron springs. I often afterwards wished that that mattress had been filleted, as the spiral springs had a nasty way of bursting through the striped cover and coming at you like the lid of a Jack-in-the-box. However, such is war.

Above this roof I determined to pile up sandbags against the wall, right away up to the roof of the cottage. This necessitated about forty sandbags being filled, so it may easily be imagined we didn't do this all at once. However, in time, it was done - I mean after we had paid one or two more visits to the trenches. We all felt safer after these efforts. I think we were a bit safer, but not much. I mean that we were fairly all right against anything but a direct hit, and as we knew from which direction direct hits had to come, we made that wall as thick as possible. We could, I think, have smiled at a direct hit from an 18-pounder, provided we had been down our funkhole at the time; but, of course, a direct hit from a 'Johnson' would have snuffed us completely (mattress and all).

Life in this house and in the village was much more interesting and energetic than in that old trench. It was possible, by observing great caution, to creep out of the house by day and dodge about our position a bit, crawl up to points of vantage and survey the scene. Behind the cottage lay the wood - the great Bois de Ploegstert - and this in itself repaid a visit. In the early months of 1915 this wood was in a pretty mauled-about state, and as time went on of course got more so. It was full of old trenches, filled with water, relics of the period when we turned the Germans out of it. Shattered trees and old barbed-wire in a solution of mud was the chief effect produced by the parts nearest the trenches, but further back 'Plugstreet Wood' was quite a pretty place to walk about in; birds singing all around, and rabbits darting about the tangled undergrowth. Long paths had been cut through the wood leading to the various parts of the trenches in front. A very quaint place, take it all in all, and one which has left a curious and not unpleasing impression on my mind.

This ability to wander around and creep about various parts of our position led to my getting an idea, which nearly finished my life in the cottage, village, or even Belgium. I suddenly got bitten with the sniping fever, and it occurred to me that, with my facilities for getting about, I could get into a certain mangled farm on our left and remain in the roof unseen in daylight. From there I felt sure that, with the aid of a rifle, I could tickle up a Boche or two in their trenches hard by. I was immensely taken with this idea. So one morning (like Robinson Crusoe again) I set off with my fowling-piece and ammunition, and crawled towards the farm. I got there all right, and entering the dark and evil-smelling precincts, searched around for a suitable sniping post. I saw a beam overhead in a corner from which, if I could get on to it, I felt sure I should obtain a view of the enemy trenches through a gap in the tiled roof. I tied a bit of string to my rifle and then jumping for the beam, scrambled up on it and pulled the rifle up after me. When my heart pulsations had come down to a reasonable figure, I peered out through the hole in the tiles.

An excellent view! The German parapet a hundred yards away! Splendid!

Now I felt sure I should see a Boche moving about or something; or I might possibly spot one looking over the top. I waited a long time on that beam, with my loaded rifle lying in front of me. I was just getting fed up with the waiting, and about to go away, when I thought I saw a movement in the trench opposite. Yes! It was. I saw the handle of something like a broom or a water scoop moving above the sandbags. Heart doing overtime again! Most exciting! I felt convinced I should see a Boche before long. And then, at last, I saw one - or rather I caught a glimpse of a hat appearing above the line of the parapet. One of those small circular cloth hats of theirs with the two trouser buttons in front.

Up it came, and I saw it stand out nice and clear against the skyline. I carefully raised my rifle, took a steady aim, and fired. I looked: disappearance of hat! I ejected the empty cartridge case, and was just about to reload when, whizz, whistle, bang, crash! A shell came right at the farm and exploded in the courtyard behind. I stopped short on the beam. Whizz, whistle, bang, crash! Another, right into the old cowshed on my left. Without waiting for any more I just slithered down off that beam, grabbed my rifle and, dashing out across the yard back into the ditch beyond, started hastily scrambling along towards the end of one of our trenches. As I went I heard four more shells crash into that farm. It was at this moment that I coined the title of one of my sketches, *"They've evidently seen me."* for which I afterwards drew the picture near Wulverghem. I got back to our cottage, crawled into the hole in the floor, and thought things over. They must have seen the flash of my rifle through the tiles, and, suspecting possible sniping from the farm, must have wired back to their artillery, "Snipingberg from farmenhausen hoch!" or words to that effect. Altogether a very objectionable episode.

Chapter 13

THE RUINED CHATEAU ~ ROBINSON CRUSOE ~ THAT TURBULENT TABLE

By this time we had really got our little house quite snug. A hole in the floor, a three-legged chair, and brown paper pushed into the largest of the holes in the walls - what more could a man want? However, we did want something more, and that was a table. One gets tired of balancing tins of pl . . . (nearly said it again) -

marmalade on one's knee and holding an enamel cup in one hand and a pocket-knife in the other, so we all said how nice a table would be. I determined to say no more, but to show by deeds, not by words, that I would find a table and have one there by the next day, like a fairy in a pantomime. I started off on my search one night. Take it from me - a fairy's is a poor job out there, and when you've read the next bit you'll agree.

Behind our position stood the old ruined château, and beyond it one or two scattered cottages. I had never really had a good look at all at that part, and as I knew some of our reserve trenches ran around there, and that it would be a good thing to know all about them, I decided to ask the Colonel for permission to creep off one afternoon and explore the whole thing; incidentally I might by good luck find a table. It was possible, by wriggling up a mud valley and crawling over a few scattered remnants of houses and bygone trenches to reach the Colonel's headquarters dugout in daytime. So I did it, and asked leave to go off back to have a look at the château and the land about it. He gave me permission, so armed with my long walking-stick (a billiard cue with the thin part cut off, which I found on passing another château one night) I started off to explore.

I reached the château. An interesting sight it was. How many shells had hit it one couldn't even guess, but the results indicated a good few. What once had been well-kept lawns were now covered with articles which would have been much better left in their proper places. One suddenly came upon half a statue of Minerva or Venus wrapped in three-quarters of a stair carpet in the middle of one of the greenhouses. Passing on, one would find the lightning conductor projecting out through the tapestried seat of a Louis Quinze chair. I never saw such a mess.

Inside, the upstairs rooms were competing with the ground-floor ones, as to which should get into the cellars first. It was really too terrible to contemplate the fearful destruction.

I found it impossible to examine much of the interior of the château, as blocks of masonry and twisted iron girders closed up most of the doors and passages. I left this melancholy ruin, full of thought, and proceeded across the shell-pitted gardens towards the few little cottages beyond. These were in a better state of preservation, and were well worth a visit. In the first one I entered I found a table! The very thing I wanted. It was stuck away in a small lean-to at the back. A nice little green one, just the size to suit us.

I determined to get it back to our shack somehow, but before doing so went on rummaging about these cottages. In the second cottage I made an enormously lucky find for us. Under a heap of firewood in an outhouse I found a large pile of coal. This was splendid, and would be invaluable to us and our fire-bucket. Nothing pleased me more than this, as the cold was very severe, and a fire meant so much to us. When I had completed my investigations and turned over all the oddments lying about to see if there was anything else of use to us, I started off on the return journey. It was now dark, and I was able to walk along without fear of being seen. Of course, I was taking the table with me. I decided to come back later for the coal, with a few sandbags for filling, so I covered it over and hid it as much as possible. (Sensation: Ali Baba returns from the forest.) I started off with the table, and had about three-quarters of a mile to go, although every hundred yards I had to sit down and rest. A table is a horrible thing to accompany one on a mile walk.

I reached the château again, and out into the fields beyond, resting with my burden about three times before I got to the road which led straight on to our trenches. My task was a bit harder now, as I was in full view of the German trenches. Had it been daylight they could have seen me quite easily.

Fortunately it was dark, but, of course, star shells would show one up quite distinctly. I staggered on down the road with the green table on my back, pausing as little as possible, but a rest had to be taken, and this at a very exposed part of the road. I put the table down and sat panting on the top. A white streak shot into the air - a star shell. Curse! I sprang off the green top and waltzed with my four-legged wooden octopus into the ditch at the side, where I lay still, waiting for the light to die out. Suspense over, I went on again.

At last I got back with that table and pushed it into our hovel under the sack doorway.

Immense success! "Just the thing we wanted!"

We all sat down to dinner that night in the approved fashion, whilst I, with the air of a conspirator, narrated the incredible story of the vast Eldorado of coal which I had discovered, and, over our shrimp paste and biscuits we discussed plans for its removal.

Chapter 14

A BAD BIT OF TRENCH ~ THE AMPHIBIANS ~ FED-UP, BUT DETERMINED ~ THE GUN PARAPET ~ BUOYANT AS EVER

So you see, life in our cottage was quite interesting and adventurous in its way. At night our existence was just the same as before; all the normal work of trench life. Making improvements to our trenches led to endless work with sandbags, planks, dugouts, etc. My particular job was mostly improving machine-gun positions, or selecting new sites and carrying out removals;

BRUCE BAIRNSFATHER,
MACHINE GUNS REMOVED
AT SHORTEST NOTICE.
ATTACKS QUOTED FOR.

And so the long, dark, dreary nights went on. The men garrisoning the little cracked-up village lived mostly in cellars. Often on my rounds, during a rainy, windy, mournful night, I would look into a cellar and see a congested mass of men playing cards by the light of a candle stuck on a tin lid. A favourite form of illumination I came across was a lamp made out of an empty tobacco tin, rifle oil for the illuminant, and a bit of a shirt for a wick!

People who read all these yarns of mine, and who have known the war in later days, will say, "Ah, how very different it was then to now." In my last experiences in the war I have watched the enormous changes creeping in. They began about July, 1915. My experiences since that date were very interesting; but I found that much of the romance had left the trenches. The old days, from the beginning to July, 1915, were all so delightfully precarious and primitive. Amateurish trenches and rough-and-ready life, which to my mind gave this war what it sadly needs - a touch of romance.

Way back there, in about January, 1915, our soldiers had a perfectly unique test of human endurance against appalling climatic conditions. They lived in a vast bog, without being able to utilise modern contrivances for making the fight against adverse conditions anything like an equal contest. And yet I wouldn't have missed that time for anything, and I'm sure they wouldn't have either.

Those who have not actually had to experience it, or have not had the opportunity to see what our men 'stuck out' in those days, will never fully grasp the reality.

One night a company commander came to me in the village and told me he had got a bit of trench under his control which was altogether impossible to hold, and he wanted me to come along with him to look at it, and see if I could do anything in the way of holding the position by machine guns. His idea was that possibly a gun might be fixed in such a place behind so as to cover the frontage occupied by this trench. I came along with him to have a look and see what could be done. He and I went up the rain-soaked village street and out on to the field beyond. It was as dark as pitch, and about 11.00pm. Occasional shots cracked out of the darkness ahead from the German trenches, and I remember one in particular that woke us up a bit. A kind of derelict road-roller stood at one side of the field, and as we passed this, walking pretty close together, a bullet whizzed between us. I don't know which head it was nearest to, but it was quite near enough for both of us. We went on across the field for about two hundred yards, out towards a pile of ruins which had once been a barn, and which stood between our lines and the Germans.

Near this lay the trench which he had been telling me about. It was quite the worst I have ever seen. A number of men were in it, standing and leaning, silently enduring the following conditions. It was quite dark. The enemy was about two hundred yards away, or rather less. It was raining, and the trench contained over three feet of water. The men, therefore, were standing up to the waist in water. The front parapet was nothing but a rough earth mound which, owing to the water about, was practically non-existent. Their rifles lay on the saturated mound in front. They were all wet through and through, with a great deal of their equipment below the water at the bottom of the trench. There they were, taking it all as a necessary part of the great game; not a grumble nor a comment.

The company commander and I at once set about scheming out an alternative plan.

Some little distance back we found a cellar which had once been below a house. Now there was no house, so by standing in the cellar one got a view along the ground and level with it. This was the very place for a machine gun. Se we decided on fixing one there and making a sort of roof over a portion of the cellar for the gunners to live in. After about a couple of hours' work we completed this arrangement, and then removed the men, who, it was arranged, should leave the trenches that night and go back to our billets for a rest, till the next time up. We weren't quite content with the total safety of our one gun in that cellar, so we started off on a further idea.

Our trenches bulged out in a bit of a salient to the right of the rotten trench, and we decided to mount another gun at a certain projection in our lines so as to enfilade the land across which the other gun would fire.

On inspecting the projected site we found it was necessary to make rather an abnormally high parapet to stand the gun on. No sandbags to spare, of course, so the question was, "What shall we make a parapet of?"

We plodded off back to the village and groped around the ruins for something solid and high enough to carry the gun. After about an hour's climbing about amongst debris in the dark, and hauling ourselves up into remnants of attics, etc., we came upon a sewing-machine. It was one of that sort that's stuck on a wooden table with a treadle arrangement underneath. We saw an idea at a glance. Pull off the sewing-machine, and use the table. It was nearly high enough, and with just three or four sandbags we felt certain it would do. We performed the necessary surgical operation on the machine, and taking it in turns, padded off down to the front-line trench. We had a bit of a job with that table. The parapet was a jumbled assortment of sandbags, clay, and old bricks from the neighbouring barn; but we finally got a good sound parapet made, and in about another hour's time had fixed a machine gun, with plenty of ammunition, in a very unattractive position from the Boche point of view. We all now felt better, and I'm certain that the men who held that trench felt better too. But I am equally certain that they would have stayed there *ad lib* even if we hadn't thought of and carried out an alternative arrangement. A few more nights of rain, danger and discomfort, then the time would come for us to be relieved, and those same men would be back at billets, laughing, talking and smoking, buoyant as ever.

Chapter 15

ARRIVAL OF THE 'JOHNSONS' ~ SKETCHING THE SCENE ~ "WHERE DID THAT ONE GO TO?" ~ THE FIRST '*FRAGMENT*' DISPATCHED ~ THE EXODUS ~ A MIDNIGHT MARCH ~ WHERE?

Shortly after these events we experienced rather a nasty time in the village. It had been decided, way back somewhere at headquarters, that it was essential to hold the village in a stronger way than we had been doing. More men were to be kept there, and a series of trenches dug in and around it, thus forming means for an adequate defence should disaster befall our front-line trenches, which lay out on a radius of about five hundred yards from the centre of the village. This meant working parties at night, and a pretty considerable collection of soldiers lurking in cavities in various ruined buildings by day.

Anyone will know that when a lot of soldiers congregate in a place it is almost impossible to prevent someone or other being seen, or smoke from some fire showing, or, even worse, a light visible at night from some imperfectly shuttered house.

At all events, something or other gave the Boches the tip, and we soon knew they had got their attention on our village. Each morning as we clustered round our little green table and had our breakfast, we invariably had about half a dozen rounds of 18-pounders crash around us with varying results, but one day, as we'd finished our meal and all sat staring into the future, we suddenly caught the sound of something on more corpulent lines arriving. That ponderous, slow rotating whistle of a 'Johnson' caught our well-trained ears; a pause; then a reverberating, hollow-sounding 'crumph!' We looked at each other.

"Heavies!" we all exclaimed.

"Look out! Here comes another!" And sure enough there it was, that gargling crescendo of a whistle followed by a mighty crash, considerably nearer.

We soon decided that our best plan was to get out of the house, and stay in the ditch twenty yards away until it was over.

A house is an unwholesome spot to be in when there's shelling about. Our funkhole was all right for whizz-bangs and other fireworks of that sort, but no use against these portmanteaux they were now sending along.

Well, to resume; they put thirteen heavies into that village in pretty quick time. One old ruin was set on fire, and I felt the consequent results would be worse than just losing the building; as all the men in it had to rush outside and keep darting in and out through the flames and smoke, trying to save their rifles and equipment.

After a bit we returned into the house - a trifle prematurely, I'm afraid - as presently a pretty large line in explosive drainpipes landed close outside, and, as we afterwards discovered, blew out a fair-sized duck-pond in the road. We were all inside, and I think nearly everyone said a sentence which gave me my first idea for a '*Fragment from France*' - a sentence which must have been said countless times in this war - *"Where did that one go to?"*

We were all inside the cottage now, with intent, staring faces, looking outside through the battered doorway. There was something in the whole situation which struck me as so pathetically amusing, that when the ardour of the Boches had calmed down a bit, I proceeded to make a pencil sketch of the situation. When I got back to billets the next time I determined to make a finished wash drawing of the scene, and send it to some paper or other in England. In due course we got back to billets, and the next morning I fished out my scanty drawing materials from my valise, and sitting at a circular table in one of the rooms at the farm, I did a finished drawing of *"Where did that one go to?"* occasionally looking through the window on to a mountain of manure outside for inspiration.

The next thing was to send it off. What paper should I send it to? I had had a collection of papers sent out to me at Christmas-time from someone or other. A few of these were still lying about. A copy of *The Bystander* was amongst them. I turned over the pages and considered for a bit whether my illustrated joke might be in their line. I thought of several other papers, but on the whole concluded that *The Bystander* would suit for the purpose, and so, having got the address off the cover, I packed up my drawing round a roll of old paper, enclosed it in brown paper, and put it out to be posted at the next opportunity. In due course it went to the post, and I went to the trenches again, forgetting all about the incident.

Next time in the trenches was full of excitement. We had done a couple of days of the endless mud, rain, and bullet-dodging work when suddenly one night we heard we were to be relieved and go elsewhere. Everyone then thought of only one thing - where were we going? We all had different ideas. Some said we were bound for Ypres, which we heard at that time was a pretty 'warm' spot; some said La Bassée was our destination - 'warm', but not quite as much so as Ypres. Wild rumours that we were going to Egypt were of course around; they always are. There was another beauty: that we were going back to England for a rest!

The night after the news, another battalion arrived, and, after handing over our trenches, we started off on the road to 'Somewhere in France'. It was about 11.30pm before we had handed over everything and finally parted from those old trenches of ours. I said good-bye to our little perforated hovel, and set off with all my machine-gunners and guns for the road behind the wood, to go - goodness knows where. We looked back over our shoulders several times as we plodded along down the muddy road and onto the corduroy path which ran through the wood. There, behind us, lay St Yvon, under the moonlight and drifting clouds; a silhouetted mass of ruins beyond the edge of the wood. Still the same old intermittent cracking of the rifle-shots and the occasional star shell. It was quite sad parting with that old evil-smelling, rain-soaked scene of desolation. We felt how comfortable we had all been there, now that we were leaving. And leaving for what? That was the question. When I reached the road, and had superintended loading up our limbers, I got instructions from the Transport Officer as to which way we were to go. The battalion had already gone on ahead, and the machine-gun section was the last to leave. We were to go down the road to Armentières, and at about twelve midnight we started on our march, rattling off down the road leading to Armentières, bound for some place we had never seen before. At about 2.00am we got there; billets had been arranged for us, but at two in the morning it was no easy task to find the quarters allotted to us without the assistance of a guide. The battalion had got there first, had found their billets and gone to bed. I and the machine-gun section rattled over the cobbles into sleeping Armentières, and hadn't the slightest idea where we had to go. Nobody being about to tell us, we paraded the town like a circus procession for about an hour before finally finding out where we were to billet, and ultimately we reached our destination when, turning into the barns allotted to us, we made the most of what remained of the night in well-earned repose.

Chapter 16

NEW TRENCHES ~ THE NIGHT INSPECTION ~
LETTER FROM *THE BYSTANDER*

Next day we discovered the mystery of our sudden removal. The battle of Neuve Chapelle was claiming considerable attention, and that was where we were going. We were full of interest and curiosity, and were all for getting there as soon as possible. But it was not to be. Mysterious moves were being made behind the scenes which I, and others like me, will never know anything about; but, anyway, we now suddenly got another bewildering order. After a day spent in Armentières we were told to stand by for going back towards Neuve Eglise again, just the direction from which we had come. We all knew too much about the war to be surprised at anything, so we mutely prepared for another exit. It was a daylight march this time, and a nice, still, warm day. Quite a cheery, interesting march we had, too, along the road from Armentières to Neuve Eglise. We were told that we were to march past General Sir Horace Smith Dorrien, whom we should find waiting for us near the Pont de Nieppe - a place we had to pass en route. Everyone braced up at this, and keenly looked forward to reaching Nieppe. I don't know why, but I had an idea he would be in his car on the right of the road. To make no mistake I muttered, "Eyes right" to myself for about a quarter of a mile, so as to make a good thing of the salute. We came upon the Pont de Nieppe suddenly, round the corner, and there was the General - on the left! All my rehearsing useless. Annoying, but I suppose one can't expect Generals to tell you where they are going to stand.

We reached Neuve Eglise in time, and went into our old billets. We all thought our fate was "back into those *@$#@*! old Plugstreet trenches again," but *mirabile dictu* - it was not to be so. The second day in billets I received a message from the Colonel to proceed to his headquarters farm. I went, and heard the news. We were to take over a new line of trenches away to the left of Plugstreet, and that night I was to accompany him along with all the company commanders on a round of inspection.

A little before dusk we started off and proceeded along various roads towards the new line. All the country was now brand new to me, and full of interest. After we had gone about a mile and a half the character of the land changed. We had left all the Plugstreet Wood effect behind, and now emerged on to far more open and flatter ground. By dusk we were going down a long straight road with poplar trees on either side. At the end of this stood a farm on the right. We walked into the courtyard and across it into the farm. This was the place the battalion we were going to relieve had made its headquarters. Not a bad farm. The roof was still on, I noticed, and concluded from that that life there was evidently passable. We had to wait here some time, as we were told that the enemy could see for a great distance around there, and would pepper up the farm as sure as fate if they saw anyone about. Our easy-going entry into the courtyard had not been received with great favour, as it appeared we were doing just the very thing to get the roof removed. However, the dusk had saved us, I fancy.

As soon as it was really dark we all sallied forth, accompanied by guides this time, who were to show us the trenches. I crept along behind our Colonel, with my eyes peeled for possible gun positions, and drinking in as many details of the entire situation as I could. We walked about ten miles that night, I should think, across unfamiliar swamps and over unsuspected antique abandoned trenches, past dead cows and pigs. We groped about the wretched shell-pitted fields, examining the trenches we were about to take over. You would be surprised to find how difficult a simple line of trenches can seem at night if you have never seen them before.

You don't seem able to get the angles, somehow, nor to grasp how the whole situation faces, or how you get from one part to another, and all that sort of thing. I know that by the time I had been along the whole lot, round several hundred traverses, and up dozens of communication trenches and saps, all my mariner-like ability for finding my way back to Neuve Eglise had deserted me. Those guides were absolutely necessary in order to get us back to the headquarters farm. One wants a compass, the pole star, and plenty of hope ever to get across those enormous prairies - known as fields out there - and reach the place at the other side one wants to get to. It is a long study before you really learn the simplest and best way up to your own bit of trench; but when it comes to learning everybody else's way up as well (as a machine-gunner has to), it needs a long and painful course of instruction - higher branches of this art consisting of not only knowing the way up, but the *safest* way up.

The night we carried out this tour of inspection we were all left in a fog as to how we had gone to and returned from the trenches. After we had got in we knew, by long examination of the maps, how everything lay, but it was some time before we had got the real practical hang of it all.

Our return journey from the inspection was a pretty silent affair. We all knew these were a nasty set of trenches. Not half so pleasant as the Plugstreet ones. The conversations we had with the present owners made it quite clear that warm times were the vogue round there. Altogether we could see we were in for a 'bit of a time'.

We cleared off back to Neuve Eglise that night, and next day took those trenches over. This was the beginning of my life at Wulverghem. When we got in, late that night, we found that the post had arrived some time before. Thinking there might be something for me, I went into the back room where they sorted the letters, to get any there might be before going off to my own billets.

"There's only one for you, sir, tonight," said the Corporal who looked after the letters. He handed me an envelope. I opened it. Inside was a short note and a cheque.

"We shall be very glad to accept your sketch, *'Where did that one go to?'* From *The Bystander*." The foundation-stone of *'Fragments from France'*.

Chapter 17

WULVERGHEM ~ THE DOUVE ~ NEW GROUND ~ CORDUROY BOARDS ~ SKELETON FARMS ~ FIXING THE GUNS ~ STRAY BULLETS ~ BACK AT OUR FARM ~ SLEEP

We got out of the frying-pan into the fire when we went to Wulverghem - a much more exciting and precarious locality than Plugstreet. During all my war experiences I have grown to regard Plugstreet as the unit of tranquillity. I have never had the fortune to return there since those times mentioned in previous chapters. When you leave Plugstreet you take away a pleasing memory of slime and reasonable shelling, which is more than you can say for the other places. If you went to Plugstreet after, say, the Ypres Salient, it would be more or less like going to a convalescent home after a painful operation.

But, however that may be, we were now booked for Wulverghem, or rather the trenches which lie along the base of the Messines ridge, about a mile in front of that shattered hamlet. Two days after our tour of inspection we started off to take over. The nuisance about these trenches was that the point where one had to unload and proceed across country, man-handling everything, was abnormally far away from the firing line. We had about a mile and a half to do after we had marched collectively as a battalion, so that my machine-gunners were obliged to carry the guns and all the tackle we needed all that distance to their trenches. This, of course, happened every time we 'came in'.

The land where these trenches lay was a vast and lugubrious expanse of mud, with here and there a charred and ragged building. On our right lay the River Douve, and,

The Sentry. What he doesn't know about fire-buckets and the time the rum comes up isn't worth knowing.

on our left, the trenches turned a corner back inwards again. In front lay the long line of the Messines ridge. The Boches had occupied this ridge, and our trenches ran along the valley at its foot. The view which the Boches got by being perched on this hill rendered them exactly what their soul delights in, i.e., 'über alles'. They can see for miles. However, those little disadvantages have not prevented us from efficiently maintaining our trenches at the far end of the plain, in spite of the difficulty of carrying material across this flat expanse.

I forget what night of the week we went in and took over those trenches, but, anyhow, it was a precious long one. I had only seen the place once before, and in the darkness of the night had a long and arduous job finding the way to the various positions allotted for my guns, burdened as I was with all my sections and impediments. I imagine I walked about five or six miles that night. We held a front of about a mile, and, therefore, not only did I have to do the above-mentioned mile and a half, but also two or three miles going from end to end of our line. It was as dark as could be, and the unfamiliar ground seemed to be pitted like a Gruyère cheese with shell-holes. Unlimbering back near a farm we sloshed off across the mud flat towards the section of trench which we had been ordered to occupy. I trusted to instinct to strike the right angles for coming out at the trenches which henceforth were to be ours. In those days my machine guns were the old type of Maxim - a very weighty concern. To carry these guns and all the necessary ammunition across this desert was a long and very exhausting process. Occasional bursts of machine-gun fire and spent bullets 'zipping' into the mud all around hardly tended to cheer the proceedings. The path along to the right-hand set of trenches, where I knew a couple of guns must go, was lavishly strewn with dead cows and pigs. When we paused for a rest we always seemed to do so alongside some such object, and consequently there was no hesitation in moving on again. None of us had the slightest idea as to the nature of the country on which we were now operating. I myself had only seen it by night, and nobody else had been there at all.

The commencement of the journey from the farm of disembarkation lay along what is known as corduroy boards. These are short, rough, wooden planks, nailed crossways on long baulks of timber. This kind of path is a very popular one at the Front, and has proved an immense aid in saving the British army from being swallowed up in the mud.

The corduroy path ran out about four hundred yards across the grassless, sodden field. We then came suddenly to the beginning of a road. A small cottage stood on the right, and in front of it a dead cow. Here we unfortunately paused, but almost immediately moved on. (Gas masks weren't introduced until much later!)

From this point the road ran in a long straight line towards Messines. At intervals, on the right-hand side only, stood one or two farms, or, rather, their skeletons. As we went along in the darkness these farms silhouetted their dreary remains against the faint light in the sky, and looked like vast decayed wrecks of antique Spanish galleons upside down. On past these farms the road was suddenly cut across by a deep and ugly gash: a reserve trench. So now we were getting nearer to our destination. A particularly large and evil-smelling farm stood on the right. The reserve trench ran into its back yard, and disappeared amongst the ruins. From the observations I had made, when inspecting these trenches, I knew that the extreme right of our position was a bit to the right of this farm, so I and my performing troupe decided to go through the farmyard and out diagonally across the field in front. We did this, and at last could dimly discern the line of the trenches in front. We were now on the extreme right of the section we had to control, close to the River Douve, and away to the left ran the whole line of our trenches.

Along the whole length of this line the business of taking over from the old battalion was being enacted. That old battalion made a good bargain when they handed over that lot of slots to us. The trenches lay in a sort of echelon formation, the one on the extreme right being the most advanced. This one we made for, and as we squelched across the mud to it a couple of German star shells fizzed up into the air and illuminated the whole scene. By their light I could see the whole position, but could only form an approximate idea of how our lines ran, as our parapets and trenches merged into the mud so effectively as to look like a vast, tangled, disorderly mass of sandbags, slime and shell-holes. We reached the right-hand trench. It was a curious sort of a trench too, quite a different pattern to those we had occupied at St Yvon. The first thing that struck me about all these trenches was the quantity of sandbags there were, and the geometrical exactness of the attempts at traverses, fire-steps, bays, etc. Altogether, theoretically, much superior trenches, although very cramped and narrow. I waited for another star shell in order to see the view out in front. One hadn't long to wait around there for star shells. One very soon sailed up, nice and white, into the inky sky, and I saw how we were placed with regard to the Germans, the hill and Messines. We were quite near a little stream, a tributary of the Douve, in fact it ran along the front of our trenches. Immediately on the other side the ground rose in a gradual slope up the Messines hill, and about three-quarters of the way up this slope were the German trenches.

When I had settled the affairs of the machine guns in the right-hand trench I went along the line and fixed up the various machine-gun teams in the different trenches as I came to them. The ground above the trenches was so eaten away by the filling of sandbags and the cavities caused by shellfire, that I found it far quicker and simpler to walk along in the trenches themselves, squeezing past the men standing about and around the thick traverses. Our total frontal length must have been three-quarters of a mile, I should think. This, our first night in, was a pretty busy one. Dugouts had to be found to accommodate everyone; platoons arranged in all the sections of trench, all the hundred-and-one details which go to making trench life as secure and comfortable as is possible under the circumstances, had to be seen to and arranged. I had fixed up all the sections by about ten o'clock and then started along the lines again trying to get as clear an idea as possible of the entire situation of the trenches, the type of land in front of each, the means of access to each trench, and possible improvements in the various gun positions. All this had to be done to the accompaniment of a pretty lively mixture of bullets and star shells. Sniping was pretty severe that night, and indeed, all the time we

were in those Douve trenches. There was an almost perpetual succession of rifle-shots, intermingled with the rapid crackling of machine-gun fire. However, you soon learn out there that you can just as easily 'get one' on the calmest night by an accidental spent bullet as you can when a little hate is on, and bullets are coming thick and fast. The first night we came to the Douve was a pretty calm one, comparatively speaking; yet one poor chap in the leading platoon, going through the farm courtyard I mentioned, got shot right through the forehead. No doubt whatever it was an accidental bullet, and not an aimed shot, as the Germans could not have possibly seen the farm owing to the darkness of the night. Just as I was finishing my tour of inspection I came across the Colonel, who was going round everything, and thoroughly reconnoitring the positions. I went with him right along the line. We stood about on parapets, and walked all over the place, stopping motionless now and again as a star shell went up, and moving on again just in time to hear a bullet or two whizz past behind and go 'smack' into a tree in the hedge behind, or 'plop' into the mud parados. When the Colonel had finished his tour of inspection he asked me to walk back with him to his headquarters.

"Where are you living, Bairnsfather?" the Colonel asked me.

"I don't know, sir," I replied. "I thought of fixing up in that farm (I indicated the most aromatized one by the reserve trench) and making some sort of a dugout if there isn't a cellar; it's a fairly central position for all the trenches."

The Colonel thought for a moment, "You'd better come along back to the farm on the road for tonight anyway, and you can spend tomorrow decorating the walls with a few sketches," he said. This was a decidedly better suggestion, a reprieve, in fact as prior to this remark my bedroom for the night looked like being a borrowed groundsheet slung over some charred rafters which were leaning against a wall in the yard.

I followed along behind the Colonel down the road, down the corduroy boards, and out at the old moated farm not far from Wulverghem. Thank goodness, I should get a floor to sleep on! A roof too! Straw on the floor! How splendid!

It was quite delightful turning into that farm courtyard, and entering the building. Dark, dismal and deserted as it was, it afforded an immense, glowing feeling of comfort after that mysterious, dark and wintry plain, with its long lines of grey trenches soaking away there under the inky sky. Inside I found an empty room with some straw on the floor. There was only one shell-hole in it, but some previous tenant had stopped it up with a bit of sacking. My word, I was tired! I rolled myself round with straw, and still retaining all my clothes, greatcoat, balaclava, muffler and trench boots, I went to sleep.

Chapter 18

THE PAINTER AND DECORATOR ~ WEIRD NOISES ~ *'FRAGMENTS'* FORMING ~ GOING THE ROUNDS ~ NIGHT ON THE MUD PRAIRIE ~ BACK TO DOUVE FARM

Had a fairly peaceful night. I say fairly because when one has to get up three or four times to see whether the accumulated rattle of rifle-fire is going to lead to a battle, or turn out only to be merely 'wind up', it rather disturbs one's rest. You see, had an attack of some sort come on, yours truly would have had to run about a mile and a half to some central spot to overlook the machine-gun department. I used to think that to be actually with one gun was the best idea, but I subsequently found that

A Messines memory:
"'Ow about shiftin' a bit further down the road, Fred?"

this plan hampered me considerably from getting to my others; the reason being that, once established in one spot during an open trench attack, it is practically impossible to get to another part whilst the action is on. At the Douve, however, I discovered a way of getting round this which I will describe later.

On this first night, not being very familiar with the neighbourhood, I found it difficult to ignore the weird noises which floated in through the sack-covered hole. There is something very eerie and strange about echoing rifle-shots in the silence of the night. Once I got up and walked out into the courtyard of the farm, and passing through it came out on to the end of the road. All was as still as still could be, except for the distant intermittent cracking of the rifles coming from away across the plain, beyond the long straight row of lofty poplar trees which marked the road. A silence of some length might supervene, in which one would only hear the gentle rustling of the leaves; then suddenly, far away on the right, a faint surging roar can be heard, and then louder and louder. "Wind up over there." Then, gradually, silence would assert itself once more and leave you with nothing but the rustling leaves and the crack of the sniper's rifle on the Messines ridge.

My first morning at this farm was, by special request, to be spent in decorating the walls. There wasn't much for anyone to do in the daytime as nobody could go out. The same complaint as the other place in St Yvon: "We mustn't look as if anyone lives in the farm." Drawing, therefore, was a great aid to me in passing the day. Whilst at breakfast I made a casual examination of the room where we had our meals. I was not the first to draw on the walls of that room. Someone in a previous battalion had already put three or four sketches on various parts of the fireplace. Several large spaces remained all round the room, however; but I noticed that the surface was very poor compared with the wall round the fireplace.

The main surface was a rough sort of thing, and on regarding it closely, it looked as if it was made of frozen porridge, being slightly rough, and of a grey-brown colour. I didn't know what on earth I could use to draw on this surface, but after breakfast I started to scheme out something. I went into the back room, which we were now using as a kitchen, and finding some charcoal I tried that. It was quite useless - wouldn't make a mark on the wall at all. Why, I don't know; but the charcoal just glided about and merely seemed to make dents and scratches on the 'frozen porridge'. I then tried to make up a mixture. It occurred to me that possibly soot might be made into a sort of ink, and used with a paint-brush. I tried this, but drew a blank again. I was bordering on despair, when my servant said he thought he had put a bottle of Indian ink in my pack when we left to come into the trenches this time. He had a look, and found that his conjecture was right; he had got a bottle of Indian ink and a few brushes, as he thought I might want to draw something, so had equipped the pack accordingly.

I now started my fresco act on the walls of the Douve farm. I spent most of the day on the job, and discovered how some startling effects could be produced. Materials were: a bottle of Indian ink, a couple of brushes, about a hundredweight of useless charcoal, and a GS (General Service) blue and red pencil. Amongst the rough sketches that I did that day were the original drawings for two subsequent *'Fragments'* of mine.

One was the rough idea for *"They've evidently seen me."* and the other was *"My dream for years to come."* The idea for *"They've evidently seen me."* came whilst carrying back that table to St Yvon, as I mentioned in a previous chapter, but the scenario for the idea was not provided for until I went to this farm some time later. In intervals of working at the walls I rambled about the farm building, and went up into a loft over a barn at the end of the farm nearest the trenches. I looked out through a hole in the tiles just in time to hear a shell come over from away back amongst the Germans somewhere, and land about five hundred yards to the left. The sentence, *"They've evidently seen me."* came flashing across my mind again, and I now saw the correct setting in my mind: i.e., the enthusiastic observer looking out of the top of a narrow chimney, whilst a remarkably well-aimed shell leads 'him of the binoculars' to suppose that they *have* seen him.

I came downstairs and made a pencil sketch of my idea, and before I left the trenches that time I had done a wash drawing and sent it to England. This was my second '*Fragment*'.

The other sketch, *"My dream for years to come."* was drawn on one wall of a small apple or potato room, opening off our big room, and the drawing occupied the whole wall.

I knocked off drawing about four o'clock, and did a little of the alternative occupation, that of looking out through the cracked windows on to the mutilated courtyard in front. It was getting darker now, and nearing the time when I had to put on all my tackle, and gird myself up for my round of the trenches. As soon as it was nearly dark I started out. The other officers generally left a bit later, but as I had such a long way to go, and as I wanted to examine the country while there was yet a little light, I started at dusk. Not yet knowing exactly how much the enemy could see on the open mud flat, I determined to go along by the river bank, and by keeping among the trees I hoped to escape observation. I made for the Douve, and soon got along as far as the row of farms. I explored all these, and a shocking sight they were. All charred and ruined, and the skeleton remains slowly decomposing away into the unwholesome ground about them. I went inside several of the dismantled rooms. Nearly all contained old and battered bits of soldiers' equipment, empty tins, and remnants of Belgian property. Sad relics of former billeting: a living reminder of the rough times that had preceded our arrival in this locality. I passed on to another farm, and entered the yard near the river. It was nearly full of black wooden crosses, roughly made and painted over with tar. All that was left to mark the graves of those who had died to get our trenches where they were - at the bottom of the Messines ridge. A bleak and sombre winter's night, that courtyard of the ruined farm, the rows of crosses - I often think of it all now.

As the darkness came on I proceeded towards the trenches, and when it had become sufficiently dark I entered the old farm by the reserve trench and crossed the yard to enter the field which led to the first of our trenches. At St Yvon it was pretty airy work, going the rounds at night, but this was a jolly sight more so. The country was far more open, and although the Boches couldn't see us, yet they kept up an incessant sniping demonstration. Picking up my Sergeant at Number 1 trench, he and I started on our tour. We made a long and exhaustive examination that night, both of the existing machine-gun emplacements and of the entire ground, with a view to changing our positions. It was a long time before I finally left the trenches and started off across the desolate expanse to the Douve farm, and I was dead beat when I arrived there. On getting into the big room I found the Colonel, who had just come in.

"Where's that right-hand gun of yours, Bairnsfather?" he asked.

"Down on the right of Number 2 trench, sir," I answered, "just by the two willows near the sap which runs out towards Number 1."

"It's not much of a place for it," he said. "Where we ought to have it is to the right of the sap, so that it enfilades the whole front of that trench."

"When do you want it moved, sir?" I asked.

"Well, it ought to be done at once; it's no good where it is."

That fixed it. I knew what he wanted; so I started out again, back over the mile and a half to alter the gun. It was a weary job; but I would have gone on going back and altering the whole lot for our Colonel, who was the best line in commanding officers I ever struck. Everyone had the most perfect confidence in him. He was the most shell, bullet and bomb defying person I have ever seen. When I got back for the second time that night I was quite ready to roll up in the straw, and be lulled off to sleep by the cracking rifle-fire outside.

Chapter 19

VISIONS OF LEAVE ~ DICK TURPIN ~ ALL LEAVE'S CANCELLED ~ I EXPLAIN MY CASE ~ LEAVE!

Our first time in the Douve trenches was mainly uneventful, but we all decided it was not as pleasant as St Yvon. For my part, it was fifty per cent worse than St Yvon; but I was now buoyed up by a new light in the sky, which made the first time in more tolerable than it might otherwise have been. It was getting near my turn for leave! I had been looking forward to this for a long time, but there were many who had to take their turn in front of me, so I had dismissed the case for a bit. Recently, however, the powers that be had been sending more than one officer away at a time; consequently my turn was rapidly approaching. We came away back to billets in the usual way after our first dose of the Douve, and all wallowed off to our various billeting quarters. I was hot and strong on the leave idea now. It was really getting close, and I felt disposed to find everything *couleur de rose*. Even the manure heap in the billeting farmyard looked covered with roses. I could have thrown a bag of confetti at the farmer's wife - it's most exhilarating to think of the coming of one's first leave. One maps out what one will do with the time in a hundred different ways. I was wondering how I could manage to transport my souvenirs home, as I had collected a pretty good supply by this time - shell-cases, fuse-tops, clogs, and that Boche rifle I got on Christmas Day.

One morning (we had been about two days out) I got a note from the Adjutant to say I could put in my application. I put it in all right and then sat down and hoped for the best. My spirits were now raised to such a pitch that I again decided to ride to Nieppe - just for fun.

I rode away down the long winding line, smiling at everything on either side - the three-sailed windmill with the top off; the estaminet with the hole through the gable end - all objects seemed to radiate peace and goodwill. There was a very bright sun in the sky that day. I rode down to the high road, and cantered along the grass at the side into Nieppe. Just as I entered the town I met a friend riding out. He shouted something at me. I couldn't hear what he said.

"What?" I yelled.

"All leave's cancelled!"

"*@$#@*!" That was enough for me. I rode into Nieppe like an infuriated cowboy, went straight for the divisional headquarters, flung away the horse and dashed up into the building. I knew one or two of the officers there.

"What's this about leave?" I asked.

"All about to be cancelled," was the reply. "If you're quick, you may get yours through as you've been out here long enough, and you're next to go."

"What have I got to do?" I screamed.

"Go to your Colonel, and ask him to wire the Corps headquarters and ask them to let you go; only you'll have to look sharp about it."

He needn't have told me that. He had hardly finished before I was outside and making for my horse. I got out of Nieppe as quickly as I could, and lit out for our battalion headquarters. About four miles to go, but I lost no time about it. "Leave cancelled!" I hissed through the triangular gap in my front tooth, as I galloped along the road, "leave cancelled!"

I should have made a good film actor that day: 'Dick Turpin's ride to York' in two reels. I reached the turning off the high road all right, and pursued my wild career down the lanes which led to the Colonel's headquarters. The road wound about in a most ridiculous way, making salients out of ploughed fields on either side. I decided to throw all prudence to the winds, and cut across these. My horse evidently thought this an excellent idea, for as soon as he got on the fields he was off like a trout up stream. Most successful across the first salient, then, suddenly, I saw we were approaching a wide ditch. Leave *would* be cancelled as far as I was concerned if I tried to jump that, I felt certain. I saw a sort of a narrow bridge about fifty yards to the right. Tried to persuade the horse to make for it. No, he believed in the ditch idea, and put on a sprint to jump it. Terrific battle between Dick Turpin and Black Bess!

A foaming pause on the brink of the abyss. Dick Turpin wins the argument and, after a few prancing circles described in the field, manages to cross the bridge with his fiery steed. I then rode down the road into the little village. The village school had been turned into a battalion stores, and the Quartermaster-Sergeant was invariably to be found there. I dismounted and pulled my horse up a couple of steps into the large schoolroom. Tied him up here, and last saw him blowing clouds of steam out of his nose on to one of those maps which show interesting forms of vegetable life with their Latin names underneath. Now for the Colonel. I clattered off down the street to his temporary orderly room. Thank heaven, he was in! I explained the case to him. He said he would do his best, and there and then sent off a wire. I could do no more now, so after fixing up that a message should be sent me, I slowly retraced my steps to the school, extracted the horse, and wended my way slowly back to the Transport Farm. Here I languished for the rest of the day, feeling convinced that 'all leave was cancelled'. I sat down to do some sketching after tea, full of marmalade and depression. About 6.00pm I chucked it, and went and sat by the stove, smoking a pipe. Suddenly the door opened and the bicycle orderly came in. "There's a note from the Adjutant for you, sir."

I tore it open. "Your leave granted; you leave tomorrow. If you call here in the morning, I'll give you your pass."

LEAVE!!

Chapter 20

THAT LEAVE TRAIN ~ MY OLD PAL ~ NOT NAUTICAL ~ LONDON AND HOME ~ THE CALL OF THE WILD ~ BACK AGAIN

One wants to have been at the Front, in the nasty parts, to appreciate fully what getting seven days' leave feels like. We used to have to be out at the Front for three consecutive months before being entitled to this privilege. I had passed this necessary apprenticeship, and now had actually got my leave.

The morning after getting my instructions I rose early, and packed the few things I was going to take with me. Very few things they were, too. Only a pack and a haversack, and both contained nothing but souvenirs. I decided to go to the station via the orderly room, so that I could do both in one journey. I had about two miles to go from my billets to the orderly room in the village, and about a mile on from there to the station. Someone suggested my riding - no fear; I was running no risks now.

I started off early with my servant. We took it in shifts with my heavy bags of souvenirs. One package (the pack) had four 'Little Willie' cases inside, in other words, the cast-iron shell-cases for the German equivalent of our 18-pounders. The haversack was filled with aluminium fuse-tops and one large piece of a 'Jack Johnson' shell-case. My pockets - and I had a good number, as I was wearing my greatcoat - were filled with a variety of objects: a pair of little clogs found in a roof at St Yvon, several clips of German bullets removed from equipment found on Christmas Day, and a collection of bullets which I had picked out with my pocket-knife from the walls of our house in St Yvon. The only additional luggage to this inventory I have given was my usual copious supply of Gold Flake cigarettes, of which, during my life in France, I must have consumed several army corps.

It was a glorious day - bright, sunny, and a faint fresh wind. Everything seemed bright and rosy. I felt I should have liked to skip along the road like a young bay tree - no, that's wrong - like a ram, only I didn't think it would be quite the thing with my servant there (King's Regulations: Chapter 158, paragraph 96, line 4); besides, he wasn't going on leave, so it would have been rather a dirty trick after all.

We got to the village with aching arms and souvenirs intact. I got my pass, and together with another officer we set out for the station. It was a leave train. Officers from all sorts of different battalions were either in it or going to get in, either here or at the next stop.

Having no wish to get that station into trouble, or myself either, by mentioning its name, I will call it Crême de Menthe. It was the same rotten little place I had arrived at. It is only because I am trying to sell the 'station-master' a copy of this book that I call the place a station at all. It really is a decomposing collection of half-hearted buildings and moss-grown rails, with an apology for a platform at one side.

We caught the train with an hour to spare. You can't miss trains in France: there's too much margin allowed on the timetable. The 10.15 leaves at 11.30, the 11.45 at 2.20, and so on; besides, if you did miss your train, you could always catch it up about two fields away, so there's nothing to worry about.

We started. I don't know what time it was.

If you turn up the word 'locomotion' in a dictionary, you will find it means 'the act or power of moving from place to place' - from *locus*, a place, and *motion*, the act of moving.

Our engine had got the *locus* part all right, but was rather weak about the *motion*. We creaked and squeaked about up the moss-grown track, and groaned our way back into the station time after time, in order to tie something else behind the train, or to get on to a siding to let a trainload of trench floorboards and plum and apple jangle past up the line. When at last we really started, it was about at the speed of the 'Rocket' on its trial trip.

Our enthusiastic 'going on leave' ardour was severely tested, and nearly broke down before we reached Boulogne, which we did late that night. But getting there, and mingling with the leave-going crowd which thronged the buffet, made up for all travelling shortcomings. Every variety of officer and army official was represented there. There were colonels, majors, captains, lieutenants, quantities of private soldiers, sergeants and corporals, hospital nurses and various other people employed in some war capacity or other. Representatives from every branch of the Army, in fact, whose turn for leave had come.

I left the buffet for a moment to go across to the Transport Office, and walking along through the throng ran into my greatest friend. A most extraordinary chance this! I had not the least idea whereabouts in France he was, or when he might be likely to get leave. His job was in quite a different part, many miles from the Douve. I have known him for many years; we were at school together, and have always seemed to have the lucky knack of bobbing up to the surface simultaneously without prior arrangement. This meeting sent my spirits up higher than ever. We both adjourned to the buffet, and talked away about our various experiences to the accompaniment of cold chicken and ham. A merry scene truly, that buffet - everyone filled with thoughts of England. Nearly everyone there must have stepped out of the same sort of mud and danger bath that I had. And, my word! It is a first-class feeling: sitting about waiting for the boat when you feel you've earned this seven days' leave. You hear men on all sides getting the last ounce of appreciation out of the unique sensation by saying such things as, "Fancy those poor blighters, sitting in the mud up there; they'll be just about getting near 'Stand to' now." You rapidly dismiss a momentary flash in your mind of what it's going to be like in that buffet on the return journey.

Early in the morning, and while it was still dark, we left the harbour and ploughed out into the darkness and the sea towards England.

I claim the honoured position of the world's worst sailor. I have covered several thousand miles on the sea, "brooked the briny" as far as India and Canada. I have been hurtled about on the largest Atlantic waves; yet I am, and always will remain, absolutely impossible at sea. Looking at the docks out of the hotel window nearly sends me to bed; there's something about a ship that takes the stuffing out of me completely. Whether it's that horrible pale varnished woodwork, mingled with the smell of stuffy upholstery, or whether it's that nauseating whiff from the open hatch of the engine-room, I don't know; but once on a ship I am as naught . . . not nautical.

Of course the Channel was going to be rough. I could see that at a glance. I know exactly what to do about the sea now. I go straight to a bunk, and hope for the best; if no bunk - bribe the steward until there is one. I got a bunk, deserted my friend in a cheerless way, and retired till the crossing was over. It *was* very rough . . .

In the cold grey hours we glided into Dover or Folkestone (I was too anaemic to care which) and fastened up alongside the wharf. I had a dim recollection of getting my pal to hold my pack as we left Boulogne, and now I could see neither him nor the pack. Fearful crush struggling up the gangway. I had to scramble for a seat in the London train, so couldn't waste time looking for my friend. I had my haversack - he had my pack. The train moved off, and now here we all were, back in clean, fresh, luxurious England, gliding along in an English train towards London. It's worth doing months and months of trenches to get that buoyant, electrical sensation of passing along through English country on one's way to London on leave. I spent the train journey thinking over what I should do during my seven days. Time after time I mentally conjured up the forthcoming performance of catching the train at Paddington and gliding out of the shadows of the huge station into the sunlit country beyond - the rapid express journey down home, the drive out from the station, back in my own land again!

We got into London in pretty quick time, and I rapidly converted my dreams into facts. Still in the same old trench clothes, with a goodly quantity of Flanders mud attached, I walked into Paddington Station, and collared a seat in the train on Number 1 platform. Then, collecting a quantity of papers and magazines from the bookstalls, I prepared myself for enjoying to the full the two hours' journey down home.

I spent a gorgeous week in Warwickshire, during which time my friend came along down to stay a couple of days with me, bringing my missing pack along with him. He had had the joy of carrying it laden with shell-cases across London, and taking it down with him to somewhere near Aldershot, and finally bringing it to me without having kept any of the contents . . . such is a true friend.

As this book deals with my wanderings in France I will not go into details of my happy seven days' leave. I now resume at the point where I was due to return to France. In spite of the joys of England as opposed to life in Flanders, yet a curious phenomenon presented itself at the end of my leave. I was anxious to get back. Strange, but true. Somehow one felt that slogging away out in the dismal fields of war was the real thing to do. If someone had offered me a nice, safe, comfortable job in England, I wouldn't have taken it. I claim no credit for this feeling of mine. I know everyone has the same. That buccaneering, rough-and-tumble life out there has its attractions. The spirit of adventure is in most people, and the desire and will to biff the Boches is in everyone, so there you are.

I drifted back via London, Dover and Boulogne, and thence up the same old stagnant line to Crême de Menthe; once more back in the land of mud, bullets, billets and star shells. It was the greyest of grey days when I arrived at my one-horse terminus. I got out at the 'station', and had a solitary walk along the empty, muddy lanes, back to the Transport Farm. Plodding along in the thin rain that was falling I thought of home, London, England, and then of the job before me. Another three months at least before any further chance of leave could come my way again. Evening was coming on. Across the flat, sombre country I could see the tall, swaying poplar trees standing near the farm. Beyond lay the rough and rugged road which led to the Douve trenches.

How nice that leave had been! Tomorrow night I should be going along back to the trenches before Wulverghem.

Chapter 21

BACK FROM LEAVE ~ THAT "BLINKIN' MOON" ~ AN UNLUCKY SHOT ~ JOHNSON 'OLES ~ TOMMY AND 'FRIGHTFULNESS' ~ EXPLORING EXPEDITION

As I had expected, the battalion were just finishing their last days out in rest billets, and were going 'in' the following night. Reaction from leave set in for me with unprecedented violence. It was horrible weather, pouring with rain all the time, which made one's depression worse.

Leave over; rain, rain, rain; trenches again, and the future looked like being perpetually the same, or perhaps worse. Yet, somehow or other, in these times of deep depression which come to everyone now and again, I cannot help smiling. It has always struck me as an amusing thing that the world, and all the human beings thereon, do get themselves into such curious and painful predicaments, and then spend the rest of the time wishing they could get out.

My reflections invariably brought me to the same conclusion, that here I was, caught up in the cogs of this immense, uncontrollable war machine, and like everyone else, had to, and meant to stick it out to the end.

The next night we went through all the approved formula for going into the trenches: started at dusk, and got into our respective mud cavities a few hours later. I went all round the trenches again, looking to see that things were the same as when I left them, and, on the Colonel's instructions, started a series of alterations in several gun positions. There was one trench that was so obscured along its front by odd stumps of trees that I decided the only good spot for a machine gun was right at one end, on a road which led up to Messines. From here it would be possible for us to get an excellent field of fire. To have this gun on the road meant making an emplacement there somehow. That night we started scheming it out, and the next evening began work on it. It was a bright moonlight night, I remember, and my Sergeant and I went out in front of our parapet, walked along the field and crept up the ditch a little way, considering the machine-gun possibilities of the land.

That moonlight feeling is very curious. You feel as if the enemy can see you clearly, and that all eyes in the opposite trench are turned on you. You can almost imagine a Boche smilingly taking an aim, and saying to a friend, "We'll just let him come a bit closer first."

Everyone who has had to go 'out in front', wiring, will know this feeling. As a matter of fact, it is astonishing how little one can see of men in the moonlight, even when the trenches are very close together. One gets quite used to walking freely in this light, going out in front of the parapet and having a look round.

The only time that really makes one apprehensive is when some gang of men or other turn up from way back somewhere and have come to assist in some operation near the enemy. They, being unfamiliar with the caution needed, and unappreciative of what it's like to have neighbours who 'hate' you sixty yards away, generally bring trouble in their wake by one of the party shouting out in a deep bass or a shrill soprano, "'Ere, chuck us the 'ammer, 'Arry," or something like that, following the remark up with a series of vulcan-like blows on the top of an iron post. Result: three star shells soar out into the frosty air, and a burst of machine-gun fire skims over the top of your head.

We made a very excellent and strong emplacement on the road, and used it henceforth. I had a lot of bother with one gun in those trenches, which was placed at very nearly the left-hand end of the whole line. I had been obliged to fix the gun there, as it was very necessary for dominating a certain road. But when I took the place over from the previous battalion, I thought there might be difficulties about this gun position, and there were. The night before we had made our inspection of these trenches, a shell had landed right on top of the gun emplacement and had 'outed' the whole concern, unfortunately killing two of the gun section belonging to the former battalion. For some reason or other that end of our line was always being shelled. Just in the same way as they plunked shells daily into St Yvon, so they did here. Each morning, with hardly ever a miss, they shelled our trenches, but almost invariably in the same place: the left-hand end. The difference between St Yvon and this place was, however, that here they always shelled with 'heavies'. Right back at the Douve farm a mile away, the thundering crash of one of these shells would rattle all the windows and make one say, *"Where did that one go to?"*

All round that neighbourhood it seemed to have been the fashion, past and present, to use the largest shells. In going along the Douve one day, I made a point of measuring and examining several of the holes. I took a photograph of one, with my cap resting on one side of it, to show the relative proportion and give an idea of the size. It was about fourteen feet in diameter, and seven feet deep. The largest shell-hole I have ever seen was over twenty feet in diameter and about twelve feet deep. The largest hole I have seen, made by an implement of war, though not by a gun or a howitzer, was larger still, and its size was colossal. I refer to a hole made by one of our trench mortars, but regret that I did not measure it. Round about our farm were a series of holes of immense size, showing clearly the odium which that farm had incurred, and was incurring; but, whilst I was in it, nothing came in through the roof or walls. I have since learnt that that old farm is no more, having been shelled out of existence. All my sketches on those plaster walls form part of a slack heap, surrounded by a moat.

Well, this persistent shelling of the left-hand end of our trenches meant a persistent readjustment of our parapets, and putting things back again. Each morning the Boches would knock things down, and each evening we would put them up again. Our soldiers are only amused by this procedure. Their humorously cynical outlook at the Boche temper renders them impervious to anything the Germans can ever do or think of. Their outlook towards a venomous German attempt to do something 'frightfully' nasty, is very similar to a large and powerful nurse dealing with a fractious child - sort of: "Now, then, Master Frankie, you mustn't kick and scream like that."

One can almost see a group of stolid, unimaginative, non-humorous Germans taking all things with their ridiculous seriousness, sending off their shells, and pulling hateful faces at the same time. You can see our men sending over a real stiff, quietening answer, with a sporting twinkle in the eye, perhaps jokingly remarking, as a shell is pushed into the gun, "'Ere's one for their Officers' Mess, Bert."

On several evenings I had to go round and arrange for the reconstruction of the ruined parapet or squashed-in dugouts. It was during one of these little episodes that I felt the spirit of my drawing, *"There goes our blinkin' parapet again."* which I did sometime later. I never went about looking for ideas for drawings; the whole business of the war seemed to come before me in a series of pictures. Jokes used to stick out of all the horrible discomfort, something like the points of a harrow would stick into you if you slept on it.

I used to visit all the trenches, and look up the various company commanders and platoon commanders in the same way as I did at St Yvon. I got a splendid idea of all the details of our position; all the various ways from one part of it to another. As I walked back to the Douve farm at night, nearly always alone, I used to keep on exploring the wide tract of land that lay behind our trenches. "I'll have a look at that old cottage up on the right tonight," I used to say to myself, and later, when the time came for me to walk back from the trenches, I would go off at a new angle across the plain, and make for my objective. Once inside, and feeling out of view of the enemy, I would go round the deserted rooms and lofts by the light of a few matches, and if the house looked as if it would prove of interest, I would return the next night with a candle-end, and make an examination of the whole thing. They are all very much alike, these houses in Flanders; all seem to contain the same mangled remains of simple homely occupations: strings of onions, old straw hats and clogs, mixed with an assortment of cheap clothing, with perhaps here and there an umbrella or a top hat. That is about the class of stuff one found in them. After one of these expeditions I would go on back across the plain, along the corduroy boards or by the bank of the river, to our farm.

Chapter 22

A DAYLIGHT STALK ~ THE DISUSED TRENCH ~ "DID THEY SEE ME?" ~ A GOOD SNIPING POSITION ~ A SNIPER'S POST

Our farm was, as I have remarked, a mile from the trenches at the nearest part, and about a mile and a half from the furthest. Wulverghem was about half a mile behind the farm.

As time went on at these Douve trenches, I became more and more familiar with the details of the surrounding country, for each day I used to creep out of the farm, and when I had crossed the moat by a small wooden bridge at the back, I would go off into the country nearby looking at everything. One day the Colonel expressed a wish to know whether it was possible to get up into our trenches in daytime without being seen. Of course anyone could have gone to the trenches, and been momentarily seen here and there, and could have done so fairly safely and easily by simply walking straight up, taking advantage of what little cover there was; but to get right up without showing at all, was rather a poser, as all cover ceased about a hundred yards behind the trenches.

The idea of trying attracted me. One morning I crept along the ragged hedge, on the far side of the moat which led to the river, and started out for the trenches. I imagined a German with a powerful pair of binoculars looking down on the plain from the Messines Hill, with nothing better to do than to see if he could spot someone walking about. Keeping this possibility well in mind, I started my stalk up to the trenches with every precaution.

I crept along amongst the trees bordering the river for a considerable distance, but as one neared the trenches, these got wider apart, and as the river wound about a lot there were places where to walk from one tree to the next, one had to walk parallel to the German trenches and quite exposed, though, of course, at a considerable range off. I still bore in mind my imaginary picture of the gentleman with binoculars, though, so I got down near the water's edge and moved along, half-concealed by the bank. Soon I reached the farms, and by dodging about amongst the scattered shrubs and outhouses, here and there crawling up a ditch, I got into one of the farm buildings. I sat in it amongst a pile of old clothes, empty tins and other oddments, and had a smoke, thinking the while on how I could get from these farms across the last bit of open space which was the most difficult of all.

I finished my cigarette, and began the stalk again. Another difficulty presented itself. I found that it was extremely difficult to cross from the second last farm to the last one, as the ground was completely open, and rather sloped down towards the enemy. This was not apparent when looking at the place at night, for then one never bothers about concealment, and one walks anywhere and anyhow. But now the question was, how to do it. I crept down to the river again, and went along there for a bit, looking for a chance of leaving it under cover for the farm.

Coming to a narrow, cart-rutted lane a little further on, I was just starting to go up it when, suddenly, a bright idea struck me. An old zigzag communication trench (a relic of a bygone period) left the lane on the right, and apparently ran out across the field to within a few yards of the furthest farm. Once there, I had only a hundred yards more to do. I entered the communication trench. It was just a deep, narrow slot cut across the field, and had, I should imagine, never been used. I think the enormous amount of water in it had made it a useless work. I saw no sign of it ever having been used. A fearful trench it was, with a deep deposit of dark green, filthy, watery mud from end to end.

This, I could see, was the only way up to the farm, so I made the best of it. I resigned myself to getting thoroughly wet through. Quite unavoidable. I plunged into this unwholesome clay ditch and went along, each step taking me up to my thighs in soft dark ooze, whilst here and there the water was so deep as to force me to scoop out holes in the clay at the side when, by leaning against the opposite side, with my feet in the holes, I could slowly push my way along. In time I got to the other end, and sat down to think a bit. As I sat, a bullet suddenly whacked into the clay parapet alongside of me, which stimulated my thinking a bit. "Had I been seen?" I tried to find out, and reassure myself before going on. I put my hat on top of a stick and brought it up above the parapet at two or three points to try and attract another shot; but no, there wasn't another, so I concluded the first one had been accidental, and went on my way again. By wriggling along behind an undulation in the field, and then creeping from one tree to another, I at last managed to get up into our reserve trenches, where I obtained my first daylight, close-up view of our trenches, German trenches, and general landscape; all laid out in panorama style.

In front of me were our front-line trenches, following the line of the little stream which ran into the Douve on the right. On the far side of the stream the ground gently rose in a long slope up to Messines, where you could see a shattered mass of red-brick buildings with the old grey tower in the middle. At a distance of from about two to four hundred yards away lay the German trenches, parallel to ours, their barbed-wire glistening in the morning sunlight.

"This place I'm in is a pretty good place for a sniper to hitch up," I thought to myself. "Can see everything there is to be seen from here."

After a short stocktaking of the whole scene, I turned and wallowed my way back to the farm. Some few days later they did make a sniper's post of that spot, and a captain friend of mine, with whom I spent many quaint and dismal nights in St Yvon, occupied it. He was the 'star' shot of the battalion, an expert sniper, and, I believe, made quite a good bag.

Old soldiers never die, they simply fades away.

Chapter 23

OUR MOATED FARM ~ WULVERGHEM ~ FRENCH GRAVES ~ THE CURE'S HOUSE ~ A SHATTERED CHURCH ~ MORE 'HEAVIES' ~ A FARM ON FIRE

Our farm was one of a cluster of three or four, each approximately a couple of hundred yards apart. It was perhaps the largest and the most preserved of the lot. It was just the same sort of shape as all Flemish farms - a long building running round three sides of the yard, in the middle of which there was an oblong tank, used for collecting all the rubbish and drainage.

The only difference about our farm was, we had a moat. Very superior to all the cluster in consequence. Sometime or other the moat must have been very effective; but when I was there, only about a quarter of it contained water. The other three-quarters was a sort of bog, or marsh, its surface broken up by large shell-holes. On the driest part of this I discovered a row of graves, their rough crosses all battered and bent down. I just managed to discern the names inscribed; they were all French. Names of former heroes who had participated in some action or other months before. Going out into the fields behind the farm, I found more French graves, enclosed in a rectangular graveyard that had been roughly made with barbed-wire and posts, each grave surmounted with the dead soldier's hat. Months of rough wintry weather had beaten down the faded cloth cap into the clay mound, and had started the obliteration of the lettering on the cross. A few more months; and cross, mound and hat will all have merged back into the fields of Flanders.

Beyond these fields, about half a mile distant, lay Wulverghem. Looking at what you can see of this village from the Douve farm, it looks exceedingly pretty and attractive. A splendid old church tower could be seen between the trees, and round about it were clustered the red roofs of a fair-sized village. It has, to my mind, a very nice situation. In the days before the war it must have been a pleasing place to live in. I went to have a look at it one day. It's about as fine a sample of what these Prussians have brought upon Belgian villages as any I have seen. The village street is one long ruin. On either side of the road, all the houses are merely a collection of broken tiles and shattered bricks and framework. Huge shell-holes punctuate the street. I had seen a good many mutilated villages before this, but I remember thinking this was as bad, if not worse, than any I had yet seen. I determined to explore some of the houses and the church.

I went into one house opposite the church. It had been quite a nice house once, containing about ten rooms. It was full of all sorts of things. The evacuation had evidently been hurried. I went into the front right-hand room first, and soon discovered by the books and pictures that this had been the Curé's house. It was in a terrible state. Religious books in French and Latin lay about the floor in a vast disorder, some with the cover and half the book torn off by the effect of an explosion. Pictures illustrating Bible scenes, images, and other probably cherished objects, smashed and ruined, hung about the walls, or fragmentary portions of them lay littered about on the floor.

A shell-hole of large proportions had rent a gash in the outer front wall, leaving the window woodwork, bricks and wallpaper piled up in a heap on the floor, partially obliterating a large writing-desk. Private papers lay about in profusion, all dirty, damp and muddy. The remains of a window blind and half its roller hung in the space left by

Taken at St Yvon, Christmas Day, 1914.
Officers, 2nd Lieutenant - 1. Bairnsfathers, Bruce - 1. Holes, Shell - 1.

the absent window, and mournfully tapped against the remnant of the framework in the light, cold breeze that was blowing in from outside. Place this scene in your imagination in some luxuriant country vicarage in England, and you will get an idea of what Belgium had had to put up with from these Teutonic madmen. I went into all the rooms; they were in very much the same state. In the back part of the house the litter was added to by empty tins and old military equipment. Soldiers had evidently had to live there temporarily on their way to some part of our lines. I heard a movement in the room opposite the one I had first gone into; I went back and saw a cat sitting in the corner amongst a pile of leather-backed books. I made a movement towards it, but with a cadaverous, wild glare at me, it sprang through the broken window and disappeared.

The church was just opposite the priest's house. I went across the road to look at it. It was a large, reddish-grey, stone building, pretty old, I should say, and surrounded by a graveyard. Shell-holes everywhere; the old, grey gravestones and slabs cracked and sticking about at odd angles. As I entered by the vestry door I noticed the tower was fairly all right, but that was about the only part that was. Belgium and Northern France are full of churches which have been sadly knocked about, and all present very much the same appearance. I will describe this one to give you a sample. I went through the vestry into the main part of the church, deciding to examine the vestry later. The roof had had most of the tiles blown off, and underneath them the roofing-boards had been shattered into long narrow strips. Fixed at one end to what was left of the rafters they flapped slowly up and down in the air like lengths of watch-spring. Below, on the floor of the church, the chairs were tossed about in the greatest possible disorder, and here and there a dozen or so had been pulverized by the fall of an immense block of masonry. Highly coloured images were lying about, broken and twisted. The altar candelabra and stained-glass windows lay in a heap together behind a pulpit, the front of which had been knocked off by a falling pillar. One could walk about near some of the broken images, and pick up little candles and trinkets which had been put in and around the shrine, off the floor and from among the mass of broken stones and mortar. The vestry, I found, was almost complete. Nearly trodden out of recognition on the floor, I found a bright coloured hand-made altar cloth, which I then had half a mind to take away with me, and post it back to some parson in England to put in his church. I only refrained from carrying out this plan as I feared that the difficulties of getting it away would be too great. I left the church, and looked about some of the other houses, but none proved as pathetically interesting as the church and the vicar's house, so I took my way out across the fields again towards the Douve farm.

Not a soul about anywhere. Wulverghem lay there, empty, wrecked and deserted. I walked along the river bank for a bit, and had got about two hundred yards from the farm when the quiet morning was interrupted in the usual way, by shelling. Deep-toned, earth-shaking crashes broke into the quiet peaceful air. "Just in the same place," I observed to myself as I walked along behind our left-hand trenches. I could see the cloud of black smoke after each one landed, and knew exactly where they were. "Just in the same old - hullo! Hullo!"

With that rotating, gurgling whistle a big one had just

sailed over and landed about fifty yards from our farm! I nipped in across the moat, through the courtyard, and explained to the others where it had landed. We all remained silent, waiting for the next. Here it came, gurgling along through the air; a pause, then 'CRUMPH!' - nearly in the same place again, but, if anything, nearer the next farm. The Colonel moved to the window and looked out.

"They're after that farm," he said, as he turned away slowly and struck a match by the fireplace to light his pipe with. About half a dozen shells whizzed along in close succession, and about four hit and went into the roof of the next farm.

Presently I looked out of the window again, and saw a lot of our men moving out of the farm and across the road into the field beyond. There was a reserve trench here, so they went into it. I looked again, and soon saw the reason. Dense columns of smoke were coming out of the straw roof, and soon the whole place was a blazing ruin. Nobody was in the least perturbed; we all turned away from the window and wondered how soon they'd 'have our farm'.

Chapter 24

THAT RATION FATIGUE ~ SKETCHES IN REQUEST ~ BAILLEUL ~ BATHS AND LUNATICS ~ HOW TO CONDUCT A WAR

They seemed to me long, dark, dismal days, those days spent in the Douve trenches; longer, darker and more dismal than the Plugstreet ones. Night after night I crossed the dreary mud flat, passed the same old wretched farms, and went on with the same old trench routine. We all considered the trenches a pretty rotten outfit, but everyone was fully prepared to accept far rottener things than that. There was never the least sign of flagging determination in any man there, and I am sure you could say the same of the whole Front.

And, really, some jobs on some nights wanted a lot of beating for undesirability. Take the ration party's job, for instance. Think of the rottenest, wettest, windiest winter's night you can remember, and add to it this bleak, muddy, war-worn plain with its ruined farms and shell-torn lonely road. Then think of men, leaving the trenches at dusk, going back about a mile and a half, and bringing sundry large and heavy boxes up to the trenches, pausing now and again for a rest, and ignoring the intermittent crackling of rifle-fire in the darkness, and the sharp *'phit'* of bullets hitting the mud all around. Think of that as your portion each night and every night. When you have finished this job, the rest you get consists of coiling yourself up in a damp dugout. Night after night, week after week, month after month, this job is done by thousands.

As one sits in a brilliantly illuminated, comfortable, warm theatre, having just come from a cosy and luxurious restaurant, just think of some poor devil halfway along those corduroy boards struggling with a crate of biscuits; the ration 'dump' behind, the trenches on in front. When he has finished he will step down into the muddy slush of a trench, and take his place with the rest, who, if need be, will go on doing that job for another ten years, without thinking of an alternative.

The Germans made a vast mistake when they thought they had gauged the English temperament.

*

We went 'in' and 'out' of those trenches many times. During these intervals of 'out' I began to draw pictures more and more. It had become known that I drew these trench pictures, not only in our battalion but in several others, and at various headquarters I got requests for four or five drawings at a time.

About three weeks after I returned from leave, I had to move my billeting quarters. I went to a farm called 'La petite Monque'; I don't know how it's really spelt, but that's what the name sounded like. Here I lived with the officers of 'A' Company, and a jolly pleasant crew they were. We shared a mess together, and had one big room and one small one between us. There were six of us altogether. The Captain had the little room and the bed in it, whilst we all slept round the table on the floor in the big room. Here, in the daytime, when I was not out with the machine-gun sections, I drew several pictures. The Brigadier-General of our brigade took a particular fancy to one which he got from me. The divisional headquarters had half a dozen; whilst I did two sets of four each for two officers in the regiment. Sometimes we would go for walks around the country, and occasionally made an excursion as far as Bailleul, about five miles away. Bailleul held one special attraction for us. There were some wonderfully good baths there. The fact that they were situated in the lunatic asylum rather added to their interest.

The first time I went there, one of the subalterns in 'A' Company was my companion. We didn't particularly want to walk all the way, so we decided to get down to the high road as soon as we could, and try and get a lift in a car. With great luck we managed to stop a fairly empty car, and got a lift. It was occupied by a couple of French soldiers who willingly rolled us along into Bailleul. Once there, we walked through the town and out to the asylum close by. I expect by now the lunatics have been called up under the group system; but in those days they were there, and pulled faces at us as we walked up the wide gravel drive to the grand portals of the building. They do make nice asylums over there. This was a sort of Chatsworth or Blenheim to look at. Inside it was fitted up in very great style: long carpeted corridors opening out into sort of domed winter gardens, something like the snake house at the Zoo. We came at length to a particularly lofty, domed hall, from which opened several large bathrooms. Splendid places. A row of large white enamelled baths along one wall, cork mats on the floor, and one enormous central water supply, hot and cold, which you diverted to whichever bath you chose by means of a long flexible rubber pipe. Soap, sponges, towels, *ad lib.* You can imagine what this palatial water grotto meant to us, when, at other times, our best bath was of saucepan capacity, taken on the cold stone floor of a farm room. We lay and boiled the trenches out of our

systems in that palatial asylum. Glorious! Lying back in a long white enamel bath in a warm foggy atmosphere of steam, watching one's toes floating in front. When this was over, and we had been grimaced off the premises by 'inmates' at the windows, we went back into Bailleul and made for the 'Faucon d'Or', an old hotel that stands in the square. Here we had a civilised meal. Tablecloth, knives, forks, spoons, waited on, all that sort of thing. You could have quite a good dinner here if you liked. A curious thought occurred to me then, as it occurs again to me now I write it down. Here it is: if the authorities gave one permission, one could have rooms at the 'Faucon d'Or' and go to the war daily. It would be quite possible to, say, have an early dinner, table-d'hôte (with, say, a half-bottle of Salmon and Gluckstein), get into one's car and go to the trenches, spend the night sitting in a small damp hole in the ground, or glaring over the parapet, and after 'stand to' in the morning, go back in the car in time for breakfast. Of course, if there was an attack, the car would have to wait - that's all; and of course you would come to an understanding with the hotel management that the terms were for meals taken in the hotel, and that if you had to remain in the trenches the terms must be reduced accordingly.

A curious war this; you *can* be at a *table-d'hôte* dinner, a music-hall entertainment afterwards, and within half an hour be enveloped in the most uncomfortable, soul-destroying trench ever known. I said you can be; I wish I could say you always are.

The last time I was at Bailleul, not many months ago, I heard that we could no longer have baths at the asylum; I don't know why. I think someone told me why, but I can't remember. Whether it was the baths had been shelled, or whether the lunatics objected, it is impossible for me to say, but there's the fact, anyway. 'Napoo' baths at Bailleul.

Chapter 25

GETTING STALE ~ LONGING FOR A CHANGE ~ WE LEAVE THE DOUVE ~ ON THE MARCH ~ FINDING BILLETS ~ SPOTTED FEVER ~ TEN DAYS' REST

The Douve trenches claimed our battalion for a long time. We went in and out with monotonous regularity, and I went on with my usual work with machine guns. The whole place became more and more depressing to me, and yet, somehow, I have got more ideas for my pictures from this part of the line than any other since or before. One's mental outlook, I find, varies very much from day to day. Some days there were on which I felt quite merry and bright, and strode along on my nightly rambles, calmly ignoring bullets as they whisked about. At other times I felt thoroughly depressed and weary. As time wore on at the Douve, I felt myself getting into a state when it took more and more out of me to keep up my vigour, and suppress my imagination. There were times when I experienced an almost irresistible desire to lie down and sleep during some of my night walks. I would feel an overwhelming desire to ignore the rain and mud, and just coil up in a farm amongst the empty tins and rubbish and sleep, sleep, sleep. I looked forward to sleep to drown out the worries of the daily and nightly life. In fact, I was slowly getting ill, I suppose. The actual rough-and-ready life didn't trouble me at all. I was bothered with the *idea* of the whole thing. The unnatural atmosphere of things that one likes and looks upon as pleasing, peaceful objects in ordinary times, seemed now to obsess me. It's hard to describe; but the following gives

Off 'in' again.

a faint idea of my feelings at this time. Instead of deriving a sense of peace and serenity from picturesque country farms, old trees, setting suns, and singing birds, here was this wretched war business hashing up the whole thing. A farm was a place where you expected a shell through the wall any minute; a tree was the sort of thing the gunners took to range on; a sunset indicated a quantity of light in which it was unsafe to walk abroad. Birds singing were a mockery. All this sort of thing bothered me, and was slowly reducing my physical capacity to 'stick it out'. But I was determined I would stick to the ship, and so I did. The periodical going out to billets and making merry there was a thing to look forward to. Everyone comes up in a rebound of spirits on these occasions. In the evenings there, sitting round the table, writing letters, talking, and occasionally having other members of the regiment in to a meal or a call of some sort, made things quite pleasant. There was always the post to look forward to. Quite a thrill went round the room when the door opened and a sergeant came in with an armful of letters and parcels.

Yet during all this latter time at the Douve I longed for a change in trench life. Some activity, some march to somewhere or other; anything to smash up the everlasting stagnant appearance of life there. Suddenly the change came. We were told we had to go out a day before one of our usual sessions in the trenches was ended. We were all immensely pleased. We didn't know where we were bound for, but, anyway, we were going. This news revived me enormously, and everything looked brighter.

The departure-night came, and company by company we handed over to a battalion that had come to relieve us, and collected on the road leading back to Neuve Eglise. I handed over all my gun emplacements to the incoming machine-gun officer, and finally collected my various sections with all their tackle on the road as well. We merely marched back to our usual billets that night, but next morning had orders to get all our baggage ready for the transport wagons. We didn't know where we were going, but at about eleven o'clock in the morning we started off on the march, and soon realised that our direction was Bailleul.

On a fine, clear, warm spring day we marched along, all in the best of spirits, songs of all sorts being sung one after the other. As I marched along in the rear of the battalion, at the head of my machine-gun section, I selected items from their repertoire and had them sung 'by request'. I had some astonishingly fine mouth-organists in my section. When we had 'On the Trail of the Lonesome Pine' sung by half the section, with mouth-organ accompaniment by the other half, the effect was enormous. We passed several battalions of my regiment on the road, evidently bound for the Armentières direction. Shouts, jokes and much mirth showed the kindred spirits of the passing columns: all battalions of the same regiment, all more or less recruited in the same counties. When we reached Bailleul we halted in the Square, and then I learnt we were to be billeted there. There was apparently some difficulty in getting billets, and so I was faced with the necessity of finding some for my section myself. The Transport Officer was in the same fix; he wanted a large and commodious farm whenever he hitched up anywhere, as he had a crowd of horses, wagons and men to put up somehow. He and I decided to start out and look for billets on our own.

I found a temporary rest for my section in an old brickyard on the outskirts of the town, and the Transport Officer and I started out to look for a good farm which we could appropriate. Bailleul stands on a bit of a hill, so you can get a wide and extensive view of the country from there. We could see several farms perched about in the country. We fixed on the nearest and walked out to it. No luck; they were willing to have us, but it wasn't big enough. We tried another; same result. I then suggested we should separate, and each try different roads, and thus we should get one quicker. This we did, I going off up a long straight road, and finally coming to a most promising-looking edifice on one side - a real large size in farms.

I went into the yard and walked across the dirty cobbles to the front door. The people were most pleasant. I didn't understand a word they said; but when a person pushes a flagon of beer into one of your hands and an apple into the other, one concludes he means to be pleasant, anyway. I mumbled a lot of jargon to them for some time, and I really believe they saw that I wanted to use their place for a billet. The owner, a man of about forty-five, then started a long and hardy discussion right at me. He put on a serious face at intervals, so I guessed there was something rather important he was trying to convey to me. I was saved from giving my answer by catching sight of my pal, the Transport Officer, crossing the yard. He came in.

"I've brought Jean along to talk," he announced. (Jean was our own battalion interpreter.) "I can't find a place; but this looks all right."

Jean and the owner at once dived off into a labyrinth of unintelligible words, from which they emerged five minutes later. We sat around and listened. Jean turned to us and remarked: "They have got fever here, he says, what you call the spotted fever - how you say, spotted fever? - and this farm is out of bounds."

"Oh! Spotted fever! I see!" we both said, and slid away out of that farm pretty quick. So that was what that farmer was trying to say to me: spotted fever! I went down the road wondering whether cerebral meningitis germs preferred apples or beer, or perhaps they liked both; awful thought!

We went back to our original selection and decided to somehow or other squeeze into the farm which we thought too small. Many hours later we got the transport and the machine-gun section fixed up. We spent two nights there. On the second day I went up into Bailleul. Walking along in the Square, looking at the shops and market stalls, I ran into the brigade machine-gun officer.

"Topping about our brigade, isn't it?" he said.

"What's topping?" I asked.

"Why, we're going to have about ten days' rest. We clear off out of here tomorrow to a village about three miles away, and our battalion will billet there. Where we go after that I don't know; but, anyway, ten days' rest. Ten days' rest!!"

"Come and split one at the 'Faucon d'Or'?"

"No thanks, I've just had one."

"Well, come and have another."

Chapter 26

A PLEASANT CHANGE ~ FIXED UP ~ SUZETTE, BERTHE AND MARTHE ~ 'LA JEUNE FILLE FAROUCHE' ~ ANDRE

On the next morning we left Bailleul, and the whole of our battalion marched off down one of the roads leading out into the country in a westerly direction. The weather was now excellent; so what with the prospect of a rest, fine weather and the departure from the Wulverghem trenches, we were all very merry and bright, and 'going strong' all round. It seemed to us as if we had come out of some dark, wet underworld into a bright, wholesome locality, suitable for the habitation of man.

Down the long, straight, dusty road we marched, hop-yards and bright coloured fields on either side, here and there passing prosperous-looking farms and estaminets: what a pleasant change it was from that ruined, dismal jungle we had so recently left!

About three or four miles out we came to a village; the main road ran right through it, forming its principal street. On either side small lanes ran out at right angles into the different parts of the village. We received the order to halt, and soon learnt that this was the place where we were to have our ten days' rest. A certain amount of billets had been arranged for, but, as is generally the case, the machine-gun section have to search around for themselves; an advantage really, as they generally find a better crib this way than if somebody else found it for them. As soon as we were 'dismissed', I started off on a billet search. The Transport Officer was again with me on the same quest. We separated, and each searched a different part of the village, The first house I went into was a dismal failure. An old woman of about eighty-four opened the door about six inches, and was some time before she permitted the aperture to widen sufficiently to allow me to go inside the house. A most dingy, poky sort of a place, so I cleared off to search for something better. As I crossed the farmyard behind, my servant, who had been conducting a search on his own, suddenly appeared round the corner of the large barn at the end of the yard, and came towards me.

"I've found a place over 'ere, sir, I expect you'll like."

"Where?" I asked.

"This way, sir!" and he led the way across a field to a gate, which we climbed. We then went down a sort of back lane to the village, and turned in at a small wicket-gate leading to a row of cottages. He led me up to one in the centre, and knocked at the door. A woman opened it, and I told her what I was looking for. She seemed quite keen for us to go there, and asked if there was anyone else to come there with me. I told her the Transport Officer would be coming there too, and our two servants. She quite agreed to this, and showed me the rooms we could have. They were extremely small, but we decided to have them. 'Them' consisted of one bedroom, containing two beds, the size of the room being about fourteen feet by eight, and the front kitchen-sitting-room place, which was used by everybody in the house, and was about twice the size of the bedroom. I went away and found the Transport Officer, brought him back and showed him the place. He thought it a good spot, so we arranged to fix up there.

Our servants started in to put things right for us, get our baggage there, and so on, whilst I went off to see to billets for the machine-gun section. I had got them a pretty good barn, attached to the farm I first called at, but I wanted to go and see that it was really large enough and suitable when they had all got in and spread themselves. I found that it did suit pretty well. The space was none too large, but I felt sure we wouldn't find a better. There was a good field for all the limbers and horses adjoining, so on the whole it was quite a convenient place. The section had already got to work with their cooking things, and had a fire going out in the field. Those gunners were a very self-contained, happy throng; they all lived together like a family, and were all very keen on their job.

I returned to my cottage to see how things were progressing. My man had unrolled my valise, and put all my things out and about in the bedroom. I took off all my equipment, which I was still wearing; pack, haversacks, revolver, binoculars, map-case, etc., and sat down in the kitchen to take stock of the situation.

I now saw what the family consisted of; and by airing my feeble French, I found out who they were and what they did. The woman who had come to the door was the wife of a painter and decorator, who had been called up, and was in a French regiment somewhere in Alsace. Another girl who was there was a friend, and really lived next door with her sister, but owing to overcrowding, due to our servants and some French relatives, she spent most of her time in the house I was in.

The owner of the place was Madame Charlet-Flaw, Christian name Suzette. The other two girls were, respectively, Berthe and Marthe. Ages of all three in the order I have mentioned them were, I should say, twenty-eight, twenty-four, and twenty. The place had, I found, been used as billets before. I discovered this in two ways.

Firstly; on the mantelpiece over the old stove I saw a collection of many kinds of regimental badges, with a quantity of English magazines. Secondly; after I had been talking for some time, Suzette answered my remarks with one of her stock English sentences, picked up from some former lodgers, "And very nice too," a phrase much in vogue at that time.

The Transport Officer, who had been out seeing about something or other, soon returned, and with him came the regimental doctor, who had got his billets all right, but had come along to see how we were fixed up. A real good chap he was, one of the best. All six of us now sat about in the kitchen and talked over things in general. We were a very cheery group. The Transport Officer, doctor and myself were all thoroughly in the mood for enjoying this ten days' rest. To live amongst ordinary people again, and see the life of even a village, was refreshing to us. We had a pretty easy afternoon, and all had tea in that kitchen, after which I went out and round to look up my old pals in 'A' Company. They had, I found, got hold of the Curé's house, the village parson's rectory, in fact. It was a square, plain-looking house, standing very close to the church, and they all seemed very comfortable there. The Curé himself and his housekeeper only had three rooms reserved for themselves, the rest being handed over to the officers of 'A' Company. I stayed round there for a bit, having a talk and a smoke, and we each of us remarked in turn, about every five minutes, what a top-hole thing it was that we had got this ten days' rest.

I then went back to our cottage, where I had a meal with the Transport Officer, conversing the while with Suzette, Berthe and Marthe. I don't know which I liked the best of these three, they were all so cheery and hospitable. Marthe was the most interesting from the pictorial point of view. She was so gypsy-like to look at: brown-skinned, large dark eyes, exceeding bright, with a sort of sparkling, wild look about her. I called her 'La jeune fille farouche' (looked this up first before doing so), and she was always called this afterwards. It means 'the young wild girl' (at least I hope it means that). The doctor came back again after dinner, and we all proceeded to fill the air in the small kitchen with songs and tobacco-smoke. The Transport Officer was a 'Corona Corona' expert, and there he would sit with his feet up on the rail at the side of the stove, smoking one of these zeppelins of a cigar, till we all went to bed.

There was an heir to the estate in that cottage - one André, Suzette's son, aged about five. He went to bed early, and slept with wonderful precision and persistence whilst we were making noise enough to wake the Curé a hundred yards away. But, when we went to bed, this little demon saw fit to wake, and continue a series of noises for several hours. He slept in a small cot alongside Suzette's bed, so it was her job, and not mine, to smack his head. Anyway, we all managed very comfortably and merrily in those billets, and I look back on them very much as an oasis in a six months' desert.

"Poor old Maggie!
She seems to be 'avin' it dreadful wet at 'ome!"

Chapter 27

GETTING FIT ~ CARICATURING THE CURE ~ 'DIRTY WORK AHEAD' ~ A PROJECTED ATTACK ~ THE COMING 'SHOW' ~ UNLOOKED FOR ORDERS

Military life during our ten days was to consist of getting into good training again in all departments. After long spells of trench life, troops get very much out of strong, efficient marching capabilities, and are also apt to get slack all round. These rests, therefore, come periodically to all at the Front, and are, as it were, tonics. If men stayed long enough in trenches, I should say, from my studies in evolution, that their legs would slowly merge into one sort of fin-like tail, and their arms into seal-like flappers. In fact, time would convert them into intelligent sea lions, and render them completely in harmony with their natural life.

Our tonic began by being taken, one dose after meals, twice daily. In the morning the battalion generally went for a long route-march, and in the afternoon practised military training of various kinds in the fields about the village. My whole time was occupied with machine-gun training. Morning and afternoon I and my sections went off out into the country, and selecting a good variegated bit of land proceeded to go through every phase of machine-gun warfare. We practised the use of these weapons in woods, open fields, along hedges, etc. It was an interesting job. We used to decide on some section of ground with an object to be attacked in the distance, and approach it in all kinds of ways. Competitions would follow between the different sections. The days were all bright, warm and sunny, so life and work out in the fields and roads there was quite pleasant. Each evening we assembled in our cheerful billet, and thus our rest went on.

My sketching now broke out like a rash. I drew a great many sketches. I joked in pencil for everyone, including Suzette, Berthe and Marthe. I am sorry to say I plead guilty to having cast a certain amount of ridicule at the Curé. He was so splendidly austere, and wore such funny clothes, that I couldn't help perpetrating several sketches of him. The disloyalty of his parishioners was very marked in the way they laughed at these drawings, which were pinned up in the row of cottages. Sometimes I would let him off for a day, and then he would come drifting past the window again, with his 'Dante' face, surmounted by a large curly, faded black hat, and I gave way to temptation again.

He didn't like soldiers being billeted in his village, so Suzette told me. I think he got this outlook from his rather painful experiences when the Germans were in the same village, prior to being driven north. They had locked him up in his own cellar for four or five days, after removing his best wine, which they drank upstairs. This sort of thing *does* tend towards giving one a bitter outlook. He preached a sermon whilst we were there. I didn't hear it, but was told about it simultaneously by Suzette, Berthe and Marthe, who informed me that it was directed against soldiery in general. His text had apparently been, "Do not trust them, gentle ladies." A gross libel. I retaliated immediately by drawing a picture of him, with a girl sitting on each knee, singing, "The soldiers are going, hurrah! Hurrah!" (To the tune of 'The Campbells are coming'.) I'm afraid I was rather a canker in his village.

One day, my dear old friend turned up, the same who accompanied me on leave to England. He didn't know we were having our rest, and searched for me first behind

Wulverghem. He there heard where we were, and came on. He was rather a star in a military way, and could, therefore, get hold of a car now and again. I was delighted to see him, as it was possible for me to go into Bailleul with him for the afternoon. We went off and had a real good time at the 'Faucon d'Or'. We went out for a short drive round in the evening, and then parted. He was obliged to get back to somewhere near Bethune that night. The next day I was just starting off on my machine-gun work when an orderly arrived with a message for me. The Colonel wanted to see me at headquarters. I went along, and arriving at his house found all the company commanders, the second in command, and the Adjutant, already assembled there.

"Dirty work ahead," I thought to myself, and went into the Colonel's room with the others. Enormous maps were produced, and we all stood and listened.

"We are going to make an attack," started the Colonel, so I saw that my conjecture wasn't far wrong. He explained the details to us all there, and pointed out on the maps as many of the geographical features of the forthcoming 'show' as he could, after which he told us that, that very afternoon, we were all to go on a motor-bus, that would come for us, down to the allotted site for the 'scrap', to have a look at the ground. This was news, if you like: a thunderbolt in the midst of our rural serenity.

At two o'clock the bus arrived, and we, the chosen initiated few, rattled off down the main street of the village and away to the scene of operations. Where it was I won't say (cheers from Censor) but it took us about an hour to get there. We left the motor-bus well back, and walked about a couple of miles up roads and communication trenches until we reached a line of trenches we had never seen before. A wonderful set of trenches they were, it seemed to us; beautifully built, not much water about, and nice dugouts. The Colonel conferred with several authorities who had the matter in hand, and then, pointing out the sector in front which affected us, told us all to study it to the best of our ability. I spent the time with a periscope and a pair of binoculars drinking in the scene. It's difficult to get a good view of the intervening ground between opposing lines of trenches in the daytime, when one's only means of doing so is through a periscope. Night is the time for this job, when you can go in front and walk about. This ground which we had come to see was completely flat, and one had to put a periscope pretty high over the parapet to see the sort of thing it was. It was no place to put your head up to have a look. A bullet went smack into the Colonel's periscope and knocked it out of his hand. However, with time and patience, we formed a pretty accurate idea of the appearance of the country opposite.

Behind the German trench was the remains of a village, a few of the houses of which were up level with the Boche front line. A great scene of wreckage. Every single house was broken, and in a crumbling state. This was the place we had to take. Other regiments were to take other spots on the landscape on either side, but this particular spot was our objective. I stared long and earnestly at the wrecks in front and the intervening ground. "About a two-hundred-yard sprint," I thought to myself. We stayed in the trenches an hour or two, and then all went back to a spot a couple of miles away and had tea, after which we mounted the motor-bus and drove back home to our village.

We had got something to think about now all right; the coming 'show' was the feature uppermost in our lives now. Everyone was keen to get at it, as we all felt sure we could push the Boches out of that place when the time came. We, the initiated few, had to keep our 'inside' information to ourselves, and it was supposed to be a dark mystery to the rest of the battalion. But I imagine that anyone who didn't guess what the idea was must have been pretty dense. When a motor-bus comes and takes off a group of officers for the day, and brings them back at night, one would scarcely imagine that they had been to a cricket match, or on the annual outing.

Well, the 'tumbril', as we called it, arrived each day for nearly a week, and we drove off gaily to the appointed spot and saturated ourselves in the characteristics of the land we were shortly to attack. In the mornings, before we started, I took the machine-gun sections out into the fields, and by mapping out a similar landscape to the one we were going to attack, I rehearsed the coming tribulation as far as possible. My gunners were a pretty efficient lot, and I was sure they would give a good account of themselves on 'der Tag'. We practised bolting across a ploughed field, and coming into action, until we could do it in record time. My Sergeant and Senior Corporal were both excellent men.

The whole battalion was now in excellent trim, and ready for anything that came along. A date had been fixed for the 'show', and now, day by day, we were rapidly approaching it. It was Friday, I remember, when, as we were all sitting in our billets thinking that we were to leave on Sunday, a fresh thunderbolt arrived. A message was sent round to us all to stand-to and be ready to move off that evening. Before the appointed day! What could be up now? I was full of enthusiasm and curiosity, but was rather hampered by having been inoculated the day before, and was feeling a bit quaint in consequence. However, I pulled myself together, and set about collecting all the machine-gunners, guns and accessories. We said good-bye to the fair ones at the billets, and by about five o'clock in the evening the whole battalion, transport and all, was lined up on the main road. Soon we moved off.

Why were we going before our time? Where were we going to?

Nobody knew except the Colonel, but it was not long before we knew as well.

Chapter 28

WE MARCH FOR YPRES ~ HALT AT LOCRE ~ TOWARDS YPRES ~ A BLEAK CAMP AND MEAGRE FARE ~ SURVEYING THE SCENE ~ MAKING FOR YPRES ~ SIGNS OF BATTLE ~ FIRST VIEW OF YPRES

We marched off in the Bailleul direction, and ere long entered Bailleul. We didn't stop, but went straight on up the road, out of the town, past the asylum with the baths. It was getting dusk now as we tramped along.

"The road to Locre," I muttered to myself, as I saw the direction we had taken. We were evidently not going to the place we had been rehearsing for.

"Locre? Ah, yes; and what's beyond Locre?" I pulled out my map as we went along. "What's on beyond Locre?" I saw it at a glance now, and had all my suspicions confirmed. The word YPRES stood out in blazing letters from the map. Ypres it was going to be, sure enough.

"It looks like Ypres," I said, turning to my Sergeant, who was silently trudging along behind me. He came up level with me, and I showed him the map and the direction we were taking. I was mighty keen to see this famous spot. Stories of famous fights in that great salient were common talk amongst us, and had been for a long time. The wonderful defence of Ypres against the hordes of Germans in the previous October had filled our lines of trenches with pride and superiority, but no wonderment. Everyone regarded Ypres as a strenuous spot, but everyone secretly wanted to go there and see it for themselves. I felt sure we were now bound for there, or anyway, somewhere not far off.

The tin-opener.

We tramped along in the growing darkness, up the winding dusty road to Locre. When we arrived there it was quite dark. The battalion marched right up into the sort of village square near the church and halted. It was late now, and apparently not necessary for us to proceed further that night. We got orders to get billets for our men. Locre is not a large place, and fitting a whole battalion in is none too easy an undertaking. I was standing about a hundred yards down the road leading from the church, deciding what to do, when I got orders to billet my men in the church. I marched the section into a field, got my Sergeant, and went to see what could be done in the church. It was a queer sight, this church; a company of ours had had orders to billet there too, and when I got there the men were already taking off their equipment and making themselves as comfortable as possible under the circumstances, in the main body of the church. The French clergy had for some time granted permission for billeting there; I found this out the next morning, when I saw a party of nuns cleaning it up as much as possible after we had left it. The only part I could see where I could find a rest for my men was the part where the choir sits. I decided on this for our use, and told the Sergeant to get the men along, and move the chairs away so as to get a large enough space for them to lie down in and rest.

It was a weird scene, that night in the church. Imagine a very lofty building, and the only light in the place coming from various bits of candles stuck about here and there on the backs of the chairs. All was dark and drear, if you like: a fitting setting for our entry into the Ypres Salient.

When I had fixed up my section all right, I left the church and went to look about for the place I was supposed to sleep in. It turned out to be a room at the house occupied by the Colonel. I got in just in time to have a bit of a meal before the servants cleared the things away to get ready for the early start the next day. I spent that night in my greatcoat on the stone floor of the room, and not much of a night at that. We were all up and paraded at six, and ready to move off.

We soon started and trekked off down the road out of Locre towards Ypres. I noticed a great change in the scenery now. The land was flatter and altogether more uninteresting than the parts we had come from. The weather was fine and hot, which made our march harder for us. We were all strapped up to the eyes with equipment of every description, so that we fully appreciated the short periodic rests when they came. The road got less and less attractive as we went on, added to which a horrible gusty wind was blowing the dust along towards us, too, which made it worse. It was a most cheerless, barren, arid waste through which we were now passing. I wondered why the Belgians hadn't given it away long ago, and thus saved any further dispute on the matter.

We were now making for Vlamertinghe, which is a place about halfway between Locre and Ypres, and we all felt sure enough now that Ypres was where we were going; besides, passers-by gave some of us a tip or two, and rumours were current that there was a bit of a bother on in the salient. Still, there was nothing told us definitely, and on we went, up the dusty, uninteresting road. Somewhere about midday we halted alongside an immense grassless field, on which were innumerable wooden huts of the simplest and most unattractive construction. The dust whirled and swirled around them, making the whole place look as uninviting as possible. It was the rottenest and least encouraging camp I have ever seen. I've seen a few monstrosities in the camp line in England, and in France, but this was far and away a champion in repulsion. We halted opposite this place, as I have said, and in a few moments were all marched into the central, baked-mud square, in the midst of the huts. I have since learnt that this camp is no more, so I don't mind mentioning it. We were now dismissed, whereupon we all collared huts for our men and ourselves, and sat down to rest.

We had had a very early and scratch sort of a breakfast, so were rather keen to get at the lunch question. The limbers were the last things to turn up, being in the rear of the battalion, but when they did the cooks soon pulled the necessary things out and proceeded to knock up a meal.

I went outside my hut and surveyed the scene whilst they got the lunch ready. It *was* a rotten place. The huts hadn't got any sides to them, but were made by two slopes of wood fixed at the top, and had triangular ends. There were just a few huts built with sides, but not many. Apart from the huts the desert contained nothing except men in war-worn, dirty khaki, and clouds of dust. It reminded me very much of India, as I remembered it from my childhood days. The land all around this mud plain was flat and scrubby, with nothing of interest to look at anywhere. But, yes, there was - just one thing. Away to the north, I could just see the top of the towers of Ypres.

I wondered how long we were going to stay in this Sahara, and turned back into the hut again.

Two or three of us were resting on a little scanty straw in that hut, and now, as we guessed that it was about the time when the cooks would have got the lunch ready, we crossed to another larger hut, where a long bare wooden table was laid out for us. With sore eyes and a parched throat I sat down and devoured two chilly sardines, reposing on a water biscuit, drank about a couple of gallons of water, and felt better. There wasn't much conversation at that meal; we were all too busy thinking. Besides, the CO was getting messages all the time, and was immersed in the study of a large map, so we thought we had better keep quiet.

Our Colonel was a splendid person, as good a one as any battalion could wish to have. (He's sure to buy a copy of this book after that!) He was with the regiment all through that 1914-1915 winter, and is now a Brigadier.

We had made all preparations to stay in the huts at that place for the night, when, at about four o'clock in the afternoon, another message arrived and was handed to the CO.

He issued his orders. We were to march off at once. Everyone was delighted, as the place was unattractive, and what's more, now that we were on the warpath, we wanted to get on with the job, whatever it was.

Now we were on the road once more, and marching on towards Ypres. The whole brigade was on the road somewhere, some battalions in front of us and some behind. On we went through the driving dust and dismal scenery, making, I could clearly see, for Ypres. We ticked off the miles at a good steady marching pace, and in the course of time turned out of our long, dusty, winding lane on to a wide, cobbled main road, leading evidently into the town of Ypres itself, now about two miles ahead. It was a fine sight, looking back down the winding column of men. A long line of sturdy, bronzed men, in dust-covered khaki, tramping over the grey cobbled road, singing and whistling at intervals; the rattling and clicking of the various metallic parts of their equipment forming a kind of low accompaniment to their songs.

We halted about a mile out of the city, and all 'fell out' on the side of the road, and sat about on heaps of stones or on the bank of the ditch at the roadside.

It was easy enough to see now where we were going, and what was up. There was evidently a severe 'scrap' on. Parties of battered, dishevelled-looking men, belonging to a variety of regiments, were now streaming past down the road - many French-African soldiers amongst them. From these we learnt that a tremendous attack was in progress, but got no details. Their stories received corroboration by the fact that we could see many shells bursting in and around the city of Ypres. These vagrant men were wounded in a degree, inasmuch as most of them had been undergoing some prodigious bombardment and were dazed from shellshock. They cheered us with the usual exaggerated and harrowing yarns common to such people, and passed on. This was what we had come here for - to participate in this business; not very nice, but we were all 'for it', anyway. If we hadn't come here, we would have been attacking at that other place, and this was miles more interesting. If one has ever participated in an affair of arms at Ypres, it gives one a sort of honourable trademark for the rest of the war as a member of the accepted successful Matadors of the Flanders Bullring.

We sat about at the side of the road for about half an hour, then got the order to fall in again. Stiff and weary, I left my heap of stones, took my place at the head of the section, and prepared for the next act. On we went again down the cobbled road, crossed a complicated mixture of ordinary rails and tramlines, and struck off up a narrow road to the left, which apparently also ended in the city. It was now evening, the sky was grey and cloudy. Ypres, only half a mile away, now loomed up dark and grey against the skyline. Shells were falling in the city, with great hollow-sounding crashes. We marched on up the road.

Chapter 29

GETTING NEARER ~ A LUGUBRIOUS PARTY ~ STILL NEARER ~ BLAZING YPRES ~ ORDERS FOR ATTACK

After about another twenty minutes' march we halted again. Something or other was going on up the road in front, which prevented our moving. We stood about in the lane, and watched the shells bursting in the town. We were able to watch shells bursting closer before we had been there long. With a screeching whistle a shell shot over our heads and exploded in the field on our left. This was the signal, apparently, for shrapnel to start bursting promiscuously about the fields in all directions, which it did.

Altogether the lane was an unwholesome spot to stand about in. We were there some time, wondering when one of the bursts of shrapnel would strike the lane, but none did. Straggling, small groups of Belgian civilians were now passing down the lane, driven out no doubt from some cottage or other that until now they had managed to persist in living in. Mournful little groups would pass, wheeling their total worldly possessions on a barrow.

Suddenly we were moved on again, and as suddenly halted a few yards further on. Without a doubt, strenuous operations and complications were taking place ahead. A few of the officers collected together by a gate at the side of the lane and had a smoke and a chat.

"I wonder how much longer we're going to stick about here," someone said. "What about going into that house over there and see if there's a fire?" He indicated a tumbled down cottage of a fair size, which stood nearly opposite us on the far side of the lane. It was almost dark by now, and the wind made it pretty cold work, standing and sitting about in the lane. Four of us crossed the roadway and entered the yard of the cottage. We knocked at the door, and asked if we might come in and sit by the fire for a bit. We asked in French, and found that it was a useless extravagance on our part, as they only spoke Flemish, and what a terrible language that is! These were Flemish people - the real goods; we hadn't struck any before.

They seemed to understand the signs we made; at all events they let us into the place. There was a dairy alongside the house belonging to them, and in here our men were streaming, one after another, paying a few coppers for a drink of milk. The woman serving it out with a ladle into their mess-tins was keeping up a flow of comment all the time in Flemish. Nobody except herself understood a word of what she was saying. Hardy people, those dwellers in that cottage. Shrapnel was dropping about here and there in the fields nearby, and at any moment might come into the roof of their cottage, or through the flimsy walls.

We four went inside, and into their main room - the kitchen. It was in the same old style which we knew so well. A large square, dark, and dingy room, with one of their popular long stoves sticking out from one wall. Round this stove, drawn up in a wide crescent formation, was a row of chairs with high backs. On each chair sat a man or a woman, dressed in either black or very dark clothes. Nobody spoke, but all were staring into the stove. I wished, momentarily, I had stayed in the lane. It was like breaking in on some weird sect - 'Stove Worshippers'. One wouldn't have been surprised if, suddenly, one member of the party had removed the lid of the stove and thrown in a 'grey powder', or something of the sort; this to be followed by flames leaping high into the air, whilst low-toned monotonous chanting would break out from the assembly: feast in honour of their god 'Shrapnel', who was 'angry'. I suppose I shouldn't make fun of these people though. It was enough to make them silent and lugubrious, to have all their country and their homes destroyed. We sat around the stove with them, and offered them cigarettes. We talked to each other in English; they sat silently listening and understanding nothing. I am sure they looked upon all armies and soldiers, irrespective of nationality, as a confounded nuisance. I am sure they wished we'd go and fight the matter out somewhere else. And no wonder.

We sat in there for a short time, and stepped out into the road again just in time to hear the order to advance. We hadn't far to go now. It was quite dark as we turned into a very large flat field at the back of Ypres, right close up against the outskirts of the town. Just the field, I felt sure, that a circus would choose, if visiting that neighbourhood.

The battalion spread itself out over the field and came to the conclusion that this was where it would have to stay for the night. It was all very cold and dark now. We sat about on the great field in our greatcoats and waited for the field kitchens and rations to arrive. As we sat there, just at the back of Ypres, we could hear

and see the shells bursting in the city in the darkness. The shelling was getting worse, fires were breaking out in the deserted town, and bright yellow flames shot out here and there against the blackened sky.

On the arrival of the field kitchens we all managed to get some tea in our mess-tins; and the rum ration being issued, we were a little more fortified against the cold. We sat for the most part in greatcoats and silence, watching the shelling of Ypres.

Suddenly a huge fire broke out in the centre of the town. The sky was a whirling and twisting mass of red and yellow flames, and enormous volumes of black smoke: a truly grand and awful spectacle. The tall ruins of the Cloth Hall and Cathedral were alternately silhouetted or brightly illuminated in the yellow glare of flames. And now it started to rain. Down it came, hard and fast.

We huddled together on the cold field and prepared ourselves to expect anything that might come along now. Shells and rain were both falling in the field. I think a few shells, meant for Ypres, had rather overshot the mark and had come into our field in consequence.

I leant up as one of a tripod of three of us, my face towards the burning city. The two others were my old pal, the platoon commander at St Yvon, and a subaltern of one of the other companies. I sat and watched the flames licking round the Cloth Hall. I remember asking a couple of men in front to shift a bit so that I could get a better view.

It poured with rain, and we went on sitting in that horrible field, wondering what the next move was to be.

At about eleven o'clock, an orderly came along the field with a mackintosh groundsheet over his head, and told me the Colonel wished to see me.

"Where is he?" I asked.

"In that little cottage place at the far corner of the field, near the road, sir."

I rose up and thus spoilt our human tripod.

"Where are you going 'BB'?" asked my St Yvon friend.

"Colonel's sent for me," I replied.

"Well, come back as soon as you can."

I left and never saw him again. He was killed early the next morning; one of the best chaps I ever knew.

I went down the field to the cottage at the corner, and entering, found all the company commanders, the second in command, the Adjutant and the Colonel.

"We shall attack at 4.00am tomorrow," he was saying.

This was the moment at which I got my *'Fragment'* idea, *"The push, by one who's been pushed! We shall attack at dawn!"*

The Colonel went on to explain the plans. We stood around in the semi-darkness, the only light being a small candle, whose flame was being blown about by the draught from the broken window.

"We shall move off from here at midnight, or soon after," he concluded, "and go up the road to St Julien."

We all dispersed to our various commands.

I went and got my Sergeant and section commanders together, and explained the coming operations to them. Sitting out in the field in the rain, the map on my knees being occasionally brightly illuminated by the burning city, I looked out the road to St Julien.

Subterranean voice, commenting on the abnormal activity of the mortar across the way:
"They're devils to snipe, ain't they, Bill?"

Chapter 30

RAIN AND MUD ~ A TRYING MARCH ~ BATTLE OF YPRES ~ A PERFECT DELUGE ~ IN THE THICK OF IT ~ SPRAYS OF BULLETS ~ HEAVY SHELLING ~ A WOUNDED OFFICER ~ I GET MY 'QUIETUS!'

At a little after midnight we left the field, marching down the road which led towards the Yser Canal and the village of St Jean. Our transport remained behind in a certain field that had been selected for the purpose. The whole brigade was on the road, our battalion being the last in the long column. The road from the field in which we had been resting to the village of St Jean passes through the outskirts of Ypres, and crosses the Yser Canal on its way. I couldn't see the details as it was a dark night, and the rain was getting worse as time went on. I knew what had been happening now in the last forty-eight hours, and what we were going to do.

The Germans had launched gas in the war for the first time, and, as everyone knows now, had by this means succeeded in breaking the line on a wide front to the north of Ypres. The Germans were directing their second great effort against the Salient.

The Second Battle of Ypres had begun. We were making for the threatened spot, and were going to attack them at four o'clock in the morning.

Ypres, at this period, ought to have been seen to get an accurate realisation of what it was like. All other parts of the front faded into a pleasing memory; so it seemed to me as I marched along. I thought of our rest at the village, the billets, the Curé, the bright sunny days of our country life there, and then compared them with this wretched spot we were in now. A ghastly comparison.

We were marching in pouring rain and darkness down a muddy, mangled road, shattered poplar trees sticking up in black streaks on either side. Crash after crash, shells were falling and exploding all around us, and behind the burning city. The road took a turn. We marched for a short time parallel to now distant Ypres. Through the charred skeleton wrecks of houses one caught glimpses of the yellow flames mounting to the sky. We passed over the Yser Canal, dirty, dark and stagnant, reflecting the yellow glow of the flames.

On our left was a church and graveyard, both blown to a thousand pieces: tombstones lying about and sticking up at odd angles all over the torn-up ground. I guided my section a little to one side to avoid a dead horse lying across the road. The noise of shrapnel bursting about us only ceased occasionally, making way for ghastly, ominous silences. And the rain kept pouring down.

What a march! As we proceeded, the road got rougher and narrower: debris of all sorts, and horrible to look upon, lay about on either side. We halted suddenly, and were allowed to 'fall out' for a few minutes. I and my section had drawn up opposite what had once been an estaminet. I entered, and told them all to come in and stay there out of the rain. The roof still had a few tiles left on it, so the place was a little drier than the road outside. The floor was strewn with broken glass, chairs and bottles. I got hold of a three-legged chair, and by balancing myself against one of the walls, tried to have a bit of a doze. I was precious near tired out now, from want of sleep and a surfeit of marching. I told my Sergeant to wake me when the order came along, and then and there slept on that chair for twenty minutes, lulled off by the shrapnel bursting along the road outside.

My Sergeant woke me. "We're going on again, sir!"

First discovered in the alluvial deposits of southern Flanders. Feeds almost exclusively on jam and water biscuits. Hobby: filling sandbags on dark and rainy nights.

"Right oh!" I said, and left my three-legged chair. I shouted to the section to 'fall in', and followed on after the battalion up the road once more. After we had covered another horrible half-mile we halted again, but this time no houses were near. How it rained! A perfect deluge. I was wearing a greatcoat, and had all my equipment strapped on over the top. The men all had mackintosh capes. We were all wet through and through, but nobody bothered a rap about that. Anyone trying to find a fresh discomfort for us now, that would make us wince, would have been hard put to it.

People will scarcely credit it, but times like these don't dilute the tenacity or light-heartedness of our soldiers. You can hear a joke on these occasions, and hear the laughter at it too.

In the shattered estaminet we had just left, one of the men went behind the almost unrecognisable bar-counter, and operating an imaginary handle, asked a comrade, "And what's yours, mate?"

Again we got the order to advance, and on we went. We were now nearing the village of Wieltje, about two miles from St Jean, which we had passed. The ruined church we had seen was at St Jean.

The road was now perfectly straight, bordered on either side by broken poplar trees, beyond which large flat fields lay under the mysterious darkness. As we went on we could see a faint, red glow ahead. This turned out to be Wieltje: all that was left of it, a smouldering ruin. Here and there bodies of dead men lay about the road. At intervals I could discern the stiffened shapes of corpses in the ditches which bordered the road. We went through Wieltje without stopping. Passing out at the other side we proceeded up this awful, shell-torn road, towards a slight hill, at the base of which we stopped.

Now came my final orders.

"Come on at once. Follow up the battalion, who, with the brigade, are about to attack."

"Now we're for it," I said to myself, and gave the order to unlimber the guns. One limber had been held up some little way back I found, by getting jammed in a shell-hole in the road. I couldn't wait for it to come up, so sent my Sergeant back with some men to get hold of the guns and tackle in it, and follow on as soon as they could. I got out the rest of the things that were there with us and prepared to start on after the battalion.

"I'll go to the left, and you'd better go to the right," I shouted to my Sergeant. "Here, Smith, let's have your rifle," I said, turning to my servant. I decided that he had best stay and look after the limbers. I seized his rifle, and slipping on a couple of bandoliers of cartridges, led on up the slight hill, followed by my section carrying the machine guns. I felt that a rifle was going to be of more use to me in this business than a revolver, and, anyway, it was just as well to have both.

It was now just about four o'clock in the morning. A faint light was creeping into the sky. The rain was abating a bit, thank goodness!

We topped the rise, and rushed on down the road as fast as was possible under the circumstances. Now we were in it! Bullets were flying through the air in all directions. Ahead, in the semi-darkness, I could just see the forms of men running out into the fields on either side of the road in extended order, and beyond them a continuous heavy cracking of rifle-fire showed me the main direction of the attack. A few men had gone down already, and no wonder - the air was thick with bullets. The machine-gun officer of one of the other regiments in the brigade was shot right through the head as he went over the brow of the hill. I found one of his machine-gun sections a short time later, and appropriated them for our own use.

After we had gone down the road for about two hundred yards I thought that my best plan was to get away over to the left a bit, as the greatest noise seemed to come from there.

"Come on, you chaps," I shouted, "we'll cross this field, and get to that hedge over there." We dashed across, intermingled with a crowd of Highlanders, who were also making to the left. Through a cloud of bullets, flying like rice at a wedding, we reached the other side of the field. Only one casualty - one man with a shot in the knee.

I couldn't get a good view of the enemy from the hedge, so I decided to creep along further to the left still, to a spot I saw on the left front of a large farm which stood about two hundred yards behind us. The German machine guns were now busy, and sent sprays of bullets flicking up the ground all round us. Lying behind a slight fold in the ground we saw them whisking through the grass, three or four inches over our heads. We slowly worked our way across to the left, past an old, wide ditch full of stagnant water, and into a shallow gully beyond.

Dawn had come now, and in the cold grey light I saw our men out in front of me advancing in short rushes towards a large wood in front. The Germans were firing star shells into the air in pretty large numbers; why, I couldn't make out, as there was quite enough light now to see by. I ordered the section out of the gully, and ran across the open to a bit of old trench I saw in the field. This was the only suitable spot I could see for bringing our guns to bear on the enemy, and assisting in the attack. We fixed up a couple of machine guns, and awaited a favourable opportunity.

I could see a lot of Germans running along in front of the wood towards one end of it. We laid our aim on the wood, which seemed to me the chief spot to go for. One or two of my men had not managed to get up to the gun position as yet. They were ammunition carriers, and had had a pretty hard job with it. I left the guns to run back and hurry them on. The rifle-fire kept up an incessant rattle the whole time, and now the German gunners started shelling the farm behind us. Shell after shell burst beyond, in front of, and on either side of the farm. Having got up the ammunition, I ran back towards the guns past the farm.

In front of me an officer was hurrying along with a message towards a trench which was on the left of our new-found gun position. He ran across the open towards it. When about forty yards from me I saw him throw up his hands and collapse on the ground. I hurried across to him, and lifted his head on to my knee. He couldn't speak and was rapidly turning a deathly pallor. I undid his equipment and the buttons of his tunic as fast as I could, to find out where he had been shot: right through the chest, I saw. The left side of his shirt, near his heart, was stained deep with blood. A captain in the Canadians, I noticed. The message he had been carrying lay near him. I didn't know quite what to do. I turned in the direction of my gun section without disturbing his head, and called out to them to throw me over a water-bottle. A man named Mills ran across with one, and took charge of the Captain, whilst I went through his pockets to try and discover his name. I found it in his pocket-book. His identity disc had apparently been lost.

With the message I ran back to the farm, and, as luck would have it, came across a colonel in the Canadians. I told him about the Captain who had been carrying the message, and said if there was a stretcher about I could get him in.

All movement in the attack had now ceased, but the rifle and shellfire was on as strong as ever. My Corporal was with the two guns, and had orders to fire as soon as an opportunity arose, so I thought my best plan was to see to getting this officer in while there was a chance. I got hold of another subaltern in the farm, and together we ran back with a stretcher to the spot where I had left Mills and the Captain. We lifted him on to the stretcher. He seemed a bit better, but his breathing was very difficult. How I managed to hold up that stretcher I don't know; I was just verging on complete exhaustion by this time. I had to take a pause about twenty yards from the farm and lie flat out on the ground for a moment or two to recuperate sufficiently to finish the journey. We got him in and put him down in an outbuilding which had been turned into a temporary dressing-station. Shells were crashing into the roof of the farm and exploding round it in great profusion. Every minute one heard the swirling rush overhead, the momentary pause, saw the cloud of red dust, then, 'CRUMPH!'

That farm was going to be extinguished, I could plainly see. I went along the edge of the dried-up moat at the back, towards my guns, I couldn't stand up any longer. I lay down on the side of the moat for five minutes. Twenty yards away the shells burst round and in the farm, but I didn't care, rest was all I wanted.

"What about my Sergeant and those other guns?" I thought, as I lay there. I rose, and cut across the open space again to the two guns.

"You know what to do here, Corporal?" I said. "I am going round the farm over to the right to see what's happened to the others."

I left him, and went across towards the farm. As I went I heard the enormous ponderous, gurgling, rotating sound of large shells coming. I looked to my left. Four columns of black smoke and earth shot up a hundred feet into the air, not eighty yards away: then four mighty reverberating explosions that rent the air. A row of four 'Jack Johnsons' had landed not a hundred yards away, right amongst the lines of men, lying out firing in extended order.

I went on, and had nearly reached the farm when another four came over and landed fifty yards further up the field towards us.

"They'll have our guns and section," I thought rapidly, and hurried on to find out what had become of my Sergeant.

The shelling of the farm continued; I ran past it between two explosions and raced along the old gully we had first come up. Shells have a way of missing a building, and getting something else near by. As I was on the sloping bank of the gully I heard a colossal rushing swish in the air, and then didn't hear the resultant crash . . .

All seemed dull and foggy; a sort of silence, worse than all the shelling, surrounded me. I lay in a filthy, stagnant ditch covered with mud and slime from head to foot. I suddenly started to tremble all over.

I couldn't grasp where I was. I lay and trembled . . .

I had been blown up by a shell.

*

I lay there some little time, I imagine, with a most peculiar sensation. All fear of shells and explosions had left me. I still heard them dropping about and exploding, but I listened to them and watched them as calmly as one would watch an apple fall off a tree. I couldn't make myself out. Was I all right or all wrong?

I tried to get up, and then I knew. The spell was broken. I shook all over, and had to lie still, with tears pouring down my face.

*

I could see my part in this battle was over.

Chapter 31

SLOWLY RECOVERING ~ FIELD HOSPITAL ~
AMBULANCE TRAIN ~ BACK IN ENGLAND

How I ever got back I don't know. I remember dragging myself into a cottage, in the garden of which lay a row of dead men. I remember someone giving me a glass of water there, and seeing a terribly mutilated body on the floor being attended to. And, finally, I remember being helped down the Wieltje road by a man into a field dressing-station. Here I was labelled and sent immediately down to a hospital about four miles away. Arrived there, I lay out on a bench in a collapsed state, and I remember a cheery doctor injecting something into my wrist.

I then lay on a stretcher awaiting further transportation.

My good servant Smith somehow discovered my whereabouts, and turned up at this hospital. He sat beside me and gave me a writing-pad to scribble a note on. I scrawled a line to my mother to say I had been knocked out, but was perfectly all right. Smith went back to the battalion, and I lay on the stretcher, partially asleep.

Night came on and I went off into a series of agonising dreams.

I awoke with a start.

I was being lifted up from the floor on the stretcher. They carried me out. It was bright moonlight, and looking up I saw the moon, a dazzling white, against the dark blue sky. The stretcher and I were pushed into an ambulance in which were three other cases beside myself. We were driven off to some station or other.

I stared up at the canvas bottom of the stretcher above me, trying to realise it all.

Presently we reached the train. Another glimpse of the moon, and I was slid into the ambulance car . . .

In three days I was back in England at a London hospital - *'A Fragment from France'*.

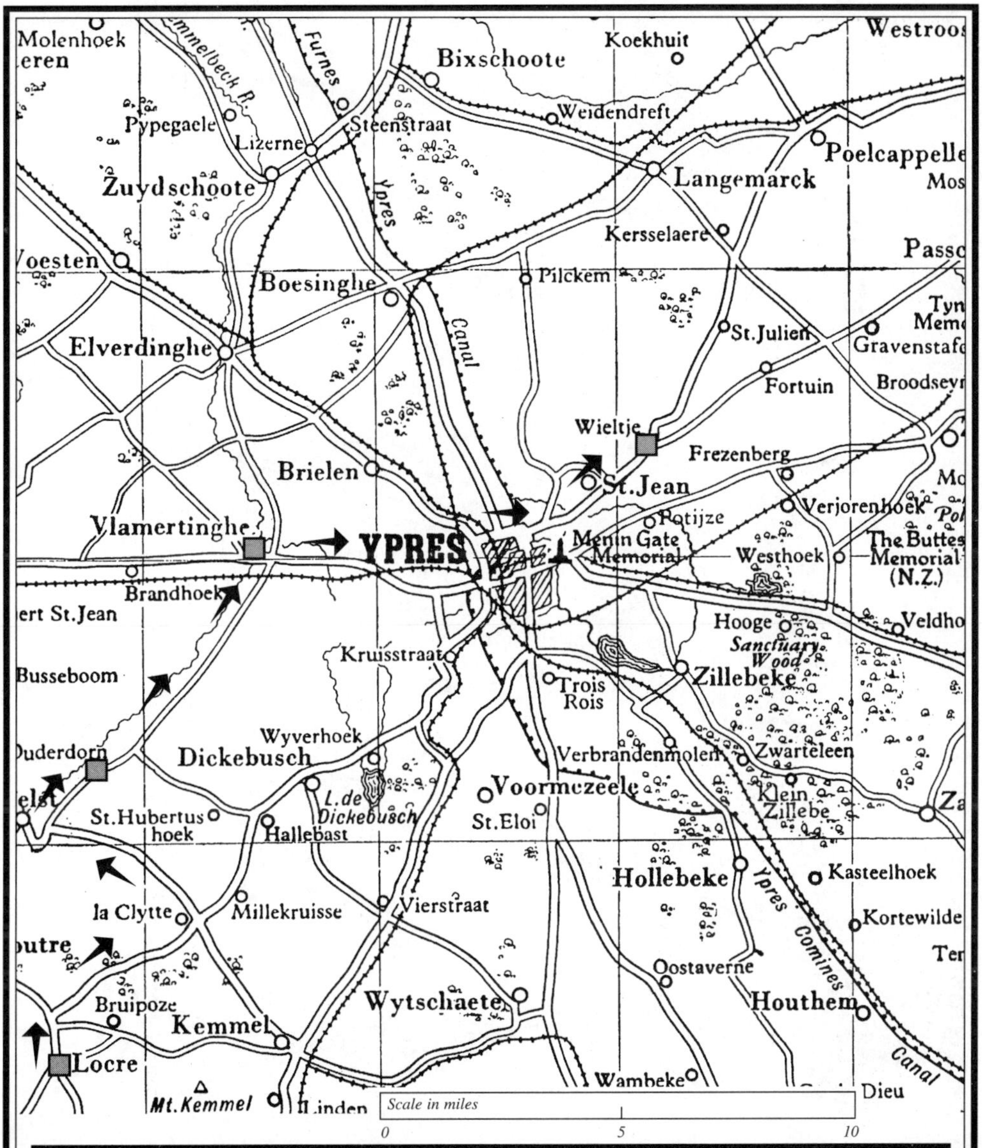

23rd April 1915: *The 1st Battalion Royal Warwickshire Regiment was ordered to hold in readiness and went into billets at Locre with the Argyll and Sutherland Highlanders.*
24th April 1915: *The Battalion left Locre at 7.00am and marched to Ouderdon, reaching it at about midday. At 4.00pm it advanced via Vlamertinghe and halted outside Ypres until midnight.*
25th April 1915: *The Battalion marched on Wieltje (Vielje) at 12.00 midnight to form part of Brigade attack launched at 4.00am. The Battalion attacked the woods on the left side of the line, supported by the 7th Argyll and Sutherland Highlanders. It was during this attack that Bairnsfather was wounded. The Seaforth Highlanders, Royal Irish Fusiliers and Royal Dublin Fusiliers attacked to the right, against St Julien. Due to the enemy's trenches having been insufficiently shelled, and with support unable to get forward, the Battalion was forced to retire to trenches in a nearby farm at 7.00pm and consolidated its position. Casualties were high, with 17 officers and 500 other ranks killed, wounded or missing.*

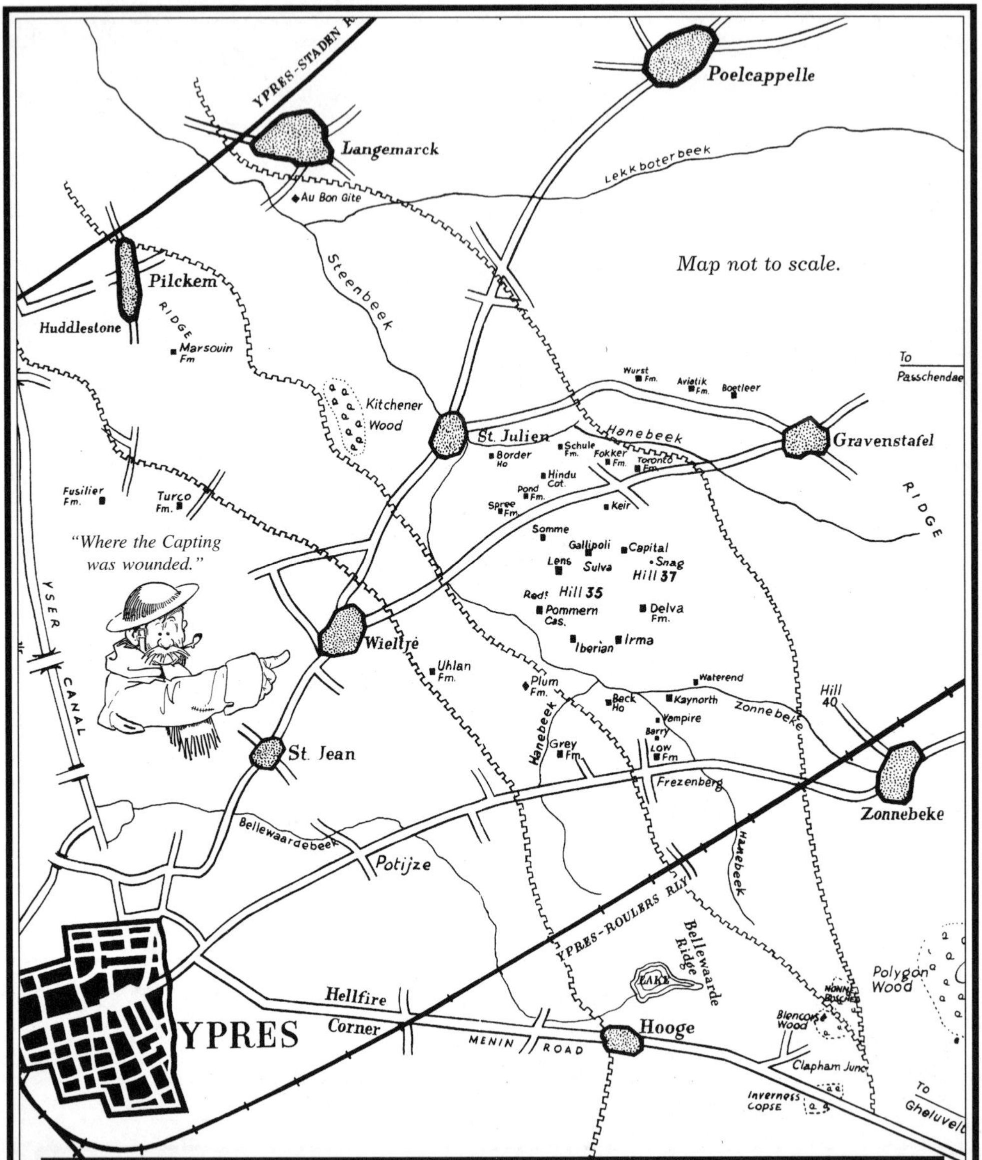

The area of the Battle of St Julien, Second Battle of Ypres, April 1915.

The Ypres Salient, a bulge out of the Allied line, was perhaps the most hotly contested area of the entire war. The ancient city of Ypres with its famous Cloth Hall and Cathedral was practically reduced to rubble by the pounding it took from the enemy guns. Ypres, or 'Wipers' as the Tommies called it, became synonymous with the British front line and came to epitomise (just as Verdun did for the French) the strength and determination of the humble Tommy to cling on despite everything the enemy and the elements could throw at him. Bruce Bairnsfather, serving with the Warwickshires, was wounded on 25th April 1915 at Wieltje (Vielje), following the enemy's second gas attack of the war in the area of Langemarck and Passchendaele (north-east of Ypres).

THE BAIRNSFATHER OMNIBUS

From Mud to Mufti

Written and illustrated by

Bruce Bairnsfather

1919

Taken from the original frontispiece for 'From Mud to Mufti', the second part of Bairnsfather's wartime experiences.

The original title page for Bairnsfather's second book, 'From Mud to Mufti', published by Grant Richards in 1919.

Preface

I write this preface after the war. Those four years of horror are over, and I doubt whether anyone is happier than myself to think so. I look back on a sea of adventures and episodes, painful and otherwise. I think of pals I have lost, and friends I have gained. In *Bullets & Billets* I have recounted my story in the mud, and here my story after I had left the mud for 'Tabs and Travelling'.

Bruce Bairnsfather

DEDICATED TO MY MASCOT MOTHER WHO, THOUGH WAY BACK AT HOME, HAS HELPED ME SO MUCH IN INSPIRATION THROUGH ALL THESE YEARS OF WAR, AND WHO, IN HER ANXIETY, HAS ENDURED MORE THAN I HAVE.

The original preface and dedication by the author.

Chapter 1

BEGINS IN HOSPITAL ~ A SURPRISE VISIT ~ FIND MYSELF IN REQUEST

Those who have endured *'Bullets & Billets'* and have possessed sufficient mental control and iron determination to have finished the last chapter, will remember that, subsequently to being wafted out of the Second Battle of Ypres (April 1915) by a 'Johnson', I was in due course deposited in a London hospital. This was a large building, one of the finest hospitals in London, I should say. One of those Olympic palaces with endless stone corridors, lifts, rice puddings and temperature charts.

But what a harbour of refuge it seemed! I really think it is quite worthwhile going through an offensive in order to get that marvellous feeling of rest, security, and the goodwill of human beings which comes slowly over you on admission to one of our British hospitals. After months of saturation in all the excessively masculine and harsh ways of war, to recline in a comfortable bed and watch a nurse moving towards you across a carpet, with nothing more dangerous than a thermometer or a tonic, one feels that the world is a nice, kind thing after all. Those marvellous hospitals!

Day after day, week after week, month after month, thousands of new cases come in and yet the staff turn on an enthusiastic and cheery welcome each time with unfailing regularity. One feels that one is the first and only case with which they have had to do. It's the same in all our hospitals, and I've had experience of one or two.

I was pretty rotten for some little time, and *had* to put up with those well-known long and weary days in bed. Days when you look forward to the doctor's visit on his rounds, after which you spend the rest of the time watching the daylight fading into the evening, and then wait for the night nurse to come and take that confounded temperature of yours again prior to wishing you goodnight.

During these days my mind seemed to be going all through the war again, from the day I began. All the varied scenes and episodes I had been in, in which I had taken part, culminating in that big brother at Ypres; all these thoughts went surging through my mind, tumbling and tossing about in fantastic profusion. I rushed into the Salient and fired machine guns into writhing, hateful masses of Boches about twice nightly . . . *in my dreams.*

I think everyone who gets 'knocked out' knows this sensation of 'fighting one's battles over again'. It's just like one of those long perforated paper rolls used in pianolas: you have the tune first, re-wind, and then have it all over again.

I wasn't allowed to see 'strangers' for some time; only my mother was allowed to be with me, and she read to me and brought me things.

At last came the time when I was pronounced 'distinctly better'. It was no longer necessary to have that Y-shaped tube thing of the doctors, groping its way through my pyjama jacket to listen to my heart. Everything seemed brighter, and I was immersed in one enormous, enthusiastic desire to go out and see the world again. Not a sandbag, shell, and corrugated iron world, but to go out and roam at ease amidst all the soft and comfortable things of peace and security.

At the Front one feels it's one's business not to live, but to die, and here I was, after an intervening mystical period of repairs in a hospital, entitled to go forth and place a

"Nao!! I ain't pinched yer blinkin' paper, and next time take yer 'at off when ye come into my 'ouse!"

greater importance on living than dying. The result was a vast sparkling joy in life, and all the things that go with it.

But one's own ideas about recovery are always in advance of the hospital's views on the same subject. I had to remain there, in spite of my daily protest of, "I'm all right now doctor."

At this time, as I mentioned in *'Bullets & Billets'*, I had done only a few sketches. The first *'Fragments'* had gone in and been accepted.

My Ypres affair and subsequent hospitalisation had temporarily knocked out my drawing desires, but now, as I revived, a torrent of ideas came pouring into my head and I started off again.

My mother brought me a sketchbook, and in it I weaved a series of rough drawings depicting various scenes, painful at the time, yet humorous to look back on; incidents in fact, of the last few months. Yet the continuance of *'Fragments from France'* was not for a moment in my mind. The wealth resulting on my first few drawings was perhaps not such as would create a wild desire to 'send up' more.

But now a certain day arrived.

I was beginning to be allowed to see people, and one morning I was told that a gentleman had called to see me. He sent up his card, with the announcement that he was a representative of *The Bystander*. I was glad I knew this, as his 'make-up' was 'an undertaker' to the life, and I should have undoubtedly thought that the doctor had been lying about my recovery. A young man of about thirty summers (as the novelists say) entered the room. He placed his funereal bowler and umbrella on a table and advanced to my bed. I shot out a tattooed arm from under the red blanket and shook hands.

The Bystander presented its compliments and hoped I was better. After which my visitor informed me that *The Bystander* had had applications for the originals of the drawings I had so far sent up, and also complimentary letters. Finally, *The Bystander* would be pleased to see any other drawings I might do.

I pointed out that I was, at the moment, closed for structural alterations, but on reopening would see what I could manage.

The mournful one left.

I recoiled into my red blanket and grinned into the pillow. I then sat up and grinned at the room, at my mother, at the bunch of grapes and the temperature chart.

"Well I'm damned! Fancy them wanting some more drawings!"

A great enthusiasm got hold of me. I should have wanted a mental tennis-racket to fence off the ideas which hurtled into my mind.

"Just wait till I get out of here," I said to myself.

And in the next few days I got out of there and went home to convalesce and to think.

Chapter 2

THE MEDICAL BOARD MYSTERY ~ AWAITING THE VERDICT ~ LIGHT DUTY

My home being in the country, a restful recovery was aided in every way. I progressed from day to day, and rapidly sailed along in the direction of one of those mysterious and problematic institutions . . . a Medical Board.

The London hospital had given me sick leave, marking its termination with a compulsory visit to the above-mentioned Medical Board.

Now, a Medical Board is a curious institution. For very good reasons, no doubt, it has the following peculiarities: you never know where it's going to be held, or when, until a few hours before it comes off. Say you have two months' sick leave; well, you get your notice to attend the Medical Board, at the last place you thought of, on the last day of that leave. A wire arrives giving time and place in such a way as to leave you a mere wisp of a chance for catching the only train that day to the appointed spot.

My Board was in Birmingham. I had for some days had my money on Salisbury or Warwick, but just as in the three-card-trick, I was 'wrong again'.

The Birmingham Medical Board was held in an enormous impregnable building. With a few others I awaited my turn in a vast stone corridor. A row of massive, polished doors faced us. On these were the various titles of the different medical and temporary owners. One by one my companions disappeared through one of these apertures. I felt like Ulysses as he watched the Cyclops daily reducing the number of his companions.

At last your turn comes. A different door opens to the one you've had your eye on, and an hilarious combatant who has just got another man's sick leave is ejected. Behind him you see the Cyclops . . . a medical major generally, who barks at you from behind the mahogany to come in. Inside you stand before an immense table covered with papers. Behind the table sit two of the Board. The third member (there is generally a third) seems to have a sort of roving commission - lurking by the window, or standing by the fire, ready, I suppose to do anything from chucking you out to calling someone else in.

You stand before the table. Nobody speaks, but the heaviest member of the Board looks through a folio of papers. This folio comprises your history. The Board read it to themselves, and mutter to themselves; then with an air of suspicion, as if they didn't believe for a moment that there had been anything the matter with you, one of them tells you to take off your coat. (Business with Sam Browne and tunic.)

You now shyly approach them from the row of clothes hooks, where you have hung your trappings, minus dignity and rank, which, of course, you have left on the sleeves of your tunic. They've got you now, and they know it. They ask you how you feel. You are mesmerised into saying cheerfully, "Quite all right."

One of them produces that Y-shaped silver tube thing, and fitting it to his ears he insinuates the loose end into the opening of your khaki shirt. A moment or two of this, then the Board exchange mystic words, and finally start writing on blue paper. One of them looks up and says, "That will do, you can put your coat on."

You retire to the clothes rack like an artist's model and put your tunic on again.

The Board suddenly barks, "Two months' light duty!"

It's over! You know your fate, and to creep from the room is all that remains to be done. I left the room with as much military demeanour and nonchalance as I could summon, but on arriving out in the stone corridor I found that the flapping noise I heard behind me came from my braces, which I had omitted to put over my shoulders before replacing my tunic. It just shows how nerves can bring about one's undoing. I regained the entrance hall and thence passed out into the open air.

Two months' light duty! Well, that meant a return to my regiment's reserve depot. I hadn't been there since the start of the war, and now I was going back after many months of wanderings, trials and adventures. I was keen and interested at the thought of going. Those far-away days at the beginning of the war seemed like weird, romantic memories. Days when we had marched around and drilled and played; each day awaiting the command for which we longed - the command to be sent to the Front!

I had left for the war, a second-lieutenant, from a bell-tent in a sodden field. I was now returning a captain, with six months' war behind me. The second lap of my war race was beginning.

Chapter 3

THE DEPOT ~ BARRACKS AND BOTANY ~ SETTLING IN

The Isle of Wight was my regimental depot, and very nice too you might think; but you must not confuse the wartime Isle of Wight with the peacetime version. White flannels, yachts and romantic hotel life, punctuated by regattas, were all sent west when the war began. Now you have a mighty armed camp; one congealed mass of khaki. You can't escape; the island is quite small, so you must cheerfully resign yourself to living under the full force of British militarism.

It had all changed immensely when I returned this time. The old, primitive collection of bell-tents, whence I had sprung, had disappeared, and my battalion was now housed in red-brick grandeur. There were large and spacious barracks at the depot, and latterly a myriad of supplementary huts. All this change was distasteful to me. No doubt things were more comfortable and all that, but I missed the old, haphazard, primitive tents in the sodden field. Things had become more businesslike and definite. The buccaneering glamour had gone. Well, I returned to 'the Island' and reported myself to the Colonel.

Reporting yourself to anyone means that you've got to find him first. Not always an easy matter at large regimental depots. An old soldier, however, gets a few elementary rules into his head for this job. If you are looking for colonels, try the orderly room first. If you are looking for second-lieutenants, try the ante-room. If you are looking for captains, have a look at the leave book before taking any further trouble!

I went across the enormous barrack square - that gravel desert which seems essential to military incubation - and entered the orderly room. There I found the Colonel, the Adjutant, and a host of minor stars. They had had notice that I was returning, so had plenty to say when I turned up.

"Glad to see you back again," said the Colonel. "Hope you're better."

I have known this Colonel for a long time as I was in the same battalion with him before the war on militia training. He and the Adjutant had evidently settled my fate long before I got there, for I was at once posted to a company and given all instructions.

I left the orderly room and set about looking for quarters. I found the Quartermaster, and also found that there was a fearful rush on quarters. The prospect of no quarters didn't in the least disturb me, and never more in this life will disturb me. To one who is versed in rolling oneself up in a mackintosh sheet in a clay hole in Belgium 'no quarters' conveys nothing disagreeable. Leaning against one of the barrack blocks in a greatcoat for the night is good enough for me. A week in a greatcoat under Westminster Bridge is better than one night in some trenches I have known.

Since I had left the island to go to war the military outfit there had grown enormously. The number of officers was treble what it used to be. All the large officers' buildings were full up. I got hold of a hut that night, and kept a greedy, jealous eye on a certain upper chamber in the main block of buildings. The owner, a captain, was about to leave for the Front, so they said. I met him in the mess frequently, and took an immense interest in his departure. He had been 'out' before, but had now finished his light duty and was waiting for the word to go out again. One day he went, and I got his room.

I know nothing, with the exception of a base camp, quite as distressingly plain and uninteresting as the average barrack quarters: this room I had got was the plainest of plain cubes. It had the barest necessities in the way of furniture, a large plain window, no blind, no carpet, and a small wooden board hanging up on which was printed a list of meagre articles which had been supplied by the Quartermaster's stores. I don't mean to say this was a unique room. All barrack rooms are the same. After all, why should they be different? They are only meant as a case to contain you at night, to keep you safely till the next day, when the Adjutant gets you in his grip again from 6.00am onwards.

You mustn't look for domestic leisure in the army. You are one of a vast horde of trained gladiators. The proper use for a soldier is putting him on to shooting, clubbing or sticking someone else who happens to get in the way of his country's welfare. Unless he is in one of these attitudes he is wasting the country's money. A certain amount of time is, of course, allowed for perfecting these arts. Anyway, bothering about such things as window blinds, carpet on the floor, etc., is sheer froth. This necessary simplicity and Spartan atmosphere doesn't end with your room. In fact you'll soon find out that this forbidding cube is about the best place in the whole barracks. Your window looks out on to about six acres of gravel. Round this barren waste are ranged a series of oblong red-brick blocks like so many workhouses. It is here that the soldiers are kept. Behind these outrageously ugly buildings are others nearly as bad, but not quite. They comprise a variety of offices and stores. The chances of the owners of living there longer than an ordinary soldier puts in, generally lead them into such non-military acts as growing a geranium in an empty ammunition box in the window, or training a bit of something up the wall. Three sides of the square have to put up with what I have described above, but on the fourth side you come to the *pièce de résistance* . . . the officers' mess.

It is just like the other huge blocks in shape, but has a few extra adornments stuck on the front. You generally have to go up some steps to the entrance hall. Some garden-beds are under the windows. Perhaps some tender-looking pansy faces gaze out from amongst a geranium or two - what a mockery! Pansy faces and geraniums for a soldier! His job is gravel squares, rations, feet inspections and shooting or getting shot. Away with all this sentimental pansy business.

The two main component parts of the officers' mess are the ante-room and the mess-room. They are both plain, but might be worse. I'll take the ante-room first. It is very large and is furnished mainly with leather chairs and divans, tables for matches and ash-trays, and tables for papers. The wall decorations nearly always consist of one or two portraits of royalty or famous generals, an engraving of Wellington meeting Blücher, and the intervening spaces are filled up with subscription lists for things you haven't either the time or the inclination to take advantage of. Now, the mess-room. Empty, except for several long tables and a sufficient number of chairs to accommodate the surging mass of officers which debouches into the room three times daily.

This is a barracks, and this was where I now had to put in two months' 'light duty'.

When you are in a precarious shell-hole, with shrapnel squibbing overhead at 4.00am in France, you look back on barracks as one of the bright spots of life. When you get back to those barracks, and have had a week of them, you'd pay quite a handsome sum of money to be miraculously transported back to the shell-hole. Anyhow, that's how I felt after the first week of two months' light duty.

Chapter 4

TAKE OVER A COMPANY ~ OLD SOLDIERS' TRICKS ~ COMPANY PAY-DAY

Being on light duty, my first job was to be put on to a company which also went in for light duty. A couple of companies were kept there in those days, which were entirely composed of men who had been out to the war, but who, having been either wounded or temporarily invalided, had gravitated back to the depot.

I was posted to one of these companies, and was now, therefore, responsible for its entire welfare. There were several men there who had been with me in France; men who had been through the winter in the trenches and who, at varying dates, had been wounded and had left the front in consequence. The whole company was a collection of 'has-beens'. This company of mine (I'll call it 'X' Company) was not remarkable for a thirst for barrack-life work. It was astonishing how bad those old wounds became on the day that the route-march came round. But how could you blame them? They had all had a fearful time in France and really did deserve a bit of a slack. To get them completely fit again was the main point, and this with the minimum amount of toil to them. I confess I am leniently inclined to these people. I think others who have 'been out' and 'had some' feel the same. But at that period there were a good many in authority who had not been to France, and who consequently had little sympathy for easy work.

Everyone, now, has 'been out', but the time I write about is late in 1915. Those veterans I had in my company were the most work-evading group that ever existed, yet if they had been ordered out to an attack they would have sailed into it with the good old original 'Battle of Mons' spirit, or held any line till all was blue. I love those old work-evading, tricky, self-contained slackers - old soldiers! They are the 'cutest set of old rogues imaginable, yet with it all there is such a humorous, childlike simplicity.

They can size up their officers better than any Sherlock Holmes. I'll guarantee that an 'old soldier' will know to a nicety how dirty he can keep his buttons without being hauled up by his new officer after doing one parade under him. An 'old soldier' will pinch a tunic from a man in another company because he has pawned his own, and come on parade with it, entirely to deceive you, temporarily. If you were lying wounded in the middle of a barrage, that same man would come and pull you out.

And good 'Old Bill' belongs to those lovable humorists whose total outlook is 'as little work as possible' and whose total ability is to 'fight like hell and not be beaten'.

Many is the time I have come across their quaint and cunning tricks amongst themselves, or directed against me; and many a time I have had to go off behind some huts to laugh it out to myself. Company work is all right, but company upkeep is another matter. This company of mine was about two hundred strong, and when I took over I was, of course, immediately put in charge of all the documents and books which appertain to the looking after of a company.

Now, this is where I am no good whatever. I do not think that I shall ever live to see a day when I can say I understand that backbone of the army, 'The Pay and Mess Book'. It is only one of a set of books necessary to company upkeep, but it has an atmosphere all its own. It consists simply in a statement of what a soldier ought to get, and what he does get, and I think you subtract one from the other (although I'm not quite certain). It sounds simple, but it's only in about one case in a million that a soldier gets exactly what he is, theoretically, entitled to. He has either borrowed some in advance, been fined, or has had some compulsorily deducted at the request of a turbulent wife. This makes the interior of the Pay and Mess

Memories of Rouen.

Book a treatise on mathematics to me. If you are a halfpenny out at the end of the week, you spend an afternoon with your Quartermaster-Sergeant trying to find it. You would willingly pay the halfpenny yourself and call it square, but that doesn't do at all. It would simply throw the whole thing out. At about 4.30pm, when all signs of troops have melted away, everyone has gone to play, the sun is shining outside and distant laughter comes from the football field, the Quartermaster-Sergeant looks up from the Pay and Mess Book, and turning to you declares, "I've found it, sir!"

He then points a perspiring finger at a pencilled halfpenny in one of the columns, and explains that there is a halfpenny due back from Mrs Dubbs, the washerwoman, on behalf of Private Stickleback's shirt which ought to have gone to the wash, but didn't. What a relief! The Pay and Mess Book is now temporarily correct and can be put away . . . only temporarily though. It is going to come out again next time you 'pay out'.

This 'paying-out' comes once a week. 'X' Company got paid on a Friday. Barring the part where you have to carry a couple of sacks of assorted coins up from the bank to do it with, it's a comparatively easy job. And this is how the whole operation goes: Friday comes. There's going to be no parade in the afternoon because it's pay-day, and after attending battalion orders at 2.00pm in the orderly room, you are due to go to your Sergeant-Major's hut and pay your company out.

In the morning, whilst you are drilling your company, inspecting their huts, etc., you have sent one of your Subalterns down to the bank, wherever it may be, with a cheque for the amount required. This officer goes to the bank, gets the money, and then tries to return with it. If he is in good health and hasn't any heart trouble he will probably turn up with a sack of half-crowns, shillings and sixpences before lunch, and have them ready for you. About a hundred and fifty pounds' worth of nothing larger than a half-crown is a rotten thing either to walk or bicycle with.

Orders are over and paying-out time has arrived. You and the Subaltern, who is going to help you, go to the Sergeant-Major's hut. He is there, ready for you, likewise your Company Quartermaster-Sergeant, who has covered a table with a General Service (GS) blanket and has produced that bogey - the Pay and Mess Book - and has laid it on the table. You, the Company Commander, now sit at the table, and your Subaltern shoots out all the money in front of you and starts making neat little piles of half-crowns, shillings and sixpences. The Quartermaster-Sergeant sits at your side, ready to interpret the mathematical enigmas in the Pay and Mess Book.

The Quartermaster-Sergeant, by the way, knows everything there is to know about company upkeep, book-keeping and everything else. To me he stands out like a human lighthouse in a sea of trouble.

The company is now surging about outside the hut, like hens waiting to be fed. Some of the bolder ones put their heads round the corner of the door and let their eyes feast on the dazzling array of half-crowns. They are frightened off by the Sergeant-Major who has now taken complete charge of the scene. He turns to you and says, "Are you ready, sir?"

You hastily review the piles of wealth and murmur, "Are you ready, Quartermaster-Sergeant?"

"Quite ready, sir," he murmurs.

You then suddenly remember that you must get two witnesses to the 'paying-out'. These are hurriedly obtained, after which you say, in a loud, truculent voice, "Carry on, Sergeant-Major."

You've started. Paying-out has begun.

The Quartermaster-Sergeant reads out the names. He does it like this, "Eighty-four ninety-eight Blobbs!" (8498 Blobbs). A face of avarice is framed in the doorway, salutes and comes forward. The Quartermaster-Sergeant murmurs to you, "Shilling, sir."

You hand a shilling to Mr Blobbs, who takes it, forgets to salute, makes a left-about turn and walks away; but is immediately stopped by the Sergeant-Major at the door, who makes him go all through the motions of taking a shilling on pay-day again - this time correctly - which is: salute, take money, salute, right-about turn and exit. Private Blobbs goes out and darts off amongst the huts to get some lonely corner where he can figure out how much amusement and worldly benefit can be derived from that shilling. He should have had more, only he is being fined for having three days before slit a mattress from end to end with his bayonet in an outburst of untimely jocularity.

"Forty-six eighty-three Perkins!" barks the Quartermaster-Sergeant. Then, turning to you, says, "Six shillings, sir."

You look up to see who this model of virtue may be who is entitled to all his pay and you hand him six shillings with a thrill of admiration. He salutes and departs.

"Thirty-two sixty-four Smith!"

A freckled giant shoots in at the door.

The Sergeant-Major is suspicious. "What's your number?"

"Twenty-nine thirty-five Smith," answers the freckled giant.

The Sergeant-Major, Quartermaster-Sergeant and Company Commander chorus together petulantly, "Wrong number! It's thirty-two sixty-four Smith we want!"

The real Smith appears and gets his money, and so the job goes on.

Paying out 'X' Company used to take me about an hour and a half. Paying is easy enough, but at the end you have to 'balance the books' and 'enter things up'. This, as I said before, may lead to anything. In my case it generally led to another couple of hours grappling with figures. I think this must have been the fate of anyone who had 'X' Company under his care!

Chapter 5

BARRACK ROUTINE ~ A DISCIPLINARIAN MAJOR ~ ORDERED TO SALISBURY PLAIN

Life at the Front and life in one of those enormous English depots are two very different things. And so they should be. On the island, just as at all the other home depots for training reserves and recruits, the work consists of nothing but training. Other sidelines which go on, such as 'Commanding Officer's orders', 'pay-day', 'kit inspections', etc., are all necessary accessories to the one great important feature which is tirelessly being carried out, and that is providing a ceaseless flow of efficient men for our great armies in the field.

When at a depot you are regarded as an amateur learning the art. When in France, you are there as a professional. It is, therefore, easy to see that the mode of life and work must be different in the two places. I must say I prefer the Front. I think everybody does. There is something very adventurously attractive about being in a real war. There are times though, when I admit frankly that I have thought the adventurous side a bit overdone. Being sprayed with machine-gun bullets whilst you are lying in an insufficient fold in the ground at dawn, and in a thin drizzle, throws up the life of a bank clerk in a delicious bas-relief of security!

As time went on, and my light duty was waning, I was shifted to a more arduous company. I was now much better, but far from quite right. Anyhow, I was better, and was now on quite a different line in companies. This time I was posted to a recruit company, full of activity and ambition. I was a Company Commander, but two companies were clubbed together and the whole outfit was under a higher command - that of a Major. Some Major too! One of the real old chutney variety. The old British Army epitomised. One felt something like a Zulu must have felt at a witch hunt, when the devil doctors 'smell you out' to be thrown to the crocodiles - on one of the Major's parades. I don't know who was the most frightened, my company or myself . . . I think I was. Discipline was, and is, his motto, and quite right too. There's nothing like it for winning wars, but it's damned uncomfortable when you are on parade.

If that Major thought you a bit shaky about company drill, out you'd come; and there, standing in the middle of the square, you'd have a good chance of improving yourself. And moving companies about a square is no easy matter, as all who have tried will know. It's easy enough to start them moving, but to move 'em where you want to, and get them back where you want to, 'aye, there's the rub'.

You stand about the centre of the gravel desert and with one mighty lung-tearing shout you order the company to move. Before you can think of the next command to get them back again, and before you have recovered from the first exhausting vocal outburst, the company is 'marking time' against the barrack wall as they can't march through it!

"Bairnsfather! You must give your commands quicker and louder." To which I blush and try again.

In the evenings, when all this strafing was over, I and a few pals went off down to the town about a mile and a half away and played about till time for mess. At weekends we progressed further and perhaps went over to Cowes, Ryde or Ventnor. So the time went on. I was slowly getting through my light duty, and the question was now looming up, "What next, when this is finished?" In the ordinary course of events I should be put on the list of those ready to return to France again, but of course, with the date uncertain.

Anyway, the prospect of nearing the end of my time on the island was exciting. The idea of something new happening, of some new move in existence, always cheers when one's bored. I was bored. There's a very bottled-up sensation on the Isle of Wight, after you have been there some time. It's aggravated by seeing one's pals disappearing out to the Front at odd moments on the receipt of a telegram. You yourself, somehow, always seem to be the last to go. It's strange, the magnetic influence of those torn and mutilated plains of France and Belgium. I can see the old cracked remnant of Smelly-Pig farm in my mind's eye as I write, and I feel I want to be there.

One day the call came. A telegram came to the orderly room and it contained a message for me . . . to go to the Front? No! I went to the orderly room and there heard the worst. I was to go to a new division, then forming, as machine-gun instructor.

A good job, I thought, as I had been a machine-gun officer all my time in the trenches so far. I found out all about this division, or rather as much as I could, and eventually when I was to go. It appeared that I had to be off as soon as possible. That evening I packed my traps and pondered on the coming move. Machine-gun instructor to a new division; a division that would shortly be going to France. An interesting job, forsooth, and as I had had a pretty varied experience in this business, from the practical point of

By means of a Turkish bath Old Bill hopes some day to boil the effects of 'plum and apple', Bolshevism and demobilisation completely out of his system.

view, I felt that I could be of some use in this new departure. My Isle of Wight job was over; so was the light duty, and now I was bound for a new division somewhere on Salisbury Plain. I knew, also, that I was taking another step in the direction of the front - soon I should be back again, back amongst the dilapidated estaminets, the shattered châteaux, the land of *'Bullets & Billets'*.

Chapter 6

HANDING OVER ~ ARRIVAL AT DIVISIONAL HQ ~ I DIG MYSELF IN

Instructions for most military movements are run on the same lines as instructions for attending Medical Boards; you get a curt wire about two hours before you have to start. As a general rule, the more drastic the move you have to make, the less warning you get. For instance, if you have got to be at a lecture one day, you will probably be told about it a week in advance. If you've got to go to the Front - which entails packing, collecting everything you may need, handing over your company and saying good-bye - you will probably get a wire half an hour before starting.

This exodus of mine to the new division was arranged in just this way. I had to shin off from the island with the greatest rapidity. I collected all my worldly goods and handed over my company to another captain. 'Handing over' meant, in my case, palming off a set of disorganised accounts and paying for all losses out of my own pocket. I forget exactly what it cost me this time, but I know that running a company is an expensive amusement unless you are very careful.

Early one morning, my valise and I set forth on this new life. We left from Cowes and watched the island fade into the mist as we glided up the Solent.

Salisbury Plain was where rumour said this new division lived. In due course I arrived there. Pretty vague that, I know, for Salisbury Plain is a vast expanse, larger than something or other, and nearly as big as anything you like (no, the Germans are not going to get any information out of me). At the time of which I write enormous numbers of soldiers were quartered all over the Plain, in different parts.

It was wintertime and phenomenally wet, so it really represented life in a leviathan bog. There were many divisions there. Each, of course, had a divisional headquarters and each divisional headquarters had a divisional general. It was like a lot of bees, in several different swarms. Each day the bees would stagger forth into the treacle round about and mix with each other, practising field days, route-marches and all that sort of thing, and at night all the different hives would swarm round their various queen bee divisional commanders again. It was to this humming hive of industry that I came. I arrived at the station frequented by my particular swarm and inquired the way to their hive.

The divisional headquarters was, I found, about three miles from the station. I got hold of a taxi and, putting my traps into it, drove off through the squalid little town out into the country towards divisional headquarters.

This part of Salisbury Plain I was in was certainly one of the best parts, but there is not much choice. Except for the fact that it isn't shelled and mutilated, it is nearly as bad as the Front to look at. In fact, if someone would lend me a couple of howitzers for a day, I could make a quite passable imitation of the Somme valley near Fricourt, out of Salisbury Plain. I drove along in the taxi full of interest, combined with a certain amount of nervousness at the coming new job that lay before me. It was all so very different to the Front. It's far easier to be one of the crowd doing a real job, and putting everything you do to a practical and immediate use, than having to demonstrate the same things to warfare students in the security of Salisbury Plain.

The headquarters of the division had a very charming house situated in very charming grounds. Headquarters always know what they are about as regards where they are going to fix up. No bell-tents for them, and quite right too; for the complications and impedimenta necessary for running a division, particularly a new one in the course of formation, are beyond comprehension. I shot along the curved gravel drive in the taxi and pulled up in front of the noble front door of the mansion. Here I was at last . . . no hope of escape now.

Having discharged my taxi I entered and broke the news of my arrival as gently as possible. As luck would have it, there was already an officer doing the job I was booked for and although he was leaving to return to France his departure had been postponed for another week. This was very fortunate for me as I soon found out how he had arranged things, and what was the correct method to adopt. He was a most expert machine-gunner, and had put in a long and arduous time in the Ypres Salient. He had been wounded at Ypres on the same day on which I received my 'knockout' at the same place, although he was, of course, in another regiment and in a different part of the show. I went to see him the night I arrived and finding him down at his hut, talked the whole thing over. For a week I lived up at the divisional château and daily absorbed his methods for instruction. At the end of that time he left, I bagged his hut, and started on the job by myself. A point which may strike readers here is, "Why bag his hut, when you're living at the château?"

There were two reasons. First and foremost, I far prefer a hut to a château. I am much happier in a matchboard box with a corrugated iron roof and a smoky stove than in one of England's sumptuous country-house bedrooms. My line is rough, straightforward, masculine freedom in simple surroundings, and I deteriorate, mentally and physically, to a ridiculous degree in grand houses. The other, secondary, reason for leaving the château was that it was rapidly filling up with more important people than I, and rooms were getting scarce.

I went to the huts, as I have said, and felt better all round. The huts were attached to a brigade headquarters. A division contains a number of brigades and I was now living with a brigade, although still on the divisional staff.

Chapter 7

**THOSE FIELD DAYS ~ WHO'S WON? ~
A KEEN DIVISION**

It didn't take me long to size up this new division. It was just the most hard-working and keen division that ever was, but at that time I think the whole of Salisbury Plain was crammed with such divisions. It was almost entirely composed of men from the north country, and was just bursting to reach the last stage of proficiency and go out to France or anywhere, to have a smack at the Boches.

When I arrived, the situation was that the order for the exodus might come at any time. Training and final equipage was going on with relentless vigour. The work of the divisional and brigade staffs was enormous. Enthusiasm ran like an electric current through the entire concern.

My little part consisted of getting hold of all the machine-gun sections of the division with their officers, and imparting practical tips for Prussian puncturing.

I took a group out daily into the country round about and reconstructed actual front-line scenes and episodes, coupling it all with as good word pictures and advice as I could command. I took about fourteen men out at a time. We marched off into a new bit of country daily, and there spread ourselves for perfecting the gentle art of machine gunning. I arranged 'attacks' of all descriptions on all sorts of places, and at the end of an arduous morning, sat in the middle of a perspiring group, correcting faults and illustrating them with examples from my knowledge of the Front.

The rest of the division was almost invariably out on a field day or a route-march. The machine-gun department nearly always worked on its own. Occasionally there came a great day of combined work, in the shape of a full-blown field day, in which all the component parts of the division took part. These days, though very hard and tiresome, are generally tinged with humour . . . humour arising out of pain generally!

This division I was in was great on field days. About a week before one came off, all the 'crowned heads' of the division were given what is known as the 'general idea'. This consists of a group of intricate documents laying out concisely what sort of a field day the Divisional General is going to have, say, 'next Tuesday'. Then comes the 'special idea', and finally out of all this the fact dawns on the mere regimental officer that on Tuesday next there is to be a field day when a 'Brown Force' will be opposed by a 'White Force', which is the invariable army method for distinguishing the two sides for the 'battle'.

For a week the staff officers have worked themselves to red-tabbed shadows preparing for this monster game of hide and seek, and the General's right-hand man - in army parlance 'the GSO1' - performs miracles of work on these occasions.

At last Tuesday arrives.

It is pouring with rain generally, but the plan is far too vast to be interfered with by any considerations of weather. The Brown Force has been set in motion against the White Force and now no power on earth, except the General being suddenly superseded, can possibly avert the ultimate collision of these two ponderous pieces of human mechanism that have now been set in motion.

At about 6.00am the Brown and White forces, numbering thousands each, covered with equipment and ammunition, exuding profanity and determination, stagger forth into the surrounding morass and disappear into the neighbouring country. The two forces, of course, take different paths immediately. They will ultimately meet in a fearful mock collision (arranged by the GSO1) in about three hours' time.

The great charm about these onslaughts is that from that day on you never really know who has won the battle. There being no convincing arguments such as real barrages and devastating machine-gun fire, it is always possible for each side ever afterwards to prove to its own satisfaction that it 'won hands down'.

A whole battalion, with enormous self-satisfaction, storms a hill and refuses staunchly to believe (though repeatedly told) that a solitary machine gun concealed in a hedge has entirely murdered them (in theory) whilst they were approaching said hill. In actual war one is apt to get painful and convincing arguments of an exceedingly practical nature, but at home, rehearsing, it's left to words and superior judgement.

I have often thought that, if only we were Spartan enough, what a valuable training a *real* scrap would be. There is nothing in the world that illustrates better what a mistake it is to march in fours down an enfiladed road than a couple of real live machine guns at the end of it. The appearance of a red-tabbed military apostle in an apoplectic temper at the end of the road announcing in uncomplimentary terms that, "the whole lot of you would have been simply wiped out!" leaves one cold.

But anyway, one learns a lot on these field days. They are great training in endurance. Nothing could keep one in better training. My only comment is that they rarely, if ever, are the least bit like the real thing in the way of an attack. It is quite impossible to make them so. Other wars may have been a bit on the lines of a field day, but not this one. War wouldn't be half so bad if it was like a field day, with all its marching and 'outflanking movements', etc., etc. There is some sporting adventure and 'go' about that. But the Germans have, wisely for themselves, taken to mud and mechanics and have thereby spoilt the true sporting idea of a battle.

My division always threw themselves with whole-hearted enthusiastic vigour into these field days. These were days before the great battle of the Somme. How little those fine chaps knew of the kind of thing the real field days would shortly be!

I used to try, by means of sketches and word pictures, to give my machine-gunners as clear a vision as possible of the Front and what it means; but it's very, very hard - nearly impossible - to convey the correct idea. Nobody who has not actually been to the Front can know what it is really like, and by going to the Front I don't mean going to some headquarters and being taken to 'as near as it's safe', and then being given a pair of field glasses. A visitor to the Front knows he can leave when he has seen it. A soldier knows that he can't and isn't going to. There's the difference.

Being accidentally caught in a bit of shelling whilst visiting the Front doesn't give you the idea either. You are buoyed up by the knowledge that a car is waiting back there, near the crossroads, to whisk you off to security and a good lunch.

You want to be in a morning's shelling and then, having escaped when it stops, realise that you'll probably get the same thing again to-morrow morning. I have heard of people saying, when shown Ypres, that they thought it would be much worse. If they will come to me, I will soon tell them how to get that opinion altered.

This division of course, didn't know and couldn't appreciate it, but what they did know was that they were ready for anything, and would go through anything. They fully acted up to it too, in their splendid performance on the Somme a few months later.

Chapter 8

MY SOLDIER SERVANT ~
BLOBBS' LOVE AFFAIR

Field days on the grand scale came off about once a week. The intervening times were filled up with all sorts of highly important training, so life for the division was one ceaseless activity and hard labour. I used to be free at about 4.00pm, when I would retire to my wooden hut to have a rest, decide what I was going to do that evening and plan the next day. It was the usual simple sort of officer's hut, and all I had inside was a camp-bed, a washstand, a tin bath and a table. My bag and valise was all my luggage and that was in the corner. It was wintertime and pretty cold too, so a fire was urgently necessary in the little stove.

A few days after I had adopted the hut for a home, I had procured my 'soldier servant'. He belonged to a regiment coming from one of England's eastern counties. He was the most charming example of that rapidly dying class, the ploughboy yokel, that you could possibly find. The whole simplicity of his life and mind, combined with the constitution of a rhinoceros, gave him a most lovable aspect to me.

Until I caught this specimen I didn't know that such things still lived, and when I found that they did, I was annoyed and troubled to think of the danger that such a genuine, simple creature ran of having his outlook altered by this ideal-shaking war. He was about twenty years old, and as strong as an ox. Thickset, short, with a healthy red complexion, he was just the sort of rustic type that, on the stage, sucks a straw and wears a smock. His head was delightfully thick as well. It took him a long time to fully grasp anything you wanted him to do, but when he had got hold of the idea and digested the fact that you wanted him to do whatever it might be, he went at it with the relentless vigour of a charging bison.

This blossom hadn't done any soldier-servant work before, so all was new to him, and I used to derive considerable amusement by knowing full well that he thought I was insane in most of my desires and tastes. I told him how to look after the hut and when to light the stove. He thought it all slowly over and then carried out these items with unfailing precision and thoroughness. I remember the first time I told him I wanted a bath. He was standing in the doorway, having finished whatever it was, and was evidently waiting for me to give him something else to do.

"Blobbs," I said, "I want a bath. Hot water, do you see, and then fill up this tin thing here." I indicated the bath.

In a queer, hesitating manner he repeated, "Oi see, you wants a bath."

"Yes, I want a bath," I said.

He fingered the bath about a bit, half went to the door and then stood looking at me in a hesitating way. After a few moments' pause he suddenly jerked out, "I'd better get it now." And with that he disappeared like a Jack-in-the-box through the doorway.

He returned later with a vast volume of scalding water, about enough for three baths, all having been conveyed there by himself in a collection of canvas buckets. I wished I'd asked him for the bath itself as well! I'm sure he would have gone to some house and severed a porcelain one from its pipe connections and brought it along.

He had no personal initiative, but when guided and commanded he was nearly as

"I don't think I'll dress for dinner tonight, Bert."

good as the dear old genie in the *'Arabian Nights'* . . . 'rub the lamp and see it appear' sort of thing. He woke me in the mornings by a method all his own. I watched him once or twice with eyes feigning sleep. He would bring along my clothes and boots and put them near the one and only chair, then he would bring a pail of hot water and then hesitate a bit. He appeared to be thinking deeply. After a minute or two's hesitancy he would suddenly come to the side of my bed and say in a loud voice, "Shall you be wantin' the stove?" This sentence, you will observe, combined waking me with getting instructions.

Why he always did it this way goodness knows; I soon ceased to try and probe his beautiful mind. He interested me intensely, this man. I soon began leading him on into conversations about himself and about his private and home life. Later on I encouraged him into discourses on his love affairs. It appeared he had a "gurl", or, in other words, he was "a-courtin'."

"Splendid!" I thought, "now I'll get some funny stuff out of this cove." And I did. I recall a conversation we had one morning which went something like this:

"Have you had any leave yet, Blobbs? I expect you'd like to go back to your home for a day or two eh? Go back and see that girl of yours."

"Oi!" replied Blobbs with a rubicund grin, "I shouldn't 'arf loike a bit o' leave. The Sergeant says the other night that 'e thought as 'ow Oi was a-goin' soon, and," he added bashfully, "she won't 'arf be pleased to see me too, I reckon . . ." he finished, critically examining a row of chilblains on the back of his hand.

"What did she say when you joined the army, Blobbs?"

"Just afore I joined she wouldn't speak to me. It was because I was drivin' Dad's thrashin' machine down the road past 'er 'ouse. She says, "Arthur, you never looks at me now that you are a-drivin' that there thrashin' machine." You see, she thought I was a-doin' the grand, soon as I got to drivin' Dad's big engine. One day I sees 'er by the rick in 'er Dad's farm, and I picks up a pitchfork and runs at 'er like this . . ." Whereupon he made an imitation of a savage running with the pitchfork. "She says, "Why do you do that Arthur?" I says, "'Cos I'm goin' to join the Army, Ciss, that's why." So I chucks down me pitchfork and she says as she was proud o' me, and now she writes to me reg'lar every week."

"That's right, Blobbs. You stick to her and she'll stick to you. Now, you might just go and get me a bucket of water as I want to have a wash before lunch-time."

Thus the dialogue closed.

I have often wished that I could hear that that splendid country jake got safely back to Ciss and his thrashing machine out of all this devastating turmoil.

Chapter 9

THE CENSOR DEFIED ~ MACHINE-GUN TRAINING ~ RUMOURS OF WAR ~ BLOBBS GETS INTO TROUBLE

Now I wonder if I shall incur the odium of the authorities or prolong the war by saying where it was that we lived in those days on Salisbury Plain. I should like to say the name, as it was a nice place, the nicest in the neighbourhood. I wonder if I dare . . . shall I?

No . . . yes, I will. It was Sutton Veney! No doubt the German Mark will go up in value on all the exchanges and there will consternation on Wall Street. I wish I hadn't said it now!

Well, I've done it, so there you are. Sutton Veney was the place; a delightful little English village it must have been before all we khaki locusts settled upon it. It was quite a pleasure having all this military training set in such delightful surroundings. The headquarters themselves possessed most charming gardens, but as I have said in a previous chapter, such luxuries always seem painful to me. Mailed fist work and charming gardens are so desperately out of harmony with each other. Yet all the Sutton Veney times seemed mighty pleasant to me. Perhaps it was that I had not long since come out of that drab whirl of events, the Front; houses without roofs and châteaux turned inside out, still lingered in my mind's eye. On the whole, it was a short but happy time at Sutton Veney, standing out with pleasing brightness in all my war life.

I do not write all this sort of stuff which you've just read (or slurred over) with the idea of demonstrating that I am thinking differently to anyone else about the war. I do so in the hopes and, indeed, with the knowledge, that there were, and are, many who have looked on their various war experiences in the same way that I have. I was merely a common-or-garden captain, leading a common-or-garden captain's life, and now as I write I wonder why the devil I have the cheek to write about it at all. I have apologised once in the preface of *'Bullets & Billets'*. I won't do it again.

Here at Sutton Veney, and all over the Plain, thousands of men were leading the most arduous and dullest of lives imaginable. It was a new picture altogether to me. Previously I had only seen the practical application of warlike skill. Now, here at Sutton Veney, all the technique was being acquired.

In my daily work with the machine-gunners I used to make desperate attempts to brighten up the job for them by giving them as vivid word pictures of the Front and its ways as possible. Occasionally I organised and ran a small 'battle' in some part of the surrounding country. This led to quite exciting times. I galvanised the opposing teams into enthusiastic action by means of competitions and prizes.

Whilst all this training was in progress an assistant trainer joined me - a second-lieutenant, who had been wounded and was on light duty like myself. He was a most efficient machine-gunner, in fact, I have never seen his equal at machine-gun mechanism.

We both went out and each took a hand in the competitions. Over a wide tract of variegated land, two sides, composed of two gun teams in each, would attack each other. We invented a series of rules so that decisions could be arrived at, and then had breathlessly exciting mornings. We crept about the country after each other, and butchered each other silently round hedges and ditches, until the overwhelming superiority of one side over the other became apparent owing to someone sticking a head lathered in mud out of a culvert and announcing that, "We've been enfilading you for at least half an hour." This was followed by much dispute, the verdict and then, "Fall in on the road."

So, we'd all march back to the barracks beguiling the tedium of the way home by arguments as to which side had really won.

Things were now getting pretty shipshape with the division all round and the air was full of rumours, such as:

"I hear we're going to Egypt," or, "I shouldn't be surprised if we had orders to go to France any day now."

All this made life much more interesting and exciting.

Leave was being granted in great profusion, which was a good sign. It looked as if 'they' were trying to let everyone have some home leave before going out. The whole circus was bristling with equipment and excitement.

Amongst the gentlemen to have leave was Mr Blobbs, my servant. That dense but happy rubicund face burst into my hut one morning and gave forth the following:

"Sergeant says as I'm in the next lot for leave."

"Are you, Blobbs?" I asked. "That's a good job. You'll be able to go along and see that girl of yours, and go for a spin in your father's thrashing machine if you're lucky."

Blobbs' face was covered in a bovine grin, "That's roight, sir."

In due course Blobbs got his leave and went to his home in Suffolk. Like all good soldiers he, of course, overstayed his pass. (One should always suspect a soldier who comes back on the day he's been told to.) Then, like all good soldiers, he had to be hauled up and punished. The first step in this procedure consists of the offender coming up before his immediate commander. In this case Blobbs had to be 'got at' by me. He had returned two days late, so I sternly asked him why.

"Well, it was like this, sir," he replied. "Me and my mate started to come back, and we left Bury St Edmunds in the mornin' to come along to Lunnon. When we got there a bloke on the platform says to us, "Where are ye for?" And I, silly like, says, "Bury St Edmunds" and he took us along to a train and the next thing was we was back at Bury. You see, sir, I thought as the man was askin' us where we 'ad come from, not where we was a-goin' to. Well, there weren't a train back to Lunnon not till night-time, so we comes on that, and we got to Lunnon about six o'clock in the mornin'. Me and my mate 'ad never been to this 'ere station before, and we wasn't goin' to ask no more questions again, we'd 'ad enough o' being sent back to Bury. Presently up comes a lady, an' she says as she would show us 'ow to go. She says, "Where are you goin'?" So I says, "Sutton Veney." So she says, "Come along with me then," and we went down a lot of tunnels to where the trains was a-runnin' into a 'ole like. She says as she couldn't stop, but she says, "Take the next train as comes in." Well sir, I reckon we watched about 'alf a dozen of them trains go out afore we got into one."

"What made you do that, Blobbs?" I inquired. "What did you want to wait there for?"

"Well, sir," replied Blobbs, "this is 'ow it was. A carriage would come into the station, shuntin' like, without any injun on, and I says to my mate, "There's 'eaps of time, the train can't go without an injun on." And just as we was sittin' on that there seat, the carriage would go off by itself down the 'ole at the end. I knows what it was now, but ye see sir, I didn't understand anythin' about them 'lectric trains as 'aven't got no injuns, and no more did my mate."

Poor old Blobbs and his mate! They know something about trains by now. The knockabout wanderings that will have led them through Southampton, Havre, Rouen and Amiens will have gone a long way to destroying the old-world, cabbage-like simplicity which at that time they both possessed.

Chapter 10

THE FINAL POLISH ~ A ONE-HORSE TOWNSHIP ~ IN 'THE ISLAND' AGAIN ~ DETAILED FOR ALDERSHOT ~ THE OLD GUARD

Now came a day of fearful excitement and anticipation. Not an order for the division to leave, but a much more delicate hint that departure was at hand. Sun helmets were issued all round. They spelt two things: the East! and that an early departure was likely. All was joy. The months of mud and training were nearly over, and now for the war!

I was still on 'light duty', so was a bit nervy as to what my chances were of being allowed to go with them. I hoped for the best, and looked forward with a buoyant interest to the departure. The time was now entirely filled up, so far as I was concerned, in machine-gun firing on the ranges. We were served out with great masses of practice ammunition and a full rig-out of guns, so the machine-gun end of the butts gave forth a splendidly nerve-shattering rattle for the surrounding neighbourhood until we left. The inhabitants of Sutton Veney however, had no hope of escape. We were not the first division to be there, nor were we to be the last. When we left another division took our places.

The weather was terribly wet. We stood about in pouring rain squirting lead into the hillside from our Maxims for about a week. The entire division was firing all day long in ceaseless practice, until the word came for departure. As is the way with all military movements, you never know exactly what is going to happen till it happens. Suddenly all the sun helmets were 'called in'. Hullo! Egypt was off, everyone thought, and they were quite right.

The soldiers didn't mind where they went, as long as they went somewhere. They were all for 'up and at 'em' now. They would willingly part with all the simple joys provided by the neighbouring township of Warminster. They would cheerfully relinquish the pleasures of the penny shows and cheap cinemas which grew thickly in the neighbourhood. What they wanted now was to have a real live try-out of their skill and energy combined with all the romantic attraction of 'foreign parts'.

Every evening, when work is over, the one idea possessing the minds of all the soldiers is to walk into the nearest town. This crowd that I was with walked into Warminster, which was only about three miles distant from our huts. Apart from this, Warminster had little else to recommend it. In the dark winter evenings, with its anti-Zeppelin lighting arrangements and squalid streets, this little one-horse township presented as rotten and unattractive an appearance as you could wish for. It served as a very good incentive to hurry back to the camps at the time requested by the authorities.

A sharp rise in tin.

The road from Sutton Veney to Warminster was, at about 6.00pm, almost a solid mass of soldiers, all walking in to partake of the meagre delights of the town. A few movable sideshows, seeking to add to the paucity of Warminster's attractions, had taken root in the fields on either side of the road. A few men were seduced off into these places, lured by the light of a naphtha flare, or the exaggerated announcements shouted out by a half-caste Negro showman. The bulk of the division however, got down into Warminster itself and flooded out the various cinema palaces.

Rain, soldiers, mud and poor lighting, gaudy-fronted cinemas with Charlie Chaplin posters, those are my impressions of Warminster. I went down several times whilst I was at Sutton Veney. I suppose even now it is still the same old thing. Now that our departure was imminent, I went down more frequently. It seemed to look a bit brighter somehow - brighter, I suppose, because we were leaving. Anyway, the vast congealed masses of soldiers on the road were brighter. They knew they were going, and that was all they wanted.

In a few days they left, and a finer division never went anywhere. About half of it was composed of Scottish regiments, so when the whole lot took to the road with their bands and pipes playing and skirling, the division presented as fine an assortment of British Army types as one could wish to see. The East was 'off', as the sun helmet episode had foreshadowed, and now it was to be France. On the day of departure I got my orders. I was not to go with them, as I had only been attached and did not belong to the division. Where was I to go? Back to the Isle of Wight they said. I could have 'cried my eyes out' as they say of children.

The Isle of Wight again! Oh help! I should have liked to have rushed into the headquarters and flung myself at the feet of the General, imploring him to stay this dread sentence. Instead of which I walked away amongst the huts and pondered on the advisability and possibility of stowing away in a machine-gun case, or a blanket wagon, and thus 'getting over'.

The Isle of Wight! The Isle of Wi . . . oh, curse the . . . no I won't say it again.

The division went.

So did I, and although I didn't know it at the time, I too was to be in France within three weeks. I sorrowfully trekked off back to the island, and rolled up to the red-brick barracks on the square again. Things hadn't changed much. Several officers had gone, others had come, and the Roll of Honour in the ante-room had grown a bit longer. Somehow I found the island was not now so objectionable as I had anticipated, and I couldn't make this out at the time. But I know what it was now. I was feeling better and my nerves were settling into a more placid condition. Sutton Veney had done me good. I had been a long time in getting right after my knockout at Ypres - far longer than I knew myself at the time. I became quite exuberant in the island on this tour, and took a lively and active part in a series of soldiers' 'gaffs' which were held in the barracks. Merry shows these were. You suddenly find on these occasions that quite half the regiment are comedians. When feeling particularly hilarious, I am 'induced to give a song', and when I do it always takes a comic turn. Red nose, bowler hat and umbrella effect, I find is about my mark when I'm roped into a soldiers' gaff. We were now having these convivial evenings about once a week and I was invariably to be found at them. Huge audiences crushed their way into the large gymnasium and sang the choruses through clouds of smoke.

Sometimes we took these shows over to one of the towns on the island, and one particular occasion I remember well was when we 'did a show' at Ryde. The proceeds were, of course, for charity, and at this entertainment my job was to draw lightning sketches on the stage, to be auctioned amongst the audience. Yes, I was altogether much brighter on my second return to the Isle of Wight.

Just when I was really thinking that, "Jove, this isn't half a bad place," I got orders to join a Works company and take them to Aldershot. It's a curious thing, that you always seem to like a place best when you know you've got to leave it. Join a Works company and go to Aldershot - that didn't sound particularly attractive. I went to influential quarters and tried to get a reprieve, but it was no good, I had to go.

The Works company was a sort of company used for doing odd jobs and 'dirty work' such as carrying uninteresting military objects from one place to another, clearing up mangled roads and being generally useful. Sort of scene-shifters and stage-carpenters to the army. They were non-combatants - they wouldn't have been able to be combatants if you'd paid 'em any amount. No doubt they had all fought splendidly in the Crimea, but I could see at a glance that they would never wield a battle-axe against Prussian militarism. Dear old chaps they were, but taking them to Aldershot caused me great anxiety. I managed to get to Southampton without losing any in the Solent, but when we arrived there we had unfortunately very little time to catch the train which left the station a long way from the docks. This brought on a sort of rout of the company down the main streets of Southampton - with all the appearance of 'Napoleon's retreat from Moscow', or a 'Chelsea Pensioners' hundred yards handicap at the annual sports'. It was a fearful rush, but thanks to the RTO (Rail Transport Officer), who kept the train back a little, we caught it, baggage and all, and glided off to Aldershot.

We arrived at Farnborough and apparently weren't in the least expected.

We waited about for a bit, hoping for someone to say something about us, but as nothing happened I lined the Old Guard up outside the station, stood them at ease, and went off to telephone in all directions to find out who would like a Works company. In a couple of hours I found out that the aerodrome at Farnborough wanted one. A lot of aerial goods had to be shifted. I took the company along to this place about a mile and a half away. Here, in a worn-out field, were a set of empty bell-tents. We collared the tents and the company collapsed inside them in batches of ten.

I went and reported the arrival of the company, found out what they were to do, when they had to start, and then set about arranging for their life there.

It was first of all necessary to see about rations for them, also plates and cups and knives and things. Here was a Works company, homeless and destitute as it were. Nobody knew, and nobody cared. We had nothing but a set of old bell-tents pitched in a squalid field of the sort that you generally find round a gas-works.

I went off that evening to Aldershot, and by visiting several offices, eventually obtained a permit to get camp equipment at a certain store. I and the driver of a motor-lorry I had got hold of spent a heated hour packing assorted bowls, plates, knives and forks into the lorry, and wrapping the lot up in straw. We then returned and tackled the local canteen for food. The outfit was now complete and the Works company was saved. That night I got an empty room in one of the huts at the aerostores, and rolling out my valise on the floor in the corner, went to sleep.

I awoke early, as the floorboards were somehow particularly hard in that hut. A valise on the ground is alright, but is mighty hard on floorboards. I lay awake, thinking and very fed up with my prospects now. I took another Gold Flake from the yellow packet always beside me and inhaled it as an antidote to my temper.

"Curse this aerodrome! Why can't I go to France? I wish I had gone with that division."

Later I rose and went on with my job of seeing to the welfare of the Works company.

Chapter 11

**THOSE AUTOGRAPH ALBUMS ~ FITS ~
A WIRE FROM WAR OFFICE ~ NEW APPOINTMENT**

For a couple of days I stuck pretty solidly to my Works company and my little wooden hut, as there was a lot to be done in getting the men's domestic affairs in order; also I wanted to grasp fully the 'ins' and 'outs' of the whole job myself, and to see what was required by the aerial potentates of the neighbourhood.

After a few days things straightened out, and I was then free to spend the evenings more or less as I liked. 'As I liked', of course, meant going off to Aldershot. I walked up the Farnborough road and in due course reached the Queen's Hotel. Many of my readers will know this 'resort of the élite'. I admit I am at times lured by a whisky and soda, but in this case I expected a letter or two as I had given the hotel as an address.

Not knowing the neighbourhood, it was a good central spot to call at.

I went in and up to the box-office.

"Any letters for me?" I asked.

The 'Sweet Maiden with a smile' (and a brooch made out of a second-lieutenant's metallic star culled from a 'British Warm') replied, "Are you Captain Bairnsfather?"

"Guilty, me lord."

The Sweet Maiden's smile widened, "Here are three letters for you, and I wonder if I dare ask you . . . but would you be awfully good and put something in my autograph album? Any little thing will do."

Smiling I replied, "Righto, with pleasure." False creature that I am, I don't say that this makes the five hundredth album I've seen, and that the sight of one more will make me commit some diabolical atrocity. I can't say that, as the owners of those five hundred albums would think me 'stuck up' and I should hate to be thought of as 'stuck up'.

So, I take the morocco-bound volume scented with Shem-el-Nessim, with the golden word 'Album' scrawled about its concave padded cover, and turn over the multi-coloured pages in the hopes of finding one on which it may be possible to make a rapid scribble. I held converse with the damsel and then had dinner. By easy stages I returned to my wooden hut, slipped myself into my canvas scabbard - my valise - and went to sleep.

Next morning, as usual, I emerged into the daylight and confronted my Works company. I found them standing in two ranks at a variety of angles and I proceeded to inspect them. I had to be careful whom I spoke to about dirty buttons, or no buttons at all in that group. I knew by rumour that at least one member of the party went in for having fits. I saw a fit in progress on one occasion, but owing to the crowd surrounding the patient I couldn't see what he was like, so I was never able to recognise him on parade. And I wasn't going to risk a strafe on buttons which might end in one member of the party flipping about on the ground like a landed trout; particularly in front of the Commander of the aerial stores.

I had hardly begun the parade, when an orderly approached from the main offices across the field and handed me a military telegram.

Having squirted out that time-honoured formula, "Carry on Sergeant-Major," I turned away to read the wire. I can't remember the exact wording, but it was very much to this effect:

'Captain Bairnsfather to proceed at once to join the Expeditionary Force, Staff Captain, Fourth Army Railheads.'

I nearly had a fit myself. My great wish had been granted. I was to go at once to France, and be amongst the real stuff once more. But what was all this about 'Staff Captain', and 'Fourth Army Railheads?'

All that was Greek to me. I felt frightened of the job. I knew the ordinary regimental Front, but this Staff Captain business was something quite different. However, I didn't worry about that; all I cared about was the fact that I was going out.

It's a curious feeling, this wanting to go back. Nobody could possibly want to go back to life in the trenches or to participate in an offensive, if one looks at it from that point of view alone. But it's because all your pals are out there at the Front, and all the people who really matter are at the Front; that's why you long to be one of them, and in with them, in the big job on hand. The satisfaction of feeling that you are in the real, live, and most important part of the war, is very great. The feeling that you are amongst all the gang who have the nasty part to do, and that you are accepted by them as one of the throng, is enormous.

But people must never be misled into thinking that just being 'out in France' is sufficient to produce this feeling of satisfaction. Oh dear no! You must have been either in the infantry or the flying corps. Infantry is the thing. You can take your hat off to anyone in any infantry battalion anywhere at the Front, to a distance of not more than two miles from the firing line. You can then be certain that you have saluted men who have gone to the hub of the show. Those are the chaps to be amongst.

That I was to go to France again was my one great joy, but I could see by the wire I was not going as I had done before. I was now a Staff Captain! No more sitting through long days and nights in waterlogged trenches with Bill, Bert and Alf. No more picking my way past the stiff and swollen cows at Dead Pig Farm, on my way to the ration dump. No more sandbag filling on rainy nights. I was both pleased and sorry - sounds curious, but it's true. I was pleased at the honour of being promoted to Staff Captain (vision of red tabs), but sorry that I should not be one of the 'jungle folk of the trenches', as I always used to call them.

However, I knew I should be right up close to the Front, and would see it all, and I was also glad to think that I should now be able to observe the war from a different and wider point of view. I was red-hot keen for going out, and forthwith began to set about making arrangements for handing over the Works company.

I left next day, and as the train slid out of the station I felt that now at last I was off to where this war life appealed to me most. The Isle of Wight, Salisbury Plain, Aldershot, all this was over. Now for France, Flanders and adventure.

A chaplain to the Forces that would have been welcome

Chapter 12

OVERSEAS ONCE MORE ~ OUR EVER-GROWING ARMY ~ TRAINS AND TRIBULATIONS ~ MY DESTINATION AT LAST

Being a rotten sailor I was relieved to find that I was to go out at the narrow end of the Channel; by the Folkestone-Boulogne route. By setting my teeth and staring intently at some object on deck, such as a lifebelt, or a deckchair, I can generally survive this passage, if the sea is calm. A Staff Captain with red tabs, and a red hat, leaning against the bulwarks like a gymkhana dummy, is lowering to oneself and encouraging to the enemy. I kept well, thank goodness, and staggered down the corrugated gangway at Boulogne in a most efficient manner. I have crossed to France about eight times so far in this war, and up to the time of writing this have drawn it lucky.

I walked down the wharf I knew so well, and on past the 'Hotel de Louvre' to the station. Near the AMLO's office (I don't know what that means, but countless thousands will know the place), I stumbled across a *'Fragment from France'* right away. A war-weary 'Bert' elated by prospects of going on leave, was approaching the docks. He had just asked the French porter some question. A torrent of explanatory French followed. Our Bert, weighed down by haversacks and equipment, stood stolidly listening and gazing intently at the porter. The verbal torrent ceased, and Bert slowly asked, "And 'ow does the chorus go?" A slight effect, but it amused me at the time, and making a mental note of the scene, I drew a picture of it later.

I got all my ticket business fixed up by the Railway Transport Officer (RTO) and found I had some time to wait for a train. I took a stroll through Boulogne. Very amusing it was to me. This was the place where I stopped for a day when I first came out to the war.

I mentally fought those days over again. But Boulogne was altered. Everywhere were the signs of the growing British army. Things were looking more settled and business-like. The primitive military arrangements which we had of necessity when the war broke out, were all gone. Once could feel that the ever-growing British army was 'digging itself in' and slowly but surely getting down to 'make a job of beating the Bounder Boche'. I lurked about the town for a bit and then returned to the 'Hotel de Louvre' and had a final meal before pushing off on the train in the Amiens direction.

All *good* trains in France seem to start in the evening, and you get to wherever you want to go some time the next morning.

I had never been to the battle area between Arras and Amiens before, as all my time previously had been put in between Ypres and Epinette (south of Armentières). This journey in a new direction was quite a novel experience to me. I found it just like all other wartime French journeys; twelve hours in an overcrowded first-class carriage with all the windows shut.

The RTO had grasped where I wanted ultimately to get to, and had made out one of those bilious-looking yellow forms entitling me to go to a place called Longpré. When I arrived there I was, possibly, to be met by a car. Longpré conveyed nothing to me, except that I knew it was somewhere down Amiens way.

An overcrowded train pushed off from Boulogne some time in the evening, and we drivelled about through Etaples and Abbeville all through the night. I have done a fair amount of travelling in France in wartime, but if you really want a good sample of a

boring journey, Boulogne to Amiens or vice versa is as good as any to experiment with. You leave Boulogne - late in all probability - and after gazing for about two hours at some grass-grown derelict railway siding just outside the station, the train moves on until you get a commanding view of a sodden cabbage patch in a fifteen-acre field, from which mammoth faded wooden hoardings regale you with allurements such as: *'Chocolat Menier'*, or *'The Heliopolis Hotel Cairo (close to the golf course)'*. These are varied with, *'The Lipton'*, or *'Heinz Pickles, 57 Different Varieties'*. You now move on another hundred yards in the twilight and come opposite a vast yellow board with faded and scabby chocolate-coloured lettering, exhorting you to take *'Dubonnet après le bain'*.

Sleep now overpowers you, and by means of balancing your head against the screwed-on ashtray in the 'Fumeur' carriage, you doze and finally slumber.

You awake with a start and remove your legs from the French major's lap, who is sleeping next to you and who, through continental politeness, has raised no objection to them being placed there. You rub your eyes and try to look out of the window. *Great scare!* "What time is it? Wonder how long I've been asleep; wonder if we've passed Longpré." Your watch tells you that you have been asleep for four hours. You rub the fog off the carriage window in panic.

"Great Scott! We may have passed Longpré and be at Amiens!!"

As you can't see through the foggy window you rise and open the one over the door. Some weed-overgrown lines and the sharp end of a low platform are visible, but not a soul is about.

Presently a figure looms out of the darkness and comes along the line at the side of the train. You don't know the French for "Is this Longpré?", so you blurt out, "Longpré Monsieur?" with as much interrogation about it as possible.

There comes an indignant answer from the figure on the line, "Non! Non! Non! Etaples!"

"Merci, Monsieur."

You collapse into the carriage.

"Etaples!! Ceasar's ghost! Etaples! Why that's the next station to Boulogne." Then you sleep again.

The train rattled and jolted its shameless way into Longpré at about eight o'clock in the morning, as far as I can remember.

Longpré is a ridiculously small place with an importance quite out of proportion to its size, owing to the war. It happens to be a junction.

I got out on to the line (there is never a platform near the train when it stops) and pulling out my meagre belongings after me deposited them on the track. There's something about the way a valise flops on to the grass-covered line that says, "Here you are now, and it's going to be a hell of a time before you go away again."

I wandered to the RTO's office, a small wooden hut complete with telephone and maps. I told him who I was and where I was going, a very nice chap he was too. He started off a telephone call to the place I was bound for, asking whether they would send a car or whether I should go on by train, and then he invited me to have some breakfast in his place, which was a small cottage about a hundred yards away.

I went with him when he had finished with that train and after an excellent breakfast kicked around the place until an answer rolled up on the 'phone. The answer, when it arrived, was pleasing. A car was being sent and would be there at three o'clock.

This was now the last lap of my journey. In a few hours I should start off for Montrelet, the place where I was to carry out my new job. The RTO had told me that Montrelet

"What the 'ell are you doin', spinnin' a web?"
"Nao! My puttee's undone, sargint."

was my headquarters, but beyond that he knew nothing, except that it was a very small village on the way to Doullens and that it was in my army area.

At three o'clock the car arrived, and bundling my valise and bag into it, I started off for Montrelet, which was to be my home for some little time to come.

Chapter 13

THE LAST LAP ~ A PEACEFUL SCENE ~ MEET MY COMMANDING OFFICER ~ A FRENCH BED

The car buzzed along the dusty country roads under the efficient guidance of an Army Service Corps (ASC) chauffeur and I surveyed the scenery at ease. It all struck me as so very, very different from the Ypres-Armentières sector. This was far more France, and consequently prettier. The little villages amongst the valleys and the wooded hills and streams all combined to give an entirely different tone to the war in this area.

I talked to the driver. Montrelet, I found, was a small village not far from Candas, which in turn was not far from Doullens. It was there that the present Army Administrative Commandant had fixed up his temporary abode. How long he was staying there the chauffeur didn't know. He, the chauffeur, had to drive about all over the army area and knew it all, so I soon got the hang of things. I gazed around me at the scenery; it was really quite nice. For the first time in the war I was able to get an idea of the country in which hostilities were being carried on. That's the advantage of a staff job. If you are bound for the trenches and a battalion life, your horizon is extremely limited. You go by night into the war zone, and your life from then onwards is cast amongst mangled estaminets, ruined villages and trenches. On a staff job, although you see all the mangled-up part, yet now and again you do catch sight of what the normal country looks like.

It is fairly hilly country about Montrelet and the road twisted about amongst valleys and in and out of woods, until at last we reached a pretty little village, with a few scattered cottages and an ancient church, and turned into a farmyard. Hens scattered hysterically in all directions, and the car pulled up at the farmhouse front door. The village was Montrelet, and this farmhouse was to be my billet. My things were carried in and, entering the house, I met a corporal in the hall. It appeared that the Colonel was out. He had to be out nearly all day and every day, but would be back in the evening. So I left my traps in a heap at the foot of the stairs and strolled out to look around. "This is a curious job I'm in now," I thought to myself. "How different from my last time out here! Fancy being able to live in a house like this!" For the house was certainly a good one. I have always thought that houses without the front torn out and a couple of holes in each gable end are much better than those possessing

that doubtful decoration. This was a real old square-built farmhouse with the farm sprawling round it on three sides and with a garden behind. Beyond the garden was a little old grey stone church which stood on the edge of a very large wood.

It was a beautiful evening in early summer, and the whole outfit was really very pretty and peaceful. I strolled about the garden and mused around the church and wood. It all struck me forcibly as beautiful, but sad. There was such an air of melancholy about this place, an effect produced, I think, by the close proximity of war to this scene without that proximity having disturbed the place or knocked it about. Here was normal, peaceful French village life. Only a few miles away were the trenches before Albert, with all the mangled-up desolation which surrounds them. Somehow I found that the village of Montrelet, on this summer evening, with its little cottages in the sunlit valley, its old grey church and the peaceful farmyard, had the effect of emphasising the pathos of this devastating war in a greater degree than many a ruined landscape that I had previously seen.

I returned to the farmhouse after my stroll around, and sat down to smoke in one of the front rooms. Quite a good room it was, with a lavish distribution of looking-glass in gilt frames, and a highly-coloured ornamental ceiling like the top of a Christmas cake.

Presently a car rolled into the yard and up to the door. The Colonel had returned. I felt, somehow, that he would be a terrifying person who would come into the hall and be heard saying, "Fee, fi, fo, fum, I smell the blood of an Englishman," or something on those lines; but he didn't. Instead, he walked into the room where I was and I introduced myself to him. He was as nice a Colonel as ever I have met. A Scotsman, in a Highland regiment. Discipline with understanding were his chief props, and he was a real good sort. I will always allude to him as 'the Colonel' after this, which saves me putting down his real name or inventing a false one (tricky fellows these authors you know).

It was about 7.30pm now, so it was dinner-time, and the Colonel's batman proceeded to get the meal ready. He disappeared into the room across the hall, and one could hear him working off crude French with a Scottish accent on to the people of the farm. A pretty considerable quantity of this farmload of soldiers were Scottish as I soon found out. The Colonel, his servant, and a party of soldiers billeted in a loft, completed the military outfit which came from the north of the Tweed. There were a couple of other fellows who could claim nothing more than Middlesex, Essex or Suffolk for their origin.

The dinner appeared and was spread on the table by Clark, the Colonel's man, who darted about the room in a kilt, full of timidity of the Colonel and a desire to please. We sat down to a plain but efficient meal, and the Colonel outlined the job that lay before me, after which we got to discussing things in general, including, of course, the war. The Colonel, I found, had been serving in many parts of the show where I myself had been, and had experienced all sorts of wild and strenuous times. We coincided, as regards knowledge of the Front, at Messines and Ypres, and I soon saw that he had had what the vulgar might term 'a skinful' of the Ypres Salient - so had I - and our conversation resulted in considerable mutual understanding. He had had a terrific overdose of Hooge, a spot I have never been to, but I can thoroughly guarantee that part of the line as a first-class sample of modern war.

For an hour or two we regaled each other with stories of trials, tribulations and grim jokes, in the manner that you will notice any two do who find that they both have known the same part of the Front, and we laughed a lot about it too. When one looks back on some of the pickles one has been in, they do seem funny. They are anything but amusing at the time, but everyone laughs at them after. I remember trying to smile in the middle of the second Ypres tornado, just to see whether my face *could* crack up into that facial contortion known as a grin. I was curious to see whether the death-charged and hateful atmosphere pervading the Salient had permanently stopped my capabilities in this direction. I tried to think of something to smile at. I looked around me as I lay in a fold of the ground under a machine-gun deluge and surveyed the scene, 'crumphs' exploding in all directions; every house with the roof off, or in the act of coming off and then I thought, "What a world! We build houses to live in and enjoy ourselves and have doctors to mend us as much as possible to prevent decease, and yet here we are; all trying to knock everything down and kill as hard as we can." I smiled at the incongruity. The Colonel and I aired these thoughts to each other that night and we smiled again.

I was to start on my job the next day. I knew nothing about it as yet, but I was to go with the Colonel in the morning to a railhead south of Albert and so I would pick up what I had to do. We sat and smoked a bit and then went to bed. It was a curious old place, this farmhouse, with good old-fashioned rooms. My bedroom overlooked the farmyard and contained two huge wooden beds with those canopy sort of structures sticking up at the pillow end from which curtains hang in regal festoons.

I had my valise and boxes dragged upstairs and by the light of a candle proceeded to 'dig myself in.' The chief ingredient of a French bed seems to be a nondescript sort of pillow-eiderdown-mattress; an enormous feather-stuffed cushion which is a mile too large for a pillow and not large enough for anything else. What you are supposed to do with it I don't know. You are nearly smothered if you use it as a pillow and your feet would be frozen if you used it as a counterpane. Each of the beds had one of these monstrosities and feather beds as well. I decided to be continental and risk it. I chose the bed nearest the window, sank out of sight into the feathers and pulled the other thing over the top of me; thus enveloped I went to sleep.

Chapter 14

MY NEW JOB ~ A TYPICAL DAY'S PROGRAMME ~ HOW '*FRAGMENTS*' ARE EVOLVED

I discovered in the morning that the Colonel maintained an office in the place. What had been a sort of jam and pickle storeroom had been given over to us, and in this I found the Colonel writing at one table by the window, whilst a youthful clerk encased in khaki was toiling at a tall sloping desk on which was strewn all the inevitable impedimenta of a military office. Blue forms, white forms, buff forms and buff 'slips', all were here. A gaudy assortment of coloured pencils and rubber stamps, files and OHMS (On His Majesty's Service) envelopes; in fact everything that can bring joy to the heart of a quartermaster-sergeant or an orderly-room clerk. Now I am sorry

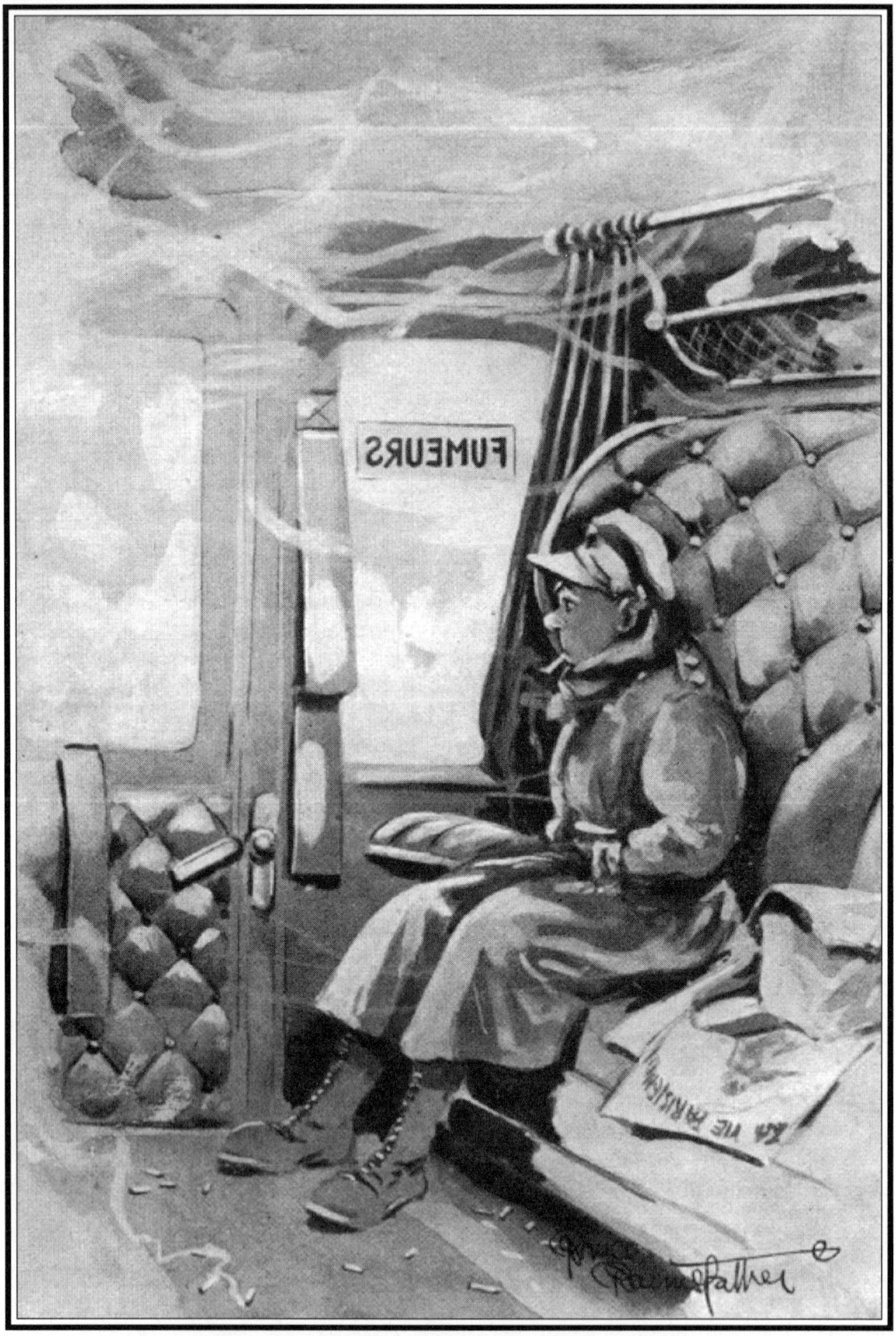

A Hopeless Dawn.
Just back off leave. Amiens is only 34 hours more in the train now.
You know that because you can see the Cathedral quite clearly.

to say I'm very poor at this sort of thing, in fact it might be said, I am rotten at it; so I saw at once that to stay efficiently in this new job of mine, without incurring the odium of British militarism, I should have to buckle to, and pump up as much knowledge and enthusiasm as possible over all these buff slips and indent forms.

The Colonel, it appeared, came down early and did a bit before breakfast, as he had to be out so much in the day, so I made a mental note, "I must do the same."

I turned over a variety of papers dealing with the work until breakfast was ready, and tried to get the hang of things. The Colonel at breakfast amplified my scanty knowledge by giving an outline of the job. It appeared that he was responsible for discipline on all the communications in the area, approximately between Doullens and Amiens. I was to be his Adjutant, as it were. Each army has an administrative commandant and each one of them has a staff officer.

Now, I do not want to be confused with the real staff officer. By real, I mean those on Corps, Divisional or Brigade staffs. They are all 'combatant' officers. My job was now on communications. I had gone from 'strafe' to 'staff' and this was as much staff as my physical ability at that time would permit. I was a staff officer right enough as per 'the book', but I never can consider anyone quite the real thing, quite the neat stuff, who is in any job other than the active strafing department. Of course, an army must have people behind it. If you took the ASC (Army Service Corps) away the army would be done in a week. Anyway this job was as much as I could do, and I soon found that it was going to provide me with a view of the war such as I had never had before.

After breakfast the Colonel ordered his car round and we both started off for one of the daily jobs. He had chosen Montrelet as his headquarters, as it was about central for the whole area he had to see to. This day we had about twenty miles to go, and this was my first view of the Somme country. A country shortly to be made famous by our mighty effort, 'The Battle of the Somme'.

It was very hot and dusty. The car buzzed along through long poplar-lined lanes, and in and out of ramshackle dusty villages. The Colonel, with a map spread on his knee, would every now and then shout instructions to the driver. Sometimes we were on a broad, white high road, passing a whole stream of giant motor-lorries taking supplies to the dumping grounds, and at other times going slowly through a billeting village crammed with dusty khaki-clothed soldiers resting from a spell in the trenches. As we neared the Front all the villages seemed to be hives of soldiery. The land seemed alive with men in khaki, and out in the fields vast groups of horses were tethered or limbers stacked in rows. There was dust and ponderous motor-traffic everywhere. Mile after mile we sped on through this varied scene, and now we were approaching the place we were making for - a certain railhead. What horrible, dry, dusty, uninteresting places railheads are, and how fearful it must be to be an RTO! Imagine a paltry French wayside station for a home. A railhead is a place where stuff of any description for the Front arrives and is subsequently taken over for distribution by motor-lorries and wagons.

The station selected may be small or large; it all depends on the position of the trench line in that area. If the station is small, then an army of assorted huts springs up around it, and in these lurk the individuals who operate the railhead. Presiding over this industrious scene is the RTO. He is usually selected from the ranks of those who have 'done their bit' and are only fit for something a bit milder than life in the trenches.

It all depends on the railhead as to what sort of a time this cove has. Some railheads have a frenzied hour's work a day, when everything seems to happen at once, after which there is nothing to do but take a pride in the dandelions on the siding, or get on with the latest E. Phillips Oppenheim sent out from home. Other railheads never leave off being a pandemonium day and night. Six howitzers arrive from the Sinai Peninsula at four o'clock in the morning, or an Army Corps of Portuguese Infantry are passing through and have to change at midnight.

The railhead we visited the morning I write about was a cross between the two. There was a good bit of ammunition work to see to there, and that is a more regular sort of occupation. We stopped the car by a goods shed and the Colonel and I got out. The Colonel was monarch of all railheads; they were one of the units under his command. I trailed along beside him, absorbing the scene and trying to learn the job for the future.

I looked around at the huts and the station. A face, distorted by the hate of many inquisitive interruptions, suddenly appeared at a window and hastily disappeared again. I guessed it was the RTO, and I was right. The door of the hut opened and this potentate came out. We now, all three, had to evince an interest in the deadly dull details of the railhead. I have, of course, percolated through a host of railheads, so I will only describe, not an individual, but a typical one.

A railhead nearly always gives you the impression that it is a station which the railway company have been disappointed with, and have readily given away to the military authorities. It mostly consists of apparently inconsequent sidings, no platforms and a row of uninteresting huts. It appears to be always a kind of derelict terminus in a forty-acre field. When it's not raining all day this enthralling scene is enveloped in an opaque cloud of dust. The occupation of the inhabitants, moreover, is most inartistic, and soul-destroying. Counting rusty truck-loads of howitzers, or tins of jam; anxiously regarding a prodigious quantity of fifteen-inch shells and wondering when they can be got rid of; those are the daily joys and sorrows of the RTO and his assistants. Added to these activities, he of course worries over an interminable correspondence which he finds on many coloured forms (chiefly buff and white) which come floating in to him from all parts of France and from every angle imaginable; i.e. *'We have as yet received no news of the trench mortar dispatched from Khartoum and last seen at Abbeville,'* or, *'Re your indent for a drinking trough for sparrows at your railhead. Please state size.'*

The Colonel, the RTO and myself, all three fully conscious of these dull and uninteresting shortcomings, but determined to serve our King and country, wandered round the railhead. The three parts played by the Colonel, the RTO and myself were as follows: the Colonel, to summon as much mailed fist and military severity as possible, and to frame cunning, terrifying questions to the RTO on the details of his work; the RTO, to attractively walk alongside the Colonel and be ready with a plausible answer - with a substratum of truth - for everything; occasionally volunteering to show something which he had previously ascertained was in perfect order; myself: to walk along looking as clever as possible and refrain from letting the least sign leak out that I knew less than either about the job. And so these visits proceeded, week after week, and after each inspection the Colonel and I would return across the miles of that sad, bleak country, back to our headquarters at Montrelet. During this time I employed all my leisure drawing further *'Fragments from France'*. How little people knew where the jokes that appeared week after week in *The Bystander* were made, and how! It somehow pained me, when I knew the result spelt laughter, to think how often the idea had come to me through the infinite sadness of the Somme valley. In

the evenings I have often wandered around a mutilated little village, and gone off by myself to inspect the deserted and partially smashed church, or the silent weed-grown courtyard of an old farm, and have sat and reflected on the whole monstrous conflict, and as often as not with that same feeling that prompted me to smile during the Second Battle of Ypres. I have smiled here, and thought of a ridiculous and amusing situation - amusing to those who know, because it was founded on truthful pain, but merely light comedy to those who don't and can't know.

I have now emerged from the war, and look back on a vast sea of episodes and curious incidents, but nothing strikes me more forcibly than the various and extraordinary places in which I have drawn my pictures. In weird, safe, dangerous and unique spots, which range from the North Sea to Goritzia and the Austrian Alps.

But more of that anon . . .

Chapter 15

DIVERSIONS IN AMIENS ~ HOTEL DU RHIN ~ A CLEAR PERSPECTIVE ~ AN EXTENDED INSPECTION TOUR ~ BIRTHPLACE OF 'OLD BILL'

For many, many weeks this job went on, full of a variety of small incidents, good, bad and indifferent. I got to know my work and continued to persevere with life in that peculiar resigned, but optimistically determined fashion which is common to all the component parts of the Allied armies in the field. I liked the job, I liked those I lived with and those I met. Now and again we went into Amiens, and this was always a great event for us. Something like market-day to a farmer, who lives a crowded rural life ten miles from a station and drives a consumptive horse in once a week to the nearest apology for a town.

Whenever the Colonel had to visit a railhead near Ameins he went there either before or after his inspection, and you can bet I was always on for being in that expedition. I am glad I saw Amiens in those days, because I saw it afterwards and I can feel for the inhabitants in that terrible trial which befell the city during the last big dying flicker of the Prussian push.

Amiens was about fifteen miles from our headquarters, but it was well worth the trouble of getting there. Montrelet was very nice and picturesque and all that, but I confess I like a bit of crowded humanity and sparkle now and again. Not that one got much in Amiens, but still, it was better than nothing. We used to go there after a devastating and dry visit to Longeau or Heilly, or some miserable oasis near by. The great thing was to lunch somewhere. If anybody ever reads this book he is almost sure to have a gladiator relation or friend who has been to Amiens and has had a lunch at one of the restaurants or at the 'Hotel du Rhin'. All my pals seem to have drifted in to the 'Hotel du Rhin' - in fact if I come across an old sport who knows the Front I succulently murmur something about the 'Hotel du Rhin' and it at once conveys visions to his feverish mind of the gladdest nights that were then permissible.

How many, many of those wonderful, courageous chaps have wandered in to Amiens and had what was to them the best of fun - a lunch in Amiens - and then gone back to their squadron, battalion or platoon, never to return. The buccaneering romance of this is enormous, and sad. Well, anyway, we used to go to Amiens, and in a crowded, frowsy restaurant down one of the main streets, we would lunch, and revel in the joys of fried fish, mysterious meat and red wine.

It was a dear old town, and to see the Cathedral with a pyramid of sandbags at the front door makes one very annoyed at these perpendicular-haired gentlemen who have elected to disturb the world so violently.

And so the weeks went on. Work and travel, evenings full of war gossip and rumours of great events to come, now and again punctuated by these visits to Amiens. I went on with it all, but slowly, and bit by bit, the whole environment was reducing me to a very low ebb. Those who read may wonder why - and possibly those who read may never understand - but to me, the sum total of the 'idea' and real horrible reality of this terrible, elementary and brutal war was burning a hole in my mind and system which time can never heal. Somehow, when I sat in that dreadful death-charged mud, I felt it less, but here - outside and behind it - I got a clear perspective of the frightfulness of the thing. It's not the actual danger or the death and sorrow, it's the idea of this drastic antagonism of humanity, separated by merely national aims.

But why should I bore or wound people with these thoughts of mine? I will return to the real great and inspiring idea of war; bright uniforms, heroic victories, medals and cheering multitudes. I write these lines as our mighty and wonderful nation, with the assistance of others, has just reached the glorious and hard-fought conclusion which was vitally necessary. I have only digressed for a few moments in order not to forget the amazing wonder of those simple valorous souls who, as component parts, did things the greatness of which few realise and none can grasp, things which in their country- and home-loving way (although submerged owing to their smallness) are mightier than the war itself.

There came a time at Montrelet when it became necessary for the Colonel to wander further afield. There was a tendency for journeys to be taken north of Doullens. I welcomed this, and was still further elated when one morning he announced that he had to go right up north, to Ypres in fact. This was splendid, I was more than keen to see once more the old stamping ground of Amentières, Bailleul, Locre and Ypres, for they were all places with a big fascination for me.

The day came when we started out. The Colonel, the driver and myself slid off in a large car and were soon rolling along the winding, dusty road from Montrelet. It's a great game, being able to go about the Front in a car, you can loll back amongst the upholstery and calmly survey the ruins as they flash past you, now and again having the satisfaction of being accidentally mistaken for a general, as some dust-covered pedestrian catches sight of you as you flit past. When one really has acquired that 'limousine loll' it's a great sensation. Beats sitting in a frozen dugout with 'stand to' at 4.00am, beats it hollow I can tell you. We went through a vast mass of dull, blackened country and wound our way over the cobbled streets of innumerable small towns and villages, now and again stopping to try and reconcile an unintelligible signpost with the road on our map,

or listening to the still more unintelligible explanations and directions of some Frenchman, from whom, in a weak moment, we had asked the way.

Anyway, on we went, and bit by bit approached that mystic and romantic area known as the Ypres-Armentières sector. As I began to recognise the once familiar landmarks the whole of the old-time war atmosphere came back with clear vigour. Here were the roads I knew so well, the broken houses, shelled-out woods, etc. Here was the land of *'Bullets & Billets'* - that weird country which holds in its keeping a certain dank and mysterious horror, 'Plugstreet Wood', the birthplace of 'Old Bill'.

Chapter 16

THE OLD FIGHTING GROUNDS ~ SOMETHING WRONG ~ HOSPITAL IN BAILLEUL ~ HOMESICKNESS

We arrived at Bailleul. In those days it was still a respectable and reasonable town. In fact, it was much the same as when I had been there before. A few more restaurants and officers' clubs had sprung up, but that was all. It had not been much shelled. Of course it occasionally had to go through an air-raid or something of that sort, but on the whole it was still quite a presentable spot. We didn't stop, but went straight on to the Colonel's destination, which was Locre. It was here that a certain division had its headquarters and it was here that the Colonel had someone he particularly wanted to see. Locre is a nasty spot, becoming nastier still towards the end of the war; but at this period, and even before, it was charged with a most unpleasant atmosphere; air-raids, and back-area shelling were its specialities. I remember disliking this spot intensely when I spent the night with my machine-gun section in its unwholesome surroundings on the night before the Second Battle of Ypres; but now I found myself disliking it still more. The place looked horribly mutilated and dismal. The Colonel went to a headquarters - I waited outside. As he was going to be some time, I went to have a look at the various parts of the place I knew. I went to the large church there, and entered. It was here that I had billeted on that turbulent night, the 23rd April 1915, and had stabled my machine-gun section by means of piling up some pews and chairs around the part where the organ is fixed. It was from this place that, at dawn, we had all moved off to Vlamertinghe, the day before that scrap in front of St Julien.

Outside the church several long rows of crosses (new ones were being added daily) testified to the severity of holding that part of the line. Later on I joined the Colonel, who asked me to come with him to a house where a certain staff was located. I went, and there had the honour of meeting Colonel Congreve, the famous and valorous son of the equally famous General of that name. Congreve was perhaps one of the most wonderful and courageous characters in the war. With a row of decorations, earned during the war, he was one of the youngest senior staff officers in the army. An unaffected, courtly young man, with a lion's courage (shortly after this he was killed on the Somme).

While sitting in this office I noticed that I was feeling very quaint. This wasn't due to the office, for I had suspected, whilst coming along in the car, that I was not very well. I remember feeling astonishingly bad as I left that office and, waiting by the car outside, I realised I was feeling worse every moment, and a fearful pain had started at the back

"Look out, Bill, you're sittin' on a wasp's nest!"

of my neck. Feeling for the cause of this disorder, I found a nasty sort of swelling below the hair at the back of my head. It was most annoying just when I wanted to be going strong for my visit to the Salient. "What the devil is it?" I wondered to myself.

However, I didn't say anything, and we all went off to see a battalion headquarters near Kemmel. My! But I did feel bad, and got worse every minute. I can scarcely remember that old farm we went into - near the front-line trenches. I can dimly recollect a hospitable but drastically plain lunch, a crowd of officers and seeing a lot of my cartoons torn from the papers and pinned up on the dilapidated walls. I don't know how I pulled through that meal.

Somehow we eventually got back to Bailleul and, not being able to stick the pain any longer, I told the Colonel that I had symptoms of an obscure and unattractive kind, and that I thought I was going to be ill. He immediately said he thought I ought to see a doctor in Bailleul. He was right; for by the time we reached Bailleul I felt like a dead fly in a cream jug. They took me to a hospital (a converted convent or monastery or something) and there I waited in a collapsed heap on a form till my turn came for inspection.

At last a doctor came and examined me with evident suspicion. "Very feverish," was the verdict, "with a carbuncle on the back of his neck."

If you look up the word carbuncle in a reasonable dictionary you will see that it means; 'A beautiful gem of a deep-red colour' or 'A painful and highly inflamed tumour.' I had the latter - in fact I had, I think, a mixture of the two, something that might be described as, 'A gem of a highly inflamed tumour, of a beautiful deep-red colour.'

I felt rotten. They gave me some medicine and said I must go to a clearing station (a field hospital). Here was a disaster! Me, ill! Got to leave my job and be sent to hospital, what a blow! I knew this would mean weeks, and heaven knows what might happen after that. However, there it was, and as by now I was feeling thoroughly ill, I resigned myself to my fate. I spent the night in a bunk at the Bailleul hospital.

This was my second time of collapsed removal from the Salient - which was evidently an unsuitable place for me. My first exit was after that little affair I had with a shell near St Julien. The second, this infernal carbuncle. But how unheroic this second exit! To have to leave the Ypres Salient owing to a carbuncle on the back of the neck is to my mind one of the most degraded forms of heroism. There are worse places than the back of the neck to have carbuncles. I found that out most painfully later, whilst languishing on the Italian alpine Front; but I will come to that in time.

Next morning I was taken in an ambulance from the monastic Bailleul hospital, off along the dusty, dreary roads, down to the old sector around Doullens, and as I was carted along I dwelt with some sadness and depression on my bad fortune. Here was the end of my first staff job. I somehow felt that, once inside the hospital, I should lose all the ground I had gained and return, when repaired, to my same old life - that of a regimental captain. Visions of interminable months of trenches, billets and ordering people to carry corrugated iron, floorboards or something . . . Well, anyway, here I was now, a Staff Captain, complete with carbuncle, turning in at the gates of a beautiful château which at that time had just been converted into a hospital.

The ambulance stopped at the front door. I got out and entered. In half an hour I was in a suit of pyjamas (giant's size) and lying on an iron bed by a window. One of the hospital doctors was coming to see me shortly. I lay and pondered. I thought of the farm at Montrelet. I thought of the Colonel. What would happen now? Would I return there when I was well again, or not?

Outside the sun was shining in the beautiful grounds of the beautiful chateau. On the spacious lawn several nurses were walking about - those who at the moment were off duty. Several officers were out there too, convalescents and others. At the far end of the lawn, under the shade of a clump of lofty trees, a regimental band was assembling. The scene was one of delightful summer calm.

"What band is that?" I asked.

Somebody answered me through the window, "The Royal Warwickshire Regiment."

That was my own regiment, and as I lay there they started up the Warwickshire march. Warwickshire is my county and I love everything belonging to it.

I don't know why - perhaps because I was ill - but that tune, floating across that sunny, tranquil lawn, made me nearly cry with an intense love and longing for England.

Chapter 17

EVACUATED TO BASE ~ MONASTIC SECLUSION ~ A NICE OLD TOWN ~ RETURN TO LONDON ~ CONVALESCENCE

The doctor came and examined me. He did a few conjuring tricks with that half golf ball at the back of my neck and gave me things to take. I read, and thought, and slept, and incidentally, felt very ill. Time went on, and after a week I appeared to be no better. I was apparently very 'run down'.

After ten days there the doctor who watched me came and said that any idea of my going back to Montrelet was 'off' and that I must be 'evacuated to the base'.

'That's done it,' I thought; but I little knew that that moment was the turning-point in the whole of my war career, and that I was soon to find myself in a position which I had never dreamt of.

What I took to be an unfortunate termination to my staff career was in reality the first premonitory sign of being wafted into a job which was the only one of its kind in the army. I didn't know it then, and with a depressed spirit I went off with a gang of others, all correctly labelled with our various complaints, down to the base. You never could say what base it was going to be, or what hospital there. Those mysterious labels they tie on you may convey a wealth of meaning to the medical authorities, but nothing to yourself.

After the usual form of train journey (I refer to the sixty-miles-with-sixty-hours-to-do-it-in variety) we arrived at Rouen, and were split up into several different groups and sent in ambulances to the various hospitals. I went to a fine big one on the hill above the town. This one, again, was a trifle ecclesiastical; it had been, I think, a sort of incubator for would-be monks. These hermits had all been roped in for service with the French Army, and the building was rented at a preposterous figure by the British authorities for use as a base hospital. It was a fine hospital too, with platoons of nurses and VADs (Volunteer Aid Detachments), doctors and the whole outfit.

I was put into a room by myself. That sounds very grand, but in reality it was a sort of cubicle in a long corridor. There were open wards there as well, but a lot of us were kept in the cubicles. I imagine these box-like creations were, in ordinary times, used by the budding monks - they were austere enough for anything! One almost wanted to get up twice a night to scourge oneself so as to complete the picture.

In this harbour of refuge they were all very good to me. The doctors said I was very run down and must rest quietly. There was really no physical reason for this, but I have had such miserable times with my state of mind and imagination about the war that it is difficult for me to explain to others what a terrible ordeal it can be. There is no reason why one should not attempt to explain this phenomenon. It is simply this: there are types of men who can go to a war such as this and only see its practical and physical side. Such a man, on returning home, will say, "It was terrible at Ypres!" Somebody will ask, "Why?" And he will then explain that the mud was something awful, and that they had to be up all night in pouring rain, and never had a wink of sleep. Moreover, the ceaseless shelling necessitated them working on the trenches every day. I envy that man. For I know there are others, like myself, to whom all that, though objectionable, is not the worst feature. It's the horrible *idea* of the thing - the sudden reduction in the value placed on human life. The thoughts on the devastating pain and sorrow caused away back at home at each casualty. The precarious conditions regarding the mode of burial, which all depend on the local conditions prevailing at the time. These thoughts, and a host of others, make such a mess of one that physical ills are nothing compared to them.

I would, in fact, sum it up thus; that the pain and devastation to the individual is directly proportional to the amount of imagination that individual possesses. The most suitable man for a war is a butcher, whilst the most unsuitable is a poet.

And so it was that I was ill and run down. But thanks to an inherited juvenile spirit, I can permanently camouflage a lot of troubles, come up to the surface and drink in the joys of life. Under the soothing influences of kind-hearted nurses, aided by succulent substantial assets,

such as chicken and occasional champagne, I slowly recuperated in my cubicle, and in a few days began to look back on past events and ache for pencils, paints and paper. I got these, and dived off into a volume of scribbles, sketches and jokes on a host of topics which ironically amused me. If ever that monk goes back to that cubicle of his, he's going to find a fine mess on the walls for I perpetrated a series of most worldly drawings on the sides of his ethereal cell.

I added enormously to the already nauseating number of autograph albums which I have from time to time scribbled in. Later on I was better still and went out. The medical officers very kindly invited me to their mess. I disgraced their walls with further efforts, and later still I reached that state of physical fitness which entitled me to go outside the grounds and roam around the town. I wasn't long in taking advantage of this and daily went for a couple of hours off into Rouen. It's a nice old town, and was very pleasing in those summer days. I examined it all thoroughly. I sat in cafés and amused myself as I always do with Pelmanizing the place and the people. I wandered around and observed the life of the place.

Rouen had been swooped down upon by the British army and had become a large military base. This, of course, leads to a lot of 'back to front' departments. 'Brass hats' shone all over the place. The 'Hotel de la Poste' fairly glittered with them. Some of them were ex-gladiators from the front, and others, who had only heard about the Front through the papers or from their friends. It was a merry town.

So the time passed. I was better, but again the Medical Board at the hospital decided that I ought not to return to the Front. Now this showed me a new and painful difficulty. I knew that if sent to England, by the approved rules of the game, this would automatically cause me to be struck off the lists of the BEF (British Expeditionary Force), and I should be put back in the home forces. More depression and forebodings ensued.

However, I am very fatalistic, and I curled up mentally in order to await the day which I knew was coming, i.e. to have a label tied on my tunic directing me to England. At last it came and I left that kind, hospitable Red Cross monastery and was shipped with a crowd of others for England. We all went on the *Asturias*, which most people will remember was subsequently torpedoed. The boat was crowded, almost entirely with wounded returning from the battle of the Somme, that great and glorious conflict which cost us so much.

I had a bunk in a crowded ward on the ship, and we all were very cheerful. A hospital boat returning to England contains an astonishing amount of cheer and brightness. The idea in every man's mind that he is being taken by Englishmen back to England, and the visions that he sees of dear old Blighty, are enough to make them cheerful. It's the best tonic I know.

A chap with an arm in a sling and with all his clothes torn to ribbons would be sitting on the side of a bed smoking a 'stinker' and recounting, laughingly, exactly how they all got held up on the barbed-wire in front of a Boche machine gun.

His companion would follow up this story with a grouse that his 'push' had all been north of the battle, and he'd " . . . heard all the row goin' on, but hadn't had a look-in."

That's the stuff to give 'em.

When the *Asturias* reached Southampton we were all put into ambulance trains and sent to various parts of the country. My lot was London. At midnight I and a few others were removed from the station by motors and taken to a hospital, but with the strange coincidence, in my case, that it was the same hospital which had received me after my blowing-up at Ypres.

I entered that hospital at Camberwell and when I left, cured, it was to start on the most extraordinary part of my war life, viz., my tours round all the Fronts. Before the end of the war I was to see the Fronts from the North Sea to the Adriatic and the backs of the Fronts from Rome to New York; and so I began another chapter.

Chapter 18

SICK LEAVE ~ SUMMONED TO WAR OFFICE ~ AMAZING INTERVIEW ~ A UNIQUE JOB

In due course I was better, and after going before a Medical Board I was given sick leave. I then went home and wondered about the future. It was "Good-bye, Montrelet!" I knew that, but what would be my next job? Back in the old 'apple and plum,' I supposed.

I spent two weeks amongst the leafy calm of Warwickshire, getting better every day. In a few days now I should have my final Medical Board and then report at the headquarters of my Battalion Reserve Depot. The days slid on and I was just about to go through the above formula when the blow fell, or the squib exploded, or whatever you like to call it. I awoke one morning to find, amongst other letters, a long envelope with OHMS (On His Majesty's Service) on the cover.

I was summoned to London, to the War Office!

Now, my feeling about the War Office is almost identical with that I had at school when requested to visit the headmaster's study after 'prep' with a view to being caned. I don't know why, but perhaps it's that wonderful and unique chill which one associates with long unfurnished stone corridors.

The War Office is well worth a visit to those who haven't been there. It is a vast pile with an intricate labyrinth of long, dull-coloured corridors, something like entering the Great Pyramid at Giza - one almost expects to find the mummified corpse of a king when one gets to the centre. You feel that somewhere in the middle there must be some vast and highly-coloured potentate - maybe a super-general - who is, perhaps, dead in a sarcophagus, or even alive like a queen bee; but anyway, one who is guarded by a host of officials, minor satellites and girl guides. You, of course, never get near or see this personage; you merely feel the gloom and awe which his presence creates. I haven't been to the War Office very often, but I have never lost this sensation.

You enter the building and fill in a form. In time you are boisterously told by a Boer War veteran to "follow the girl." The girl, a guide of sorts in a dark brown engineer's overall, sets off sullenly down a cement passage with a group of assorted officers pursuing her. She, I fancy, revels in the intricacies of these stone catacombs. Having apparently described a complete parallelogram by means of walking round the edifice in a forbidding-looking corridor, you suddenly come upon a lift. It is always disappearing upwards when you arrive, so the whole group silently waits for its return. It comes down suddenly and disgorges an assorted crowd, when, headed by the girl guide, you enter and are taken up. Now we all repeat the corridor and parallelogram business again; only this time you have to abandon trying to realise where you are. Nothing but the girl guide can save you now. Lost in the War Office! How awful that would be!

I can imagine a visitor, having lagged behind the guide a bit, suddenly realising that he was lost. How he would vainly beat on those stone walls and scream for help - how his skeleton would be found by a typist, weeks later, in an attitude which evidently showed that he had succumbed while endeavouring to gnaw his way through a door.

I followed the guide, and after being handed to several officials whose job it is to take you to other officials, at last came up with *the* official whose duty it was to prevent, if possible, anyone seeing the officer who had summoned me by letter from my rural retreat. The official took my form and reverently asked me to "wait a minute." He then disappeared through a door ten feet high and five feet wide, closing it behind him.

I now sat on a chair and idly listened to the suburban gossip of a couple of typists, which floated out from behind a couple of screens.

"Have you been to *Chu Chin Chow,* dear?"

"No, darling, I was going but something happened, I don't know what. Harold told me he had seen you there."

A sudden rattling burst of typewriting indicates that another monstrous door has opened down the passage and a staff officer has come out. He passes the typists and me carrying an armful of buff-coloured papers, then all is still again.

My door opens. The official comes out. He beckons me in. I go in. I am in. I hear the ponderous door close softly behind and I am now face to face with the occupants of the room.

The interview was brief, but to the point. I was complimented on the effect of my pictures. I was told that the War Office would not only like me to continue as I pleased with my ordinary cartoons, but that I was to be placed in the Intelligence Department, to be used, pictorially, for certain work which they wanted done. They then hinted that in the near future they might require me to visit the French and Italian armies, and to produce similar work to that which, during many months, had grown out of the mud, as it were, of the British front line. I was then told of certain work to get on with immediately, and was initiated into a lot of details dealing with the Intelligence Department.

I left the War Office as an official and fully-licensed humorous cartoonist, and continued in that capacity up to the end of the war.

I left Whitehall and nearly ran down the street outside, I was so bucked. I went into the 'Old Ship', a restaurant which you will find nearly opposite Cox's bank. Here, with a cup of coffee and a Gold Flake, I sat and thought it all over. I looked back at the start of it all. Back into those dank dark days of early 1914, when I, as a very poor and submerged second-lieutenant, slushed around the Messines mud, and at night drew my first sketches by the light of a candle-end, stuck on an empty tin, whilst keeping myself warm by the heat of a fire-bucket.

'From that to this,' I thought, and smiled with sadness as I recollected the various ups and downs and trials of those early days. Here I was now, attached to the Intelligence Department of the War Office!

"The War Office like my drawings!" Overcome with pride I paid my bill and went across the road to draw as much as I could out of that one pound nineteen and elevenpence that still remained to my credit at Cox's.

Chapter 19

OFF TO FRENCH FRONT ~ LONELINESS IN PARIS ~ FOLIES BERGERES

Now I want to ask all readers of this book to exonerate me from any charge of egoism. I feel that many will be interested to hear exactly all about what my job as a cartoonist was like, and how and where the pictures were drawn; also, it is necessary for me to give a general idea of the results of the pictures and a variety of personal details, if I am to explain fully. The vast mass of letters that I have received from all over the world has emboldened me to put as much as I can of the personal note into these pages. I have felt there are so many who would like to know the 'inside' of *'Fragments from all Fronts'* that I am going to describe the actual work in connection with my drawings, as well as the geographical adventures which led to them.

My first return to the Continent after the events related in the last chapter was to the French Army. The French Army Intelligence Department applied for me to be sent to their Front, to live amongst the troops there and to bring out pictorially, and in my own way, a series of cartoons. At the time this came about as an order; my pictures in *The Bystander* had been bound into several books under the title of *'Fragments from France'*, and had had an enormous circulation. The French papers had commented on them, and ultimately the application which I have mentioned above occurred.

I went to the War Office and having received my pass and certain papers, I set off for France. A large and complicated paper had been given to me amongst the others, which told me of the number of a certain corps in the French army to which I had to report. It said nothing about the part of the line where I should find this corps; but somehow or other I got it into my head that this particular corps lurked about somewhere near Rheims or Soissons.

After a suffocating all-night journey, following a nauseating passage to Boulogne, I arrived at the Gare du Nord in Paris, where I reported to the French Provost Marshal's headquarters. I was shown into an office where a very courtly French Colonel explained most politely and gently to me that the corps in question was near Rosendael.

"And where is that?" I asked.

He turned to a large map and pointed a finger practically at Ostend.

"Heavens! Near Ostend! And here have I come all the way down to Paris!" I had a

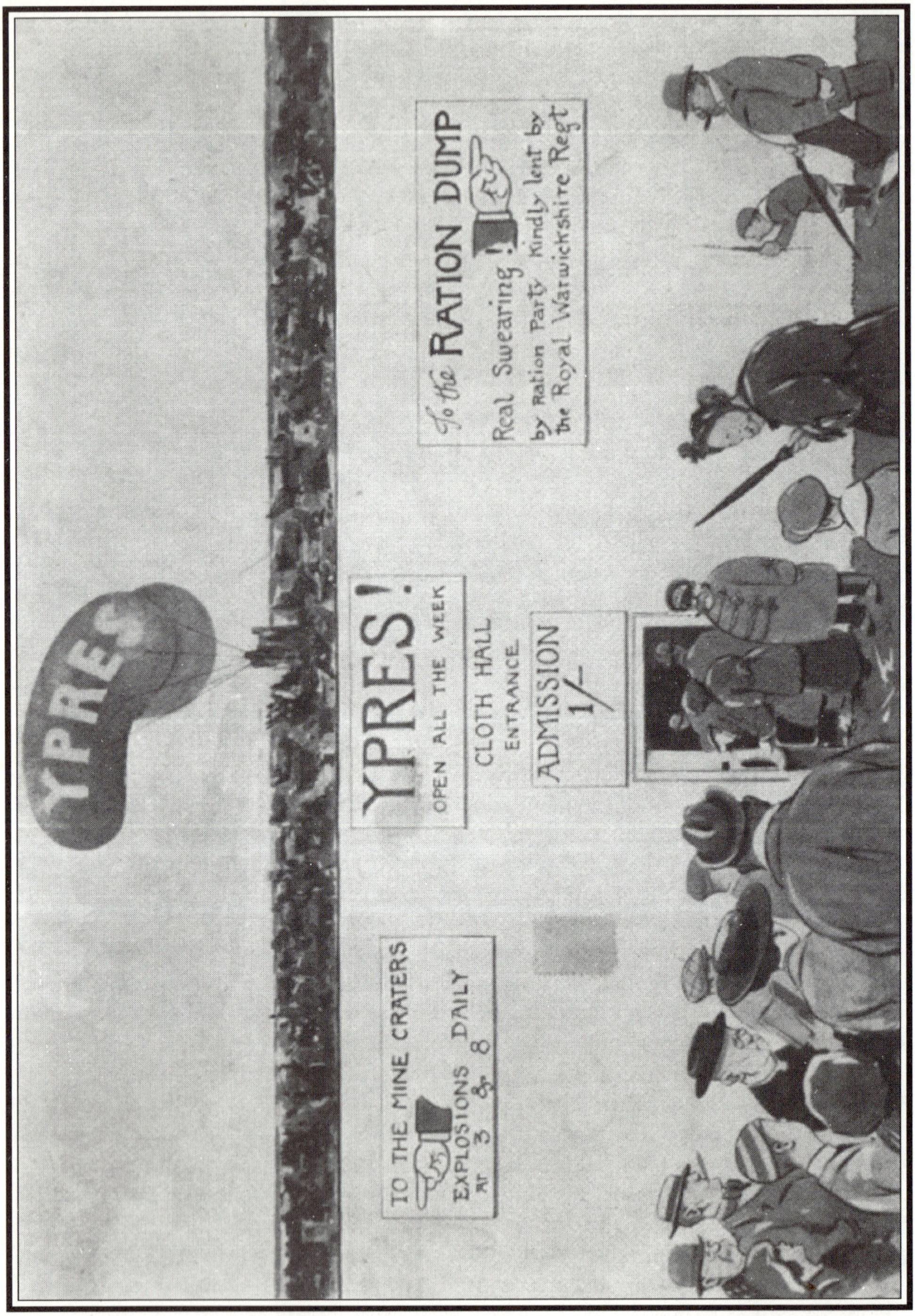

A prophecy . . . but I won't guarantee Old Bill taking the commissionaire's job.

vision of another long, suffocating journey with a suitcase, almost back to where I had started from. I thanked the Colonel and returned to the station to find out the trains for the next morning. I really couldn't get into a train again that night.

"I'll stay the night in one of these pubs here," I thought to myself, and, acting on this impulse, selected the 'Hotel Terminus du Nord', which faced the station.

Mine was to be a lonely job. During all my wanderings from this date on, I was cast for long, solitary train journeys and nights in various hotels, estaminets and billets, all on my own. Here I was now in Paris, just about to have a sample of the kind of evening I have had so many of.

I went that night to the Boulevards and wandered around. I sat in several cafés, always with my notebook and pencil, and watched the cosmopolitan and semi-military crowd as it moved in an apparently endless stream down the Boulevard des Italiens. It was late autumn, and the interior of the cafés were crowded. Looking out from the brightly lighted interior the street seemed to be a joyous mass of humanity, all forever moving onward. I sat back on the frowsy seats, and with a sheet of paper and a drink on the marble-topped table in front, followed my customary habit of weaving pictures in the tobacco smoke around.

Later I went to the 'Café de Madrid' and had dinner. Tomorrow I was starting for Rosendael and the Front.

After dinner, shunning the dull quiet of the 'Hotel Terminus du Nord', I decided to go to a show somewhere, and soon concluded that what would be about my mark would be the 'Folies Bergères'. So off I went, and after the usual robbery at the entrance, roamed around the palm court, listened to the band and with the aid of a whisky and soda, watched the fountains squirting water out into the smoke-laden atmosphere. What a mass of women they have in that place, somehow! Gaudy, doubtful women, fountains and lazy bands form a very curious background to that Front which, not so many miles away, is dealing exclusively in death, toil and devastation.

But here it was; all going strong. "Eat, drink and be merry, for tomorrow somebody else dies."

There was some show going on on the stage, but as I can't understand a word of French at the speed the natives talk it, I contented myself with absorbing the sights of the palm court. Having sat in the palm court at the 'Folies Bergères' and in kindred theatres a score of times, I have come to the conclusion that there are other dangers beside the trenches. This fancy (it's probably only a stupid hallucination of mine) I have recorded in the shape of a drawing which you will find in one of my books of *'Fragments'*, namely, *"Come on Bert, it's safer in the trenches!"*

I left before the end of the show, and walked back to the hotel. Having overhauled my baggage and told the swarthy rogue of a Boots to call me in the morning, I went to bed, and recuperated for my journey to Rosendael in the morning.

All this herbage - and then perhaps only a second-lieutenant!

Chapter 20

WHERE WIRE MEETS SEA ~ CRACKED COXYDE ~ CORDIAL RECEPTION ~ CHILLY QUARTERS

Rosendael is a paltry, unattractive little town near the sea in the Dunkirk direction. I and my suitcase arrived there in due course and I presented myself to the Corps General who graciously saw me to the château just outside the town which he used as his headquarters. He was a very famous French General, but there is no need to mention his name. I showed him my papers and explained to him, at his request, exactly what I would like to do.

I wanted to go into the French trenches in that sector, and thoroughly get into the spirit of what holding that part of the line was like; also I wanted to familiarise myself with the way the French soldiers lived and fought. He quite understood and gave a few rapid orders to an officer who was in the room. He then told me that he had decided that I should go to a certain division who were at the time holding that part of the line which runs alongside the Yser canal, and which had its left flank on the sea. This sounded very interesting, as this sector comprised places of such war-historic interest as Dixmude, Nieuport and Furnes.

A car was placed at my disposal and I was whirled off along the flat, bleak and occasionally poplar-lined roads up towards the Front and towards the great Yser canal, the scene of so much Belgian gallantry. It was very, very cold, and the long drive in the open car as the evening came on was not a particularly exhilarating performance.

We at last arrived at a lot of sandhills, amongst which were some scattered villas of the sort that you will inevitably find at Belgian seaside resorts. This place, the driver announced, was Coxyde - and this was where the division had its headquarters. My destination at last!

Personally, the architecture and total surroundings of a Belgian seaside resort in peacetime, I consider fairly unattractive, but under war conditions I confess that I was bordering on a feeling of absolute revulsion at the town's general appearance. A cheap stucco and red-tiled villa on a wind-swept sandhill is bad enough at any time, but when there is a shell-hole through the roof, a couple of windows missing and a corner chipped off, its appearance is still more repulsive.

There were a good number of these seaside atrocities standing about, and it was in one of these that I found the divisional commander and all his staff, to whom I reported myself. They had heard that I was coming, and as luck would have it knew all about my pictures, and therefore I was saved that painful explanation which I have from time to time had to indulge in - that of telling officials what my work consists of. To explain my business to a man who has never heard of me or my work is a terrible ordeal. The subject is so large and the whole story so peculiar, that I never know where or how to begin. Fortunately nowadays there don't seem to be many people who are unaware that there is such an individual existing as Bruce Bairnsfather, and that he happens to make a series of marks on bits of paper which a kind-hearted world had taken to calling cartoons. Things are not so bad for me now as they used to be. But you can imagine that for some time after I began to draw cartoons, it was a bit trying to explain to some fire-eating general who had never heard of me, and whose *'bête noir'* was cartoons, that I was a licensed military cartoonist, and wished to be allowed to wander all around his trenches so as to get the *atmosphere* and feeling of that particular sector. After a life spent in pondering on the theory of howitzers, road-maps, discipline and battles, a general is naturally a bit strange to the flimsy unreality and apparent uselessness of art.

Oh yes, I've had some trying times, believe me!

However, here at Coxyde, I was most cordially, understandingly and enthusiastically received by this French army commander, and my introduction was followed by my being allotted quarters and then going to lunch with the staff. They were a most happy, light-hearted group of officers, and all worked hard. The General himself, a short, thickset, swarthy, strong man, was one of the brightest and most cheerful ornaments of the mess; a general at his work, and a human being when it was over. All the group of officers connected with him were perfectly free and happy at that mess. All was brightness and freedom, with, whenever necessary, a rigid and vigorous return to work and hard discipline.

I was very much struck with that headquarters mess. I had occasion to have many meals there and I also saw all the members at work, and was most forcibly impressed by the difference between their headquarters and the equivalent in the English army. Since then, having had similar experiences with the Italian and American armies, I am still more struck with the same difference to our own English equivalent. That frigid atmosphere which some of our 'headquarters' can and do assume is entirely lacking in any foreign army. In any other army but ours, a second-lieutenant, when at some 'off-duty' period, say at dinner, can talk with his general and be answered and talked to by his general like two human beings who have respect for each other's knowledge, each in his own sphere. You will frequently find with us that, under similar circumstances, a gloomy, unintellectual silence is maintained, with an occasional remark from the general which is followed by a sycophantic answer from someone of a rank no lower than a captain; whilst a second-lieutenant (if there is one present) munches his toast in dead silence, consigned as he is to unquestionable ignorance at the far end of the table. I've 'ad some myself. No offence meant, only a slight digression on insularity.

The worst of Kultur is it's almost unrecognisable at times!

After lunch at that Coxyde villa, I was taken round and shown where I was to be stabled, and from where I would make excursions to the various trenches in the sector. The place I was to live at was a hotel on the sea front. You will notice I say 'was', and I still stick to that word. Of all the chilly, horrible hotels, I think this one was the peach. Being almost winter it was dark when I and my guide got there and as I was taken up the uncarpeted, creaky, cheap stairs, with a Zouave leading

In the next war.

the way with a candle stuck in a bottle, I couldn't help thinking how unfavourably the place compared to the 'Savoy'. A long, bare corridor with the wind whistling down it through a window with no glass in it greeted us at the top of the stairs. Macbeth's castle was a cosy invalids' home compared with this place. The Zouave, with his dark red, Turkish-looking hat, led the way. The candle spluttered and blew about in the breeze. He opened a door on the right and the candle went out in the draught.

The Zouave entered and re-adjusted the sheet of sacking across a broken pane of glass in the window at the far end. He then relit the candle and showed me my room. A bed, one chair, and a washstand, all made out of a horrible, bilious yellow-coloured wood, and standing on a carpetless floor.

Those were the contents, the other attractions consisting of a rattling window and a mouldy smell such as one, I imagine, would associate with a derelict hotel. The Zouave of course, could speak nothing but French. I can't do much at that, and as I fancy he threw in a little Arabic now and again, I found I could do nothing to establish an 'entente'. I indicated with a smile and a few gestures that I was 'quite alright now, thanks very much' and leaving me the candle he went away. I sat on the bed which was damp from the sea air blowing through the open window. Outside I heard the waves breaking on the shore, whilst inside the hotel was emitting a variety of creaky, weird noises.

The candle, burning with sullen dullness, was standing on the cheap washstand, and apparently it was all it could do to illuminate the surface of that unattractive piece of furniture.

"Here I am at Coxyde, and this is where I have got to live with the French soldiers, find ideas and draw them," I thought to myself. "If you knows of a better 'ole, go to it."

There was no better 'ole, and if there had been I couldn't go to it, so I resigned myself to forthcoming life at 'Coxyde les Bains'.

Chapter 21

GOING THE ROUNDS ~ MUD AND MONOTONY ~ VERDUN HEROES ~ THOUGHTS ON SHELLING

The next day I began my work. The General had arranged for me to have a guide, and to be taken to a regiment that was in front-line trenches to the right and in front of Nieuport. It was a bleak, grey, dismal day as we went down the long, monotonous, shell-pitted road towards Nieuport. What a dreary waste that country round the Yser Canal is, particularly in all the wild, wet weather of winter. We went as far as we safely could in the car, and then walked a short way to the place where the regimental commander lived. He had a fairly large, well-built subterranean dugout, where my guide explained all about me and what I wanted to see and do.

It appeared that the Colonel had been rung up on the telephone already and told all about me, and he readily grasped the idea. He prepared to come round with us and show us all over his particular command. All through my many visits to the various parts of the stupendous battle-line from Ostend to Goritzia, I have been particularly impressed by the willing courtesy shown by the different commanders whom I have had the pleasure of meeting. In spite of the strenuous lives they had to live, they always found time to do all that was possible to show me everything in their power, and were invariably most hospitable. Trench hospitality is a wonderful and touching thing. Every one of my official hosts would turn out extraordinarily good meals in my honour, and on many occasions I have known that this must have meant curtailing their own none too luxurious rations.

The Colonel got ready, gave some orders, and then started to show us round. We followed close behind. I shall never forget that waterlogged, dreary waste near Nieuport; a vast, perfectly flat country, with long, mournful grass waving about in the cold wind under a lead-coloured sky. We went along 'duck-boards' most of the way, occasionally passing groups of war-worn poilus, who were toiling at that everlasting necessity, the battle between man and mud. To these men the Colonel would always say something, perhaps praise, perhaps criticism. But to those poor, cold, wet devils, even a harsh corrective word of command must have been a relief. Those winter months on the Yser were a triumph for our Belgian and French allies.

We went on and at last slushed our way into a series of muddy trenches. It is hard for those who have never seen those trenches to imagine the fearful conditions under which the soldiers lived; no worse, indeed, than what our own army has had to contend with, but they were just as bad as you could get. There is so much marshland in these parts, that to make anything but a sloppy bog for your home is nearly impossible. Dark days, mud, rain, danger and death. When you add those ingredients together and multiply it by the length of a whole winter, you'll find it wants a lot of beating.

And these were the soldiers, some of those amazing fellows who had 'stuck out' so much. These were some of those wonders who astonished the world by their heroic performance at Verdun. I looked at them all keenly, and thought hard as I followed behind the Colonel down trench after trench. Here were these splendid men, in old, dirty uniforms covered with mud; some sitting down on ledges at the back of the mud and sandbag parapet, and others standing about with their hands in their pockets, stamping their feet on the old worn 'duck-boards' to keep warm; while others, again, were occupied on their ceaseless watch for the enemy over the parapet. An English officer following their Colonel around was an unusual sight - I was the first they had ever seen there, and they all looked with silent curiosity as I passed, and then muttered something amongst themselves. I don't know what they said, but if it had been me I should probably have said, "What's this bloody fool doin' muckin' around here!"

I expect they said something like that. I hope so anyway for it's human and friendly.

I don't know many things more tiring than being shown round miles and miles of trenches. To begin with, you can't walk normally. You always seem to be stepping over things or stooping under things; added to which, you have occasionally to do about half a mile in a bent-up attitude, because the parapet is low. This latter procedure is

Portrait of a gentleman who knows that Morocco is a far, far 'better 'ole' than Verdun.

advisable owing to a latent desire on the part of those Rhineland gentlemen to snipe your head if it shows.

I got tired out that day, but I saw and learned a lot. I scrambled about in various ditches known technically as communication trenches. I went on 'all fours' into sundry dugouts or trench mortar emplacements. I slushed through hundreds of yards of dirty, marshy, shell-torn ground, tripped on old rusty barbed-wire, and, in fact, *saw* those trenches thoroughly.

We stopped for lunch at the dugout of a company commander, and there we sat round a low table - a survivor of some mutilated home close by - and partook of a plain but very welcome ration lunch, given to us with the utmost cordiality and hospitality; after which we enjoyed a smoke, and attempted the removal of as much mud as one could.

They are invariably a cheery and friendly crowd, these French officers, and there is invariably a 'happy family' atmosphere in all French regiments.

During this visit of mine to these Nieuport trenches there was very little shelling or violent interruptions of any kind - a little rifle-firing and a little 'back-area' strafing, that was all. That form of amusement indulged in by the artillery and known as 'back-area shelling', consists of lobbing nice, large, juicy shells over the heads of the trench holders, way back on to some town, village, camp or building; occasionally varying this by deluging a certain road so as to make it unattractive if not impossible to use.

Of the various forms of irritant which this war has possessed, I hate shelling the most. Against one of those large, flying umbrella-stands, in the shape of a fifteen-inch shell, you can do nothing. It's mere delusion to think you are safe in a house, dugout or cellar. These shells have a persistent and noisy way of penetrating anywhere, with the almost inevitable result that you go out either bodily or in pieces.

I can laugh, and have laughed, at the rattling splutter of machine-gun bullets against a wall when I have been on the other side, but when those mammoth howitzers start squirting those explosive drainpipes over at you, I confess my smile fades. That *BOOM*, very soft in the distance, then that swirling, rotating, swishing crescendo overhead; the ghastly momentary pause as you see an earth fountain waft a cottage a hundred yards into the air, followed by a crash like a battleship being dropped into Olympia. No! No! I don't like it at all.

These Nieuport trenches were comparatively quiet that day, but when the time came for us to retrace our steps along the sodden 'duck-boards' I wasn't sorry. They were a clammy, horrible, depressing sight, and very reminiscent to me of those dark, dank ditches I used to live in before Messines.

I looked back when we had gone about half a mile; under the darkening, dreary, wet sky the flat war-torn country lay in gloomy silence. The long wavering grass, a skeleton farm roof silhouetted against the lemon-coloured light of the setting sun, and beyond, the dark, hazy mystery of where those primitive trenches lay, and where, night after night, week after week, month after month, those muddy, weather-beaten, war-worn poilus for ever 'held the line'.

Chapter 22

METHODS OF WORK ~ A WONDERFUL TUNNEL ~ AN 'AIRY' BIT OF LINE ~ BACK TO COXYDE

My life now consisted of going daily to some new part of the line, seeing different regiments and noting a host of various incidents. At night, back in that drastic hotel by the light of two candles stuck in their own grease, I worked away on my detailed drawings and wrote notes on all the little effects and points which I had observed in character and design amongst the soldiers and in the trenches. I have sketchbooks and notebooks full of the various characteristics of different trenches, localities and soldiers.

Thinking it may interest readers of this book, I am having a typical page from one of my sketchbooks reproduced. It is a hurried, detailed drawing, made at about the time of which I have just written. A cracked and deserted cold hotel is not the best studio on earth, but here it was that I collected all the material that I wanted in the way of technical detail. I made no attempt to get ideas for pictures; I never do at this period. I just go in for letting the whole scene and conditions of life soak into my system; live with them all, and feel what it is to live there with them all. Then, afterwards, when I come away, a clearer vision of what it was that struck me most comes along and then I can carry on.

The times I have had in fearful 'studios', from that dugout where I drew my first *"Where did that one go to?"* picture, to a cabin in mid-Atlantic. Incidentally, having perpetrated sketches in a broken-down estaminet in the Vosges, a swimming-bath on the Carso and a host of other weird and unstimulating spots along the way.

I thoroughly investigated that Yser area, and will not describe any more of the ordinary trench life there, as it is all much the same everywhere. I will, however, give you an idea of what the line was like in those days on the extreme left. This, by the way, was to me a very interesting spot, for this was where the whole battle-line ended. The line was, as everyone knows, approximately from Ostend to Belfort.

The part I am about to describe was the North Sea end of it all, about eight miles westward from Ostend. Here the trenches ended because of the sea, and the barbed-wire defences of each side ran out into the sea for a finish. This thought amused me, I don't exactly know why. I somehow felt how ridiculous it was for the vast numbers of twentieth century human beings, who more or less all prided themselves on progress and enlightenment, to be facing each other in two long slots in the ground, with the ends stopped up, one by the North Sea, and the other by the Alps.

A Zouave regiment was holding these trenches, and I was most interested to see the men and to absorb all the characteristics of the places around. As before, we went in a car as close to the line as possible, and afterwards had to walk, but this time we had to leave the car a long way behind the Front. This precaution was very necessary, as a lot of shelling went on here, and the Germans, having a good view from some high sandhills and towers in the distance, were able to send a pretty nasty occasional burst of shelling down into the lines which led to the Zouave trenches. To circumvent this, the regiment had made a long tunnel under the sand, over a mile in length. This was really a wonderful piece of work. It was impossible to detect the tunnel from the outside, and yet inside it was big enough for two people to walk abreast, and was completely wood-lined from end to end, with electric light and telephone wires running its whole length. The carpentry of it and its general structure were excellent; truly it was a wonderful bit of work for an infantry battalion to have accomplished. Now and again in the course of its length there was a slot left open on the seaward side from which, as you passed, you could see the ocean.

I went along this tunnel affair, and came out at the far end, just at the mouth of the Yser Canal. A few terribly mutilated houses, miniature lighthouses and ruined canal lock-gates marked the end of this historic canal.

Beyond the canal, about a thousand yards away, were the sandhills which formed the Allied front line. I don't claim to be a military genius, but I confess that, at the very time I first saw those trenches it struck me as a dangerously airy place to have them. For against the advantage of having got a thousand yards of sandhill beyond the canal towards the enemy, there was the obvious disadvantage that the canal was behind our lines. It was very wide at that part, and, moreover, supplies were entirely dependent on our being able to maintain intact a series of bridges across the water. I said nothing of course, and imagined that there was some good reason for our line being thus thrown forward, but subsequently when we got that very nasty smack from the Huns in these very sandhills, I read the account and saw that the canal and the ruptured bridges had been the cause of the trouble.

The Germans had concentrated artillery fire on the only bridges by which reinforcements could come to the aid of the garrison of the sandhills which was held in a deathly struggle with overwhelming numbers.

The Zouaves are a magnificent crowd, and this particular crew had done wonders at Verdun. They were here 'resting'. Holding these trenches compared to Verdun was indeed resting, but 'resting' in this war has been a much abused word. A few of my pals in the trenches will endorse that sentence, I know.

I spent the day crashing about amongst Zouaves and sand, and began my journey back to Coxyde towards evening. I was now accompanied by my guide and a Zouave officer. We thought we would chance it and go above ground instead of bothering to walk back along the tunnel. We started off, but about three-quarters of a mile back, as we walked down the main but completely shattered street of Nieuport Bains, a shell or two whizzed over our heads and landed with a nasty bang a hundred yards ahead of us. We all thought the tunnel

The 'Regimental Mascot' finds it cold on the Yser

advisable after this, I most certainly did. We dived down a hole in the basement of a house and by means of an underground passage constructed out of a series of cellars, reached the tunnel by the sea again. In due course we emerged, and as we got into the car we saw another couple of shells burst in the road we had lately left. We motored off back to Coxyde, arriving there without further incident.

Before leaving that sector I was taken to see the old city of Nieuport. I have seen a lot of ruined cities, but this one wants a deal of competing with for thorough ruination. I asked the commandant, more jokingly than otherwise, if there was such a thing as a whole unbroken house in the town. He said that a careful examination had been made and it had been found that there was not.

The town was in a fearful mess. Every house was knocked to pieces, and the streets were a mass of shell-holes. The town hall and church were appalling wrecks. I took a lot of photographs, made sundry sketches and left. I left by moonlight and an eerie sight it was. A clear night, and a large, full moon shining down on the deserted, ruined, silent city. Far away in the trenches out in front, an occasional rifle-shot would cause a harsh echo amongst the still, cold ruins as they stood there under the moon.

Chapter 23

AN INVITATION TO DINNER ~ IN PARIS AGAIN ~ OFF TO VERDUN ~ BAR-LE-DUC

My time in this North Sea area was drawing to a close. I had got all I wanted, a crowd of impressions and a forest of detail. Now came the big event, the star turn, the thing I was longing to do. I was now to go to Verdun! Verdun, with all its epic story of cast-iron endurance and its mighty battles! Verdun, the Ypres of the French army!

I was glad, in a way, to leave that damp and dismal Rosendael sector, but I was sorry to leave the jolly, friendly crowd of French officers at Coxyde who were more than good to me. Before leaving I received an invitation on which I will say a few words. I was invited to dine with Prince Alexander of Teck who lived over at La Panne, and was the British representative with the King of the Belgians. His senior staff officer was a friend of mine, and I went over one night and enjoyed a very pleasant evening. I had the honour of sitting next to the Prince, who told me a lot of interesting things about the sector and the Belgian army.

I mention this dinner, you see, to show that I don't always live on bully beef in dugouts, but now and again glide off up into the realms of *table-d'hôte*. This pleasant little episode happened just before I left. I had another invitation to go to the Naval Division, who operated some venomous-looking naval guns in the sandhills close by, but had to cancel, as I was leaving for Paris. After a variety of small bothers, such as getting one's papers and 'authority to proceed', etc., I left Rosendael for Paris.

*Why is this sort of thing always down at the base,
where medals keep coming out on him like a rash?*

I went to the French authorities and saw an Intelligence Department lieutenant who gave me a couple of reams of paper entitling me to go to Verdun. I managed to snatch a night in Paris. I wanted something to contrast with the joys of the Rosendael mud wastes. What a rotten thing loneliness in great cities is! One night is quite enough for me, but circumstances have caused me to have a great many.

After one evening in Paris I started for Verdun. I rattled off from my hotel in one of those reckless petrol-driven bathing machines known as taxis, and having paid my Jehu a hundred per cent over his fare (I daren't argue, as I don't know enough French), I walked into the station. It's a mighty station is the Gare de l'Est, and I have never seen it without its being packed to suffocation with people. All the Paris stations seemed to be the same during the war. One large seething mob of soldiers, civilians, women and children. Trains about a mile long are always standing at the platforms and are allowed about two hours to load up with passengers. They seem to believe in a few trains of staggering length, to a greater number of reasonable proportions. My heart bleeds for the engine that has to start pulling that enormous dead-weight out of the station. I'm sure the station-master must give the train a bit of a shove so as to make things easier.

It is very rare that I have managed to evade carriages with eight a side, the floor covered with baggage, and a family of assorted babies sprawling over it. I have done hundreds of miles in carriages like the Black Hole of Calcutta.

This journey to Verdun was crowded, but minus babies. I think that sector is unsuitable for babies, but it apparently deals largely in farm labourers, who seem to live exclusively on garlic and onions (at least so I surmise from my travelling experiences and a keen sense of smell). A boisterously healthy, swarthy Hercules, with a luxuriant moustache, will sit in a first-class carriage and open a parcel in which is wrapped a lunch enough to feed a platoon. Then, with a brigand-like pocket-knife he will proceed to cut the cheese against a monstrous, dirty thumb, looking blandly out of the window with eyes like 'The Soul's Awakening'.

It was just such a journey as this that I made towards Verdun. You can't go the whole way to Verdun by train - only as far as Bar-le-Duc - then hope for the best. I arrived at Bar-le-Duc in the evening, and was motored out that night to a certain army headquarters which was established in an old stone town hall in a small town. An effective, romantic sort of a place - I remember noticing a lot of shields and old historical spears hung on the walls. Everything was very solid and gloomy.

I was told what the necessary procedure was before being allowed to enter and see Verdun. In about half an hour I was in the French staff car again, and being motored back to Bar-le-Duc. It was late at night when I got there, and I found a room in one of the few hotels in the main street. Somehow the whole air seemed charged with a quaint air of excitement and mystery. Bar-le-Duc tonight, and tomorrow I was to be called for and taken to Verdun. I was mighty keen on this visit. Verdun spelt to me such a mysterious, romantic charm, and at this time the world was echoing the great story of the ceaseless German attacks, and the amazing tenacity of the French troops in holding the town and the salient.

Verdun, Douaumont, Vaux; all magic, terrifying names, each one conveying a wealth of martial meaning to every man and woman in France. One big story of the courageous spirit of undefeatable France, and one big necropolis for the Germans.

I spent a fairly reasonable night in a fairly reasonable hotel, and when daylight broke again I prepared myself for my visit to the mighty fortress of Verdun.

Chapter 24

**VERDUN ~ UNDERGROUND HALLS ~
DEATH AND DEVASTATION**

A large French staff car appeared before the hotel at about nine o'clock in the morning. I left with a French officer guide and a chauffeur. The road was long and winding, and it is a famous road that, being the main artery which feeds the salient. As we went along we passed an incessant stream of motor-lorries proceeding in both directions. A vast traffic was here, I could see, and my mind immediately flew to thoughts of the mighty mechanism behind it all. Long, apparently never-ending, streams of motor-lorries carrying food and ammunition, followed by another stream carrying fresh soldiers for the fray.

The backward freight consisted of battle-worn poilus being taken back for short but urgent rest. That road was charged with all the tense, electrical seriousness of the great battle of Verdun. Our car dashed along past all this traffic, and I gathered from the milestones that we would soon be in sight of the historic city.

At last we were there. We entered under a huge, stone-built gateway, giving entrance through the walls of the citadel. Guards challenged us and looked at our passports. All was well, and entering the town we proceeded slowly along. Huge, massive walls were on either side; walls built for defensive purposes at a very much earlier date. We stopped before an arched, dark opening on the left. This opening was the entrance to a massive stone tunnel and led to the interior of the underground fortress. We got out of the car and the French officer led me into the tunnel.

That underground system at Verdun is truly wonderful. Long, electrically lit passages take one into great arched stone halls where there is room and equipment for everything and everybody. We went along a series of passages and up sundry stone stairs, down others - along more passages - until we arrived at the quarters of the French General commanding the citadel. Here I was introduced to the General and my visit was explained.

The General expressed a wish to show me the town and fortress that day; this more than pleased me, as of course, I wished to see everything, and as soon as possible.

The General ordered his car round and was good enough to ask me to come with him on a tour of inspection. We drove slowly through the town. It was impossible for the Germans to see into the town, as they had been prevented from gaining the heights commanding the place, but from the monstrous shell-holes and demolition round about I clearly saw that they went in for extensive shelling on the off-chance of making themselves a nuisance.

I was shown a lot of the interesting, historic buildings of Verdun, all more or less knocked about. The old walls of the city were very curious; the terrific shelling had blown away so much masonry and so many houses, that another set of ancient walls had been exposed to view!

Verdun is a most ancient town, and has a very great historical interest. Mr Atilla and his Huns originally dashed through this place, in their customary rude and pushing way, and were ultimately defeated utterly at Chalons-sur-Marne - which is not very far away.

I went into the Cathedral. Such a pitiful mess it was in! Piles of smashed and twisted metal, originally priceless wrought-iron work, were lying on the chipped and scarred stone floor. The great decorative domed ceiling had a huge, gaping shell-hole in it, whilst several of the altars were torn and lacerated by shrapnel. It is a very ancient cathedral, and is most massive and magnificent in structure.

We spent the rest of the day cruising around the various spots of interest in the city. Verdun stands on the Meuse river and is surrounded by a series of hills, all about two miles away from the town and all held by the French. It was these hills that the Germans were after, and had they ever got them they could have dominated the town and knocked the bottom out of all the defences. This they were precious near doing at one time, but the magnificent courage and heroic endurance of the French were too much for them.

Towards evening we drove back to the underground department. The General invited myself and my officer guide to dinner that night, and ordered someone to show me where I was to sleep. I was led into a sort of dormitory full of wooden cubicles; one of these was to be mine. I sat on my bed and made some notes and rough sketches, then had a wash and brush-up for dinner.

At a little before the time a French soldier called for me; something like the jailer coming for the doomed man to take him to the scaffold. I followed the soldier to my doom. We went down another set of maze-like passages and ultimately entered the dining-hall. A huge, vaulted hall, with several rows of tables met my gaze. The room was rapidly filling with a great number of French officers. The whole scene was full of life and bustle. The pulsating flicker of rather yellow electric light flooded the place. Soldier servants and cooks were working with enthusiastic vigour at preparing the feast. Two tables ran down the centre of this vaulted hall, and one across the top end at right angles to the others. The room was soon full and the General entered. He took his seat at the centre of the top table and summoned me to sit beside him. The dinner started.

I wish he had let me be at the far end of the junior officers' table, or amongst the cooks and waiters. High places at these functions always end in my eating nothing. A great rattling roar of people talking and eating now filled the place, and I worked hard at my poor French to evolve sentences for the benefit of the General and the other officers round about. I'm sure that dear old General mistook me for an ambassador or something. At the end of dinner he made a speech, referring to me in the middle of it, and later on a band played 'God save the King' during which I had to bear the scrutiny of about two hundred pairs of eyes, whilst all stood to attention. I was honoured, but uncomfortable. The evening concluded in a most cordial and happy way with a smoking concert.

The next few days I spent in examining the outer defences of Verdun. I went to see the famous forts of Douaumont and Vaux. I was shown where the various German attacks had been beaten, and all the ground over which the French had fought during those long anxious months which were vital to the whole cause of the Allies. And what a dreadful country it was! I looked out from Souville fort on to the ground around Fleury and Douaumont. The land seemed to radiate nothing but an atmosphere of death and decay from its dull brown, shell-churned surface. As I looked heavy shells were bursting continuously over the French advance trenches, and over the broken remains of Douaumont fort. Souville marked the spot that had proved a Waterloo for the Germans. Out on the ground in front lay the unburied remains of many who had fallen, and everywhere the ground was littered with old, rusty, broken rifles, bayonets and bombs.

Mud was everywhere in gigantic quantities, and everything within sight seemed to be blasted and destroyed. A truly ghastly sight was this land around those outer forts, steeped as it was in all the full fury of the worst kind of war that man could make. As I had anticipated, this Verdun salient was quite on a par with the horror of Ypres. I picked up an old bayonet to take away with me as a souvenir, and it now hangs, with other trophies, in my Warwickshire home. We had just left Souville to return, and had hardly gone thirty yards when a heavy shell crashed alongside the place where we had been standing. Almost immediately the woods behind seemed to burst into life with French guns, barking more death and more destruction at the Germans. And so that relentless argument went on, and day after day the death-charged atmosphere reigned over the Verdun salient, ultimately bringing the world's greatest disappointment to Germany and its gospel of brute force. I was glad to leave that area. It was a long time before I could forget the horrible look of that unearthly ground before the forts.

We returned through the mutilated Souville forest into Verdun - I went to see the General, and, thanking him very much for the facilities he had so kindly granted me, awaited the car to take me away. I was glad now, and very pleased with things in general. I had spent a night in Verdun, and had seen it all; this seemed to form the cap to my interesting French experiences. Now I would return to Paris and then to England, after which I should begin my series of drawings from the French Front. I had seen them in comparative quiet on the Yser, and in hell at Verdun. I knew their story. I knew their feelings and outlook. I was charged with the *atmosphere* and had amassed a great volume of detail. My job was over for the present. Now for civilisation - by which I mean escape from the devastating mental nausea of the war areas.

The car came round, and took me to Bar-le-Duc, from where I went by train to Paris. In a few days I was back in England once more.

Chapter 25

SUPPLYING 'COPY' ~ A CROWDED EXISTENCE ~ ORDERED TO ITALY

All through these wanderings and adventures I was always at work on my weekly contributions to *The Bystander*. I worked in any old place that I could find, and by means of a compact portable set of implements and paints, spread myself out into an artist in a 'studio'.

From the day I began to the present time I have never missed getting a drawing back somehow or other to *The Bystander* offices in time for the weekly publication. Once or twice I got men, going on leave to England, to take a parcel and post it in London; and once, when I drew a picture in my cabin, somewhere off Newfoundland, I got the Turkish bath attendant on the ship to post it on his return to Liverpool; so you see, what with my own precarious existence, followed by the equally precarious posting and delivery, those weekly cartoons have seen a bit of life before they emerged in the paper.

Having returned from this French visit I started out full steam ahead to work out my finished pictures, and in due course they were completed.

I have a sort of idea that a lot of people imagine that this job of mine is a delightful, easy and simple occupation. Along the lines of this sort of thing: "Fancy! How topping

The Spahi:
The most picturesque man in the war.

it must be to be a cartoonist; nothing to do but draw pictures; no fighting, only going on visits to the Fronts and making jokes; isn't he a lucky chap?"

In case I am right (and this idea undoubtedly does prevail) I will tell you the real story.

First of all, it would have been wholly and completely impossible for me to have made one joke or drawn one line on the subject, had I not originally been burnt in the fire of the war, and badly burnt too. My life in the original mud, and the consequent strafing, pain and anguish, were the foundations of my war drawings. If I had started life in any other capacity than the infantry, these drawings would have been impossible. No amount of looking *at* the war is any good, you must have been *in* it, with a darn good chance of never leaving it. I believe this to be the one and only reason for the popularity of my war drawings.

Following this initial necessity comes the actual work; few can realise how much and how hard it is, and nobody except myself and a very intimate few will ever know what I have been through. Work of this class has to be in your system all the time. You don't leave an office at six o'clock, as it were, and then forget all about your work till nine o'clock the next morning.

For over three years now I have done on an average three or four drawings a week, out of which, possibly, two have been what I thought suitable to use. Added to this, I have been deluged with letters and autograph albums from all parts of the world. These cannot be ignored, and I have always done my best to get all such applications attended to in some way or other. Each drawing takes me about two days to complete. In the 'spare time' resulting on all this I have worked on another book, *'Bullets & Billets'*, the forerunner to this volume. I have written the play entitled *'The Better 'Ole'*, and also one or two short theatrical sketches. Add to all this innumerable drawings for charities of all kinds, and you will observe that I have had rather a crowded existence, and by the time it is realised that the material for all these activities has been collected by personal visits to the war zones on all the Fronts, with the consequent fatiguing journeys and hard fare, you will see that to be *Bruce Bairnsfather* has been an intricate and arduous job. But I am lucky, though, I fully appreciate that.

Here I am, at the end of the war, with a complete set of component parts: two legs, two arms, two eyes, a nose and a mouth. How many of my pals have been less fortunate!

After a short session of work in England I was told by the War Office that I was shortly to go to the Italian front. I was most elated at this, as I was longing to see Italy and the war there. The accounts of the fighting on the Carso and in the mountains seemed to be full of interest compared with the mud scrambles in France. Italy, with its warm sun and bright days! I felt things couldn't be quite so bad there as elsewhere, and that the grandeur of the scenery would outweigh a lot of the nasty parts which are inseparable from visits to war zones.

I was keen on the Italian job, and presently the day arrived when I was to start. I went to the War Office and was told a lot of things that I must observe, and given details in connection with my journey. I got my passport and papers, and went back to my hotel. Here I overhauled my 'props' and having procured various articles I wanted for my work, I left Charing Cross on my way to Italy. Same old Folkestone and Boulogne journey, with Paris to follow. I arrived at the Gare du Nord, Paris, and dragged myself and baggage into the same old hotel.

I always make for railway hotels as they are generally more 'up' on the trains, and in my case are easier to do things from. The next morning I drove off in a taxi for the Gare de Lyon, there to catch a train for the frontier on my way to Italy.

Chapter 26

EN ROUTE TO MILAN ~ HOTEL BRIGANDS ~ SPAGHETTI ~ ON TO UDINE

By some extraordinary lucky chance I got a seat in the train. The usual trouble was prevailing, and you almost needed a shoehorn to get the last few people into that train. We pushed off.

It's a beautiful journey, the run from Paris to Milan. First of all, of course, one passes down through the best part of France; trees, meadows, old towns, villages and châteaux. Right down through the centre of France one goes and then comes the Riviera. Splendid scenery here. At last the train reached Modane.

This place is a very important feature *en route* to Italy, as it is the frontier station and here in wartime it was necessary to change trains. In the days before the war one could go from Paris to Rome without a change, but now it was different. I got out at Modane, and was crowded, pushed and banged about on a super-crowded platform, in an endeavour to board the train which was to take me on to Italy.

The scenery had all changed now. Huge mountains on either side, and the line running along cuttings in the sides of the cliffs, over precarious-looking bridges, or through long tunnels. This was Italy!

Everything looked different now, even the character of the houses; I was mighty pleased to have got as far as this on the journey. We went on through a host of wonderful mountain sights and arrived at Turin (I call it Torino at times, like the Italians; sounds well, I think). Turin is a fine, bright-looking town. I didn't stop there, but went on to Milan, which brought me to the end of the first half of my journey.

Udine, on the Carso, was my destination, but a pause in Milan was necessary for the purpose of picking up a train to that area. I wasn't sorry either. Milan is good enough for me for twenty-four hours. I got out of the train, and was nearly bitten in half by a swirling mass of hotel porters. Brigands in all sorts of uniforms, with the name of their hotel written in gold letters round a military-style hat. I got my back against the train and turned to face my attackers (the effect was rather one of 'Horatius Cockles defending his suitcase'). I didn't know which hotel would suit me best, so I got out of the difficulty by asking in French which hotel was the nearest to the station. A tall, dark, thin outlaw immediately sprang at me and grabbed my baggage. He evidently was unquestionably the clutching hand belonging to the nearest hotel. The rest of the group looked menacingly at this man, and sullenly began to move off. Some, however, still skulked along close to me and my porter as if there might be a chance that either I should change my mind, or that the porter would drop my baggage, in which case they would spring in and seize it. One swarthy child of Milan followed me and my porter right across the station square outside, keeping up a seductive barrage of Italian as to the absurdity of my going to any other hotel but his, and occasionally glancing venomously at my own porter with all the hate and vendetta of ages in his eyes. I suppose that after trains have come in and travellers have been dragged in to the various hotels, these men go to some lonely spot and fight it out. The mortality amongst foreign hotel porters must be terrible. My hotel was quite a nice one, and the management could speak English. This, of course, is a blessing to one who doesn't know a word of Italian. A good mixture of French and English can get you to most places nowadays though.

It was a beautiful evening when I arrived at Milan, and the whole scene was most pleasing. The feeling of the South was borne in upon me strongly. My mother has told me that I was born somewhere in India. For several years I lived there, and I fancy that the frying I had in the days of my infancy has never quite got out of my system. I like the sun, and warm, balmy breezes. One seems to be able to swell out two sizes larger in that sort of a climate, and to look altogether more blandly and lazily on life.

I had dinner outside on a sort of terrace where all the tables were set, and remember being most interested in an Italian officer dining at a table a few feet away. The object of my interest was his marvellous dexterity with his macaroni, or rather spaghetti. I didn't dare to eat mine after watching him. He could dip a fork into about a hundredweight of this stuff in a bowl in front of him, and bring it out with a tight knot wound round the end. My fork had a lot of strings dangling from the prongs like a dozen anaemic worms. He could do it every time with deadly precision - practice, I suppose. Before going to Italy again I shall attend a college and take a spaghetti course, because one is always up against having to eat this stuff there. I wandered round Milan and went, of course, to see the Cathedral. I mingled with the crowds taking their evening strolls, sat about in various cafés and had a touch of the 'lonely' nuisance again.

It's extraordinary how, when one is by oneself in a crowded city, everyone else seems to have someone to be with or talk to, and all are apparently laughing in your face with the sheer joy of life. I liked Milan, but was anxious to get along up to the Front and see the wonders of the war in the mountains.

The next morning I caught the train for Udine. From Milan to Udine takes the best part of a day. Udine is on the Carso, and at that period was very close to the Front, which ran from Monfalcone on the Adriatic, through Goritzia up towards the mountains. You miss Venice by about twelve miles on your right, on the journey to Udine. I arrived that evening, and drove from the station in an open, tumbledown carriage to the headquarters of the British Mission. I drove sedately along behind what sounded like a three-legged horse, looking at the town as I passed. A very old place is Udine, full of odd corners and ancient monuments. The Romans spread themselves a good bit around here in days gone by.

I found the British Mission headquarters and reported myself. There was a British general there who helped me very much during my visit to the Italian Front. He was head of the Mission, and as such was very much in touch with the Italian Army Command. I dined with the General that night, and he very kindly set about making arrangements for me to visit various parts of the Front, beginning on the morrow. I was given a room in the building, which had been appropriated as the Mission's billets, and passed off into a pleasant sleep, dreaming mostly of spaghetti, hotel porters, generals and Alps.

Chapter 27

ARRIVAL ON CARSO ~ BERSAGLIERI ~ A HEATED WAR ~ TRANQUIL UDINE

It wasn't long before I started my examination of the Italian Front. The next morning the General very kindly arranged for me to go down in a car to see life on the Carso. He had fixed it all up with the Italian authorities, and I was free to go right up to the Front towards Trieste. We set off in an English car, and made for some spot with a name something like sarsaparilla, in order to see a famous regiment of Bersaglieri who were then in trenches south of Goritzia. Any liking I had about warmth and sunshine was fully gratified here. It was scorching hot. The roads were white with burning dust, the trees simply frizzling in the summer sun. To touch the leather upholstery or the metal sides of the car was nearly impossible. The heat was immense. Fighting battles in this weather must be a 'poor line' I thought.

And now was to come my first view of the Italian army in the field. I conjured up ideas, founded mostly on coloured pictures I had seen of the famous Bersaglieri with their plumed hats and gallant charges across open country, shouting soul-stirring phrases as they pushed heroically for ever onward, the flag of Italy waving proudly in the breeze. I arrived on the Carso and found, apparently, a group of organ-grinders playing cards under a tree, all very swarthy, healthy and happy. "These are Bersaglieri," said my officer guide . . . You should never go by appearances. A Guards' parade outside Buckingham Palace is a very sorry indication of the same regiment in billets behind Ypres.

These Bersaglieri were resting, and even if they weren't, they did the battle business minus any of the highly-coloured heroism beloved of artists. Those wonderful plumed hats, where were they? Back in Milan or Rome, I suppose, in a wardrobe with camphor bags. There was a great mob of these men sitting about under shrubs and trees, in the blazing heat.

The trenches were a short way off, being held in shifts, as it were. There was no shelling - no rifle-fire. A delightful calm Italian day with the sun shining down on the tranquillity of the Carso. This is the sort of war I like, much better than that noisy, dangerous running about waterlogged ploughed fields I had been used to. Unfortunately, I found it had not always been like this. There had been some terrific scraps with the Austrians around this spot, and I was shown how far these people had been driven back. The Bersaglieri, which are some of the finest troops in Europe, had, to put it plainly, 'wiped the floor' with the Austrians around there, and had suffered very heavily in doing so.

I went all around that area and saw thousands of Italian soldiers, some resting, some in their trenches. They are a wonderfully swarthy, healthy crowd.

But what a different landscape to fight in from our Front! Instead of the sticky mass of sloppy sandbags along the edge of a narrow canal which constitute the normal trench on the Western Front, these men had nothing but rocks and sand to deal with. The Carso has about two inches of soil over solid rock, so you can imagine what making trenches is like. Moreover, when a shell lands on ground like this, the resulting explosion is greatly augmented by flying bits of rock.

The first thing that struck me about the Carso itself was, what on earth did anybody want to fight about it for? I would willingly give it away, if I owned it. It's a huge, barren, rocky desert, that's all.

The part I was now inspecting was just opposite Goritzia. To the south lay Trieste, and it was possible to see from this place I was in, the mountainous difficulties lying between the Italians and the capture of that city. There is a nasty-looking mountain called the Hermada which is right in the way of a march on Trieste. The Italians had made wonderful progress prior to my visit, but were now sitting down a bit to consider what was the best way to snooker the Austrians who had fortified this Hermada with howitzers and barbed-wire to an alarming degree.

A day doesn't go very far when one starts looking at a Front. I spent the whole of this first day squinting about round this one regiment, its trenches, and its billets, and in the wonderful Italian evening drove back to Udine. Those warm southern days breed wondrous evenings. There is a still, clear warmth under the glorious deep night blue; the people are all sitting outside their houses, and everything is bathed in a sort of Venetian tranquillity. When I got back it was about six o'clock, and I went out for a prowl around the town.

I have most pleasing memories of Udine; so picturesque and so tranquil. Except for the fact that there were a good many assorted kinds of Italian soldiers strolling about, you wouldn't have known there was a war on. The architecture, too, was old-world and pleasing. A lot of Roman efforts still remained, and a goodly sprinkling of the Venetian period. What bold lads those Romans were! I stood bashfully in the main square of the town looking at a group of rude statues, and dwelt upon the lack of YMCAs and the absence of Mrs Grundy in the days of Vespasian.

They are a happy, healthy crew these Italians, and I've half a mind to live in Udine when I retire.

I had dinner in some café or other, and sat out in the courtyard under the wonderful sky. A distant song, or perhaps a mandolin being played, were the only noises which broke on that calm evening air.

In this curious, unwarlike scene, full of all the beauty of this wonderful land, I couldn't help visioning my past career in the war. How little I thought as I went forth to the war, an impecunious, submerged second-lieutenant, that one day I should see all the Fronts, have dinners with the Great Ones and be sitting in the character of a 'freelance' under the southern evening sky in old Udine. I even thought further back still; back to the weird, dark abyss in my life when, as an electrical engineer earning two pounds ten shillings a week, I returned in a wood pulp carrying ship from Canada just in time to participate in this mighty conflict.

If someone had come to me whilst I sat on that ship with the cook who was peeling potatoes, and told me that one day I should be having dinner with the Duke of Milan in an old Italian garden near Venice, I should have told him to go to - well, never mind; anyway, I shouldn't have believed him. It's a comic world, but there are times when the comedy is hard to see. And yet these things have actually happened to me.

I wandered back to my billets late at night, and keenly awaited the next day. I was to go to see Monfalcone which was the nearest point possible to Trieste, and there would be able to survey the whole of the battle-line, which meant so much to Italy. I should also be able to get a distant view of Trieste which can be seen from Monfalcone. This, then, was my programme for the following day.

Chapter 28

MONFALCONE ~ CAMOUFLAGED ROADS ~ A PEEP AT TRIESTE

The car turned up in good time, and the officer guide and myself were driven off in the direction of Monfalcone. On the way we stopped at the interesting old village of Aquila. This is the site of an old Roman town of the same name, and contains a wonderful old church dating from that period. Part of this church was once a Roman swimming-bath or something of the kind, and had an amazing mosaic floor. When I was there some antique employees of the church were endeavouring to restore this marvellous floor which had been broken and obscured in many parts. Restoring it mainly consisted of searching through endless piles of rubbish for the minute particles of mosaic, and piecing them together. Solving a jigsaw puzzle is child's play compared to this. Outside the church, in a charming cypress-tree graveyard, one of the ancient walls had a large marble slab fixed to it, bearing a short, inspired verse by Gabriel d'Annunzio, the famous Italian poet. A few minutes afterwards I saw the poet himself inside the church, looking round its ancient, inspiring relics.

We went on from here to Monfalcone. What a mess it was in! Here was the same old war that I knew. Tangled masses of plaster, iron, and brickwork that once were houses. It is a typical Italian-looking town, and before being demolished in this way must have been a pleasant spot to live in. Judging by the look of the camouflaged roads which we encountered on the way there, the Austrian artillery must have been a big nuisance. The town, of course, was entirely denuded of civilians, which fact was very apparent as we drove through its deserted streets.

We had to be careful though, as at any moment a bother might break out and a lively shelling commence. The car was left at a good hiding spot where chances of its being hit were remote, and we got out to walk the rest of the time. We examined the town and I made sundry sketches and took a few photographs. Nothing but ruin and desolation everywhere.

Now for the docks; that was the 'star turn' of Monfalcone, which boasts of quite a big shipping yard situated, of course, on the Adriatic. The docks are some way from the town, so we fished the car out again for this job. We drove down an elaborately camouflaged road. These are just ordinary roads with a screen constructed from a kind of rush matting fixed up on the side nearest the enemy.

The appearance of these roads from a distance is just like the rest of the country. Of course this doesn't prevent the enemy from firing at such roads which they know exist, but it prevents deliberate aim at a definite object and therefore it would probably be a sheer waste of shells to fire on the off-chance of hitting something. It's not a very nice sensation driving along these camouflaged roads, but there it is, and the danger is not really great.

We reached the outskirts of the docks, hid the car and walked on to them. We had now arrived at the nearest point for a view of Trieste.

It was a stifling hot day. A blazing sun shone out of a cloudless blue sky with true southern vigour. The ground had that trembling haze over it from the heat. We entered the ship-building sheds and the first thing that caught my eye was a bit of machinery stamped with the name of a famous English firm of shipbuilding engineers. I roamed about all over these yards. Several Austrian submarines, all rusty and derelict, in dry dock, caught my eye. The Austrians had shinned off out of Monfalcone very quickly, and had been obliged to leave these things behind them. We were joined by an Italian officer or two who knew all about this place. They led us further into the maze of silent, deserted dockyards. I listened to an unintelligible torrent of sound from one of these men who was talking to my officer guide. When interpreted I

found it meant that there was a large, half-finished liner in the docks, inside which the Italians had made an observation post, and from which it was possible to get the best view of Trieste. I was keen on this, so we all made for the ship.

It was a monster. A great wall of rusty iron plates seemed to spring out of the earth and tower upwards above our heads. We walked alongside this metallic mammoth, and arrived at a set of wooden steps which ran up its side. I followed the others up this stairway: temperature about 400 degrees I should think. It was a real scorching day - impossible to touch the iron side of the ship without burning your fingers. The ladder led us up on to some deck or other, and we proceeded along a dark corridor towards the sharp end of the boat, by which I mean the part furthest from the rudder.

The walk down this stifling corridor being over we arrived at a sort of wooden hut built up inside the ship, and turned into a telegraphist's and observer's office. The heat here was almost unbearable. The sun was streaming down on this huge iron box of a ship, and inside there was not a breath of air. It was all I could do to evince an interest in Trieste. Someone handed me a pair of German binoculars, and I looked out through a narrow slot cut in the side of the ship. I saw Trieste. It was about as interesting as seeing Tunbridge Wells from Clapham on a clear day. However, I did not want to dishearten the Italians in their quest, so I remarked that it was 'very interesting'. One could just see a lot of blue hills with a town of the Monfalcone order, only larger, at their base. I turned away from the slot in the ship's side, and handed the binoculars to someone else to have a look. The close, oppressive heat was terrific. I had seen Trieste and that was enough for me. When everyone of the party had satisfied their gloating ambitions by looking at Trieste we returned from the ship to the car. No shelling interrupted our movements. All was silent, hot, and rusty in that shipyard.

We bade farewell to the officers who had kindly shown us round, and then drove back towards Udine. I knew the war in the plains fairly well by now, and subsequently had several experiences in the way of seeing more trenches and more troops. I went to all sorts of battalion headquarters and saw the Italian soldiers in every phase of their life on the plains. By the time I had seen all this I felt I 'knew' the war on the Carso. Goritzia, Monfalcone, Udine, Trieste: all this was a definite story to me. Now for what I was after most - the war in the mountains. I applied to the authorities for permission and extorted a promise that I should go there.

I waited in Udine for the day on which I should be permitted to start, and in the meantime, was invited to a famous dinner which I really must describe.

Chapter 29

AN INTERNATIONAL DINNER ~ OFF TO THE MOUNTAINS ~ MY DUCAL GUIDE ~ A PRECIPITOUS MOTOR DRIVE

Udine was the Italian General Headquarters at this time; consequently, if any foreign powers had representatives with the Italians, they were located there. Well, the Italian army did suffer from foreign representatives, and whilst I was at Udine I found a nest of them consisting of English, French, Russian, Belgian, Romanian, Serbian and Japanese. So you see the Italians were not hard up for encouragement from their Allies.

A memory of the Yser.

It was the custom once a week for a dinner to be given to this assembly, at a certain château in the town, and whilst in Udine I was honoured by being asked to join these functions. I went once, and that once I will describe.

I should have gone more often only, as I have hinted previously in this book, I prefer a 'sausage and mash' in a pub round a corner to table-d'hôte at the Ritz. I hate meals elaborated by means of marble pillars, sycophantic head waiters, and publicity.

This international dinner was a fearfully swell affair. It was held in a beautiful garden behind this old-world château, and was really a most picturesque sight: an old Venetian château which possessed an equally old garden and a lawn, with a border of tall dark cypress trees surrounding it. On the lawn was a long dinner-table, and there, prior to dinner, the international guests assembled.

One by one the guests arrived, and what a sight! Each one was attired in the full peacetime uniform affected by his particular Army. I had, of course, to turn up in khaki which had a miserably sombre effect in the midst of so much grandeur. By dinner-time the lawn was a mass of different coloured cloth and gold braid. A circus procession was tawdry compared to this.

Again, another axiom which experience has taught me: 'The gaudiness of the uniform is inversely proportional to the size and importance of the Power'.

A haughty stiffness filled the air, partly due to the starch in these fancy dresses, and partly to the different languages. In time we all folded at the middle, and sat down to dinner. I had an Italian officer on my right, a Romanian general on my left, a Cossack officer and a Serbian ADC opposite. I can only talk English properly, with merely a diabolical attempt at French, so you can imagine that the soup went down amidst almost complete silence. As I gazed at the Cossack's shaved head and grey uniform, I made a mental note; "Sausage and mash at a café in Udine for you, me lad, in the future."

The dinner progressed with all the polite stiffness inseparable from these orgies, but the scene was certainly romantic and picturesque: a wonderful setting sun behind the cypress trees, the dark olive-green lawn and these mighty ones in their fancy dresses. I again thought of that mud-hole in the trench near Messines and realised what a long way I had come.

All these Allied representatives dispersed each day to various offices and represented their different countries, which - to boil it down - I feel sure means being a 'damn nuisance' to the Italian Army Headquarters, who of course had to diplomatically please them, and at the same time get on with the war.

Am I right, Cadorna?

After this one visit to see the 'sea lions fed' I decided that I would not be lured into that again. I in my 'customary suit of solemn' khaki was a

*"There's 'eaps of ice 'round 'ere, Bill,
all we wants is a drop of vanilla."*

damper on this wonderful, kaleidoscopic colour display. Besides, dinner in a café in Udine, with a Gold Flake and coffee to follow, was much more in my line.

I now waited for the day on which I was to go off to the mountains.

One morning I heard all about it. I was to go with the Duke of Milan who was at the Italian Army Headquarters. We were to start in a car, and stay some days with the Alpine regiments who were in the line up in the Dolomite Alps. This was splendid. The Duke was an exceedingly nice companion who talked English, and the Dolomites were what I particularly wanted to see.

The day arrived, and we set off. We whirled along over the dusty flat roads, heading for the mountains. In the distance one could see the mighty forms of the red-coloured Dolomites towering high above, with their snow-capped peaks. With my faculty for seeing the ridiculous in the sublime I could not help thinking that they looked like a row of gigantic strawberry ices. We got nearer and nearer to the mountain region and at last began to leave the baking-hot plains and mount the foothills which led to the mountains. We drove along the narrow, winding roads, past innumerable beautiful villages, now and again passing over a bridge and a raging torrent of emerald-coloured water. The atmosphere was, needless to say, as clear as crystal, and as we gained in height the great heat diminished. Occasionally we would pass a stream of motor-lorries on their way to or from some part of the battle-line, and now and again we would nearly collide with an Italian staff car which was doing its usual ninety miles an hour round impossible corners.

Higher and higher we went; always spiralling upwards along the mountain roads. It seemed an endless drive. One seems to have to do so much road work to get such a little distance - always going round and round the same mountain to get to a point you have seen half an hour before. We were making for Belluno because from there we would make a second day's journey to see the Alpini. Belluno was a good convenient spot to make a start from for the last lap of the business, and moreover contained a lot of military headquarters officials with power to give permission for various visits. We scaled a crowd of mountains in that car, and crashed along through many a lonely forest glade.

The water in the radiator started to boil in the middle of one mountainous forest, and we had to explain radiators and their need for water to two aboriginal girls who were living in a wood-cutter's hut hard by. They fetched us some water, and were suitably rewarded by the Duke.

The same evening we started our spiral descent down towards Belluno which lies in a valley in the mountains. About six o'clock we crossed the bridge into the town, and glided up to the courtyard of an hotel, just off the main square. So ended the first stage in the journey.

Chapter 30

**MORE MOUNTAINS ~ ORDEAL BY MULE ~
THE ALPINI ~ A VISIT TO ROME**

Another night, in another hotel, and then came the visit to the Alpini. In the morning we went round to see some potentate or other, who lurked in the Town Hall which had been taken over by the military authorities. He gave us some permission to do something which I did not catch, and off we started.

It was necessary to do about twenty miles in the car before we got near these mountain trenches, and then came the most terrible feat of all. We had been driving along the usual mountain spiral roads, rushing through forests, over cascades on thin, flimsy-looking bridges, past vast waterfalls, half of which were usually frozen and covered with snow. At length we came to a halt. I wasn't surprised, as the road had ended, and a colossal mountain stuck up on either side.

"Are we there?" I asked.

"Not quite," replied someone, and with that I became aware of a group of mules being led towards us. I hoped they would pass, but no.

"What do we do now?" I asked again.

The Duke interpreted the cataract of conversation he had been listening to. "We now have to do about an hour and a half's ride on these mules," he said. He seemed to relish this idea. Dukes are prone to riding, I have noticed - I am not. I would have given a large sum of money to have seen a glacier or something slide down the hill and obliterate those mules.

We all got out of the car, and the Duke and I, plus a few assorted officers who were to act as guides, made for the mules. I clambered up the side of my mount, and was relieved to notice that an Alpini soldier was going to lead the beast with a rope. The Duke and the others rode these mules as if they liked nothing better. I sat like a pair of compasses on mine.

We started off. First of all over a perilous wooden bridge, and then off up a precarious slope at an angle of forty-five degrees. Oh, that ride! For one hour and a half I was busily engaged trying to avoid sliding off over the mule's tail. That road was a disgrace, if you could call it a road. It was a narrow, twisting track, winding through a pine forest at an almost impossible angle.

Many times on that journey I felt it was a toss-up as to whether my mule and I would go sliding all the way back to the bottom of the hill. The path was made of large, rough stones with occasional wood struts across it, and apparently the object of the designers had been to take one round the most frightful hair-raising corners and nerve-shattering ravines. I confess that, when crossing a mighty chasm full of a raging mountain torrent on a three-foot bridge, I was in a funk. These mules were amazing. They seemed to think nothing of crossing one of these elementary bridges with a half-melted glacier underneath, on three legs, with the other over the side.

They ought to ride monkeys, not mules, in these places. "An hour and a half of this!" I thought, as I rode along. My Alpini guide was ahead, assisting the mule and me, by means of a long rope fixed somewhere near the mule's nose (I couldn't see where). I wished he wouldn't do this, as it forced a pace on me which was very uncomfortable, especially about the seat of the trousers. I didn't like to speak about it though, as I hate hurting people's feelings, even an Alpini's. It seemed to last for hours, that trip. A never-ending forest and a path that seemed to have been designed to include everything in the way of excitement.

At last, when my stamina and nerve were at the lowest ebb, I became aware of the fact that there was humanity about. This phenomenon manifested itself by means of sundry swarthy faces which peeped at one from behind trees. The woods became alive with curious dark brown eyes, glaring out of the undergrowth. These faces belonged to the Alpini, whose forest home we had now reached. The sight of an English officer awakened them a bit. The first they had ever seen, and a poor specimen at that.

I must have looked like a sort of mascot officer on a toy mule; of the sort you might see at Gamage's. I did my best to throw an expression of 'I-love-hunting-and-am-a-devil-for-riding' into my face, but I fear I failed. These mountaineers saw through it. At last our cavalcade came to a welcome halt. The Duke, who had enjoyed the ride, I think, dismounted, and I removed my stiffened, battered body to the ground. The mules were dragged off to some cavern, but were unfortunately fostered for our return. We now had to do the rest of the journey on foot. We scaled a precipice, and at last reached what we were looking for: the forest mountain home of the Alpini.

We saw the Colonel of this regiment, and he showed us all around. I still felt I was riding the mule. The Duke, on the other hand, was walking about as if nothing had happened. I looked with pain at the various means of defence and offence employed by these wonderful mountaineers. (Oh, that mule!) I was shown ridiculous trenches which ran up to the side of an almost perpendicular mountain of solid rock. In some cases I observed that the Austrians and Italians shared a mountain. Appalling discomfort and no result. The only offensive that occurred in these volcanic regions was occasionally when an Italian would unexpectedly meet an Austrian round a boulder, and would at once engage in mortal combat, ending probably by having a dagger - or possibly a bayonet stuck in each, and both rolling down six thousand yards of mountain, there to be marked hereafter by two neat, but small wooden crosses. Such is national antagonism. After an exhausting few hours looking at these wonders we were piloted back to lunch.

These Alpini saw other human beings about once a year, so when I was dragged in to lunch they were determined to make the best of it. Being a British officer, too, the interest was intense. The Ancient Mariner, stopping one of three, was nothing to this. They held me in conversation for an incredible period. I thought that lunch would never end. From about half-past twelve till four o'clock it lasted, and during that time I had to describe what was going on on other Fronts, and war news generally. Poor devils, they were stuck away up in these impossible mountains without any chance of coming into the world; I suppose some day, years hence, they will come back to the world and find that the war's over - they will never hear about it otherwise.

I spent many days after this going to see various forms of mountain fighting, and I wandered through many miles of Alpine scenery, spent hours in many a still mountain forest glade, and pondered on this distant, obscure warfare which was being relentlessly pursued. I saw all the celebrated mountains which had been captured, and had many a meal with various mountain detachments. Night and silence midst those vast mountains was a wondrous thing - very depressing to me somehow. The futility of it all seemed to hit me hard. I remember, near Monte Piave, coming to some few isolated wooden crosses, marking a few graves on the icy shadows of the mighty mountain, and I couldn't help evolving a small verse as I looked at the scene, and have since made a large painting of the theme:

Here, amidst the frozen Dolomites,
A battered cross - some mountain flowers - a breeze;
A hero of a hundred Alpine fights;
One hears his story from the whispering trees.

I left the mountains one fine morning and returned to Udine. My time was up now on the Italian Front. I had seen many things and had absorbed the many wonderful details in connection with the peculiar war which it was necessary for Italy to cope with. The main feature which struck me most forcibly was their great engineering ability; their rapid rebuilding on devastated areas, their great wire rope transport schemes in the mountains, etc., etc. I left the Italian Front, taking my hat off deep and low to their ability.

Before leaving Italy I asked permission to visit Rome *en route* - I was very keen to do this. As I was so near, I was most anxious to have a day amidst the historic wonders of Rome. I was readily given leave, so off I started, and left Treviso in a Pullman-car seat for the ancient city on the Tiber. After Rome, I was to return to England to turn the mass of impressions and detail I had obtained into a set of pictures of life on the Italian Front. I determined to work a bit in Rome, and then return, *via* Paris, to London to complete the job. I arrived in Rome.

Chapter 31

ROME ~ RETURN TO LONDON ~
'THE BETTER 'OLE' ~ A REQUEST FROM AMERICA

What a charming spot Rome is! Here one was clean out of the war. Hotels, cafés, theatres, bright sunny days, with people all amusing themselves. I had only two days in Rome, but I got busy in that time. I bribed a motor merchant to take me everywhere worth seeing; I took his car for a morning and went off to the Appian Way. Saw the baths of Caracalla and the Coliseum. I should have liked a week in Rome to let all these wonders soak in. A good look round St Peter's and the Vatican completed my sightseeing. I stayed at the Grand Hotel near the station, and found it to be the usual sort of pomp, glitter and marble business, which apparently is inseparable from grandeur in all countries. At this date, besides my pictures, which had been appearing regularly every week, I had completed another effort with which most people are now familiar, namely the play, *'The Better 'Ole'*. It had been finished just prior to my departure for Italy, and the theatre management had been getting on with the production. I picked up papers in Rome which announced its forthcoming appearance in London. Being particularly anxious to be back in time to look over the final rehearsals and details I was not sorry that the Italian tour had ended at such an opportune moment. I was not going to stay long in Rome, but hurry along back, so that whilst getting on with my finished sketches, I could also now and again go to superintend rehearsals at the theatre.

After the usual journey - Rome, Paris, London - I settled down to work hard on all the subject matter I had culled in Italy. Each day, and all day, I have worked for months on end at the real hard labour which drawing cartoons entails. I started on my Italian drawings, and found time in the evenings to go to rehearsals of that show, *'The Better 'Ole'*. Now that it is an accomplished fact, I want you to exonerate me from any idea of ego or advertisement whilst I tell you the result of this show. It played in London for over a year, twice daily. Five touring companies toured and are touring as I write, and have played in the same towns over and over again. It is an equal success in America, Canada and Australia, whilst amongst its minor activities it has toured India. Yet on the night before the first production, I would willingly have accepted a small fee to have the whole show cancelled.

I felt that I could place little or no reliance on others sufficiently understanding to interpret the real meaning of 'Old Bill', 'Bert' and 'Alf' - for they are the embodiment of my idea of a great and curious phenomenon: the psychological temperament of the British race. Added to which there was the peculiar atmosphere and romance which this unique war has possessed. However, the play started, and has had the results above mentioned, much to the surprise of the management and sundry other individuals whose ideas, of necessity, largely rotate round girls, tights and rag music. *'The Better 'Ole'* having been fairly launched on its run, I worked all day and every day on my drawings for the War Office, which subsequently went to papers all over the world.

Now came another big and interesting move for me. I was suddenly informed that the American Propaganda Department had applied to know whether it was possible for me to go to visit and live with the American army in the field, "there to find and create similar characters to 'Bill', 'Bert' and 'Alf'." So said the cable. This was great news. I had been with the British, French and Italian armies, and now was to go to the last joined army of all - the American.

America was just beginning to send her first troops to France, and I was to be with them on their initial appearance. I received my orders and instructions, and forthwith set off to join the ever-rising tide of the American army, and to see life way out in Alsace-Lorraine. I little thought that this was to be my last Front in the war; but after the long session I spent out round this area, I left it to hear of the armistice before my return again to France. I left for the American Front full of enthusiasm, vigour and curiosity.

As far as they can make out with the binoculars, from Monte Macaroni across the valley, the man marked 'x' is almost certain to get the Italian Victoria Cross.

Chapter 32

START FOR AMERICAN FRONT ~ COMMON-SENSE METHODS ~ NEUFCHATEAU ~ A CORDIAL WELCOME

I think, perhaps, I was keener on going to this Front than any. This arrival in Europe of a vast army of our own kith and kin, from over three thousand miles away, was a great and wonderful event; and what was no small consideration in my case, I was going amongst soldiers who spoke my own mother tongue. Moreover, the American army was taking over the most romantic part of the whole French battle-line, Alsace-Lorraine.

All ways to the Front run through Paris - at least, all Fronts except the British, and, consequently, I found myself once more in the French capital, thus making the eleventh time I had crossed the Channel. Back at the old Gare du Nord, and a lonely night or two in Paris. I reported at the Headquarters of the American Intelligence Department in the Rue St Anne, off the Avenue de l'Opéra, and there received intelligent consideration and answers, which somehow one expects but does not always find in an Intelligence Department. The American staff officers were most courteous, and without any loss of time explained how I was to get to my destination. Going to the American Front was made the easiest thing in the world, if you were authorised to go, and your mission was genuine.

The American methods are direct and to the point. 'Common sense' is turned on rapidly and clearly, and a decision one way or the other arrived at without a month or two of 'passed for necessary action'.

I left Paris for the railhead most suitable for my ultimate destination, which was Gondricourt, and made very much the same journey that I had taken before, when going to Verdun. We passed through Bar-le-Duc, and trickled along a desolate line of rails until we reached the dull-looking, war-worn town known as Gondricourt. This was an American railhead, and this was my first sight of the American army. There were a few of these children of the West hanging about the station, and I could feel at once the type of soldier they were. My first big impression of America in our European war, and an impression I still retain, is that they seemed to jump in at the point which it had taken us four year to get to. Within a week of landing they looked as if they had been in the war since 1914. They wallowed off into the mud, misery and destruction, without any amateurish-looking deportment.

The men at the station were probably waiting around for the arrival of military stores, or something of that sort, whilst, of course, the collection comprised one or two military police, which you find anywhere. All fine, healthy-looking men, a hint of what I was to see later.

A car was waiting for me at the station, and in I got, with my baggage. We drove off towards Neufchâteau, which was at that time the headquarters of one of the first American divisions to arrive in France. The chauffeur had been told where to take me, so I lay back behind my suitcase and half under a rug and looked out at the scenery.

A very grey, bleak country, undulating and desolate. Now and again we would flash through a muddy, dilapidated village, frightening a lot of hens, causing a pig or two to stare, or some man or woman to pause in his or her work to gaze at us. We had several miles of this sort of thing to do, but finally we topped a rise and began a descent on a winding road into Neufchâteau. Everywhere now were the signs of the American army. Rows of motor-lorries on the road, groups of soldiers, men working on the telegraph and telephone lines at the side, men standing around their billets, a general busy confusion, getting thicker and thicker as we approached the town. We reached the main street and reduced our speed as we wended our way through the mass of soldiers moving about in the narrow, old-world street. Here I was now right amongst the Americans. First impressions: big, strong, healthy, cheerful, with all the effective cowboy looks, strap of hat behind their heads, and the familiar large felt hat.

I felt at once, "I shall be all right here." Driving down the main street we at length turned up a still narrower lane, and reached a market-square with the inevitable statue in the middle. Turning out of this square we descended a hill and came at last to an hotel. Of course, the word 'hotel' is absurd; but the proprietor's feelings might possibly be hurt if I described it as anything else.

A room had been booked for me here. My bags were dragged in, and I went to this room. It was only one stage better than the hotel at Coxyde, but had the advantage of not being shelled, or living in fear of a shelling. You can have no idea how much nicer a hotel is when there is no prospect of a few 'five-point nines' coming through the roof during your stay.

My bedroom was a plain, uncarpeted room, no fireplace, and a plain, yellow wood bed. A candle furnished the only illumination. I sat on the bed and surveyed the situation, after which I unpacked and dug myself into the room as much as possible.

After repeated imprecations down the staircase, a young, but portly, Alsatian girl brought up some hot water and placed it in the enamel tin basin. Whilst I was having a wash and brush-up, there was a knock at the door, and on opening it I found an officer from the press Censor's office, who gave me a message from the Divisional General. The General had very kindly asked me to dine with him that night. I was very tired, but still, of course, I decided at once to accept this hospitality, and consequently prepared myself to go.

The officer told me how to get to the Headquarters, and by dinner-time I reached the place. The General was most cordial and hospitable. I have seldom met a nicer man, and several times after this I had the privilege of being taken by him round the sights in his area. He, of course, had a group of staff officers around him, and they were in every way the most friendly group I have ever met. They gave me permission to do everything I liked in the divisional area. The General talked a lot about my pictures. He had a collection of them all, and was most interested in my war wanderings and the adventures I had met with. He was only just

recovering from an attack of pneumonia, and this worried him considerably, as it prevented him from being as active as he wished.

Altogether a most kindly and genial headquarters; I wish all were like this one.

I explained exactly what I had to do, and how I liked to do it. They did everything in their power to assist. The General told one of his ADCs to go with me next day, and to show me as far as possible over the various component parts of his divisional area.

Late that night I left the headquarters and wended my way back to my old hotel. I mounted the creaky stairs, entered my bleak, cold room, and crept into bed.

Chapter 33

A PRIMITIVE 'HOTEL' ~ YANKS IN TRAINING
VISIT TO MARINE HQ ~ KEENNESS AND EFFICIENCY

The weakest point in that outrageous hotel was, I found, the question of breakfast. I asked for breakfast; I talked about breakfast; I intimated that I was perfectly willing to pay for breakfast - but I couldn't ever get any. Whilst living there I had to be up early and off on some expedition or other in the cold mornings, and I never could start the day right owing to this defect in the management. The hotel was a French one, and was not patronised by the Americans, who lived in billets and arranged for their own breakfasts. For several days I made repeated attempts to encourage the management into some effort towards a breakfast, but no - it was useless. The best that happened was that I had a cup of atrocious coffee on a damp, marble-topped table, with a roll of unbreakable bread about two feet long. The room was a saloon bar, the time usually about 7.00am. Opposite me sometimes sat the manager in shirt sleeves and carpet-slippers, eating an enormous slab of repellent cheese, and washing it down by drinking a quantity of red wine. This sight alone, at 7.00am, is unnerving. Later, I bought some biscuits and a tin of jam in order to deaden the taste of the coffee.

My first views of the American army were made in the vicinity of Neufchâteau, in this divisional area. A great quantity of training was, of course, on at this time, and everywhere one could see strenuous work and enthusiasm. One felt and saw at once that these people had not come over from so far in any mood of a light and breezy expedition. There was business and determination in the air, and what was more, that which ultimately meant the crushing of Germany - I mean the 'big outlook' which you could see the American General Staff was taking. They realised that the war was going to be a big job. Everywhere were signs that the work was not going to be underdone. If need be, Germany was to be swamped by the might of America. This early, clear vision, and its resulting big, relentless, effort, was as instrumental as anything in starting the demoralisation of the enemy, which ultimately led to his downfall.

I went to a certain bayonet exercise school. Here an English sergeant was giving instruction to the American soldiers. He was a gymnastic sergeant and a 'non-com' in the old 'regulars', and I don't suppose a finer instructor could have been found anywhere. The Americans all appreciated his value, and he appreciated their rising ability. It was a vigorous school, that. Bayonet charges over fields and trenches, rifle ranges, and all the arts necessary to efficient Prussian puncturing.

Near this place I saw huge hospital arrangements, some finished, others being constructed. I drove with the General in his car one day to some of the outlying camps, and saw the American army at work on all phases of war training. It was a busy live sector, this Neufchâteau.

In the evenings, when I got back, I used to prowl around the men's billets and cookhouses and watch their life there. There was a French and American officers' club at Neufchâteau, and a great place it was, too. I had dinner here several times and met many different men. Cocktails, tobacco smoke, talking and laughter - dinner - then more cocktails, tobacco, talk and laughter: a truly cheery spot. I felt that Americans way back in the homeland would have liked to know what a cheerful job their countrymen made of things. One can say with truth in this war that the nearer one was to the Front the more cheerfulness one found around.

There were several war correspondents in this area, representing several different papers in the States, and I had the pleasure of meeting some of them. They, too, like myself, had 'hotels' as their temporary homes. On a certain day it happened that one or two of them were going over to stay at a place about twenty-five miles away, in order to live with the Marines for a bit. They asked me whether I would like to come.

"Rather!" I replied enthusiastically. So a morning was fixed for our departure. A large car stood outside one of the 'hotels' at about seven in the morning; we all got in, and started off. I had had much motoring to do during my war life, and have known what it is to be motored alongside a precipice on a four-foot road, over a yawning chasm on an amateur bridge, etc., but heaven preserve me from an American wartime chauffeur again. He *reduces* his speed to about eighty miles an hour whilst passing through towns and villages, but in the country, when he doesn't know the roads, that's when he goes 'all out'. I arrived at the Marine area in what you might have taken to be the winning car in a Cup Race; tears were pouring out of my eyes and frozen stiff on my cheeks.

The Marines are the star troops of the American army, and are simply splendid; their countrymen may well be proud of them. We went to a Battalion Colonel's house and found him in. I have seen a good many Colonels in my time, but never a better from a military point of view than this one. He had, as a regular soldier, seen service in all parts of the world, and subsequently told me many interesting adventures of his campaigns. With him were several regimental officers who all lived in quite a nice little house in the village. The Marines were billeted all around, and also occupied several wooden huts. We had a most hospitable reception, and I knew at once that this area was going to be of great use to me in my job. I went about amongst the lines, making rough notes and taking photographs.

Here was a typical sample of the American army dumped down in this strange land to take part in a most peculiar and mighty war. And a jolly good job they meant to make of it. The housing, feeding and general upkeep of the American soldier is excellent, and the health and strength of the Marines I saw was perfect. We all had lunch in the little house, and afterwards the Colonel took myself and a couple of the war correspondents for a walk around his area. The discipline he maintained was that of a battleship. He called out a few men here and there and ordered certain things to be done to show us details of their routine. He ordered out a squad of men to do some bayonet work and turned a strict, acid criticism on the performance. Everywhere the whole of his command worked with alacrity and smartness. Now and again he caught a malefactor, and in a few warm phrases made him think that perhaps there was a 'better 'ole' elsewhere than that particular spot at that particular moment. The Marines are comparable to our Guards, and one cannot say more than that.

I got a wealth of material on this visit. I made drawings from life of several of the soldiers, and listened to stories of Cuba and Mexico. I went into one billet, and after I had been talking for some time to those around me, one man asked me whether I had ever met Bairnsfather, 'the man who draws the pictures'. This was rather embarrassing. I said I had known Bairnsfather for about thirty years; in fact that I myself was Bairnsfather. This caused great merriment to those in the place, and bashful confusion to my questioner.

I had tea up at the château where the Marine Brigadier General lives, and one day attended a tea party given by the French owner of the château and his wife. They were very nice people, and made very light of the evil times they and their estate had fallen on. I found all my picture stuff well known to them, as Madame had kept on buying it at Brentanos whenever she went to Paris. Finding that I am known in advance before I arrive at a place is always a great relief to me, as I hate explaining. I have been very fortunate in this respect. The first General I met up in the Italian Alps immediately produced my book, *'Bullets & Billets'*, and told me he had got it in Rome.

The conversation amongst the Marines at this time almost entirely consisted of the theme, "when are we going to be allowed to go to the trenches and begin?" The keenness was terrific. No better news could have come to them than that a big battle called for their immediate attendance. Poor chaps; they got their wish before long, when they performed their splendid achievement at St Mihiel, and took that long-enduring salient from the Boches.

Chapter 34

VISITS TO SHELLED AREAS ~ SALVATION ARMY CANTEEN ~ A BREWERY BILLET ~ AN OMEN

One cannot recount every episode which befalls in times so varied and full as these. My visits on all Fronts have led to so many adventures and afterthoughts that the length of a book is barely space enough in which to fit them. But these chapters of mine are merely intended to pick out the salient features, and so I will not enumerate a lot of little incidents which happened on this Front, but go ahead with an account of a visit to quite another part of the American line. Afterwards I shall tell of

"Château Thierry"

my last billet in the war and how I saw in it a big omen which I correctly interpreted as foreshadowing an early termination to my war-wanderings.

One day I saw a chance of visiting a sector in which reposed much artillery. I took the chance, and went with an officer in a car. We passed through many places of interest; towns whose names I had seen on maps, and which had always pricked up my imagination. Nancy, Toul, Luneville were on the route, and I spent a few hours in each place. Luneville attracted me; it wasn't so very badly knocked about and the town was very reminiscent of historic interest. Stanislaus, the King of Poland, used to live around here, apparently preferring it to Poland. From photographs and accounts of that country I see his wisdom. We went to Baccarat, famous as everyone knows for 'shove-halfpenny' and other gambling attractions. We also paid a short visit to Vittel, the famous watering-place, where I walked through miles of deserted but beautiful Pump Room gardens.

The artillery bunch that I went to see were right up at the front line. They were actively in the war, and this fact became painfully noticeable before I left. We entered a completely ruined village, hid the car, and proceeded to the Battery Colonel's house. Here we sat and talked for a good while, and then he took us round the sights. What a mess! The whole place was nothing but a pile of blackened bricks and mud. We saw the punctured tower of the old church, and went to look through a crack in a mangled-up house at the German positions.

Whilst there, the old familiar gurgling whistle sounded in the air, and was followed by a cloud of dust and earth flying upwards. A shell had burst down the road, and we knew that the Germans had started their daily annoyance. We went back into a barn where a group of American soldiers were busy staring down the road. As we looked, another shell came over and landed on the road. Out of the ensuing cloud of dust and smoke shot a motor-bicycle. A dispatch rider had just missed the explosion. He motored past us totally unconcerned, and went on his way. The Colonel thought it inadvisable for us to move away until this riot had subsided, and I mentally conjured up a vision of what would happen if one of those shells hit our car, which it easily might. We retired to a sandbagged dugout - the Colonel's headquarters - and had a smoke.

Whilst there, the Germans endeavoured to drop shells in as many unpleasant places as possible, but in about an hour the firing ceased. This was our opportunity, so we got out the car and motored to Beauvais, a little village not far away. Near here we began to feel mighty hungry, so the allurements of a roadside Salvation Army canteen held us

With all that shortage of tonnage, too!

tightly. We halted at this canteen, which we found had been established in an old, shell-shattered barn. A large tarpaulin formed the roof, and here and there a hole in it let the bright daylight stream through down on the heads of a crowd of American 'dough-boys' who were resting from their labours. They were either eating, playing cards or lying around smoking, and it struck me as a weird scene. The tarpaulin and the patches of sunlight striking their cowboy hats and sunburnt faces gave a beautiful effect of light and shade. At the end of this room some girls were frying eggs, and making toast and coffee. It was such a human scene, and I could not help admiring the courage of these Salvation Army girls, living up at such a place, and working as they were doing.

What a terror an American soldier is for eggs! I saw a plate containing a dozen fried eggs, and found on inquiry that they were all for one man. Those hens around there must have been doing overtime for many months now.

I took away many pleasant recollections of that scene. The tired, strong soldiers in their muddy clothes and rough felt hats, the girls working away for their comfort, such as it could be, under such surroundings. We all had fried eggs and coffee and very good they were. Feeling much better after this scratch meal we started on our return to that ancient, dingy borough of Neufchâteau.

Towards the end of my visit I again went to the Officers' Club. I turned to this as a welcome relief from the chilly horrors of my 'hotel'. On this occasion I was dining with Mr Floyd Gibbons of the *Chicago Tribune*. As we left the place together late that night he asked me where I was staying. I confessed to my 'hotel'. He, an open-hearted companion in my misfortune, suggested my coming for a couple of nights to his place. He had, it appeared, discovered a 'peach' in the way of billets; an old brewery at the far end of the town. Of course no beer in it, but a few rooms, looked after by the wife of the manager, who was away fighting somewhere.

We reached the place, and Gibbons took me up to the rooms he had got hold of. Very nice too, and a hundred per cent advance on that 'hotel'. There were two chambers, one leading out of the other, with two beds in the inner one; I had one bed, he had the other, and next morning - bacon and eggs! My first decent breakfast since arrival!

Gibbons had to go off somewhere that day whilst I drew hard at sketches till the evening, when, following my usual custom, I went round seeing what I could.

These prowls on my own in Nieuport, Ypres, Verdun, Udine, Neufchâteau, etc., etc., have been perhaps the least painful parts of the war for me.

That night, again, I went to the Club and there got a message that Gibbons would not be at dinner, but that he would go straight to the brewery billets as he would be back late. Somehow or other I got enveloped in a very convivial evening. It was my last prior to my return to England, and it's a curious thing how one's last evening at a place always seems to be the best. It was very late when I emerged into the darkness, and plodded off to the brewery. Feeling sure that Gibbons would probably be in bed and have left the door open, I went along whistling and revelling in the joys of my return towards England on the morrow. A good night's rest, I thought, then every hour will bring me nearer civilisation and good old *Angleterre*.

I arrived at the brewery; all was dark and still, the huge and double doors of the yard were shut. I had forgotten about these doors, but didn't regard them as an insurmountable barrier as I felt sure that there must be a small side door somewhere that was open. So I didn't worry, but looked casually for the side door. I looked, I groped, I scratched, and then the truth, in all its chilly horror, dawned on me. I was locked out! Locked out of a brewery at midnight! I stood, silent and still, under the moonlight, coupling other words beginning with 'B' to the brewery.

"What the . . .?"

"Why the . . .?" Etc., etc.

One doesn't expect to be locked out of a brewery under the moonlight at midnight; I had a sort of feeling that something romantic ought to happen. A lattice should open somewhere above one's head, and a pale, delicate hand drop a little scented note with a seal on it; a momentary light in her window, a rustle somewhere in the shadows, and Madeline is beside you. But no! This was just a cold, dark brewery, hermetically sealed.

I began at last to be practical. I searched the brewery's outer defences for the least crack that would permit of my getting into the yard, and thus reach the door of the house. Finding nothing that would help me, I decided to climb the wall. There was a dark, narrow passage along one side of the left-hand wall, dividing the brewery from a private house. I entered this passage and kicked against some projecting wood sheds which I hadn't seen. Looking upwards, I saw the tiled top of the yard wall, grim and clear against the moonlit sky.

"Say, who are those guys over there?"
"YMCA officials."
"Yes, I know that, but I mean those two by the tree."
"Soldiers may be?"

THE MAN WHO CAME 3000 MILES.

The man who came 3000 miles.

I began to climb up these wooden outhouses. I got on the roof, but slipping, removed most of the skin from my left hand, and allowed a leg with a military top-boot on to crash through a window covered with wire netting. Then, what a tornado! The sheds were filled with rabbits and hens, which, till then, had presumably been paralysed by fright into silence. The top-boot broke the spell. A wild, scratching scamper, mixed with the hysterical clucking of terrified hens, broke the still night air, and I lay dumbfounded on the tiled roof about two yards from the top of the brewery wall. A lattice did open now, and a gnarled and twisted brown hand gesticulated wildly in emphasising a barrage of unintelligible French, which was hurled out of the window. When the first furious blast was over I, sitting on my tiled roof, endeavoured to instil calm and understanding into this proud possessor of hens and rabbits. Short gaps in his speeches (when he was pausing for breath) enabled me to get quick, jerky little conversational stabs at him, and ultimately one of these got home. He at least understood that I was an officer who lived in the brewery, and had got locked out. His grizzled head disappeared, and presently I heard the door-key of his house turn and he came outside. He wasn't at all annoyed now, but opened the door of the brewery yard. I thanked him and entered. At last! The time was about half-past one.

"I shall soon reach my bed, and tomorrow I have to get up early to drive off to Gondricourt, on my way back to England," I thought to myself.

I stood for a few moments outside the door of the house on some stone steps, moonlight and stillness flooding the large yard of the deserted brewery. An old wagon and an empty cask or two stood in the shadows of an open shed. "Here I am," I thought, "in 1918, standing in a brewery in Alsace, far, far away from the spot where I first started in the war." I thought of all the host of things that I had done and seen since those early day. As I thought on these things I suddenly remembered that *my very first billet in the war had been a brewery:* the old deserted brewery at Nieppe, near Armentières. "What an omen!" I thought, "my first billet a brewery, and now a brewery again."

Did it mean that this was to be my last war billet?

It did.

Chapter 35

EN ROUTE TO ENGLAND ~ AN UNEXPECTED MEETING

Gibbons, with his own private key, got back and to bed sometime or other during that night, as I found him there on waking next morning. He was most amused at my adventure, and was sorry he had forgotten to tell me about the yard shutting after a certain hour. These episodes amuse me too - when they are over.

This was the day I left the American Front. I had seen these Western soldiers, training, fighting, resting - I knew the story and I felt their part, and now had come the time for me to leave. I enjoyed my visits to the American army as I have enjoyed no others. I look upon those times as the best I have spent in the war. Both officers and men are a fine crowd. I thanked Gibbons for his kindness to me, and incidentally mentioned to him the omen of the night before. He smiled. Poor fellow! I'm sure he thought the war was going to last till the fall of 1925.

I left old Neufchâteau in an American Press car, and was whirled away to Gondricourt. *En route* one passes the birthplace of Jeanne d'Arc at Domremy. It's a weird little place, and most gloomy. I don't wish to be disrespectful to the Maid of Orleans, but I feel that had I been born there myself I should have been bothered with visions too. I reached Gondricourt, and of course had the usual hour's wait on a grey, bleak platform, on a grey, bleak day. At last the train of preposterous length rattled into the station, and I found a seat on it somehow. And now we left Gondricourt - farewell to the American army and all the times I had had there. We passed through Château-Thierry, of course, and I little thought that so soon would be coming that terrific German onslaught which took this place, and that, in the ensuing battles, those chaps I had left so recently would be playing such a glorious part. The American resistance at Château-Thierry forms an episode that will live in golden letters on the pages of American history. I returned to Paris and went to the Rue St Anne to thank the authorities for my visit and for all the facilities they had given me. The next day I left for England, via Boulogne, and had the good fortune to run into my young brother on the wharf there. He is one of those people of whom ladies say, "He has got on so well, you know." He is a Staff Captain. You know what I mean; a red hat, two strawberry marks on the collar of his coat, highly nuggeted top-boots, spurs and shorts. He condescended to lean against a counter in the Hotel Folkestone and have a cocktail with me. We hadn't seen each other for ages, and he was going back to his corps up north, somewhere.

Beginning his life in the war by being nearly assassinated at Morval, in the Somme battle, he, bit by bit, has 'risen high in his profession'. He's a good lad, is my brother.

England! That's where I was going now. I went, and so begin the closing chapters of my war career.

Chapter 36

START FOR AMERICA ~ HELD UP ~ A DEVIOUS COURSE ~ NEW YORK ~ LIBERTY LOAN ~ SPEECHMAKING ~ GO SICK ~ START FOR HOME

It has been a wonderful war this, full of surprises for everyone, and I somehow think the Germans have been more surprised than anybody. But, way down amongst the ordinary small mortals, who form the component parts of this monstrous catastrophe, I doubt whether anyone has been cast for a more varied or unexpected role than myself.

The sort of man I dislike intensely:
who says in a low baritone voice that he has heard from the cabin boy that it was just here that the 'Insomnia' was struck and went down in under three minutes.

"It's an 'ell of a time way back to 1914," as Old Bill would say, and when I, fastidiously but firmly, stepped into that historical Flanders mud, I little thought that, ere my part was done in this conflict, I should number a visit to the United States of America amongst my other wanderings. And yet, here I am, penning these lines on a troopship crossing the Atlantic on my return from America. ('Penning these lines', by the way, consists in searching for the paper with an oscillating fountain-pen, and occasionally stabbing it down to the bed; then waiting till the next wave comes.)

On a troopship in mid-Atlantic - that's where I start to write 'The Eleventh and Last Voyage of Sinbad the Sailor', as it were; but it is in England where this last yarn begins.

When the startling and bewildering news that I was to go to the United States was squirted at me by the powers that be, I was in London, recently returned from the American Front in France. Whilst with the Americans I had frequently wished that sometime or other I could go to the country they came from. To my mind, one's judgement of an army is quite incomplete unless one knows what sort of a thing is behind that army, what sort of a feeling those behind have for those they have sent to war, and what those behind are doing, saying and thinking. I little thought that this vague wish of mine would be so soon realised.

Anyway, events developed. One night I received my orders, and two days later off I started. Now, in these days of strife, going to America is, as everyone knows, a complicated and secretive sort of business. There is scarcely any doubt that the Germans do not like us - in fact, they have gone still further, and what's more have been very nasty about this - sailing to and from America. I shall, therefore, in accordance with what is best for all concerned, refrain from mentioning where I sailed from, the name of the ship I travelled in, and any other details which I feel might cause jubilation, information, or gratification in Cuxhaven, Berlin, or elsewhere.

I left London, swathed in the garments which we have all grown to associate with captains in the British Army, with three boxes, complete with labels.

After a frantic and exhausting rush to a certain sea-port, in order to catch the boat which threatened to leave hourly, I then languished for a week in an hotel, as the sailing was cancelled on arrival. This, of course, was part of some cunning nautical plan, but I also learnt from sundry philosophers of the neighbourhood that there was some trouble about coal - either there was no coal, or too much coal, or nobody to poke the fire, or something, I don't quite know what (I'm no sailor); but, anyway, some bother about coal had something to do with the delay. The days of ships driven by means of twisted elastic being now quite past, we all had to wait for this coal crisis to right itself. Hence that week in the hotel. I hate hotels as I have said before; I am unmanned by an hotel. Vast palm courts and marble dining-halls depress me. This hotel was one of those gigantic new structures with several revolving front doors and an array of haughty females safe behind mahogany counters, who book you a room 'if there is one'.

Time dragged along slowly in this gilded and stupendous edifice. I discovered a Turkish and swimming-bath somewhere down below in a labyrinth of halls and passages, and spent most of my time down there. At last, after several false alarms, I finally got notice of the day and time I was ordered to embark.

It's extraordinary in hotels how news of your departure leaks out, and what a lot of interest it evokes. Strangers, in Field-Marshals' uniforms, enter your room with a skeleton key, and offer to remove your luggage, order you a taxi or take your clothes away to be brushed. The whole staff of housemaids who have your room in hand - from one anaemic-looking wench to about six monarchs of physical culture - all visit your

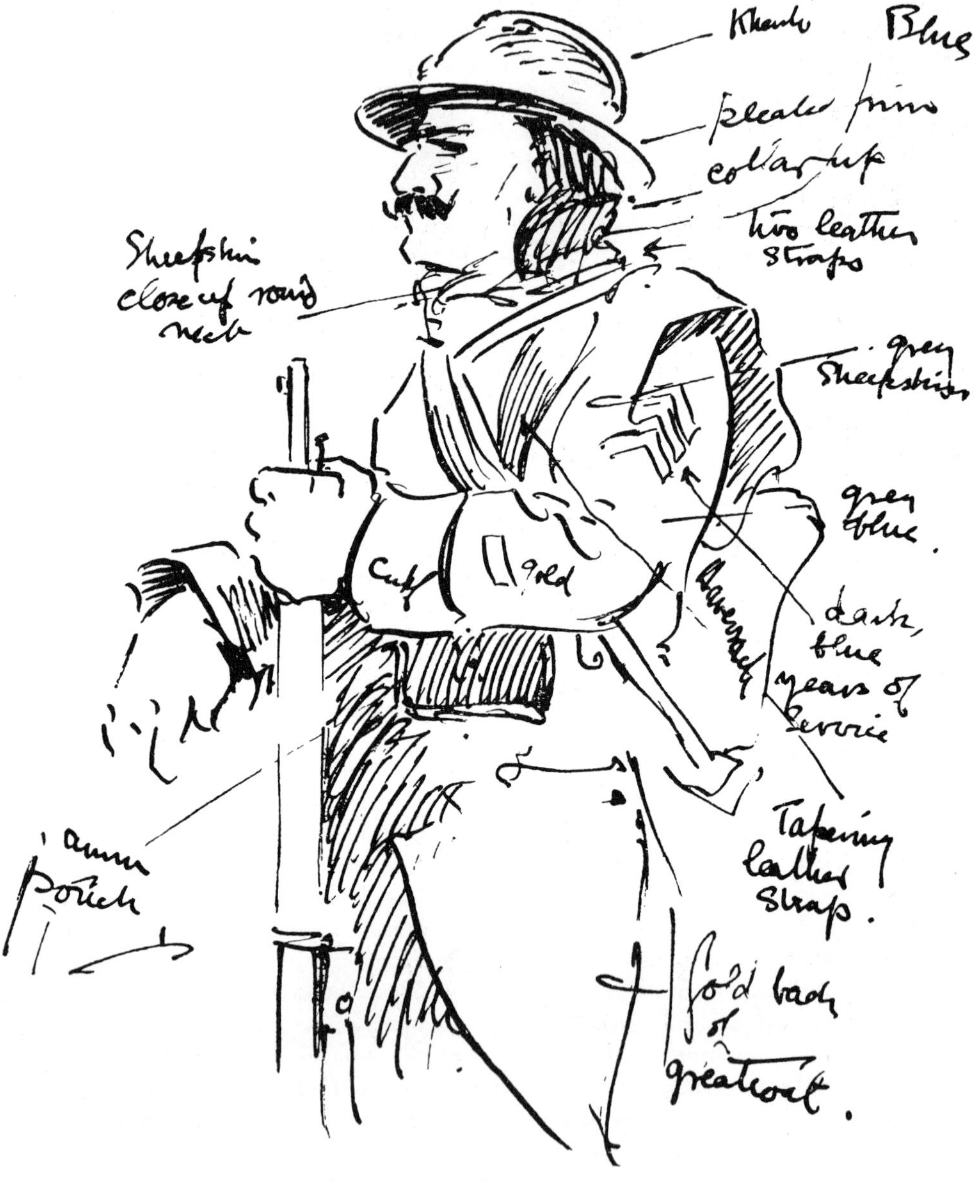

A page from one of my sketchbooks.

room. Two lift-boys take you down, and in the hall your boxes are struggled for by a platoon of swarthy foreigners in red jackets, like goldfish after crumbs. Then, finally, on both sides of the rotating doors, you encounter an array of giants in costumes of blue with gold braid, which would put to shame the diplomatic uniform of even the smallest Balkan State. You want to set aside about five pounds for this side of hotel life.

I drove off down to the docks, and was not long in getting on board. What dread words those are for me - 'getting on board'. There can never have been a worse mariner than I. If I catch sight of the funnels of a ship from the hotel windows, a mile away, I feel ill. And as for the final walk up the gangway - I am from that moment onwards a strange and unearthly being. There is something about the whole construction and personality of a ship that adversely permeates my whole system. I have endured several thousand miles on various oceans, and never have I got any better. That peculiar smell which hits you as soon as you get on a ship, that compound of paint, oil and stuffiness is worse than a gas attack to me. Well, anyway, I drove off down to the docks on this occasion, and courageously went on board. It was a big ship (the larger the better for my purpose), and was about the 25,000 tons sort of thing.

Two days were now spent slowly and laboriously extricating ourselves from the aftermath of the aforementioned coal crisis, and the complications of the local docks; then we pushed off.

The Teuton, in his agony of thwarted hate, had certainly succeeded in making the transatlantic passage peculiar, if nothing else. The submarine was conquered, but considerable strange mannerisms were still retained. The most objectionable one, to my mind, was the fact that a voyage lasted twice as long as normally. This left me with the incessant worry as to whether we can ever reach the other side before it becomes 'very rough indeed'. I live from hour to hour on a ship. I can strut truculently about the deck if the sea is as flat as a looking-glass, and can fight that nauseating gust which comes at you up a ventilator, but, if at all rough, I am down and out in a second.

I am thinking of leaving a large sum of money to establish a fund for promoting kindness to passengers amongst stewards. Oh, the anguish of a voyage, sometimes! This voyage of which I write was, fortunately, a smooth one: this was lucky as it lasted twice as long as it usually did. After an eccentric and mysterious passage we at last knew that in a few hours we would come within sight of New York.

Everything from now onwards seemed to go rapidly. I stood on the front of the ship by some railings (I don't know what the part is called, but it is towards the sharp end of the boat) watching for the first vision of New York. At last! The mammoth Woolworth building reared its head, dim and pale yellow, over a confused mass of other buildings, lost in morning haze. The voyage was over. In a few hours we had passed up the Hudson and were safely secured in a dock. An hour or two more and we had emerged from the suspicious and curt scrutiny of the Customs officials, and were, most of us, waiting for scarce taxis, surrounded with luggage and coloured porters. New York! New York in wartime, that's what I was to see. I was very familiar with the three other large capitals at war - London, Paris and Rome, and now, here was the headquarters of the newest additional nation to the determined company of Kaiser Crushers.

I drove along in a taxi, gorging on all the new sights. After a life spent mostly amongst two and four storey buildings, I confess the Woolworth building strikes one more like a nightmare than anything else. It's a bit dwarfed in New York owing to the fact that there are so many other buildings which have run to seed. An ordinary three or four storied house in New York would probably get run over by a tram or something; people's attention is centred much higher. In the distance the effect of these monstrous buildings is peculiar. They are all so geometrically uninteresting. Giant cubes, or triangles, or parallelograms; one of these habitations near my hotel was the shape of a safety-razor blade on its end, enlarged millions of times - a giant wedge, as it were. My hotel was on Broadway. A mighty cube, entrance as usual by means of rotating glass doors. My rooms in the hotel luckily looked out on Broadway, and, as Broadway crosses Seventh Avenue just in front of the Hotel Astor, the view is more varied still. The chaotic whirlpool in front of the Hotel Astor is known as Times Square.

Well, here I was at last, fixed up in New York in the Hotel Astor. Now, before going on further with this narrative, I must first explain a few little points which may not have occurred to the reader and which, if they did, he might set down as egoism or swelled head, or self-advertisement on my part. But, in order to give a clear and concise picture of my time in America, it is necessary for me to tell you exactly how things went with me. He of the domed head and starched, wide collar - Shakespeare to wit - once said, "What's in a name?" and I now know he was joking. A name can nearly kill you, that's my experience.

The news of my going to America had preceded me. I smelt a rat when I was asked to sign a volume of *'Fragments from France'* on coming down the gangway from the ship, but after a few hours at the Hotel Astor, any hope that I had ever entertained of being in America quietly was completely dispelled. The first signs of the riot which was to come took the shape of the telephone ringing incessantly. Later on, I used to spring up with a start when the telephone stopped - the silence jarred on me so.

Then came the interviews. For several days I told a sequence of pleasant but perfect strangers what I thought of New York, what I thought of the war and what I thought of the American soldiers in the field in France. Occasionally this would vary with how I came to think of Old Bill, and what places and battles I had been to. All these interviewers were very pleasant and clever people. On reading the torrent of articles which followed in the papers afterwards, I was amazed at what practice can do for them, in the taking of interviews. One man, I remember, to whom I talked solidly for nearly three-quarters of an hour, took no notes down whatever, but he had bottled all I had said, and got most of it right too.

As I sat in that room at the Astor, giving word pictures of my travels and adventures, I couldn't help thinking much of those dim, distant days, when first I slushed around on those bleak Flanders fields, and of my first meeting with Old Bill. A big jump! The trenches at Messines to the Astor, New York; but war is full of surprises.

My visit exactly coincided with the stupendous and all-absorbing movement - the raising of the Fourth Liberty Loan. I have seen war loans in various forms raised from time to time in England; I have seen our methods of doing so; I have read advertisements which pointed out in clear, dictatorial terms the small-minded stupidity of anyone who failed to be enticed by four and a half per cent. I have seen all our English methods at work; but for real, prodigious, enthusiastic effort New York, during the Loan drive, beats everything I've ever seen.

Soon after I arrived I had reason to be shot around the city in a car and, incidentally, passed down Fifth Avenue. My first impression was that the war was over. From one end to the other, on both sides of the street, and festooned down the middle, hung every flag of every size and description. A vast canopy of coloured cloth in kaleidoscopic profusion seemed to block out the sky and the walls of the cube-like, monstrous buildings on either side of the Avenue.

Here and there, through the chinks of this mammoth Joseph's coat, minor activities were rioting with each other for predominance. Here, perhaps, you might see a patriot standing on a platform in front of a picture depicting the entry of Honduras into the war, who, by means of dramatic gestures and in unintelligible words, was holding the attention of a cosmopolitan, swaying crowd, the rear ranks of which ran the risk of heavy casualties from the passing crush of taxis, lorries, decorated fire engines and private cars.

There again you might see four frantic and sexless-looking women, framed in an avalanche of flags, candidly advertising the size of their mouths as they brandished Liberty Bond forms in the air and shouted exhortations, which nobody listened to. A few yards further on you ran into a procession. No amount of inquiry could tell you *what* procession; you just had to use your judgement and experience, picked up by travel, to find out *what* procession it was. For instance, if you suddenly came upon a crashing band of cymbals, and over the sea of cars and people caught sight of a couple of hundred Mongolian faces wearing top-hats with the Stars and Stripes wound round them, you might safely conclude that this was Siam, Java, or Juan Fernandez showing unmistakably that she, too, was in favour of raising the loan; whilst a decorated furniture wagon or fire engine, with the words 'Juan Fernandez has sent more than half a platoon to the Western Front' inscribed thereon, would evoke frenzied applause and show clearly that Juan Fernandez approved of the United States, and that there was no chance of a rupture for years to come.

Fifth Avenue at Loan time is really a mighty sight. I knew that even when peace was declared London would be unable or, shall I say, unwilling to equal it.

I saw these wondrous and enthusiastic sights soon after my arrival, just before all the papers had really got going with 'Cartoonist Bairnsfather says' or 'Bairnsfather praises US soldiers', etc., etc., but I was soon to be drawn into the Liberty Loan whirlpool. Everybody had something to do with it. Everywhere all effort was directed towards the big aim in view - 'Six billion dollars' - and very soon the Big Clutching Hand said, "I see by the papers that there dwelleth in an upper chamber at the Hotel called Astor, a cartoonist by name Bairnsfather. He must forthwith be extracted and used in our enterprise."

In two days' time letters, telephone messages and callers arriving in massed formation, left me no further doubt as to my future in New York. Out of the usual average of about twenty applications a day, I selected one or two meetings at which I would speak, and determined I would do my best, such as it was, in the cause of the Liberty Loan.

I would rather have a day in the trenches than make a speech. Once I get up on the platform or whatever it is, I feel better, but in that ten minutes before I go on, I tremble like a blancmange in an east wind. All the little things which I have previously decided to say, and which I have repeated to the bedroom looking-glass with enormous success, are of course completely forgotten: instead, some lukewarm phrases are exuded through trembling lips and chattering teeth, and finally, by some miraculous piece of luck, I squirt out a lucky, pithy and perhaps pertinent or humorous remark, which saves me from a catastrophe, then sit down in a bath of perspiration.

I made speeches in various parts of New York and the country round; sometimes at theatres, sometimes on a platform in a hall, once on a platform at a railway station, and once in a church. Besides these horrible activities I held forth at innumerable dinners. The after-dinner speaking is the easiest brand, as you have nearly always got your hearers in a comatose state before you begin. I made one speech at a dinner where nothing but

If they had only electrified the barbed-wire.

iced water was provided, and found it far harder to 'get it over', as they say on the stage. I like an audience that has been built up on a good foundation of cocktails, table-d'hôte, good wine and cigars. And now, whilst all this rattle and bang was going on in New York and America generally, came the creaking and cracking of the war. The papers daily recorded signs and portents that all was not well with the Germans and their Allies. Bulgaria had left the cast, then Turkey, then Austria!

The excitement in America was intense. On all sides people felt that our turn had come at last. The Germans, deserted by their dupes, were at last ringed round by the ever-increasing power of the Allies. The weight of America at the right moment was turning the scale. I read the papers with great eagerness. I searched every line for any indication of the end. The end of the war! It hardly seemed possible that such a thing was near. The American public, I could see, couldn't fully grasp what a long business it had meant for us. The four years which Britain and France had endured were, for them, difficult to realise.

Whilst in New York I got ill. A serious trouble broke out in my left ear, and rapidly reduced me to a very low level of cheerfulness and vigour. Specialists told me that it was due to my being in a very low state of health, and excessive nerve strain. I felt very bad indeed. An acute attack of melancholia, coupled with an incessant pain from an abscess behind the drum of my ear, obliged me to cancel any further engagements. Never in my life have I felt quite so ill as I was then. I went to the British Consulate and explained the whole situation. They quite understood, and on the advice of a specialist I decided that further work out there was useless. I was really on my way across America to Australia, but I knew inwardly that my 'number was up' on this trip. I was very ill, and I realised it. People that are about me when I get ill rarely take in how bad I'm feeling as I, unfortunately, instinctively camouflage myself over with a film of jocularity.

However, some very friendly British officers understood, and did everything possible to arrange for my passage home. I went back to the hotel again and, until the boat left, made the best of it. I lay on my bed most of the time, occasionally pulling myself together to go downstairs for a meal. I think the accumulated strain of the past four years had at last got me, and that I now, for a space, had to put up with a 'nervous breakdown' and the sidelines that go with it.

I caught a Cunard boat, and started on the return voyage to England. For four consecutive days and nights I lay asleep in my cabin. I was completely exhausted. After that I began to sit up and 'take notice' as they say of babies. In two days more I pulled myself together sufficiently to draw a picture which, I am glad to say, brought £100 for the Seamen's Orphanage. It was auctioned at a 'gaff' on the ship.

They were a jolly crowd on that boat. It was a troopship, packed to the lid with American soldiers bound for France. A large, crowded convoy steadily plodded over its zigzag course on its way to England. Meanwhile, the Marconi daily news was filling the hearts of those on board with hopes of the successful termination of the war.

Chapter 37

ENGLAND ~ ARMISTICE ~ END

The crowded transports reached the Mersey. I went on deck, and lovingly gazed on the docks of Liverpool, bathed in the rose-pink light of the dawn. The forest of masts and funnels, the distant tower of the Royal Liver Building! England once more! Hours, of course, must elapse now, before they pull your boat round impossible looking corners, through absurdly narrow lock-gates, until they finally fix you up alongside a wharf, with just enough distance to prevent you jumping ashore.

At last the time came for disembarkation, and having said good-bye to the officers of the ship I went on shore with all my tackle and got a taxi.

I bought papers as soon as I got to the station - bought them in large quantities. "Yes," I thought as I read, "this war is breaking." One could feel in the air that this mighty catastrophe which had lain like a cloud over the world for four years, was drawing to a close. By an extraordinary but painful coincidence I was back in England just when all this wonderful *news* was giving England wonderful *peeps* into what would be wonderful *peace*. It seemed hard to realise that the end might be near.

I arrived in London, and felt myself slowly recovering. There is no tonic like getting back to England, but what a tonic the world was to have in a moment!

Suddenly the great news of the Armistice Terms echoed round the world, followed by those tense hours of waiting.

I was in London, spending my days resting in bed, striving for complete recovery. Then came the great news. The Germans had signed. The war was over.

My own private war was over too, for on that night I felt that there were many strains and worries that now would be no more.

The war over! I wondered what Old Bill thought. I could see those muddy, battered trenches, the land soaked with all the tragedy of years, the faces of those war-worn soldiers, as the news spread down the long line, which runs from the North Sea to Switzerland. The war was over!

Old Bill would go home to Maggie.

Epilogue

OLD BILL LOOKS BACK ~ WHAT HE THOUGHT OF THE SOMME IN 1923
(Pictorial Magazine - 6th January 1923)

During a tour of the battlefields with the 'Capting' in 1923, Old Bill revisited Albert and the Somme, and had a silent moment when he contemplated his old billet. Somewhere, deep down, he had a soft spot for the old days, where he lived in a land of mud, peopled by a great brotherhood of khaki-clad men who entered the turmoil of war with a jest and a cheery smile, and as he looked on at what used to be, Old Bill thought many things. Some thoughts he would not tell for gold, but such as may be made known he gave . . .

"The Somme was a bit off, but it weren't quite like Wipers." Old Bill let this announcement off at me as we stood in Albert, having just beaten off a sale of postcards depicting spots that we prefer to think about and not see.

"What do you mean, Bill? Do you say that Ypres was worse?" I asked.

"Well, not exactly that, Capting; but by the time this 'ere Somme was on the menu the war was bein' run up-to-date, as it were - there was corrugated iron and plenty of sandbags and all that tackle - a real, comfortable war as it were. You could ring the bell for anythin'."

"Yes, but it was a rotten battle though, Bill - in fact a fearful one! Think of Theipval, Gommecourt, Delville Wood, Peronne!" I said this with vigour and watched him closely.

"Yus, it was a rotten outfit, I know, Capting, but some'ow, somethin' 'ad left the war by then. I think p'r'aps it was the chance of losin'. It was serious and all that; but when we was stuck up at Wipers in them early times it was not only serious but a blinkin' disaster for ever if we 'ad got pushed back. Finished - napoo!"

"Yes, I see what you're meaning, Bill. But look at this place, look at poor old Albert!"

He looked around at it all sadly. "Yes, it makes ye think, don't it? You've only got to look at all that rusty barbed-wire, what we saw comin' along, to give an idea of what it was like."

Bill was right. Along those flat, desolate roads it seemed incredible that so much wire could have been used, and incredible that it was still lying there, rusty. One somehow imagined that no war traces could remain after all these years. It was possible to find shell fuse-tops almost as easily as during the war itself. Souvenirs of all kinds still litter the ground. And this after all those countless tourists! I found myself thinking what a fortune in metal lay between the North Sea and Switzerland! Think of the tons of metal in all its forms that was shot out to France during those years! Matter is indestructible, so the metal must be there - somewhere.

Bill was now wandering about amongst some house remnants, obviously impatient.

"Where would you like to go first, Bill?" I asked.

"Well, Capting, before I goes to 'ave a look at Delville Wood and all that, I just wants to drive around the back part. There's somethin' about all them old billetin' villages that gets me. I just want to see them old barns and estaminets we used to know - just want to see them places where the boys used to sit around and 'ave a sing-song, to see them cribs where we lay among the straw and waited for the sergeant to tell us to 'fall in on the road!'"

I knew what he meant.

We hope at last that Bruce and Old Bill have found that 'Better 'Ole'.

Glossary

A BRIEF GLOSSARY OF NAMES, PLACES AND TERMS USED IN THE OMNIBUS WHICH MAY BE UNFAMILIAR TO SOME READERS

ADC
Aide-de-camp - an officer who attends a general, governor, etc. and acts as a personal assistant

AMLO
Assistant Military Landing Officer

ASC
Army Service Corps

Adjutant
an officer specially appointed to assist a commanding officer

Bell-tent
a bell-shaped tent

Billets
allocated sleeping- or resting-places (for soldiers)

Bléville
town in northern France

Boches
derogatory WWI slang (originally French) - German soldiers

Bois de Ploegstert
known as Plugstreet Wood by the British

Boots
a hotel servant who cleans boots, runs messages, etc.

Boulogne
town and port in northern France

Brass hats
high ranking officers (from the gold braid on their caps)

British Warm
a heavy, knee-length greatcoat

Bully beef
canned corned beef, the main protein ration of the British army

Bystander
popular magazine/periodical

Château
a castle or large country house (especially in France)

Corduroy path
a track laid transversely with tree-trunks

Corrugated iron
sheet iron, bent by rollers into ridges for strength

Couleur de rose
rose coloured

Crystal Palace
venue for FA Cup Finals before Wembley stadium was built

Dough-boy
an American infantryman (military slang)

Dressing-station
a place where wounded were collected and tended by members of a field-ambulance

Dugout
a rough dwelling or shelter dug out of a slope or bank, or in a trench

Duck-board
a board with slats nailed across it, used for walking on swampy ground, etc.

Enfiladed
discharged firearms along the whole length of a line

Estaminet
a small bar or café

Field day
a day when troops were taken out for instruction in field exercises

Fire-bucket
a metal container (often a biscuit tin) in which a fire was lit

Fire-step
a ledge on which soldiers stand to fire over a parapet

Flanders
a region of northern Belgium

Fostered
fed

Funkhole
(military slang) a place of refuge, a dugout

Gaff
low-grade or cheap theatre

Gendarme
French policeman

Gold Flake
cigarettes/tobacco

Gordons
Gordon Highlanders (Scottish Infantry Regiment)

GSO1
General Staff Officer of 1st Grade, etc.

Hate
(usually 'morning hate' or 'evening hate') - the opening of artillery fire by both sides at dawn and dusk

Haute école
horsemanship of the most difficult kind

Indent Form
an order or official requisition for goods

Jack Johnson
nickname given to the German 150mm heavy howitzer shells, renowned for their loud noise and black smoke explosions (after the first black American heavyweight boxing champion of 1909 to 1915)

Jehu
any fast and furious coachman or driver

Johnson 'ole
a crater made by one of the above shells

Le Havre
town in north-western France, on the English Channel

Legion of Honour
French military award

Lille
city in northern France, near the Belgian border

Limber
a detachable two-wheeled vehicle containing ammunition, preceding the gun carriage and forming with it part of a field gun unit

Lit out
(colloquial) decamped

Lyddite
a powerful explosive made in Kent (tested at Lydd) and composed mainly of picric acid

Maconochie
tinned meat and vegetable stew, named after the packer, not overly palatable (it was said that MM stood for Maconochie Medal - the reward for eating it!)

Mailed fist
physical or military force

Matchboard
wooden tongue-and-groove planks

Mess-room
a place where a number or group of people take their meals together

Mess-tin
a soldier's utensil serving as plate, cup and cooking vessel

Mirabile dictu
wonderful to tell

Morphia tablets
pain relief tablets

Mrs Grundy
a prim neighbour (phrase coined from Thomas Morton's 'Speed the Plough' [1798])

'Napoo'
military slang meaning no more; used up; good for nothing; dead (from the French il n'y en a plus - there is no more)
Neuve Eglise
village in Belgium
Nieppe
town in France
Number 9
(military slang) a laxative pill (from its British Army designation)
Oppenheim, E. Phillips
a writer of thrillers, and over 100 bestsellers
Orderly Room
a room for regimental or company business
Palais de Justice
law courts
Parados
earthworks protecting against a rear attack; side of trench furthest from the enemy
Parapet
a bank or wall to protect soldiers from the fire of an enemy in front; side of trench nearest the enemy
Pelmanism
a system of mind training to improve memory devised by the Pelman Institute founded in 1898, or a card game where cards are spread face down and must be turned up in matching pairs
Platoon
a subdivision of a company
Plum and apple
the most common jam issued to British troops; 'plum 'n' apple' became almost synonymous with jam, no matter what flavour
Poilu
a French private soldier (nickname meaning 'hairy')
Prussia
a former kingdom and state in Germany
Puttee
a cloth strip wound round the leg from ankle to knee as a legging
RTO
Railway Transport Officer
Railhead
the furthest point reached by a railway under construction; the end of railway transport
Ration box
a box in which rations were kept
Red tab
staff officer (from the red patch worn on the collar)
Romerin
town in Belgium
Rouen
town in France
Salient
an outward-pointing angle, especially of a fortification or line of defences
Sam Browne
a military officer's belt with a shoulder strap
Sandbag
a bag of sand or earth, used especially to protect against bomb blasts
Sap, sapping
a trench (usually covered or zigzag) by which approach is made towards a hostile position
Seaforths
Seaforth Highlanders (Scottish Infantry Regiment)
Seine
river in northern France
Somme
river in northern France, the scene of major battles in WWI
Spahi
formerly, a Turkish or French-Algerian cavalryman
'Stand to'
a precautionary parade or taking of posts
Star shell
a shell that explodes high in the air, lighting up the scene
Strafe
to fire upon with rifle or artillery (from the German battle cry "Gott strafe England" - "God punish England")
Subaltern
a military officer under the rank of Captain
The Front
the foremost line (of soldiers or battle); the scene of hostilities
Top-boot
a knee-length boot with a showy band of leather round the top
Transport Farm
a place from where the conveyance of troops and equipment was organised
Traverse
a crossing or passage across; a parapet
Tumbril
a two-wheeled cart; the name given to the carts that conveyed victims to the guillotine during the French Revolution
VAD
Voluntary Aid Detachment, an organisation of British volunteer nurses who served in WWI
Valise
an overnight travelling bag; a kit-bag
'Wind up'
nervousness, agitation, apprehension
Ypres
town in Belgium, famous for its weavers and cloth, hence the most famous landmark of its Cloth Hall, Tower and Cathedral which were devastated during WWI. Known to the Tommies as 'Wipers'. The town is now the home of the Menin Gate memorial
Zouave
a soldier belonging to a body of French infantry, originally Algerians

References:

Brewer's Dictionary of Phrase & Fable (15th Edition)
Cassell - 1996

Chambers Dictionary
Chambers Harrap - 1993

The Wipers Times, (with notes)
Patrick Beaver - Peter Davies Limited - 1973

The World War One Source Book
Philip J. Haythornthwaite - Arms and Armour - 1994

NOTES ON THE ORIGINAL EDITIONS OF
'BULLETS & BILLETS'
and
'FROM MUD TO MUFTI'

'Bullets & Billets', with its bright red and black pictorial cover featuring a drawing of Old Bill, was first published on 4th December 1916, at the height of Bruce Bairnsfather's popularity. The publisher, Grant Richards (London), had received record advance orders for the book, and an initial print run of 50,000 copies was made, 45,000 of which were immediately bound up and made ready for sale. The paper, engravers blocks, printing and binding costs came to just over £2,300, but Grant Richards was confident of the book's success. It was priced at 5/- net, and within a week the first edition had sold out!

By the end of December 1916 the book was already in its third reprint, testament to the incredible way in which Bairnsfather had captured the attention of the British public.

Sales for 1917 exceeded 7,000 copies, and in the same year Grant Richards also produced a limited edition of 100 books, each with an original frontispiece drawing by Bairnsfather, which sold for the princely sum of £5/5s. The American rights were sold to G. P. Putnam's Sons, in New York, and by the end of the war *'Bullets & Billets'* had been reprinted eight times in all. As the war drew to a close, sales in Great Britain dropped dramatically - less than 700 copies were sold in 1918. By 1921 sales were averaging 70 copies a year. However, despite this somewhat diminished demand, *'Bullets & Billets'* was still selling ten years after its first publication.

'Bullets & Billets' was Bruce Bairnsfather's first literary work as an author, and Grant Richards' optimism in printing such a large number of copies in the first edition, was well founded. *The Bystander* magazine had published forty-three of Bairnsfather's *'Fragments from France'* cartoons in book form in February 1916, and this had been a constant bestseller for months. It was seeing a copy of *'Fragments from France'* which originally convinced Grant Richards that if Bairnsfather could come up with such imaginative captions for his drawings, he should be able to write a book. Luckily he was proved right, and his foresight made him a considerable amount of money.

The Bystander, meanwhile, was profiting from Bairnsfather's work as a cartoonist, and shortly after *'Bullets & Billets'* appeared, it issued its third collection of Bairnsfather drawings, by which time nearly two million copies of *'Fragments from France'* had been sold.

Almost immediately following the publication of *'Bullets & Billets'*, Bruce Bairnsfather was discussing plans for a second book with Grant Richards. The publisher hoped to have the sequel in bookshops within a year, but it was not until 29th September 1919 that *'From Mud to Mufti'* (price 6/ - net) was finally published. By that time there was a lull in interest in books about the war, and as a result sales of the new book suffered. The print run was only 11,350 copies, with production and material costs coming to just over £1,000. Although initial sales in 1919 exceeded 7,000 copies, only 72 books left the publisher the following year. A surge of interest in Bairnsfather in 1921 resulted in increased sales of 1,006 copies. Within three years however, sales were only averaging a dozen copies annually, and seven years after *'From Mud to Mufti'* was originally published, Grant Richards still held over two thousand stock copies.

The combined print runs for both *'Bullets & Billets'* and *'From Mud to Mufti'* here at home numbered some 64,170 copies (this figure does not include those copies of the books produced in the United States by G. P. Putnam's Sons - where Bruce had considerable success), and although not on a level with sales of *The Bystander's 'Fragments from France'*, their success confirmed Bairnsfather's credibility as an author and the books remained in print until the mid 1920's.

Mark Warby
Editor of *'The Old Bill Newsletter'*
Leicester
April 2000

Acknowledgements

TONIE and VALMAI HOLT

From the very start, when the idea of this project first took flight, Tonie and Valmai Holt have not only provided encouragement and support, but have allowed the use of their own detailed research and material which has greatly enhanced this omnibus edition. The brief biography at the front of this book is culled largely from their excellent and comprehensive biography of Bairnsfather, *'In Search of the Better 'Ole'*, and the additional photographs and illustrations which accompany it have come from their archive of memorabilia and ephemera. We acknowledge the permission of Tonie and Valmai to use photographs and illustrations which appear on pages; i, v, xvi, xx, xxii, xxvi, xxx, xxxii (2&6), xxxiv. For those readers who would like to delve deeper into the life, works and the collectables of Bruce Bairnsfather we highly recommend the couple's in-depth, lavishly illustrated biography.

'IN SEARCH OF THE BETTER 'OLE' by Tonie and Valmai Holt
ISBN: 0903852659
Hardback (260mm x 200mm) - 255 pages
£11.99 (+ £3.50 p&p)

'THE BEST OF FRAGMENTS FROM FRANCE' by Tonie and Valmai Holt
ISBN: 0906196250
Paperback (297mm x 210mm) - 160 pages
£11.90 (+ £2.50 p&p)

These books are available direct from:

TONIE AND VALMAI HOLT - Oak House, Woodnesborough, Sandwich, Kent CT13 0NJ

MARK WARBY

Mark, an avid collector and fan since his early teens, and without doubt the country's leading authority on Bairnsfather, became involved in this project prior to publication and brought his extensive knowledge to bear on correcting the errors and omissions in the original biographical portion of the Preface, whilst also loaning material from his own large collection of memorabilia and ephemera. He is also responsible for compiling the *'notes'* (opposite), which information he provided at short notice in order to enhance this work. We acknowledge the permission of Mark to use illustrations which appear on pages; xxviii, xxxii (1,3,4,5&7). We are both greatly indebted and extremely grateful to Mark for his many long hours and sleepless nights, searching his *'dugout'*, often under *'shellfire'* from a barrage of telephone calls, emails and hurried letters for the information which has made this omnibus edition what it is. Mark is also the founder and editor of the excellent *'The Old Bill Newsletter'* which is circulated throughout the world and keeps both fans and collectors informed and entertained with material on Bairnsfather, his life and his large body of work.

For details of how to subscribe to *'The Old Bill Newsletter'* please write to:

MARK WARBY - 3 Mallow Close, West Hamilton, Leicester LE5 1UY

TOM STAFFORD

Tom, another avid Bairnsfather collector, for permission to use the illustration on page 209.

NEIL PEARSON

Neil, our 'artist in residence', for his superb rendition of Bruce Bairnsfather's *'The Point of View'* for the cover.

DIANE CROWTHER

And finally, Diane, Senior Editor at Great Northern Publishing, for her many long nights in the trenches and her vigilance over the corrections.

What They've Been Saying About The Bestselling

BOMBARDMENT! The Day The East Coast Bled

Just before Christmas I obtained a copy of Bombardment! As one author to another, my congratulations on covering the subject in so thorough a fashion. I am aware of the efforts you have made in researching the book and in assembling the memories of others in a logical manner. The index of German attacks against the British mainland was of particular interest and value to me as it enabled me to place an event my grandmother witnessed as a young girl.

Stephen Fowler - Author - Surrey

I am thoroughly enjoying both books, 'Baptism of Fire' and 'Bombardment!', they make fascinating reading.

Peggy Broadhead - Wakefield

I have just taken delivery of 'Bombardment!' and am part way into it. I am very impressed with the thoroughness of your research and surprised that this bit of history is not more well known. Well done!

Frank Warriner - Ontario, Canada

Just a short note to let you know I am enjoying reading your splendid book 'Bombardment!'

Dick Bowen - York

I have just finished reading your superb 'Bombardment!' which is a masterpiece of historical research - if I may so, it is the sort of job which would earn an academic a PhD. Congratulations!

Colonel Geoffrey S. Powell
Regimental Historian, Green Howards - Gloucestershire

I have been doing a history project on the bombardment of Scarborough at school, during which I have been reading your book 'Bombardment!' which I have found very enjoyable and interesting.

Ashley Riches - Scarborough

Congratulations on your wonderful achievements with both books. Good luck and keep up the good work!

Margaret Dickinson - Author - Lincolnshire

Congratulations on your splendid book. It must really be the best researched and definitive book on the subject.

Aubrey Reeve - Survivor - Scarborough

It is obvious you have gone to considerable trouble to collect all the material for your book 'Bombardment!' Congratulations!

Stanley Sewell - Survivor - Isle of Man

I am sure 'Bombardment!' will be every bit as successful as your last book. Congratulations. It's just an amazing book.

Joy Craze - Pickering

Congratulations on another bestseller! 'Bombardment!' is superb. All our guests have been clamouring to read our copy!

Sue & Tony Hewitt - Scarborough

Congratulations on writing yet another fine book.

Paul Allen - Scarborough

Congratulations on 'Bombardment!' it is simply the best book from and about Scarborough published in the last 20 years.

Andrew Mead - bookseller - Scarborough

Many congratulations on 'Bombardment! - Superb!

Ray Westlake - Historian and author - Gwent

"Congratulations! It is a most splendid publication. When we initially spoke about this book I have to confess that I was imagining the sort of book that's normally published as a piece of local history, something about 48 pages long . . . this is 544 pages long . . . It's a magnum opus . . . A great work . . . Comprehensive is certainly the word for it. A very significant historical event. Indeed you've got an introduction by Sir Jimmy Savile OBE, and a Preface by Austin Mitchell MP, no less. Let me just say again, congratulations, it really is a splendid achievement.

Jonathon Cowup - BBC Radio York
(in an interview with the author - December 1999)

When war was declared in August 1914 a complacent nation confidently predicted it would be 'over by Christmas'. On 16th December they were shaken out of that complacency when the coastal towns of Scarborough, Whitby and Hartlepool were bombarded, resulting in extensive damage to property and the loss of innocent lives.

Bombardment! consists of a full narrative account, with extracts from letters and contemporary accounts, over 400 photographs and 36 maps which bring the incidents vividly to life. It has obviously involved an enormous amount of research as the author has worked hard to separate fact from the myth and legend of collective memory and the Chinese whispers of passed down 'eye-witness' accounts.

In the Preface former Yorkshire Television producer Austin Mitchell MP, who was involved with a 1970s TV documentary on the bombardment, pays tribute to the author's industry and diligence, and the success of the enterprise has been illustrated by the book being an outright bestseller in Scarborough over Christmas and New Year and by the book ranking number 2 in the Yorkshire Post's Top Ten book list for January 2000 - placing it higher than many well-known authors.

Detailed indexes at the end of the book identify the damage and the loss of life street by street and family by family.

I believe this book, with its often poignant personal accounts backing up official documents, is an important addition to the nation's history in its own right.

Margaret Garbett - Administrator
British Association of Friends of Museums
(Reviewed in BAFM's March 2000 issue newsletter.)

What They've Been Saying About The Award-Winning

BAPTISM OF FIRE

These Territorials landed in France less than a week before the gas attack on 22nd April; and the immediacy of that experience, and subsequent ones, is brought to life by the quotations from the diary of the author's grandfather. Other personal accounts and contemporary sources are also used to make this a very readable account. Well-produced and illustrated (with some useful maps and many photographs of the men) this book is excellent value and does the 'Yorkshire Gurkhas' much credit.

Ann Clayton - Editor - 'Stand To!'
The Journal of the Western Front Association

I read 'Baptism of Fire' within days of receiving it. It really is excellent and I must congratulate you. I do very much like the balance you have achieved in your historical narrative of the events of the 5th Battalion in the first part, and in the personal accounts in 'in their own write'. It works very well.

Major Philip Banbury - York

The book contains a lot of previously unpublished information, including first-hand accounts of the horrors of war, which will commend it to members of the regiment (past and present), students of military history and collectors of medals to the regiment.

Ian Hall - reviewer - 'Coin & Medal News' - London

I bought a copy of 'Baptism of Fire' and wanted you to know how much I enjoyed it.

Steve Metcalfe - Northallerton

I admire people who tackle local or unit history. I read much of 'Baptism of Fire' and enjoyed it. It is through work like this, set in a wider and balanced context, that a real sense of a community's or unit's war effort can be appreciated. Well done.

Dr Peter Liddle - Leeds

I have just read 'Baptism of Fire' and would like to congratulate you on its publication and to say how much I enjoyed it. There is one line which sums up for me the fact these were ordinary Yorkshire lads, no different from us today. The line is in the letter from Corporal Thomas Little on page 83 which describes the horrors he has come across, but who still tells his family, 'The most needed thing we've wanted is a good drink of tea.' My wife would tell you that when abroad I become quite painful with my complaints that nowhere outside Yorkshire can one get a decent cup of tea. Well done. I look forward to your next publication.

Michael Parkin - Scarborough

I hope your book 'Baptism of Fire' is a success as you have obviously put a lot of research and effort into its production.

David Cox - Beverley

I would like to say how much I enjoyed 'Baptism of Fire'. I found it a remarkable 'read'. I think the fact I found it so enjoyable is that it takes me back to the days when my father related his horrors of trench warfare (he served with the 5th East Yorkshires).

David Martin - Driffield

I have just read 'Baptism of Fire' and think it is an exceptional piece of research. The extracts from your grandfather's diaries and the letters of brother Territorial soldiers serving with him tell an engrossing tale of those 'Saturday Night Soldiers'. To have included so much additional information, letters, poems and photos must have been a mammoth undertaking. I hope everyone else will be as impressed as I was.

Major D. Whitehead - Bridlington

Your book 'Baptism of Fire' is a credit to you.

Richard Hall - Redcar

I have just read 'Baptism of Fire' and consider it a well-written and well-presented book which I would have no hesitation in recommending to anyone.

Tom Heron - Newcastle-upon-Tyne

I have just finished 'Baptism of Fire' and thoroughly enjoyed it. As a Green Howard and medal collector the references will certainly come in useful.

Kevin Morris - Middlesbrough

The book 'Baptism of Fire' comes alive through the words of the soldiers themselves, with letters, poems, photographs and memories from all over the region, including individual biographical details. Our battlefield tours will now be better informed, and I can use the examples to add a personal touch to my teaching. I recommend this book to all those who want to find ways of adding a 'local', and at times, very personal dimension to their teaching of the First World War.

Keith Melville
Head of History, Scalby School - Scarborough

I recently received your book on the Yorkshire Gurkhas, I must say it was well laid out and very well documented - the last remark was made by an officer of the Royal Scots Greys whom I met on a pilgrimage to my late uncle's war grave. In fact your book brought about the pilgrimage as I followed up the story of my uncle who appears in it. Thanks for the 'push' your book gave me and I am certainly awaiting the next one on the bombardment.

Pete Johnson - Kirby-in-Ashfield

Through a gripping narrative, based on official records of the battle, supported by personal letters, diaries, poems and archive photographs, Mark tells how these young men faced their baptism of fire with extreme courage; how they fought for seven days on a diet of bully beef and biscuits, sipping water from the puddles in the bottom of their hastily constructed trenches. He tells how they faced barrage after barrage of German artillery fire which not only destroyed but also prevented their resupply. It was the 5th Green Howards' first action and they suffered terribly. Yet they advanced to fill the gap and support the Canadians, and together they stopped a full-scale German breakthrough and sealed the broken front line. It was this first action which earned the 5th Green Howards the nickname the 'Yorkshire Gurkhas' - a mark of respect from their front-line colleagues. I highly commend this work to Green Howards, students of military history and the people of Yorkshire and the north-east.

Major J. Roger Chapman
The Green Howards Regimental Museum - Richmond

Great Northern Publishing wishes to acknowledge its debt to
GORDON RICHARD CROWTHER (1939-1997)
whose generosity made all this possible.
His warmth of spirit and appetite for life are sorely missed,
though he remains an inspiration and a guiding light.